THE GRAND GAME
BOOK 6: A SCION'S DUTY

THE GRAND GAME

Book 6: A Scion's Duty

Tom Elliot

COPYRIGHT

THE GRAND GAME

A burgeoning Power. Dormant followers. Ancient forces. Forgotten Allies.
And Lurking Enemies.
Will they clash?
And when they do, will the Wolf emerge triumphant?

Michael has come far in the Game since his somewhat-ignominious entry through Erebus' dungeon. Now, a force to be reckoned with, he is more than a mere player and someone the Powers would do well to fear...

But as Michael's power has grown, so too has his Pack.
Now, thousands look to him. With the fate of the House Wolf resting on his shoulders, allies left adrift awaiting his return, new friends brought into the fold, and enemies lurking in the shadows, can Michael juggle his multiplying duties and protect all those he has sworn to? All while still gathering the power he desperately needs?

Join Michael on his epic adventure and see where his journey takes him next!

PRAISE FOR THE GRAND GAME:

"Interesting portal litrpg. Well-paced and the start of a new series. Curious to see where it goes..." —**Tao Wong on goodreads.com.**

"... Great action, great storyline and I honestly binge read it, start to end..." —**Alex Kozlowski on goodreads.com.**

"Smart MC. Great Tension. Full of Action." —**CookieCrumble on RoyalRoad.com.**

"Everything I look for in a LitRPG." —**CosmereCradleChris on RoyalRoad.com.**

"Oh I liked this very much!" —**The Enlightened Beard on amazon.com.**

"One of the best in this category this year." —**kindle customer on amazon.com.**

AUTHOR'S NOTE

Dear Readers,

Thank you for reading the Grand Game. This is a self-published book. Even though care has been given to the review and editing of this novel, some mistakes may have slipped through. If you spot any grammatical errors or typos, please get in touch with me via email.

This book also contains game-like elements. They are generally unintrusive and integrated into the story, but beware, they exist. Otherwise, I hope you enjoy Michael's story.

Happy reading!
Tom (**TomLitRPG.com**)
Support me on PATREON[1]

---

[1] https://www.patreon.com/grandgame

CONTENTS

MICHAEL'S EVOLUTION

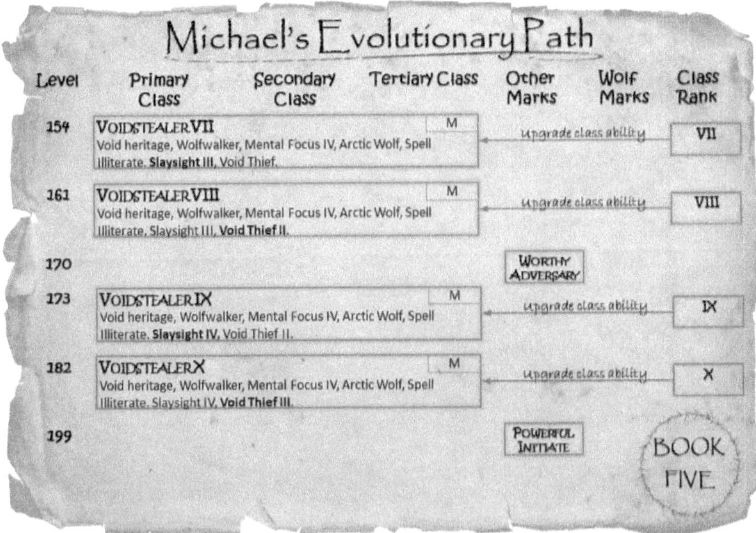

As always, Michael continues to grow during his adventures in the Forever Kingdom. The chart above only illustrates his latest achievements (as accomplished over the course of the last book). If you wish to view Michael's earlier evolutionary charts, please visit my site at the link below.

tomlitrpg.com/michael

THE SYSTEM OF THE GRAND GAME

The universe of the Grand Game continues to expand with every book in the series, and at this point, it no longer makes sense to include all the maps, charts, and diagrams in each new book.

If you wish to learn more about the world of the Forever Kingdom or understand the system of the Grand Game better, please visit my site at one of the links below.

tomlitrpg.com/game-lore
tomlitrpg.com/world-lore
tomlitrpg.com/glossary

MICHAEL AT THE END OF BOOK 5

Player Profile: Michael

Level: 199. Rank: 19. Current Health: 100%.
Stamina: 100%. Mana: 100%. Psi: 100%.
Species: Human. Lives Remaining: 2.
True Marks: Powerful Initiate.
True Marks (hidden): Worthy Adversary, Pack Alpha.
False Marks (fabricated): Lesser Shadow, Lesser Light, Lesser Dark.

Active Buffs

Damage reduction: Life: 5%. Death: 20%. Air: 45%. Earth: 45%. Fire: 45%. Water: 45%. Shadow: 15%. Light: 15%. Dark: 15%. Nether: 100%. Physical: 46%*.

Additional resistance (excluding inherent resistance provided attributes): Life: 2.5%. Death: 10%. Air: 22.5%. Earth: 22.5%. Fire: 42.5%*. Water: 22.5%. Shadow: 7.5%. Light: 7.5%. Dark: 7.5%. Nether: 70%*. Physical: 0%.

Other Boosts provided by Items*

Damage: +30% damage (ebonheart), +40% damage (faithful).
Abilities: perceive tier 6 spelled wards (sorcerer's coif), move soundlessly (wayfarer's boots), hands immune to hazardous substances (wayfarer's gloves), spellhold: empty (mage's surprise), psi-feed (psi bracelet).
Immunities: tier 2 entanglement immunity (unbound ring), tier 2 mind spells immunity (stillness ring).
Skills: +4 ranks stealth (ranger's armor).

Attributes

Available: 4 points.
Strength: 21 (13)*. Constitution: 27 (19)*. Dexterity: 84 (60)*. Perception: 40 (36)*. Mind: 119 (107)*. Magic: 48 (28)*. Faith: 0.

Classes

Available: 0 points.
Primary-Secondary-Tertiary tri-blend: voidstalker (fabricated). voidstealer X (hidden).

Traits

void heritage (hidden)**: +2 Dexterity, +2 Strength, +4 Mind, +4 Perception, +6 Magic.
beast tongue: can speak to beastkin.
Marked: can see spirit signatures.
wolfwalker (hidden)**: improved senses in all conditions.
anointed scion (hidden): bound to House Wolf.
inscrutable mind: +8 Mind.

secret blood (hidden): conceals bloodline.
mental focus IV:** increases effectiveness of Mind skills by 40%.
budding explorer: all key points in newly discovered sectors logged.
arctic wolf (hidden):** +5 Constitution, +2 Mind, +3 Strength.
spell illiterate: cannot cast mana-based spells.
potion resistance II: potency of potions reduced by 2 ranks.
spirit talker: can speak to spirits.
higher evolution: can evolve Class beyond master ranked.

** denotes boosts affected by items.*
*** denotes Class traits.*

<u>Skills</u>

Available skill slots: 0.
light armor (current: 157. max: 190. Constitution, basic).

dodging (current: 168. max: 600. Dexterity, basic).
sneaking (current: 193. max: 600. Dexterity, basic).
shortswords (current: 181. max: 600. Dexterity, basic).
two weapon fighting (current: 157. max: 600. Dexterity, advanced).
thieving (current: 118. max: 600. Dexterity, basic).

chi (current: 164. max: 1070. Mind, advanced).
meditation (current: 200. max: 1070. Mind, basic).
telekinesis (current: 169. max: 1070. Mind, advanced).
telepathy (current: 200. max: 1070. Mind, advanced).

insight (current: 200. max: 360. Perception, basic).
deception (current: 155. max: 360. Perception, master).

channeling (current: 189. max: 280. Magic, basic).
elemental absorption (current: 90. max: 280. Magic, master).
null force (current: 31. max: 280. Magic, master).
null life (current: 11. max: 280. Magic, master).
null death (current: 40. max: 280. Magic, master).
nether absorption (current: 200. max: 280. Magic, master).

<u>Abilities</u>

<u>Constitution ability slots used:</u> **10 / 19.**
load controller (10 Constitution, expert, light armor).

<u>Dexterity ability slots used:</u> **56 / 60.**
crippling blow (Dexterity, basic, shortswords).
minor piercing strike (5 Dexterity, advanced, shortswords).
improved backstab (10 Dexterity, expert, sneaking).
improved trap disarm (5 Dexterity, advanced, thieving).
superior lockpicking (5 Dexterity, advanced, thieving).
superior set trap (10 Dexterity, expert, thieving).

whirlwind (5 Dexterity, advanced, two weapon fighting).
greater fade (15 Dexterity, master, sneaking).

<u>Mind ability slots used:</u> **66 / 107.**
superior mass charm (10 Mind, expert, telepathy).
stunning slap (Mind, basic, chi).
windborne (10 Mind, expert, telekinesis).
heightened reflexes (10 Mind, expert, chi).
twin astral blades (5 Mind, advanced, telepathy).
long shadow blink (10 Mind, expert, telekinesis).
quick mend (10 Mind, expert, chi).
fortified mind (10 Mind, expert, meditation).

<u>Perception ability slots used:</u> **36 / 36.**
superior analyze (10 Perception, expert, insight).
improved trap detect (5 Perception, advanced, thieving).
conceal small weapon (Perception, basic, deception).
superior facial disguise (10 Perception, expert, deception).
superior ventro (5 Perception, advanced, deception).
lesser imitate (5 Perception, advanced, deception).

<u>Other abilities:</u>
greater slaysight (hidden) (Class, master, telepathy): shatter, sleep, terrify, blind.
superior void thief (hidden) (Class, expert, any void skill and telepathy): steal, siphon, negate.

<u>Known Key Points</u>

Dungeon Sector 14,913 (candidate's dungeon) exit portal and safe zone.
Kingdom Sector 12,560 (wolves' valley) nether portal and safe zone.
Kingdom Sector 1 (Nexus) safe zone.
Dungeon Sector 101 (scorching dunes) exit portal and safe zone.
Dungeon Sectors 102, 103, and 104 (haunted catacombs) exit portals and safe zones.
Dungeon Sector 105, 106, 107, 108, and 109 (guardian tower) exit portals.
Kingdom Sector 18,240 nether portal 1 (guardian tower), and nether portal 2 (Draven's reach).
Dungeon Sector 73,102 (Draven's Reach) one-way entrance portal and safe zone.

<u>Aetherstone Bracelet Stored Points</u>

sector 24,401 safe zone.
sector 12,560 (wolves' valley) safe zone.
sector 18,240 nether portal 1 (guardian tower).

<u>Equipped</u>

<u>Weapons</u>
ebonheart (+30% damage).

faithful (+40% damage).

Armor & Clothes
sorcerer's coif (perceive tier 6 wards).
ranger's kit (+40% damage reduction, +4 ranks stealth).
bomber's belt (4 x acid bombs, 5 x smoke bombs, 4 x ice bombs, and 4 x fire bombs).
belt of the chameleon (5 x rank 4 nether protection crystals, 11 x rank 4 disease protection crystals, 9 scent concealment crystals, 5 x mental concealment crystals, 4 x rank 6 disease protection crystals, 2 x rank 5 poison protection crystals, 1 x rank 4 strength enhancement crystals, and 2 x rank 4 magic enhancement crystals).
wayfarer's boots (legendary item, +8 Dexterity, move soundlessly).
wayfarer's gloves (legendary item, +8 Dexterity, hands immune to hazardous substances).
cloak of the Reach (legendary soulbound item, +10 Magic, +20% fire magic resistance, +20% nether magic resistance).

Rings & Accessories
goliath's ring (+8 Strength).
acrobat's ring (+8 Dexterity).
sharpshooter's band (+4 Perception).
hale stone (+8 Constitution).
savant's ring (+4 Mind).
troll's talisman bracelet (+6% damage reduction).
gift of the unbound ring (immunity to tier 1 and 2 entanglement spells).
band of stillness ring (immunity to tier 1 and 2 Mind spells).
aetherstone bracelet (3 / 5 stored locations, 2 stones charged).
simple potion bracelet (3 / 3 full heal potions).
veteran's trapper's wristband (128 / 200 trap-making crystals).
mage's surprise (+10 Magic, spellhold: empty).
psi bracelet (legendary item, +8 Mind, psi-feed).

Other
backpack, small bag of holding (50 slots), **large bag of holding** (200 slots), **hunter's alchemy stone.**
pioneer's compass (soulbound, attuned to safe zone).

Backpack Contents

<u>Money</u>: 73 golds, 5 silvers, and 3 coppers.
10 x field rations.
2 x flasks of water.
2 x iron daggers.
1 x bedroll.
goblin writ of safe passage.
bounty letter authorization.
1 x coil of rope.
tavern bill of ownership.

Tartan token.
Vivane token.
Kesh Emporium access card.
cat claws.
spectacles of ward seeing (detect tier 4 wards).
BHG ID (junior member, 1 / 10 active jobs).
simple map of Nexus.
1 x rank 6 cure disease potions.
dungeon notes.
commune rod.
greater trap detect ability tome.
enchanted leather armor set (+20% damage reduction, -35% Dexterity and Magic).
6 x acid bombs, 14 x smoke bombs, 10 x ice bombs, and 6 x fire bombs.
slotted-potion belt (2 x rank 4 cure poison).
adept's ring (+6 Magic).
mirror shield (reflect tier 4 spells).
quaker (+50% damage, paralyzing touch).
phoenix's feather shaft (soulbound).
small bag of hiding (tier 6 concealment ward).
a simple shovel.
1 x blue mages robes, 1 x black mages robes.
stygian shortsword, +3.
stygian shortsword.

<u>Miscellaneous Loot</u>

4 x legendary items.

<u>Alchemy Stone Contents</u>

(0 / 500 ingredients stored).

<u>Bank Contents</u>

<u>Money</u>: 1,655 gold, 0 silvers, and 0 coppers.
2 x full healing potions.
2 x full mana potions.

<u>Tavern Money</u>: 9,850 gold, 0 silvers, and 0 coppers.

<u>Open Tasks</u>

Find the Last Wolf Envoy (hidden) (find Ceruvax).
Heist in the Dark (steal chalice from the Power, Paya).
Silent Brethren (find out what has happened to the guardians).
A Perverted Trial (stop the Triumvirate abuse of the Combat Trial).
Brokering Peace (establish peace in sector 12,560 within 4 months).
Brotherhood Obligations (report to the brotherhood after 4 months).
Cleanse the Corruption (rid Draven's Reach of its nether infestation).

If you wish to view Michael's earlier player profiles, please visit my site at the link below.

<u>tomlitrpg.com/michael</u>

CHAPTER 379: ANTICIPATION

Awakening guardian...

Rising to my feet, I backed away from the statue. The Emblem had been inserted, the tithe made, and now all that was left was to witness the outcome.

"It is done," Adriel whispered. *"After all these long years, it is finally done."*

I glanced to my right, where the spirit hovered. The exile—former exile, I corrected—was watching the centaur guardian avidly. Unlike me, she could see him in his entirety. Although the central bank of nether was dissipating, the mists still hung heavy in the air, obscuring my sight.

"Is he awake yet?" I asked.

"He isn't," Adriel replied. *"Be patient."*

I rolled my eyes. I was not the impatient party here. *"It didn't take this long with Kolath."*

"Kolath? You mean the guardian in Nexus?" Tearing her gaze away from the statue, she glared at me. *"I doubt Kolath was ever forced to fight off—"* She broke off, noticing my grin. *"You're teasing me,"* she accused.

"Only a little," I admitted.

"Hmpf. Why don't you make yourself useful?" Swinging back around, she resumed her study of the guardian. *"Go and kill a stygian or something."*

Chuckling, I turned around to consider the mists. There was little reason for me to chase after the nether creatures—which Adriel very well knew. The stygian nest had fractured with the void tree's retreat and the harbinger's death. Still, she had a point.

A few minutes had already passed since I'd inserted the Emblem of the Reach, and as yet, the guardian showed little sign of awakening. I didn't doubt that *something* was happening—the Game message was evidence enough of that.

But that's no reason to sit around doing nothing.

Unfurling my mindsight, I let my awareness expand outwards as I walked a slow circuit around the guardian statue. A spattering of mindglows appeared—all of them stygians. But the closest was more than sixty yards away.

They're no threat, I decided.

Stopping at a random patch of ground, I dropped into a cross-legged stance and turned my focus inward. The events of the last hour had been chaotic, and I hadn't had a chance to consider my player profile yet.

You have reached level 199 and rank 19. You have 4 attribute points and 0 Class points available.

I rubbed my chin thoughtfully. I had new attribute points to invest, but my Mind did not need further advancement and of my remaining attributes, Perception, Magic, and Dexterity could all do with improvement.

What to invest in next?

Before deciding, I pulled up my skill and ability statuses for review. It had been a long time since I'd considered them.

<u>Skill Progression (total skills: 18)</u>

Tier 5 skills: 4, meditation, telepathy, insight, nether absorption.
Tier 4 skills: 9, light armor, dodging, sneaking, shortswords, two weapon fighting, chi, telekinesis, deception, channeling.
Tier 3 skills: 1, thieving.
Tier 2 skills: 1, elemental absorption.
Tier 1 skills: 3, null force, null life, null death.

<u>Ability Progression (total abilities: 25)</u>

Elite abilities: 0, none.
Master abilities: 2, greater fade, slaysight.
Expert abilities: 12, load controller, backstab, set trap, mass charm, windborne, heightened reflexes, shadow blink, quick mend, fortified mind, analyze, facial disguise, void thief.
Advanced abilities: 8, piercing strike, trap disarm, lockpicking, whirlwind, astral blades, trap detect, ventro, imitate.
Basic abilities: 3, crippling blow, stunning slap, conceal weapon.

I sighed. My skills were progressing nicely, and most were either at tier four or five. My abilities, on the other hand, lagged behind. I had *no* tier five abilities and only two tier four ones. The rest still languished between tier one and three.

While my skills and abilities both required improvement, it was my abilities that required greater work. Enhancing them, though, was easier said than done.

The biggest limiter, of course, was my unused ability slots. I had far too few available, especially considering each tier five ability required thirty slots.

It's time I reinvest in Dexterity.

While my sneaking was not yet at tier five, it was close, and as it stood, I lacked the necessary ability slots to upgrade greater fade again. Decided, I willed my choice to the Adjudicator.

Your Dexterity has increased to rank 64. Other modifiers: +24 from items.

Once I was free of the dungeon, I would have to purchase new ability tomes. That would entail visiting Nexus or possibly the wolves' valley again.

Thinking of escaping Draven's Reach naturally led to thoughts of my allies. All these long weeks, I'd actively suppressed dwelling on their fates. I couldn't afford the distraction—that was how I'd rationalized it, anyway—but now, with freedom almost within grasp, I found myself more anxious about those I'd left behind in the wolves' valley and the tundra.

I was sure the dire wolves would've adapted to the new environment. My player allies—Safyre, Terence, Teresa, and Anriq—I was less certain about.

Saya, in particular, worried me. I had not meant to leave her unguarded this long. The tavern keeper was largely alone in the wolves' valley, which was not the safest place, especially with Loken's envoy lurking about.

Shael will see her safe, I thought. I didn't know how far I could trust the bard, though. But Kesh's new agent would also be in the valley. The old Nexus merchant seemed to like the gnome, and I was sure she would do her utmost to protect Saya.

I wonder who Kesh chose to replace Safyre. Could I—

"Safyre?" a sleepy voice asked. *"Is she here?"*

Breaking off from my maudlin musings, I turned my attention to the brightening mindglow residing in my cloak. Ghost was waking up. *"Good morning,"* I greeted.

"Is it morning?" she asked grumpily. *"I can't tell."*

My lips curved upwards in a smile. *"I don't honestly know. It might be."*

Ghost yawned, or at least her mindvoice suggested she did. *"How long was I out for?"*

"Not long. A few hours, perhaps."

I felt her interest sharpen. *"Then is it done? Is the harbinger dead and the guardian restored?"*

"Yes to the first. No to the second. We're waiting for him to awaken," I said and went on to relate the outcome of the battle.

"The tree escaped?" Ghost asked when I was done. *"Does that mean we will have to cleanse the sector anew when it returns?"*

"No. Once Draven is awake and Adriel takes his place, she will see to it that the nether can never return."

"You're sure?" she asked with trepidation.

"I am."

The spirit wolf—although I didn't think it was accurate to call her that anymore—chewed over my words for a moment. *"Then... it's safe?"*

Having an inkling of where she was going, I temporized, *"Relatively safe. There are still enough other dangers about."*

"But it is safe," she said, latching onto the first part of my statement. *"I can manifest!"*

I hesitated. I was as keen to see my companion's new form as she was to assume it, but I'd not forgotten Adriel's warning. Ghost was still only a level one creature, and I had no idea how the nether would affect her. *"Better not,"* I said firmly. *"With or without the harbinger and the void tree, Draven's Reach remains a tier five dungeon, and there are still plenty of other stygians around."*

"But—" she began.

"We've come this far, Ghost," I interjected gently. *"Let's not be hasty now. Can you be patient for a little while longer? Please?"*

I felt her excitement dim. *"Alright, Prime,"* she agreed reluctantly.

"Thank you," I said gravely.

She was silent for a moment. *"I heard you mention Safyre earlier,"* a more subdued Ghost went on. *"Are we going to rejoin the pack after this?"*

I didn't question the abrupt change in topic. She likely didn't want to dwell on the thought of having to wait longer. *"We will. As soon as we wrap up matters in the dungeon."*

Ghost brightened. She had never been one to mope for long. *"I wonder what Sulan will make of my new form. Do you think she'll like it?"*

I winced, not as enthused as Ghost was at the notion of meeting Sulan again. Knowing the sharp-tongued elder, she would likely have choice words for me. Whatever Ghost was now, she was no longer a dire wolf, and while I did not doubt the pack would eventually accept her, I was not at all certain what our initial reception would be.

"I'm sure she will," I said, letting no hint of my doubts show. *"Adriel said you were unique."*

"She did?" Ghost asked, sounding pleased by the idea.

I smiled. *"She did,"* I assured her. *"Imagine how—"*

duuuu... ddddduuuu... duuuu...

I broke off. A low hum filled the air. It was almost too faint to hear, but I pinpointed the source after listening carefully for a moment. It was coming from below. Placing the palms of my hands flat against the floor, I felt the ground.

It was trembling.

Something large was on the move—or stirring.

"Prime?" Ghost asked. *"Is everything all right?"*

I rose to my feet. *"It is. But we will have to cut short our chat. It appears Draven is finally waking up."*

✳   ✳   ✳

Adriel was in the exact same position I'd left her—still staring at Draven. Only now, her face was suffused with excitement.

"It's happening," she said without looking away from the stone statue.

Saying nothing, I drew to a stop beside her, my own gaze fixing on the giant centaur. The statue had begun to shake, causing slivers of marble to break off. *Won't be long now,* I thought.

Awakening guardian...

"Remember what I told you," Adriel said. *"Let me do the talking. We don't know what state Draven's mind is in. He has been asleep so long, he might not be all there."*

I nodded. We had been over this already, and I had my instructions—more detailed and explicit instructions of what to say and how to behave than I would have accepted from anyone else. But this was Adriel, and after all she'd done for me and Ghost, I was not above humoring her.

And now that the moment the lich had been working toward for centuries was finally approaching, it seemed her nerves were getting the better of her. *"Everything will work out,"* I assured her.

"I hope so," she muttered. *"If it doesn't, I—"*

Revival complete. Draven has awoken.

The guardian's trembling stopped, and his eyes snapped open, but no new awareness appeared in my mindsight. Draven's mind was shuttered.

I couldn't see the statue's face either—the nether still obscured it—but like Kolath's, Draven's eyes shone with an inner fire so bright they were visible even through the thick mists. Stiffening to attention, I waited for the guardian's eyes to pass over me.

A hoof stomped the earth. Then another.

Marble creaked, and the trickle of falling rocks transformed into a shower. Shielding my head with my hands, I took a step back. Immaterial spirit, Adriel stayed where she was.

The guardian's forelegs disappeared.

He's reared back on his hindlegs, I thought, watching the harbinger's corpse slide unheeded off the statue's back.

My brows furrowed, and I glanced at Adriel to see what she made of this, but the lich had eyes only for the guardian. I'd not expected Draven to be this active, nor had my ally's instructions covered this eventuality.

"Adriel," I sent to her on a whisper-thin thread, *"should we—"*

"NETHERSPAWN!" Draven thundered.

The guardian's roar was an auditory assault, far louder than even a being of Draven's size should be able to manage. It was a magical projection, it had to be. Clamping my hands around my ears, I crouched down small in an attempt to shield myself from the noise.

If anything, Draven's next words were even louder, and this time, they hurt as much as I feared.

"How DARE the void come here!" the guardian spat in the resounding silence.

A guardian has injured you, inflicting sonic damage!

"This dungeon is mine. MINE!"

A guardian has injured you, inflicting sonic damage!
A guardian has injured you, inflicting sonic damage!

Hells, I groaned. I wouldn't have been surprised if they could hear him all the way in New Haven.

"Draven," Adriel greeted, finally speaking. *"Heed me!"* Her words rang across my mind, loud and undeniable.

But the guardian did not hear.

"You will rue the day you chose to come here!" Draven growled, oblivious to all but the void's presence. "I will slaughter your children and uproot your chosen. Mark me, your time in this sector is done!"

"Draven!" Adriel called sharply again.

I rose to my feet. "Guardian," I shouted, adding my voice to hers. We were well and truly off-script now. "Hear us!"

But once more, the guardian didn't respond. Or chose not to.

Dropping back to all fours, Draven brought his forelegs crashing down. The ground shook, and I lost my balance. Picking myself up, I took a deliberate step forward, intent on using a more direct approach to attract the statue's attention.

But before I could take a second step, the colossal guardian whirled about. "I'M COMING!" he yelled at his absent foes.

"They're gone, you fool!" Adriel shouted. *"The harbinger is dead, and the void tree fled."*

Paying neither her nor the large corpse behind him any heed, Draven spun about and, in a rumble of hooves, vanished into the mist.

Shaking my head in bemusement, I watched him for a moment, then turned to Adriel. She was staring off into the nether, her mouth dropped open in shock.

"Well, that was unexpected," I said lightly.

"Adriel?" I repeated when the lich did not respond.

Tearing her gaze away from something only she could see, the spirit turned about to face me. *"What?"* she asked, sounding annoyed.

"Do we chase after him?" I asked equably.

Adriel's mouth opened then snapped closed, and for one moment, she struggled silently with herself.

I didn't blame her for being out of sorts. Anyone would be after having their expectations so rudely upset. It had taken centuries of planning to bring her to this moment, and now... now, I wasn't sure what Draven's surprising behavior presaged—for her or me.

The spirit sighed, visibly releasing her pent-up tension. *"There's no point. We won't catch him."* She paused. *"Besides, he will be back."*

I tilted my head to the side. "He will?"

Adriel nodded, pointing to the stone plinth sitting forgotten in the ground. *"The Emblem is here. He has to return to retrieve it."*

I rubbed my chin thoughtfully. "I see. Any ideas of how we get him to listen to us the second time around?"

"Oh, he heard us. He just chose not to listen."

My brows lifted. "How can you—"

A flurry of Game messages interrupted.

A guardian has killed a level 163 stygian weaver with a fatal blow!
A guardian has killed a level 154 stygian crawler with a fatal blow!
A guardian has killed a level 170 stygian hydra with a fatal blow!
...

...

"What is it?" Adriel asked tersely.

"He's killing stygians," I replied.

"How pointless," she muttered. *"The damn fool is wasting what little time we have."*

Wisely, I refrained from pointing out that that was the same thing she had asked me to do only a few minutes ago. "On the bright side... Draven seems lively enough." I glanced at her. "What does that mean for you?"

Adriel fell silent for a moment. *"I don't know,"* she said quietly.

I waited to see if she would go on, but the spirit appeared lost in her thoughts. Deciding to let her be, I turned my attention outwards. I could still hear the clatter of hooves in the distance, and Game messages continued to scroll down through my vision. Draven was certainly making the most of his 'new life.'

I shrugged. The guardian would return when he did; until then, there was nothing to do but wait. Striding forward, I walked over to the spot formerly occupied by the void tree.

Now that the marble statue was no longer there to obstruct me, I could inspect the ground more closely. Kneeling, I lowered my arm into one of the many seams left in the earth by the sapling's roots.

My hand came back full of stone shards. Impressively, the sapling's roots had burrowed through solid rock—no mean feat. But other than for revealing that little tidbit of information, my investigation yielded little else.

I wasn't sure what I expected to find—bits of broken-off roots, perhaps—but after repeatedly shoving my hand into multiple cracks, it became clear that the void sapling had left nothing of itself behind.

Disappointed, I rose to my feet and moved on to my next subject of interest: the harbinger. Walking a slow circle around the corpse, I inspected it closely.

The stygian Power was as ugly in death as he had been in life. There was no blood, and although the corpse had deflated, it still made for a colossal creature. Harvesting it would yield significant rewards.

Withdrawing the alchemy stone from my pocket, I tossed it in my hands while I wondered where to place it. *At the head,* I decided, kneeling beside the harbinger's crow-like beak.

"Don't."

Hand hovering over the corpse, I looked behind to find Adriel watching me. "Why? Is it dangerous?"

She shook her head. *"No, but if you use the stone, you will lose out on the most valuable reagents."*

That was true enough. The hunter's alchemy stone was a tier four item and wouldn't gather reagents of higher tiers. But it was *also* the only means I had of harvesting the corpse. "Then, how—"

"Let Farren do it."

I frowned.

"I would do it myself," the lich added, *"but I can't, not in spiritform."*

Returning the alchemy stone to my pocket, I rose to my feet. *"It could be a couple of days before I manage to return here,"* I warned her.

"Don't worry. Nothing in the dungeon will dare to touch the body."

"Alright," I agreed reluctantly, trying to calculate how long it would take to journey to the lich's court and escort Farren back. Without the dracolich to fly us, we would have to make the journey on foot. A couple of days might've been an overly optimistic estimate. "Is it worth going to all that trouble?" I asked dubiously.

Adriel's lips twitched. *"Definitely,"* she pronounced.

Before I could ask what she meant, the clatter of hooves in the background grew louder, and Adriel's gaze flitted past me.

"He's on his way back," she said with a relieved smile. Floating forward, the spirit placed herself atop the plinth holding the Emblem and, folding her arms, waited with ill-disguised impatience for the approaching guardian.

✳   ✳   ✳

Draven's steps slowed as he drew closer. *A good sign,* I thought. At least he didn't mean to run me over. What with everything else, a mad guardian was the last thing I wanted to deal with.

A stone hoof stamped down on the plinth, passing heedlessly through Adriel's spiritform.

"Draven," Adriel began.

"WAIT," he ordered peremptorily.

Adriel's lips tightened, and she opened her mouth again, a sharp rebuke on the tip of her tongue, no doubt.

But Draven had not waited to see if his command was obeyed. Before the lich could speak again, a litany of words like a roll of thunder floated down through the mist.

Adriel's eyes narrowed, but she didn't try interrupting the guardian.

I glanced at her. "What is he doing?"

"Casting," she said absently.

I frowned. "Casting? Casting what?"

The spirit waved me to silence. *"That's what I'm trying to figure out. Now, shush and let me listen."*

I sighed. *Allies are all well and good,* I thought, pinching the bridge of my nose, *but sometimes, they can be trying indeed.* Leaving the lich undisturbed, I turned my attention back to Draven, or at least the parts of him I could see.

The guardian's mind was still hidden, but the little bit of him that was visible would suffice for an analyze attempt. *Why not?* I thought with a shrug. Reaching out with my will, I inspected him.

You cannot analyze your target! This entity is immune to this ability!

Huh, I thought dumbly. I'd only received a similar message from the Game one other time. On that occasion, I had attempted to inspect Loken. But then I'd only used a tier one analyze. This time, my analyze was a tier three ability—and not even my failed analyze attempt on the harbinger had produced a similar response.

So, what is the guardian? I wondered. A being on par with Loken, who was himself a supreme Power? I shuddered. The guardians couldn't be that powerful. Could they?

My musings were interrupted by a message from the Adjudicator.

Draven has cast purifying storm.

Howling winds descended from the sky on the tail end of the Game's alert. I staggered, pushed back by sudden gusts of air. "What's going on?" I yelled, shouting to make myself heard over the magical storm.

Adriel laughed. She, of course, was unaffected by the winds. *"It's Draven. He is expelling the fog."*

My gaze darted to the side, and sure enough, I saw the pale mists swirling upwards. Presumably, they were being sucked back into the Nethersphere through the breach in the barrier. *"That's a relief,"* I said with a smile as I switched to mindspeech. *"That leaves only the smaller fog banks to deal with."*

Adriel chuckled. *"No, Michael, it doesn't. Draven's spell extends to every corner of the dungeon. He is banishing all the nether. When he is done, the sector will be entirely cleansed of the void."*

✳   ✳   ✳

It took all of five minutes before Draven's work was complete and the dungeon purged of nether.

I sucked in a deep breath. The air tasted clean and fresh for what felt like the first time in ages. Turning my gaze upwards, I considered the horizon. There was no sign of the sickly pale strands of mist anywhere. The centaur guardian's grizzled and bearded face was finally visible, as was the violet dome surrounding the sector.

But so, too, was the deep scar directly overhead.

That's the breach, I thought. It was how the stygians had entered the sector. Even now, I could see more clouds of thick, billowing nether massing in the void beyond.

The guardian was not done yet, though, and as soon as his first spell was completed, he performed a second casting.

Draven has cast bulwark revitalization.

Before my eyes, the breach shrunk, then vanished entirely. My smile broadened, and I laughed. I couldn't help it. The sector was finally rid of the void once and for all!

As if in confirmation, a pair of Game messages unfurled in my mind.

You have completed the task: <u>Cleanse the Corruption</u>! You have purged sector 73,102 of the nether. Thanks to your efforts, the denizens of Draven's Reach no longer need to fear its vile touch. Wolf is pleased.

Your task: <u>The Silent Brethren</u>! has been updated. You have aided the guardian Draven in his mission and helped repel the stygians from his home sector. Optional objective completed.

The two alerts were just the beginning, though, and on their heels, a plethora of others followed.

Your Wolf Mark has deepened!

Congratulations, Michael! Your Wolf Mark has advanced to <u>Wolf Protector</u>. Alphas are the protectors of the Pack, responsible for shepherding their people and seeing to their welfare. But an Alpha's charge is only one Pack, and ultimately, their reach is limited. Beyond the Alphas are the Protectors, roving guardians responsible for the safety of all wolfkind.

As a result of your new Wolf Mark, your Class trait, wolfwalker, has evolved to <u>voidwalker</u>!

Your deepening Wolf Mark has unearthed a rare but not insignificant aspect of your lupine heritage, granting you the trait <u>voidwalker</u>. In

addition to enhancing your senses in all environments, this trait also grants you the ability to see through the obscuring fog of the nether.

Congratulations, Michael! You are ready to experience your first higher evolution. As the bearer of both the Mark of a Wolf Protector and a Powerful Initiate, you may acquire an epic Class.
Do you wish to begin your higher evolution now?

"Damn," I muttered, eyes widening in shock. I'd not expected a class evolution, and certainly not so quickly after obtaining the Power Mark.

"What's wrong?" Adriel asked, sensing something amiss.

"It's my Class," I whispered. "It's ready to evolve."

The spirit's eyes narrowed. *"Ready to evolve? Or already evolved?"* she asked intently.

"It hasn't changed yet if that's what you're asking."

"Then you haven't responded to the Adjudicator's request?" she persisted.

"I haven't," I agreed.

"Good. Don't. I suggest we talk before you do." Adriel's eyes darted upward. *"But later. It seems we finally have Draven's attention."*

Glancing up myself, I saw it was true. Draven was staring straight at Adriel and me. Banishing the thought of my impending evolution, I gave the guardian my full attention.

"What do we have here?" he asked. The guardian's voice was deep and hollow, as if it originated from a stone chamber, which of course, it did. Leaning down, he placed his face inches from Adriel's.

Unlike Kolath, Draven did not creak when he moved. Instead, his stone-form seemed as supple as flesh. "You smell of Death," he told Adriel. "And not Death." He turned my way. "And you, you are a Wolf."

Adriel bowed from the waist. *"You are correct, Draven. Your powers of observation are as astute as reputed."* She bowed again. *"As is your might. You have rid the sector of the foul nether for which you have our eternal gratitude."*

I hid a smile. Adriel was laying it on a bit thick, but I said nothing. As we'd agreed, she would do the talking, at least initially.

Draven grunted. "Pretty words will not aid you, lich," he spat. "I know what you are: Oath breaker. Forsworn. SCUM!"

Beside me, I felt Adriel stiffen but she didn't otherwise react to the guardian's insults. My own smile faded. Draven was proving more obnoxious than I expected, and I dearly wanted to retort, but following Adriel's lead, I stayed quiet.

"You severed your ties with your House," Draven continued, his words dropping like stones into the silence. "Why would I bother troubling myself with one such as you?"

"I had my reasons," Adriel said neutrally.

"REASONS!" Draven's roared, rearing up to his full height again. "What possible reasons could excuse your treachery?"

Once more, Adriel stayed calm. *"It's a long story and one we don't have time for now."* She gestured to the almost forgotten Emblem on which Draven's right hoof still rested. *"The tithe will not last long."*

"The tithe," Draven said, his lips curling up disdainfully. "Forget the tithe. I have time enough."

Adriel's gaze sharpened. *"You do?"* Her eyes roved over the guardian's form. *"Your energy reserves are full,"* she guessed.

"They are," Draven said smugly.

My brows drew down, and studying the guardian anew, I spotted the signs the lich must have picked up on. Draven practically thrummed with life. As I'd noticed earlier, his movements were smooth and sure. Then I'd thought that only marked him as different from Kolath. Now, I realized there was more to it.

Where Nexus' guardian had been on his last legs and fighting to conserve every iota of energy, Draven appeared to enjoy a happy surplus. Nor did he seem averse to spending it with abandon. Even now, the guardian could not remain still. His hind legs shifted restlessly, and his tail swished lazily.

"How is that possible?" Adriel asked. *"You've been asleep for centuries. And in all that time, you received no tithes. Your wells should be depleted."*

And if the guardian is as replete with energy as he claims, why didn't he respond to the nether's invasion before this? I wondered. I was sure the same question had occurred to Adriel, but for whatever reason, she'd chosen not to voice it.

Draven, though, seemed in no mood to answer even the simplest of questions put before him, and his only response was a sneering grin that irritated me no end.

I had had enough. "Answer her!" I snapped.

Turning away from Adriel, the guardian looked down his nose at me. "You do not command me, Wolf. You are no Prime."

"Perhaps not," I growled. "But it is *we* who awoke you. It is *we* who defeated the harbinger and caused the void tree to flee." I took a step forward, bristling with anger. "If not for me and Adriel, this sector would have fallen to the nether, and you would be a pile of rubble. A little gratitude would not go amiss!"

"Careful," Adriel cautioned on a whisper-thin thread. She did not urge me to stop, though. *"Don't push him too far."*

I nodded minutely but did not tear my gaze away from Draven. "Tell us, o great guardian," I said sarcastically, "why have you failed in your duty? Why did you allow the stygians to run amok in this dungeon?" I took another step forward. "Or is it *you* who is truly forsworn?"

"How DARE you!" Draven bellowed. Rearing up, he brought his forelegs crashing down less than a yard from me.

I did not retreat or flinch. Folding my arms across my chest, I glared back at him.

"I did not fail my duty!" he roared, pricked into responding by my adamant stare.

"Oh? Then what would you call it?" I asked contemptuously.

"I did not know!" Draven said, shying away from my gaze. His tone softened. "I did not know the stygians had breached the barrier."

"Did not know?" Adriel asked, floating to my side. *"How could you not—"* She broke off.

"You put yourself in stasis," she said, with dawning realization. *"Didn't you?"*

Hanging his head, Draven did not answer for a drawn-out moment. "I did," he finally whispered.

I stared at the giant statue, contrite and abashed. Was this the same Draven who had been bellowing in anger only a minute ago? Perhaps Adriel had been right to be wary about the state of the guardian's mind. Perhaps Draven was not all there.

"What's stasis?" I asked Adriel in an aside.

"It's the deepest form of slumber that guardians can assume," she replied. *"It severs all connections between them and the world. When in such a state, the guardians consume almost no energy. Their minds are asleep, the barrier defenses are not actively maintained, and they have no awareness of... well, anything, really. They cannot even awaken themselves if they want to. As you can imagine, going into stasis is fraught with peril and was only meant as a measure of last resort—for when a guardian's mind was too far gone or her energy nearly depleted."*

She turned back to Draven. *"What could have possessed you to do that?"*

"What choice was there?" the centaur answered, still not looking at us.

Adriel frowned. *"What does that mean?"*

Draven shrugged. "The Houses had fallen. The Primes were dead. The dungeons were abandoned. Something had to be done."

My brows rose. "You know about the fall of the ancients?" I asked, thinking about Kolath's ignorance.

"Of course," Draven said. "Most of us did. That was when we made the decision to go into hiding. It was that or resign ourselves to a slow decline into oblivion."

"Couldn't you have helped the Primes?" I asked. "Why didn't you fight with them against the new Powers?"

Draven raised his head then. "Oh, we wished to. But the ancients' own directives kept us confined to the dungeons. And the new Powers were smart. They knew better than to fight both us and the Primes simultaneously, which is why they and their Sworn abandoned the dungeons during the war and immediately after."

"You said we," Adriel interjected. *"Does that mean the other guardians have also put themselves in stasis?"*

Draven met her gaze, his face expressionless and absent of his earlier mockery. "Yes. Every guardian that was awake agreed to the plan. Together, we relocated ourselves to the remotest dungeons, severed the guardian network, and placed ourselves in deep slumber."

"All of you?" Adriel gasped, looking shocked by the notion. *"That would have left every dungeon vulnerable. By now, hundreds of sectors have probably fallen to the nether!"*

"Probably," Draven agreed bleakly. *"But it was that or let the network itself be compromised."*

Adriel squeezed her eyes shut, trying to come to terms with the consequence of the guardians' decision. Meanwhile, another Game message scrolled through my mind.

You have completed the task: <u>Silent Brethren</u>! You have uncovered the reason behind the silence of Kolath's brothers and sisters. Draven and the others were unresponsive to the Nexus guardian's hails because they had placed themselves in stasis.

Wolf is pleased by your effort on the guardian's behalf, and your Mark has deepened.

Draven's head jerked in my direction. "Kolath? You've met Kolath?"

I blinked, startled in turn. "You saw the task message?"

"Of course," Draven said, waving aside my question as he leaned forward intently. "Tell me about Nexus' guardian. How is my brother?"

I hesitated, then gave him the truth. "Not... good. He has been alone too long, I think."

"Ah," Draven exhaled, his eyes turning sorrowful.

"I'm guessing Kolath was one of the unlucky few who was not awake when you and the others decided to hide?" I asked, trying to fit together the pieces of both guardians' disparate stories.

Draven nodded. "Alas, given his proximity to Nexus, Kolath was more vulnerable than the rest of us. The new Powers struck at him early and cut him off from the rest of us before the war kicked off in earnest."

"I see," I murmured.

Adriel opened her eyes, calm and composed once more. *"You still haven't told us why."*

"Why what?" Draven asked, with furrowed brows.

"To what end did you and the others go into hiding?" she clarified.

"Isn't it obvious?" Draven asked. "To await the ancients' return." His gaze fell on me again. "Tell me, Wolf. Where is your Prime? I must meet him. We have much to discuss." Despite his attempt at keeping his face bland, the guardian could not conceal the glint of hope in his gaze as he awaited my answer.

"There is no Wolf Prime," I said softly. "House Wolf lies in ruins just like the other Houses." I paused. "But I mean to restore it before I'm done."

The guardian looked crestfallen at the news. His gaze flitted between me and Adriel. "I sense I may have been too... harsh in my earlier judgment, and there is much I remain ignorant of. If you two will indulge me, I think it is time I heard your tales in full."

I nodded. "I think so, too. My own story began with..."

"So, even after all these years, justice has not been served," Draven lamented once we were done.

"It has not," I agreed. Draven had listened patiently to our tales. Although Adriel's story had troubled him, my description of Nexus and the political climate amongst the new Powers seemed to disconcert him more.

"What will you do now?" Adriel asked.

"Do?" Draven repeated, shifting restlessly on his hooves. "I'm not... sure. The usurpers acted more shrewdly than I anticipated. How can the Primes return if players no longer practice our ancient traditions? Worse yet, the Houses appear to have been forgotten."

"Not entirely," I protested. "Some still remember the old ways and seek to restore it."

Draven hung his head. "Be that as it may, I fear my brethren, and I erred in our withdrawal. We gave the rebels time, and they used it." His mouth twisted. "Now, these so-called new Powers have consolidated their rule."

I had nothing to say to that. As far as it went, it was true.

"Unseating them will be difficult," Adriel agreed, *"but not impossible."*

Draven shook his head as if to banish his despair. "You are right," he said softly. "Hope remains."

Adriel floated higher, placing herself at eye level with the centaur. *"So again, I ask, guardian: what will you do?"*

"And more to the point," I added, "will you help me restore House Wolf?"

Draven's gaze flitted from the lich to me. "I will," he affirmed. "But I cannot act directly. Nor can I remain awake indefinitely. It drains me too much."

I grinned triumphantly, unbothered by the limitations he'd expressed. The aid of a being as powerful as the guardian—no matter the form it took— could not be discounted.

At the very least, I could use the Reach as a shelter for those friendly to the ancients' cause. After all, what better protection could I ask for than that of a guardian? Even better, the dungeon already housed a sizable city.

Do I need to rethink my plans?

Biting hard at my lip, I pondered the question. Instead of one sector—the hidden nether-infested one—I now had *two* possible locations for House Wolf. Nor did I need the wolves' valley as much anymore. *I could sell the tavern,* I thought, *and Saya could—*

"I have a proposal for you," Adriel said, floating closer to Draven.

Realizing what topic my companion was about to broach, I broke off from my musings to focus on her. It seemed Adriel hadn't forgotten her own plans, either.

Draven cocked his head to the side. "A proposal?"

For a moment, I contemplated interrupting. The centaur's attitude towards the lich had mellowed, especially after he'd heard her tale, but given his temperamental nature, there was no telling what his reaction would be to the former Death scion's request.

It would've been wiser to wait or abandon the notion altogether—Draven did not appear to be a spirit needing replacement—but I understood Adriel's determination. She had been looking forward to this moment for a long time. Sitting down cross-legged, I held off intervening and made myself comfortable.

"Yes," Adriel said after taking a moment to gather her thoughts. *"I offer myself in your place."*

Draven's bushy brows drew down. "Offer yourself? I do not understand."

Adriel drew herself stiffly erect. *"I propose that I take up your charge and stand watch over this dungeon and the others under your purview."* She paused. *"I wish to replace you as guardian."*

Draven's expression turned grave. "And why would you want that?"

Adriel sighed. *"To make restitution,"* she said softly. *"For abandoning my House and for the many lives I've claimed. This way, I can serve the Primes again."*

For a long moment, Draven did not respond. "Thank you for the offer," he said solemnly. "But no. Becoming a guardian is an onerous duty."

Adriel raised her arms, palms out. *"But—"* she began.

Draven held up a hand, stopping her. "It is not that I doubt your commitment. Rather, say I am not yet ready to relinquish my own burdens."

Adriel deflated. *"Oh."*

"There is a war to be fought," the guardian continued, "and I will not go to my rest easily knowing I stepped aside."

The light in his eyes flared, and I suspected something had occurred to the centaur.

"Still, your proposal is intriguing," Draven went on. "Vital even, given that there are few around able to take up the mantle of a guardian." He paused, waiting for the lich's reaction.

But lost in her despondency, Adriel failed to mark the guardian's subtle prompting.

"There are others who may take you up on your offer," Draven added more forthrightly.

That caught Adriel's attention. *"Others?"*

"Yes, others." The guardian gestured my way. "Given the young wolf's description of Kolath's condition, I suspect he will go willingly to the long sleep if offered the chance."

Adriel glanced at me, a wordless question in her gaze.

I nodded. "He was quite despondent."

"I'm sure you know this already," Draven went on, addressing Adriel again, "but do not forget Nexus is a vital cog in the guardian defense network. It is why the rebels made sure to neutralize Kolath early on. If you truly mean to serve the Primes again, then it is Kolath you should look to replace."

A complex stream of emotions crossed Adriel's face. Floating back to the ground, she bowed low to the giant statue. *"Your words are wise, guardian.*

Thank you. I will present myself to Kolath." She glanced at me. *"Assuming our 'young Wolf' is not averse to escorting me there?"*

I laughed. "Of course, I'm not."

"Excellent!" Draven pronounced. "This could work out well in our favor." He studied me thoughtfully. "Nor should we let the deed go unrewarded. Let's make it... official." Closing his eyes, the guardian caused words to appear in my mind.

Draven has allocated you a new task: <u>Restore the Nexus Guardian</u>. Draven fears that Kolath can no longer fulfill his duties as a guardian. Your objective is to reawaken the Nexus Guardian and see that the lich Adriel replaces him.

My breath caught, prompting a quizzical look from Adriel. "He's given me a task," I explained.

"Good," she said after I described the new task to her. *"That's settled, then."* She turned back to Draven. *"But was that wise? I cannot claim to know the extent of your capabilities, guardian, but I do know that the granting tasks are not without cost. How much of your energy did that consume?"*

The centaur shrugged. "I cannot act outside of the sectors I control. But that does not mean I am powerless to sway events towards a course I desire." He pointed to me. "This way, I ensure my agent does not go unrewarded."

I bristled. I certainly did not consider myself Draven's 'agent,' but this was not the time to contest the term. "Rewarded?" I asked instead.

"I cannot aid you directly," he replied.

I frowned. Draven had something similar earlier, but I still didn't understand what he meant. "Why not?"

Draven crooked one eyebrow. "You do not know?"

I shook my head.

He gestured to Adriel. "Considering your companion's proposal, I take it you know of my origins?"

I nodded. "You are a former scion."

"Correct," Draven said. "And therein lies the answer. House loyalty is not easily forgotten or relinquished. I assure you every guardian remembers their House. Despite the neutrality required by our new existence, we are all more well-disposed to our former Houses and less... charitable to its enemies." He shrugged massive shoulders. "It is because of this that Primes felt it necessary to bind us more closely when it came to the matter of players."

I tilted my head to the side. "And that means what exactly?"

"No guardian can act against a player or favor him in any way *unless* it relates directly to our core mission—protecting the dungeons—and even then, an Adjudicator-approved task is required."

"I see," I muttered.

Adriel frowned. *"But doesn't that also stop you from acting against the new Powers?"*

The centaur grinned, but the expression was devoid of mirth. "Strictly speaking, that is correct. At the war's start, though, each of the new Powers was given a task—stop their revolt against the Primes or face the consequences. Needless to say, none complied. Their failure to heed our warning makes any new Power or Sworn who enters a guardian-controlled sector fair game."

"But only if the guardian is awake," I pointed out.

Draven grimaced. "That, too, is unfortunately correct. But now that I'm out of stasis, I can awaken myself whenever necessary." He bared his teeth. "Even now, I can sense a few potential targets in some of my more populated dungeons. Destroying them will be sweet."

"Don't do that!" I exclaimed, alarmed by the guardian's bloodthirsty grin.

Draven snorted. "Don't mistake me for a pup, young Wolf. I've seen more wars in my lifetime than years you have lived. The time is not yet right to strike. When I *do* act, it will be with overwhelming force and with the support of my brethren."

"Right," I said, relaxing.

"Then you mean to awaken the rest of the guardians," Adriel surmised.

"I do," Draven confirmed.

"How?" I asked.

"With your help, of course," the guardian said. "My brothers and sisters are scattered all over the Nethersphere. It will be up to you to find and awaken each." Before I could respond, Draven waved his hand, causing another Game alert to unfurl in my mind.

Draven has allocated you a new task: <u>Revive the Guardians</u>. The guardian of the Reach is intent on restarting the now-defunct war between the Primes and new Powers. But before he does so, he has asked you to restore his brethren. Your objective is to find the remaining guardians and awaken them from stasis.

My gaze flitted between the centaur and the Game message still hanging in front of me. "That's it?" I asked, slightly incredulous. "You can't give me more information than that?"

"Sadly, I cannot," Draven said. "My brethren and I went to pains to conceal our locations from each other—in case the worst happened. However, I have a few ideas about where you should begin your search and the perfect means of getting you started."

"Did he give you another task?" Adriel asked before I could respond.

"He has," I said and went on to describe it.

"That sounds reasonable," she said.

I nodded in agreement and accepted the task.

"What is the rest of your plan then?" Adriel asked, taking up the reins of the conversation again.

The centaur tugged at his beard. "What makes you sure there is more?"

"There must be," she insisted with more of her usual assertiveness. *"Restoring the other guardians may keep the new Powers at bay for a time. But time is their ally, not yours. They will outlast you."*

The centaur inclined his head, conceding the point, then pointed one stubby finger at me. "Him. *He* is the rest of my plan."

CHAPTER 383: TOYING WITH ONE'S REWARD

I scrambled to my feet. "What does that mean?"

I was not about to become anyone's pawn, not even a guardian's, and while I had no compunctions about restoring any of the other guardians, doing so would not take precedence over my own plans.

"Awakening my brethren is only half of what needs to be done," Draven continued, ignoring my less-than-happy reaction. "If we are to defeat the new Powers, bringing about the return of the Primes is also crucial. And you, wily Wolf, are the key to that."

"I am?" I asked warily. "What about the Prime that still lives?" While retelling my tale, I had told Draven about the Prime that Kolath claimed was still alive. Unlike me, Draven didn't appear to doubt the other guardian's words, and though the news had first excited him, his interest had quickly waned. "Have you forgotten about her?"

"I have not," Draven said, shaking his head. "But wherever the Prime is sheltering, she is out of my reach." His look grew thoughtful. "She must be hiding in one of the dungeons under Kolath's control."

I frowned. "I don't follow."

Draven's voice took on a lecturing tone. "Every guardian has hundreds of dungeons under their charge. Outside of our dungeons, a guardian is nearly blind and powerless. But inside them... inside them, we are all-knowing. I, for instance, am aware of each creature in every sector forming part of my domain. None can escape my attention—unless, of course, they are a being akin to a Power and take measures to shield themselves. But even then, few Powers can hide themselves so fully as to vanish completely from a guardian's sight."

"Which is why Kolath could sense the hidden Prime but not locate her," Adriel deduced.

"That is my guess," Draven agreed.

"She must be in one of Nexus' dungeons," I mused. "But knowing that doesn't help much. There are dozens of dungeons in Nexus."

"And with most of them under the control of the new Powers' factions, getting to her will be even harder," Adriel added.

I nodded absently. What Adriel said was true enough and complicated matters significantly. Finding the lost Prime would not be easy.

"There may be a way around the factions," Draven said abruptly.

I stared at him in surprise. "How?"

The guardian waved away my question. "That's not important right now. To get back to the lost Prime—*she* is another reason why we must replace Kolath's flagging spirit with a stouter one." He glanced at Adriel. "A stronger Nexus guardian should be able to get a fix on her location."

My eyes narrowed thoughtfully. "That *is* good news."

"Finding the Prime will be your third mission." Draven held my gaze. "Will you do it?"

I didn't respond immediately. At the fore of my mind was what Adriel had told me only hours ago about the strife between the ancients. She had warned me that not every House would be keen to see Wolf rise again. Given that, there was no reason to assume the lost Prime would be friendly. Ally or foe—I wouldn't know which she was until I found her.

But *first*, I would have to find her.

And if that was all Draven was asking, then I could do as he bade. Coming to a decision, I nodded slowly.

"Thank you," the guardian said gravely. "I will grant you a task to that effect."

In response, a Game message unfurled in my mind.

The guardian, Draven, has allocated you a new task: <u>Locate the Lost Prime</u>. Draven has resolved to bring about the return of the Primes. To that end, he has tasked you with finding the hidden Prime. Your objective is to locate her and report back to Draven on her whereabouts.

"Now, finally, we come to the matter of your reward," the guardian said after I accepted the task.

My brows rose. "My reward? Reward for what?"

"For finishing Kolath's mission, of course," Draven replied. "Given the lengths you had to go to complete the task—finding me, completing the Emblem, *and* ridding the sector of the nether—you've earned a guardian's favor. Since my brother is asleep again, the Game will allow me to reward you in his stead."

Besides me, I sensed Adriel stiffen. Draven's words had caught her interest. I kept my attention on the guardian, though. I had a whole host of questions I wanted to ask.

But before I could speak, Draven held up his hand. "Be warned, a guardian's favor is not lightly earned, nor should it be frivolously spent. Do not believe completing every task from a guardian will earn you one. The Adjudicator alone assesses when granting a favor is... appropriate."

Saying nothing, I shot Adriel a sideways glance.

Her face was suffused with excitement. *"This is a great opportunity,"* she confirmed. *"The guardians' influence may be limited to the Endless Dungeon, but that does not lessen the value of their favor. Few were fortunate enough to earn a boon from them, even in my time. Those that did invariably used them to claim new sectors, acquire rare feats, or unearth legendary sets."*

"What the lich says is true," Draven said. "Most who have come before you have used their boons to access virgin dungeons—previously unexplored sectors—earning themselves a heap of feats and achievements in the process. But you need not use your own boon in that manner. There are few limits to the favor; I can send you anywhere in the Endless Dungeon, even to sectors that are inaccessible to you."

I gulped, amazed by the enormity of what Draven was offering. *"Any* sector?" I repeated, trying to come to grips with the choices on hand. "How would that even work?"

Draven shrugged. "I will create a portal to wherever you want to go."

"A portal?" I asked, struggling to contain my confusion. "But I thought opening a portal into a dungeon was impossible!"

Draven smiled. "For players and Powers, perhaps. But it is the guardians who uphold the barriers around the dungeon sectors. The barriers that stop the nether from invading also prevent anyone from teleporting into or out of a dungeon."

I shook my head. "But how would you even locate the right sector?" I asked, recalling the bit of lore I'd gained from Captain Talon and Loken. "I thought dungeons were islands lost in the dark void, with no chartable path to or from them."

"That is correct as far as it goes," Draven said. "But you are forgetting the guardian network. It is what makes this possible. The network's ley lines are the lifeblood of the Endless Dungeon, the backbone that connects every dungeon sector together. Only the guardians have access to it in its entirety."

My brows drew down uncertainly. "Didn't you and the other guardians destroy the network?"

Draven chuckled. "No, the network cannot be destroyed. It is always growing." His smile faded. "But sometimes contracting too. When my brethren and I placed ourselves in stasis, we did not pull down the network. We only severed our connections to it. Now that the Reach is secure again, I will reestablish contact with the network."

"Is that not dangerous?" Adriel asked.

"Only if I come under threat again," Draven allowed. He turned back to me. "Rejoining the network is necessary, anyway. It is the only way to find out if any of my remaining brethren are awake."

"So why haven't you done so already?" I asked curiously.

"I have already begun the process, but it will be a few hours before I am finally reconnected."

I rubbed at my temple, pondering the implications of Draven's revelations. "Will you be able to communicate with the other guardians after you do?"

"Only if they are awake or slumber lightly." Draven sighed. "I fear, though, most of my brethren will be in stasis or too close to the ragged edge—like Kolath—to respond."

I bowed my head. Draven had given me a lot to digest, and I needed to think things through carefully before making any further decisions. The guardians, I was coming to realize, could become my strongest allies yet in the fight against the new Powers. Yes, they were constructs, and yes, their primary purpose was keeping the nether out of the dungeons. But they were more than that.

They could be *made* into more than that.

Wielded correctly, they could become weapons against the new Powers.

Sure, the Game constrained what the guardians could do or how they could act. But Draven had not hidden that his brethren's first allegiance lay with the Primes, that they would do *everything* they could to bring about their return. Their willingness—eagerness even—to bring about the new Powers' downfall was the key.

I could work with that.

I would *have* to work with it and find a way around the Game's restrictions to secure the guardians' allegiance. Because what Draven's words had made clear was that it was the guardians who controlled the Endless Dungeon.

They alone could communicate across its breadth.

They alone had access to its entirety.

And they alone could open portals to and from anywhere in the Endless dungeon.

All priceless advantages in a war. I knew then that when the time came to wage open war against the new Powers, it would not be in the Kingdom sectors where we would contest their might but in the Endless Dungeon—with the guardians at our back.

"Michael?" Adriel asked, pulling me out of my musings. *"Are you still with us?"*

"Sorry," I muttered, "just daydreaming." I glanced at Draven's impatiently waiting visage. "Tell me more about the guardian's favor."

"What do you want to know?" he asked.

"Well, for instance, what *can't* I do with it?"

"A good question," the centaur chuckled. "You *can't* ask me to kill any being—dungeon creature or player—and you *can't* ask me to manufacture loot for you. Nor can you ask me to claim a sector on your faction's behalf. Beyond that, anything goes."

I eyed him askance. "Anything?"

"Almost anything," Draven corrected. "Whatever boon you choose will be confined to a single sector."

"Ah," I thought, deflating slightly. It had been on the tip of my tongue to ask for a map of the Endless Dungeon or access to the entire network. Something else occurred to me. "Is it the favor you had in mind when you said there may be a way around the factions who control access to Nexus' dungeons?"

Draven nodded. "Yes. Saving your boon until you discover the lost Prime is one of the options open to you. When you find her, I or any other guardian can teleport you to her location."

"Can't Michael use the favor to find her?" Adriel asked. *"Or your brethren, for that matter?"*

Draven shook his head. "The favor does not make the impossible possible, nor does it let me do what I cannot normally do. It only allows me—for one rare instance—to act on your behalf while unconstrained by the bindings imposed by the Game."

I rubbed my chin thoughtfully. "Could you close the entrance portal to a dungeon?" I asked, thinking of the portal between the wolves' valley and Erebus' dungeon.

Draven frowned. "Permanently, you mean?"

I nodded.

"I could," he said. "But opening a new entrance or exit would require a second favor."

I stowed away that little tidbit, then turned my attention to something else the guardian had mentioned. "When we discussed the lost Prime earlier, you said, 'one of the options.' I take it from that, you have other options in mind?"

Draven grinned eagerly. This was a question he'd been waiting for me to ask, I realized.

"I do," the guardian said, leaning forward eagerly. "If you heed my advice, you will not save your boon for visiting the lost Prime nor for plundering a virgin dungeon. Instead, I can send you to a sector where I believe one of my brethren has taken refuge."

"Oh?" I asked, curiosity piqued. "I thought you didn't know their locations?"

"I don't," Draven agreed. "But I can guess. Like me, the others would have chosen an out-of-the-way dungeon. And there are only so many of those to choose from."

"Hmm," I said, rubbing the side of my face. I didn't want to dismiss the guardian's suggestion out of hand, but I also didn't like using my favor on a guess, even a well-educated one.

I rose to my feet. "I will think upon it."

"You don't have much time to decide," Adriel warned. *"The guardian will have to go to sleep soon."*

"Correct," Draven said.

"I understand," I said, "but you still have to reconnect yourself to the guardian network, don't you?"

"True," Draven agreed.

"Then, before I decide how to use my favor, I would like to hear the outcome of that."

The guardian sighed. "Very well, young Wolf. But don't delay your decision too long. Time waits for no one."

CHAPTER 384: DOING THE UNEXPECTED

"Draven's suggestion is a good one," Adriel said. *"And perhaps the best course."*

Glancing up, I saw the spirit floating beside me. I'd left her and the guardian only a few minutes ago to ruminate over the choices he'd presented me with. I didn't know what the two had spoken about, but I could guess.

"I know," I replied, letting my gaze drift back to the landscape. Now that the nether cloud was gone, I could see the entirety of the rocky valley that had housed the void sapling. For the most part, it was flat and unbroken. Here and there, though, shards of oblong black crystal—remnants of the stygian nest—cut through the surface.

In the far distance, huddling in the shadows of the cliffs rimming the valley—and about as far away from the guardian as they could get—I spotted clumps of nether creatures. They, unfortunately, had not been banished with the nether nor destroyed entirely, even after Draven's killing spree.

How many remain? I wondered. A hundred? Two hundred? *More,* I thought. They were still a threat—if a minor one.

"Shouldn't we kill them?" Ghost asked, following my thoughts.

"We will if they are foolish enough to attack us," I assured her, *"but I suspect Draven will get around to dealing with them eventually."*

"Oh," she said, sounding disappointed. *"But what about the seeds? We shouldn't just leave them lying around. It's not safe."*

My lips twitched upwards. The spirit wolf was bored and anxious to begin her new existence, not that I could blame her. Trapped in a cloak, I would be just as restless.

Before I could respond to her, though, Adriel spoke again. *"Then, why are you reluctant?"*

I turned back to the lich, mentally backtracking to pick up on the threads of the conversation again. Her question was pertinent, but the answer was neither straightforward nor easy to define. "What Draven said was true. Time waits for no one."

Adriel cocked her head to the side. *"I don't understand."*

I sighed. "I've already lost over a month in—"

"Prime?" Ghost interjected. *"Did you hear me?"*

I broke off, losing my train of thought.

"I think we should seek out the remaining seeds," she added.

"What is it?" Adriel asked nearly at the same time.

For a moment, I sat there, mouth open, eyes unseeing, and attention split between the two disembodied entities who could neither see nor hear each other. "I'm an idiot, that's what." I laughed. "Trying to hold two conversations at once is not a good idea."

The frown marring Adriel's face vanished. *"Ah. Ghost is awake,"* she guessed.

I nodded. *"Should I let her manifest?"* I asked, projecting my voice to both of them simultaneously.

"Yes, please!" Ghost exclaimed, seeds forgotten.

Adriel's response was more tempered. *"I suppose,"* she conceded, gaze darting to the distant stygians. *"She has waited long enough."* The spirit smiled suddenly. *"And I'm as keen to see her as she is to get out."*

Grinning, I turned my attention inward. *"Adriel says you can come out—but only for a short time,"* I warned. *"And no wandering off."*

"Of course, Prime!" Ghost replied, her mindglow dancing with delight.

Saying nothing, I waited. Despite my admonishment, I, too, felt no small measure of excitement. Finally, I would get to see Ghost in her new form.

Trails of gray flowed out of the cloak—from the seams, the collar, the arms, everywhere. I glanced over my shoulder. The smoke was forming behind me, too, and if I hadn't known better, I would've thought it was *I* who was the source.

Rising to my feet, I turned around in a slow circle. The cloud about me was growing denser every second, obscuring me from sight. *Interesting,* I thought.

A moment later, Ghost's mindglow vanished from my awareness. She had slipped out of the cloak, I realized. Where she was, I couldn't tell. But I could guess.

The smoke was still gathering, growing so thick and dark that it was reminiscent of the void. I sensed no danger from it, though. If anything, it felt welcoming. Raising my arms, I waved them gently through the cloud.

Two orbs of glowing orange appeared before me.

Ghost.

I reached out to her, but before I could make contact, the cloud coalesced in a rush, sucked into and around the shining eyes.

Ghost has cast manifest and has taken the form of a level 1 stygian pyre wolf.

I blinked. A great, big wolf sat in front of me, one formed from the cold, unrelieved darkness of the void. No, that wasn't quite true. While Ghost's new body was all liquid darkness, her eyes shone with warmth—the warmth of a phoenix's undying flames.

Her breath came out in puffs of ash, and when she curled her lips, I saw her teeth bore the distinctive cast of magma. A speck of saliva dripped out of her mouth. I followed it, watching avidly as the tiny drop hit the ground. The rock hissed, then melted, leaving a shallow indentation.

Ghost was a being of fire.

One wrapped in a shell of nether.

A stygian pyre wolf indeed.

Ghost was of the void—and not. She had true mass, where most stygians didn't. She was far different from an ordinary creature of flesh and blood, though. Blood did not run in her veins; the blazing warmth of a phoenix's flames did. And where her organs should have been, only the smoky darkness of the nether was to be found.

She was both life and its antithesis, and as Adriel had said, she was truly unique, something the Game had never seen before.

"Well?" a voice demanded in my mind. *"What do you think?"*

I let my gaze drift back upward until I was staring into Ghost's orange eyes. In her new form, the spirit wolf—*pyre wolf,* I amended—was at eye level with me. "It's perfect," I said, grinning broadly. "*You're* perfect."

Ghost wagged her tail.

Adriel floated forward. Circling the pyre wolf, she studied her critically from every angle. *"Does everything work?"*

My eyes widened at the question. "Does everything—?" I broke off, deciding I didn't want to know what she meant by that.

Ghost bobbed head up and down. *"I think so. Like the Prime said, it's perfect. Thank you, Adriel!"*

Her answer did not satisfy the lich, though.

"We'll see," Adriel remarked noncommittally. Continuing her inspection, she ordered Ghost to move a foreleg forward, back, up, down, left, and right. Then, she began with the next leg, piling on instruction after instruction, all of which Ghost complied with obligingly.

I sat back down. Adriel, it seemed, was determined to be thorough, and not wanting to interfere, I watched on in silence as she ran Ghost through her paces.

✳ ✳ ✳

"She'll do," Adriel pronounced after what seemed entirely too long.

I nodded gravely, concealing a smile. *"That's good to hear."*

The spirit sank to the ground, mimicking my pose. A dozen yards away, Ghost... frolicked. That was the only word I could think of to describe it. Leaping and darting left and right, the pyre wolf pounced on random pieces of rock. Unlike an ordinary pup, though, her magma teeth crushed the stones into dust, her stygian claws dug deep grooves in the ground, and her flame breath left puddles of melted rock in her wake.

"She seems happy," Adriel commented as we watched Ghost, legs in the air, rub her liquid-black coat against a particularly sharp rock to scratch an itch.

"She is," I confirmed, feeling the glee roll off the wolf's mind in waves.

"And you? What do you think?" Adriel asked.

I turned to face her. "I think you did better than Ghost, and I had any right to expect. Thank you."

She nodded simply.

"What happens when she becomes a familiar?" I asked. "Will she change in any way?"

From what I'd observed, Ghost had a formidable arsenal of weapons at her beck, even as a level one creature. Unfortunately, I could *only* observe. I didn't have access to the pyre wolf's Game data—I wasn't even sure she would have any—nor did I know what it would mean for Ghost to become a familiar.

"You'll see," Adriel said, smiling mysteriously.

At my confounded look, she laughed. *"I wouldn't want to spoil the surprise."*

I grunted, and we both fell silent, watching Ghost again.

"You will take care of her," Adriel said finally. It was not a question.

I shot her another glance. "You will be around to help with that. For a while at least."

She grimaced. *"It seems so."*

"The idea doesn't please you?"

A welter of emotions crossed the spirit's face. *"No..."* She sighed. *"It's just that I thought I was done with this existence."*

I nodded, understanding some of what she meant. I drew out her phylactery from a pouch. "What do we do with this now?"

She glanced at the object. *"You will have to hold it safe for the time being. Once we have decided our next move, I will return to my complex and collect another flesh golem."*

"Alright," I said, stowing away the precious item again.

"Speaking of our next move..." Adriel began, resuming our interrupted conversation as I knew she would. *"Have you decided what you will do?"*

I blew out a troubled breath. "I can't do what Draven wants."

"Why not?" she asked, not looking surprised at my answer.

"I've already lost a month in Draven's Reach, and while I'm not denying the time has been well spent, there are others who need me on the outside."

Adriel didn't say anything for a moment. *"Is it your pack that worries you?"*

"Yes," I said simply.

"Then why not keep the boon for later and return to Draven once you have seen them secure?"

I sighed again. "Because the moment I leave the dungeon, everything changes. I will be amongst players again, elite players, and envoys too—not to mention Powers. I can't walk amongst them unprepared." I raised my hands. "I know, I know. All that sounds like a good argument to take my time, to go to whichever dungeon Draven sends me to and get stronger in the process, but like the guardian said, 'time waits for no one.'" I sighed. "I *can't* wait. I don't have that luxury."

"I can see that," Adriel allowed. *"But what has changed from before? What are you—"* She stopped. *"It's your new Mark,"* she continued. *"You are afraid about what it will mean for you."*

"Yes. I may be able to hide the initiate Mark from lesser players but from the Powers? *That* I'm not so sure of." I turned to face her squarely. "You know more of the Game than I do. What do you think my chances are of concealing the Powerful Initiate Mark if I came face to face with a new Power?"

"By conceal, I take it you mean hiding the Mark using lesser imitate or another deception ability?"

I nodded.

"You are not wrong to be worried. At best, your chances of hiding the Mark are negligible—at your current deception skill, anyway."

My shoulders sagged. "That's what I thought too. Now, you understand the problem."

"Perhaps," she said, studying me thoughtfully. *"Are you considering using the guardian's favor to enter a virgin dungeon and speed-running it? Do you think it will make you strong enough to face the new Powers?"*

I shook my head. "I wish there were time for that, but I don't think that's an option either."

"So, what will you do? Don't tell me you plan on hiding with your pack on the tundra?"

"I can't do that either. The pack's future must be secured. To do that, I must revisit Nexus, the wolves' valley, and other places besides. I can't hide out forever."

Adriel's brows crinkled. *"What then? I can tell you have something in mind. What is it?"*

"I need to be prepared," I reiterated softly. "That doesn't mean getting strong enough to overcome any Power I run into—which, if I'm being realistic, may take decades—but to be ready for my inevitable defeat when I do." I stared at her mutely for a second. "I need a backup plan in case I fall."

Adriel's face grew grave. *"By 'fall,' you mean die?"*

I nodded. "Yes. I have to prepare for my final death."

"You're losing me again. How can you prepare for that?"

"Seeing House Wolf established is more important than my survival," I said bluntly.

I fell silent for a moment, chewing over those weighty words. This was the first time I'd voiced the sentiment aloud—or even acknowledged what following the way of the Wolf could cost me.

But the idea did not distress me as much as I feared it would.

I'd made my peace with the risk a long time ago, I realized. In my heart, I'd always known the path I followed could lead to an untimely death. But it would not, I vowed, lead to ruin. The guardian's favor was the key. It gave me an unlooked-for opportunity to secure House Wolf's future.

And I couldn't ignore it.

I pointed to Ghost. "Protecting her future, that of the other yet-to-be-found scions, and the rest of the pack—Oursk, Aira, Sulan, Duggar—is what's crucial. If I can do that before I plunge back into the Game, I will have a freer hand to do what I must."

"I get all that," Adriel said, sounding exasperated. *"But you still haven't told me what you intend on doing. You're being awfully cryptic."*

"I guess I am," I said blandly. "A bad habit, I suppose. I wonder where I picked it up?"

She rolled her eyes. *"Just spit it out."*

I chuckled for a moment before my humor faded. "To secure House Wolf, I have to find someone to shepherd the Pack when I'm gone."

"You don't mean me," she deduced.

My lips quirked upward. "I wish it *could* be you. Or even Safyre. But no, House Wolf needs a Wolf, and that means—"

"—finding Ceruvax!" Adriel gasped. *"You mean to locate the lost Wolf envoy."* Her eyes grew distant. *"Audacious,"* she murmured. *"But it could work."* She glanced at me. *"You will use the guardian's favor to go to him?"*

"Actually, no."

Confusion colored the spirit's face again.

My smile turned wry. "I don't want to use the boon to go to Ceruvax. I want to use it to bring him *here*."

"*It could work,*" Adriel muttered, her head bowed while she considered my proposal.

"*It should be well within the limits of the boon,*" I agreed. After all, bringing Ceruvax here was not very different from teleporting me to him, and Draven had already confirmed he could send me to any dungeon.

The spirit looked up at me again. "*But are you sure you want to do this? Except for what you learned during one brief conversation, you know nothing of the Wolf envoy.*"

I didn't answer immediately, giving the question serious consideration it deserved. What Adriel said was true. I didn't know Ceruvax. But he had survived the new Powers' hunt for centuries and was a powerful player in his own right.

More importantly, though, Ceruvax was a Wolf.

And that meant something. I knew I could trust him to protect the Packs and find another scion if I fell. "Perhaps," I conceded at last. "But that one conversation was enlightening, and he *did* steer me in the right direction."

"*I'll give you that.*" Adriel shrugged. "*For all his faults, Ceruvax was always a wily one.*"

Her words piqued my interest. "You knew him?"

"*We've met,*" she admitted. "*On House business. But I never knew him well, and it's been centuries since we last spoke.*" She held my gaze. "*You should prepare for the possibility that he might not be all there. Being hunted for as long as he has been can do strange things to one's mind.*"

"It's a risk, I agree." I sighed. "But he *is* a Wolf and, by all evidence, an exceptionally loyal one. I can't just abandon him."

A smile stole onto Adriel's face. "*Already thinking like a Prime, are you?*"

"I must," I said grimly. "Too much rests on my choices to do otherwise."

Her grin faded. "*For what it's worth, I think it's the right decision.*" She glanced to the right, in the direction of Draven. In the far-off distance, the guardian was muttering to himself, presumably still busy reconnecting himself to the guardian network. "*What about him? Have you considered his reaction?*"

I winced. The centaur would no doubt be displeased by my refusal to do as he asked. Yet, as important as the guardians were, redressing their plight came second. "I have. But like you said, it's been centuries. The guardians have waited this long. They can wait a little longer still."

She nodded, not disagreeing. "*I can see your mind is set. I will not try to dissuade you further. But Michael?*" She paused, waiting for me to look at her. "*Be careful, you don't let responsibility crush you.*"

"I won't," I affirmed, then dismissed the matter from further consideration. "Now, we have another matter to discuss."

"*Your Class evolution,*" she guessed.

"Yes," I said, eyes shining. "Tell me everything."

✳ ✳ ✳

"Are you sure you want to talk about your Class now?" Adriel asked. *"This is a matter Ceruvax is better equipped to advise you on."*

I waved aside her suggestion. "I may be willing to trust House Wolf to him, but that doesn't mean I will follow the envoy's advice in all things. I know you, and I trust you. Tell me what you know, please."

The spirit inclined her head. *"Very well, if you're sure."* She paused, taking a moment to gather her thoughts. *"What do you know about higher evolutions?"*

I shrugged. "Nothing, except what you've already told me."

She nodded. *"Then, I'll start at the beginning. Ascendent Classes are—"*

"Ascendant Classes?" I cut in.

Adriel's lips turned down fractionally. *"Sorry, that was stupid of me. I forgot you might not be familiar with the term."* She closed her eyes, thinking. *"How to explain this,"* she muttered to herself.

I waited patiently.

"Powers are players," she continued a moment later. *"But they are not only players. They are more, and what distinguishes one from the other are the ascendant Classes. The best Class an ordinary player—and this includes envoys and elites—can hope for is a master Class. Powers, though, can acquire ascendant Classes which are wholly different."* She paused. *"Is this making sense?"*

I nodded. "It is. I assume it's the Powerful Initiate Mark that gives the Powers access to these Classes?"

"Correct," she confirmed.

"So, what are they?"

"Before we get to that, there is something else I should tell you." She hesitated. *"I don't want to scare you unduly, but we should discuss the envoys. Do you know what they are?"*

I frowned, not sure why she was bringing this up. "They are players trusted by the Powers to act on their behalf."

"Good. What else? Do you know why their Powers trust them?"

"Hmm, I suppose it's because they are also Sworn and bound to their Powers through a Pact."

Adriel leaned closer. *"Yes, and do you know why they've chosen to bind themselves so?"*

"Uhm... because they cannot evolve further?"

"That could be a reason," Adriel allowed, *"but is only true in a small fraction of the cases."*

I blinked. This was news to me.

Seeing my confusion, Adriel added, *"Many players choose to become envoys even though they are capable of evolving into Powers."*

My frown deepened. "Why would they do that?"

"In order to survive," Adriel said bluntly. *"Any player with an evolved Class earns their Power Mark at level two-hundred and fifty."* She held my gaze. *"That's when they become prey. To save themselves, most potential initiates give their allegiance to a Power before reaching the rank twenty-five milestone,*

becoming Sworn or, if they are fortunate, envoys. Only this will stop an evolved player from acquiring the Mark."

I rubbed my chin thoughtfully. Sworn and envoys could not become Powers; that was what Adriel was telling me. From what I knew of the Game, it made sense.

Why would any Power trust someone who could eventually become a rival with their secrets otherwise? The earlier messages I'd received from the Adjudicator regarding my evolution only seemed to confirm all this.

"I see," I murmured, returning to the topic at hand. "And I assume the reason most Powers hunt their younger kind is to deepen their own Marks?"

"Exactly. A Power Mark will only grow when you kill another Power—and growing your Power Mark is necessary if you want to evolve your ascendant Class further."

I sighed, having feared this would be the case. "Alright. I see how that will make me a juicy target for any Power. And once I evolve, I will also have to—"

I broke off as something else occurred to me. "Wait, wait! Does getting my ascendant Class mean I won't be able to attack other players anymore?" I asked, eyes widening as I considered the implications.

"Not quite," Adriel said, covering her mouth to hide her amusement. *"After your first higher evolution, you will enter the gray area that exists between players and Powers. You will be a part, yet apart, from both groups and, as such, will be vulnerable to both."*

I nodded slowly. "And when will I complete the transition? When will I truly become a Power?"

"At the second evolution of your Power Mark." I opened my mouth, but before I could speak, Adriel went on, *"Let's save discussion of what that entails for another time, shall we? Trust me, it's an entire subject all on its own."*

"Alright," I grumbled reluctantly. "One last question on the matter then: can players attack Powers?"

"They can, but few are foolish enough to do that, as doing so lifts any restrictions the Game places on the Power against said player."

"Got it." I scratched my head, thinking hard. "I take it that everything you're telling me was how things were in your time." Which, by my reckoning, was well over a millennia ago. Everything Adriel had told me could be centuries out of date. "Do you think the same applies today?"

"I do," she said. *"I can't imagine that the Game's basic mechanics have changed much even after the Houses fell. In my day, any Powerful Initiate was fair game for a rival House's Powers. In some Houses, the situation was even worse."*

"Oh?" I asked, one eyebrow raised.

"In ancient times, each House was a law unto itself, with its own rules, traditions, and practices. Some Primes forbade infighting and used a strict series of tests to decide which scions could evolve into Powers. At the other extreme, there were the Houses that preached survival of the fittest. Then, there were those that were somewhere in the middle. They formalized conflict between scions and let ritual combat decide who advanced further."

"Interesting," I mused. "Is that why you wanted Ceruvax to advise me? So, I would get the House Wolf perspective?"

"Partly, but there is more to it, as you will soon see." She paused. *"Are you ready to move on to the discussion of ascendant Classes?"*

I nodded.

"Good. First, you should know that ascendant Classes don't mix with ordinary ones. They have their separate traits and abilities. The next thing you should know is that there are only three types of ascendant Classes."

My eyebrows shot up. "Only three?"

"Broadly speaking, yes. There are three paths open to you: that of the champion, governor, or commander." She held my gaze. *"This next bit is important, so listen closely. The champion focuses on his own growth and boosting the strength of his blood memories. The governor specializes in sector development, and the commander on the advancement of his followers and Sworn. The progression path of each House is different and unique. Nonetheless, none significantly deviate from the basic template of champion, governor, and commander."* She paused. *"Every House went to great pains to hide the details of their Class variants. House Wolf, being who they are, were more successful than most in this regard."*

"Which is why you thought Ceruvax would be better placed to explain all this," I surmised.

She nodded. *"It is also important to realize that your strategy will largely be fixed once you begin your ascendancy. Swapping to an alternate path later on, while not impossible, is difficult and invariably ill-advised."*

"I can see how that would be the case," I murmured.

"It is the reason I stopped you from completing your evolution earlier. The decision you make now is as important as the choice you made when you decided to follow the way of the Wolf."

I nodded, understanding perfectly. Closing my eyes, I replayed Adriel's words in my mind while I considered the ascendant Classes. But something about the word itself was distracting. Stilling my thoughts, I tried to identify what.

I've seen the term before, I realized. What was more, it had been used in close relation to Death.

"Stayne," I muttered aloud.

Adriel raised one eyebrow. *"What's that?"*

For the first time in what felt like forever, I recalled Erebus' skeletal henchman, the Awakened Dead leader's right hand and envoy. When I'd analyzed Stayne all those many months ago, the Game had described him as an ascendant.

"What is an ascendant undead?" I asked aloud.

Adriel looked at me strangely. *"That is not an idle question."*

Exhaling, I explained the source of my curiosity.

She frowned. *"Hmm, most who become envoys usually do so before they acquire their Power Mark, but not always. There are some who, after being defeated by a fellow Power, may choose submission instead of death. That, however, may not be the case with the skeleton player you mentioned. He may have chosen submission after death."*

My brows furrowed. "What makes you say that?"

"You did. You said he also bore a Mark of Death." Her lips twisted. *"That means this Stayne of yours is of Death's bloodline. For us, death has always been more… malleable. At some point in his existence, he likely chose to become undead."*

"Right," I muttered, not understanding entirely but willing to take her word for it.

"Meeting this Stayne would be interesting," Adriel mused.

I barked a laugh. "No doubt," I said, trying to imagine what a clash between the skeleton and the lich would be like. It was a meeting I, too, would like to see, I decided.

Adriel grinned, sharing in my amusement, but only a moment later, her smile faded. *"Are you ready to begin your evolution?"*

I shook my head. "I have a few more questions."

"Go on."

I leaned forward intently. "For starters, tell me more about the champion's path."

CHAPTER 386: ANOTHER CHOICE

"I thought you might ask about that," Adriel said with a smile. Her amusement didn't last, though. *"But before we get to the matter of your ascendant Class, there is something else you must consider."*

"Oh? What's that?"

"Your blood memories. I'm afraid they will have a bearing on your choice."

I blinked. "My blood memories? Why?"

The spirit chewed on her lower lip for a moment. *"Tell me, Michael, how many blood memories do you have?"*

"Uhm... one?"

"And therein lies the problem. It's also why I suggest you don't adopt the champion's path."

"I don't—"

"In my day, most players would already have four blood memories at this stage."

"Four?" I repeated, startled.

She nodded. *"Some scions—depending on their House—would have even more than that."* She paused. *"Do you know why you are behind in this regard?"*

I did, unfortunately. "No fallen scions are around to awaken more of my blood."

"Correct. With your House in ruins, you are likely the first anointed Wolf scion in centuries. You are unlikely to find other scions outside of the Wolf trials you've told me about. It pains me to say this, Michael, but the chances of you reaching your maximum blood memory capacity are small. And unfortunately, of the three ascendant Classes, the champion's path is the one most heavily dependent on blood memories. That being the case, adopting a champion Class would only cripple you further. You see that, right?"

I sighed. "I do." Falling silent, I reconsidered the three options before me. Naturally, my interest had first gravitated towards the champion's path. It was the Class that seemed to hold the most promise, especially given how often I found myself fighting alone.

Still, while I did not doubt the truth of Adriel's words, I wouldn't rule out becoming a champion merely because it promised to be difficult. The path was still a possibility that bore consideration, and, truthfully, it was the one that appealed to me the most. First, though, I would have to learn more. "Tell me what you know of it, anyway."

Adriel did not demur again. *"The champion Class focuses on boosting the strength of your blood memories and grants you abilities and traits to that effect. Take the power word death that Loskin used on you, for instance. Cast by an ascendant champion, that blood memory would have had even more spell stages or would've conceivably affected multiple targets."*

I winced. The archlich's blood memory had been powerful enough on its own. What would it have been like in the hands of a champion?

"It's true that not all champion abilities require blood memories," Adriel went on. *"There are some that stand on their own. However, they are fewer in*

number and ignore the strong synergies that exist between the Class and a player's blood memories. More importantly, though, while Champions are undoubtedly powerful—especially early on—most don't go on to ascend to Primehood."

My face scrunched up. "They don't?"

"No Power fights alone, Michael," Adriel said softly. *"Not if they can help it. If forced into battle, most will fight with a host of Sworn and other followers by their side. As powerful as a champion may become, he or she is still only one. And one cannot stand against hundreds."*

I grunted noncommittally. "By that reasoning, the path of the commander is the strongest."

"Not necessarily," Adriel said. *"Governors are a force to be reckoned with, too, especially when fighting in their own territory. Given the host of buffs and upgrades they can institute in the sectors they rule, a governor in his home base is well-nigh unassailable."*

I stroked my chin. By Adriel's description, a governor was a stationary target, someone easily found and attacked. And fighting a pitched battle—even with the hometown advantage—was never going to be my strong suit. *No,* I decided. No matter how spectacular the Class, I couldn't see myself becoming a governor.

"Go on," I said.

"That's about all I can tell you for certain," Adriel shrugged. *"There are a lot more nuances to each ascendant Class, but they vary from House to House."* She paused. *"To sum up: champions usually end up serving on a House's strike force, while commanders become the backbone of its armies and governors, its defenders."*

I frowned. "It sounds as if all three are essential. In fact, if I'm hearing you right, you're saying the Houses typically employed all three types of Powers simultaneously?" For whatever reason, it had never occurred to me before that any one House would have multiple Powers under its roof, but now, knowing what I did of the ascendant Classes, it seemed obvious that they must have.

"They did," Adriel confirmed. *"In my day, every House would have one or more Powers assuming each ascendant aspect. If you are determined to rebuild House Wolf, you will need others to do the same for you."* She studied me seriously. *"It's a mammoth endeavor."*

"That is becoming apparent," I muttered, deflating at the enormity of the task ahead. As usual, Adriel was right. House Wolf needed more scions. Bringing Ceruvax into the fold was a good first step, but he couldn't evolve further as an envoy.

I sighed.

More and more, it was becoming apparent I could not remain a lone wolf, not if I was serious about re-establishing House Wolf. I would have to find other Wolves—young Wolves—and I would have to protect them while they came into their strength.

And you know what that means, Michael.

My lips turned down unhappily. Despite the Class's allure, I could not become a champion. It was time to focus not on my own strength but that of my allies.

It was time to become a commander.

Inhaling deeply, I faced Adriel again. "Alright, tell me everything you know about the ascendant Classes. I know, I know. Most of it will apply to House Death and not Wolf. But tell me, anyway. I'm almost ready to make my decision."

✳   ✳   ✳

Adriel spoke for nearly an hour, sharing her knowledge freely. Mostly, I listened in silence, only interrupting where necessary. Midway through, tired of her lonely play amongst the rocks, Ghost joined us as well.

While Adriel spoke, I drew pictures on the back of the New Haven map Gamil had given me weeks ago, collating the information. The lich had glanced curiously at the parchment but hadn't questioned what I was about.

"That's it," she said finally. *"That's all I know."*

Nodding absently, I added the finishing touches to the diagram I was drawing before placing it on the ground between us. It did not, of course, include everything Adriel had shared, but it did capture the essence. "Does this look right?"

The spirit peered over the drawing, studying it intently for a long moment. *"It does,"* she finally pronounced. *"Nicely done."*

I inclined my head in acknowledgment, then bent to consider the information myself.

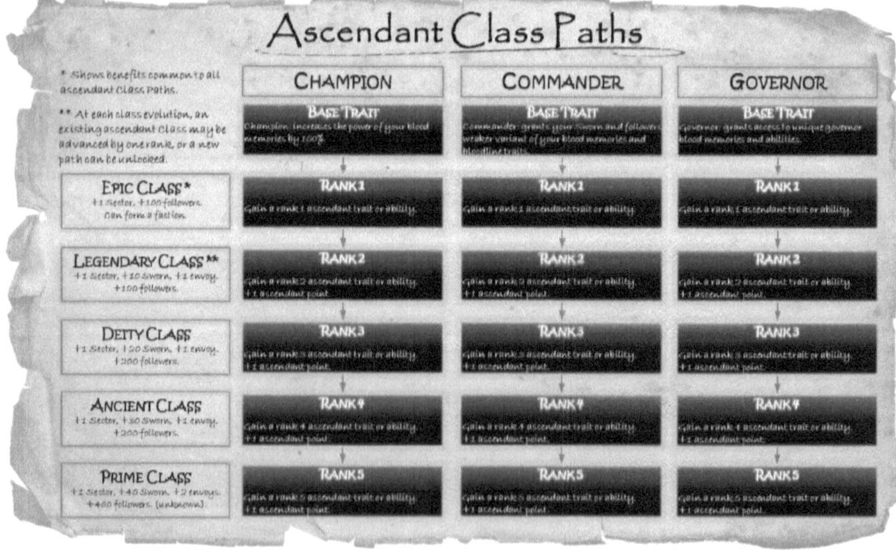

	CHAMPION	COMMANDER	GOVERNOR
	BASE TRAIT Champion: increases the power of your blood memories by 100%.	**BASE TRAIT** Commander: grants your Sworn and followers a weaker variant of your blood memories and bloodline traits.	**BASE TRAIT** Governor: grants access to unique governor blood memories and abilities.
EPIC CLASS * +1 Sector, +100 followers. Can form a faction.	**RANK 1** Gain a rank 1 ascendant trait or ability.	**RANK 1** Gain a rank 1 ascendant trait or ability.	**RANK 1** Gain a rank 1 ascendant trait or ability.
LEGENDARY CLASS ** +1 Sector, +10 Sworn, +1 envoy. +100 followers.	**RANK 2** Gain a rank 2 ascendant trait or ability. +1 ascendant point.	**RANK 2** Gain a rank 2 ascendant trait or ability. +1 ascendant point.	**RANK 2** Gain a rank 2 ascendant trait or ability. +1 ascendant point.
DEITY CLASS +1 Sector, +20 Sworn, +1 envoy. +200 followers.	**RANK 3** Gain a rank 3 ascendant trait or ability. +1 ascendant point.	**RANK 3** Gain a rank 3 ascendant trait or ability. +1 ascendant point.	**RANK 3** Gain a rank 3 ascendant trait or ability. +1 ascendant point.
ANCIENT CLASS +1 Sector, +30 Sworn, +1 envoy. +200 followers.	**RANK 4** Gain a rank 4 ascendant trait or ability. +1 ascendant point.	**RANK 4** Gain a rank 4 ascendant trait or ability. +1 ascendant point.	**RANK 4** Gain a rank 4 ascendant trait or ability. +1 ascendant point.
PRIME CLASS +1 Sector, +40 Sworn, +2 envoys. +400 followers. (unknown).	**RANK 5** Gain a rank 5 ascendant trait or ability. +1 ascendant point.	**RANK 5** Gain a rank 5 ascendant trait or ability. +1 ascendant point.	**RANK 5** Gain a rank 5 ascendant trait or ability. +1 ascendant point.

One of the first things the drawing made apparent was that the path to Primehood was both shorter and longer than I expected. I had only four more

Class evolutions ahead of me, but getting there would require climbing over the bodies of more than a few dead Powers—and I couldn't see myself facing down a Power any time soon.

Next, I noticed that all three ascendant paths employed a player's blood memories. Adriel assured me, though, that the dependency was strongest in the case of the champion Class. A commander without blood memories was still far from ideal, but that was nowhere near as problematic as in the case of a champion.

But apart from the path-specific benefits, it was the common ones that intrigued me the most—especially the ability to form a faction and claim a sector. Both would significantly ease my plans and, on their own, made the Class evolution worth it.

"Are you ready?" Adriel asked.

I glanced up at her. "I am."

She waved her hand, gesturing for me to proceed. Closing my eyes, I brought up the patiently waiting Game message.

Do you wish to begin your higher evolution now?

"I do," I murmured, willing my intent to the Adjudicator.

Commencing higher evolution...

...

...

Analysis of your player Marks completed. Viable ascendant paths determined.

Congratulations, Michael! You are now ready to begin your ascendancy and assume an epic Class. Unlike ordinary classes, ascendant Classes contain no skills. Instead, the power of your ascendant traits and abilities is determined purely by your ascendant rank and the strength of your Marks.

Three new paths lie before you.

Each focuses on a different aspect of Power and, over time, will evolve further to provide improved benefits. Note, your existing master Class will remain unaffected by your choice.

The first path is that of the <u>were gladiator</u> and will grant you the ascendant trait, <u>champion</u>. As a champion, the power of all your blood memories is doubled. You will also gain 30 attribute points and may choose 1 additional benefit unique to your chosen Class.

The second path is that of the <u>wolf lord</u> and will grant you the ascendant trait, <u>commander</u>. As a commander, you can share weaker variants of your blood memories and bloodline traits with those who follow you. You will also gain 20 attribute points and may choose 1 additional benefit unique to your chosen Class.

The third path is that of the <u>den master</u> and will grant you the ascendant trait, <u>governor</u>. As a governor, you gain access to a unique branch of blood memories and abilities that focus on sector-wide buffs and spells. You will

also gain 20 attribute points and may choose 1 additional benefit unique to your chosen Class.

Which ascendant path will you choose for your epic Class?

I opened my eyes, lips pursed. Just as Adriel had warned me, the Adjudicator did not describe the unique benefits each path provided, nor had the Game even listed the benefits I could choose from. I had to pick my epic Class first.

"Well?" Adriel asked impatiently. "*What are the Classes on offer?*"

"Were gladiator, wolf lord, and den master," I replied.

She frowned. "*I've never heard of any of them, sorry.*"

Which was not unusual, according to what Adriel had told me. Even amongst the Powers, few could divine the Class of another Power—an extremely high-tiered analyze was required—and as rare as ascendant Classes were, their details were closely guarded. Even Adriel—a player formerly destined to be a House Death Power—had been kept ignorant of Death's ascendant Classes.

"*Are you sure you don't want to wait for Ceruvax? He might know something about this that I don't.*"

I shook my head. "*It doesn't matter. I know the path I must take.*"

Adriel stayed silent, not protesting my decision. Closing my eyes, I willed my choice to the Game.

Higher evolution completed!

You are now a wolf lord! As an ascendant player, you can create a faction, claim sectors on behalf of your faction, and form Pacts with other players.

Your secret blood trait has been triggered! To conceal your bloodline, your ascendant Class will be hidden in its entirety.

You can now form Pacts with other players, and at any one time, may have a maximum of 10 active Pacts. This excludes special Pacts.

Special Pact gained: <u>follower</u> Pact. Through this Pact, you can bind a player in service to yourself. In exchange for their loyalty, you may transfer a maximum of 3 attribute points to the player at an exchange rate of 1:10, with the follower gaining 10 attribute points for every one bestowed. The attribute points are transferred permanently and are not recouped in the event of the follower's final death.

You have gained the base trait: <u>commander</u>. As a commander, you gain further options for winning the loyalty of a follower. In addition to offering attributes, you may awaken weaker copies of your bloodline traits or blood memories in exchange for the player's loyalty. Note that the player must possess wolf blood.

You have gained the epic Class, <u>Wolf Lord</u>.

There are those who command a battle through the strength of arms or the force of their charisma. This is not the wolf's way. To be a wolf lord is to master the art of subterfuge and guile. To be a wolf lord is to spurn open combat and to strike quickly and unseen from the shadows. As a wolf lord, you can mold your followers and Sworn in your image and together stalk the edges of battle, dealing death quietly and anonymously.

You have accomplished the feat: <u>Ascending to New Heights!</u> Requirement: acquire your first ascendant Class. You have been awarded 2 additional lives! Total lives: 4.

You have accomplished the feat: <u>Charging headlong into Power!</u> Requirement: adopt an ascendant Class before becoming an elite. Few in the Game dare to assume the Mark of Power as early as you have. Even fewer survive long enough to take up an epic Class. As a reward for your audacious choice, you have been awarded the trait: <u>Bold Blood</u>. This trait grants you 1 additional attribute point each time you level up.

You are now a rank 1 wolf lord and may choose your first ascendant trait or ability. 3 new ascendant Class benefits are available.

New benefit: <u>were's bite</u>. This trait activates the lycanthropy mutation in your blood. While it does not make you a werewolf, there is a small chance that your bite will permanently transform another player into one.

New benefit: <u>wolf's howl</u>. Your howl is a mighty weapon that can wreak havoc across an open battlefield, momentarily confusing, terrifying, and sometimes even charming those who hear it.

New benefit: <u>bloodlust</u>. This trait grants you a permanent aura that fortifies the attack and defensive strength of your followers and Sworn whenever they are near you.

Choose your ascendant Class benefit now.

I rocked back on my heels, dazed by the avalanche of information the Game had thrown at me.

Feats. Abilities. Traits. Lives. Attributes.

I'd gained so much and in such a short span of time that, for a second, I didn't know what to focus on.

"What is it?" Adriel asked tersely.

I looked at her sideways. "You didn't mention I would gain attributes. Or lives. Or that I would also be able to form Pacts!"

The spirit's face cleared. *"Oh, right. I forgot about all that."* She leaned forward. *"But those things aren't important right now. Tell me about your new Class benefit."*

"I haven't chosen yet. Just like you said, the Adjudicator has given me options."

"And?" she asked, gesturing for me to go on. *"What are they?"*

"An ability called wolf's howl that seems similar to my slaysight but appears more far-reaching. The other two are traits. The first grants me a buff aura." I paused. "And the second lets me create werewolves."

Adriel's jaw dropped open. *"Create werewolves? How?"*

I shrugged. "I don't know. The Game provided scant details, but I think—"

"Prime," Ghost interjected urgently.

I glanced in her direction.

"It's the guardian. He's coming this way. And he doesn't look happy."

Ghost was right.

Draven was heading our way, and from the scowl covering his face, unhappy was an understatement. "What now?" I muttered.

Adriel turned to look. *"Perhaps it has nothing to do with us,"* she said but didn't look convinced herself.

Folding my arms, I waited for the rapidly approaching centaur. "They're gone!" he snarled before he even drew to a halt. "So many of them. Just gone!"

"Who?" I asked before the belated realization hit me—Draven was speaking of his brethren.

"The others," the centaur growled. "They've vanished!"

"How can you be sure?" Adriel asked evenly. *"Aren't they in stasis? If you can't reach them, maybe it's because—"*

"No, you fools!" Draven roared, rearing up in irritation. "I'm not so ignorant as that. It's the nodes; they've gone."

My brows furrowed. "Perhaps you better back up a step."

My words seemed to infuriate the guardian even further, and he took a menacing step in my direction. Matching his growl with one of her own, Ghost stepped into his path, her liquid black coat stretching upward to give the impression of raised hackles.

Draven's gaze darted to the pyre wolf. "What's this—a nether spawn?" Raising a foreleg, he prepared to stomp down.

"Don't," I barked. Moving forward with alacrity, I placed myself beside Ghost.

The guardian's eyes locked on me. "Explain the runt," he demanded.

"She is a being of my creation," Adriel interjected smoothly.

"It's a stygian," Draven spat.

"No," Adriel refuted. *"She—not 'it'—is a wolf spirit housed in a mold of nether and fire."*

The guardian's eyes narrowed. Lowering his foreleg, he leaned forward. I tensed, hands hovering near my blades and already regretting the impulse to allow Ghost to manifest. There was nothing I could do to stop Draven if he intended her harm, but that wouldn't prevent me from trying to protect her.

The pyre wolf growled as the big guardian edged closer, flames gathering in her mouth and her eyes burning brighter.

"Back down," I hissed. *"Let's not antagonize him further."*

Still stiff with tension, Ghost did not reply, but her hackles lowered, and her growls softened.

Ignoring me entirely, the centaur placed his head an inch from Ghost and sniffed. "You speak truly, lich," he pronounced a moment later. "She is no stygian." The guardian unbent. "But I will not be threatened," he said, shooting me a warning glance.

Inclining my head in acknowledgment, I placed a restraining hand on Ghost. *"I don't like him,"* she snarled.

"He is temperamental," I agreed. That was true of both guardians I'd met so far. Whether that was because of their great age or waking up in a world so different from the one they left, I wasn't sure, but I was willing to make allowances for them.

"Now that that's been cleared up," Adriel said casually, *"will you tell us what's bothering you?"*

I winced, expecting Draven to flare up in renewed rage, but surprisingly the guardian remained calm. The interlude with Ghost seemed to have cooled his anger.

"It's the ley lines that underpin the guardian network," Draven answered at last. "Half have disappeared."

Adriel frowned. *"Disappeared as in hidden? How would that—"*

"Not hidden," Draven snarled. "Gone. Destroyed."

My own brows drew down. "But I thought you said the network can't be destroyed."

"It can't, not in its entirety." He paused, looking uncertain for the first time. "At least, I don't think so." The centaur shook his head. "But the network can contract. And it has done so now—to half its original size."

My eyes widened. "What could have caused that?"

"No Power that walks the Kingdom, that's for sure," Draven growled. "It can only be the void that is responsible."

"But half?" Adriel whispered. From her expression, she was still trying to process this startling revelation. *"That's hundreds of dungeons!"*

"And six of my brethren," Draven added grimly.

"How can you know that?" I asked, confused anew.

Draven stared at me for a moment as if contemplating how much to say. "Twelve nodes anchor the guardian network, each a hub of ley lines. Behind each node is one of my brethren. Even when we placed ourselves in stasis, the nodes remained. That they are gone..." He fell silent, eyes heavy with grief.

"... must mean the guardian behind it is dead," I finished.

He nodded mutely.

"What about the rest of your brethren?"

Draven huffed. "Their fate is still unknown. Besides me, only Kolath is connected to the network, and he remains deaf to my queries."

On the tail-end of Draven's words, a Game alert unfurled in my mind.

Your task: <u>Revive the Guardians</u>! has been updated. You have learned that 6 of the original 12 guardians have been destroyed, leaving only Kolath, Draven, and 4 others alive. Objective revised: Find the 4 guardians remaining in stasis and awaken them.

I pursed my lips, considering the message. On the one hand, my task had been simplified, but on the other, the state of the guardian network did not bode well for the Endless Dungeon—or its inhabitants.

"What about the sectors connected to the dead nodes?" Adriel asked, still fixated on their loss. *"Have they also been overrun by the void?"*

Draven grimaced. "There is no way to tell. But with the guardians dead, their protective barriers cannot be replenished." He exhaled heavily. "If they have not fallen already, they will eventually."

"How long do they have?" I asked.

The guardian shrugged. "Years? Decades? There is no telling, but once the void fathers finds them, their days are numbered." He pinned me with a hard stare. "All this makes your mission more critical. Are you ready to venture into the dungeon I've picked?"

I bowed my head, weighing the guardians' needs against my own. Matters with the void were worse than I'd thought. If left unchecked, the stygians would swallow up the Endless Dungeon. After that, it would only be a matter of time before the entire Forever Kingdom fell.

But one did not push back the void in a day or even a year. It was the work of a lifetime. And in the interim, I had more pressing needs. As dire as things were, Draven's task would have to wait.

"No," I whispered.

I sensed more than saw the guardian's frown. "I can allow you a few more days if that's what you desire, but after that, I must—"

"I will need more than that." Raising my head, I locked gazes with the giant centaur. "I'm sorry, Draven, but I cannot use my favor in the manner you wish."

✳   ✳   ✳

Silence followed in the wake of my words, a quiet that was deep, ominous, and full of threat. Neither of my companions nor I dared break it. Stiffly, we waited as Draven stared at us with smoldering eyes, the light in his eyes flaring brighter by the second.

Eventually, Ghost whined and inched backward.

I didn't blame her. Bearing the guardian's menacing regard was hard enough for me, and I could only imagine how Ghost had managed it for so long.

Draven's eyes flitted to the pyre wolf, and some of his tension dissipated. I didn't relax my own stance, though. The danger had not passed entirely.

"I did not take you for a fool, wolfling," Draven whispered, finally deigning to speak. "You would doom the Kingdom?"

I gulped. This was a side of Draven we'd not seen yet. For all that his anger appeared tightly leashed, I had the sense the guardian could explode at any moment, and none of us would survive that.

I stepped forward, palms spread. "Hear me out, please. I *will* find your surviving brethren, all of them. You have my word on that." I exhaled heavily. "But it shall take years. There is no point pretending otherwise. I can't go about your task alone either. I will need help, and securing that aid is more important right now."

"Honeyed words," Draven mused, still speaking in the frighteningly soft tone he'd adopted. "You have a silver tongue, wolfing, I'll give you that." The lines of his face hardened. "But I see through them. I see through *you*."

"I'm not trying to—" I began in protest.

"Your words are nothing more than self-serving drivel!" Draven roared.

I winced, staggering back as the centaur's cold breath washed over me.

"Guardian, trust Michael," Adriel said, floating forward. *"He is only doing what's best—"*

"Quiet, lich!" Draven ordered, his glare swapping to her.

Mid-speech, the spirit froze.

Draven, I realized, had used more than words to compel her. He had bespelled Adriel somehow.

"This is bad, Prime," Ghost moaned.

I couldn't agree more. My instincts were urging me to flee, but something else told me now was not the time to retreat. It was time to be bold.

I stepped forward.

Draven's head snapped back around to face me. "How is venturing into a virgin dungeon anything less?" he asked, picking up the conversation from where he'd left off.

I opened my mouth to reply, but before I could get the words out, Draven raged on, "How is what you intend anything but the actions of a power-drunk player? One willing to let the world burn around him while he uses *my* favor to get stronger?"

"I don't plan on—"

"Tell me, wolfling, how is it that you are any different from the new Powers? HOW?"

"I will, if you stop and listen for a second!" I snapped, finally out of patience.

Draven's expression turned frostier, but for a wonder, he stayed silent.

Grasping the opportunity, I declared, "I don't wish to use your favor to enter a dungeon, *any* dungeon—virgin or otherwise. This is not about advancing my power. It's about securing House Wolf."

The guardian's glare did not relent. "If you will not enter a dungeon, what do you intend?"

"I want you to bring someone here."

"Who?" Draven demanded, his expression still stormy.

"House Wolf's envoy."

Consternation flitted across the guardian's face for one brief second before it grew stony again.

"His name is Ceruvax," I added quickly, "and he is trapped in Nexus' saltmarsh dungeon. Will you honor your debt and bring him here?"

There, I thought, shoulders sagging in relief. I'd put my request to the guardian formally. Now, he would have no choice except to comply. But given Draven's opaque stare, I couldn't tell whether he thought the same.

"Ahh."

At the soft gasp, my gaze darted to the right. Adriel had relaxed from her frozen posture, released from whatever spell the guardian had used on her.

The lich met my eyes. *"I heard everything,"* she confirmed, projecting her words to me alone. *"You seemed to have calmed him. Well done."* Her look turned wry. *"But I think I'll stay silent for a bit. He seems to like me a lot less than he does you."*

I wasn't so sure about that, but I nodded anyway. Lifting my gaze to the guardian again, I waited. He was still staring at me.

Would he grant my boon?

He has to, I thought. The Game and the Adjudicator would see to it. Surely, they would.

"There is only one dungeon in the saltmarsh district of Nexus," Draven said at last. "But the one you named is not there."

I was so wound up it took a moment for the guardian's words to sink in. "What?" I blurted. "He has to be there!"

"He isn't," Draven denied.

"Are you sure?" I stared at the guardian suspiciously. "This isn't some ploy to get out of granting me my favor, is it?

"It isn't," he replied blandly. "In the span of time it took you to utter your request, and now, I linked to Sickening Ooze—what you call the saltmarsh dungeon—through the guardian network and searched it from end to end. There is no player named Ceruvax within."

"Then who—?"

I broke off, thoughts racing. If it wasn't the Wolf envoy in the saltmarsh dungeon, then to whom did Cyren's rumors refer? Rifling through my backpack, I extracted the dungeon notes I'd received from the gnomes, still safely stored away even after many months of adventuring.

Flipping through the scraps of paper, I found the one I wanted. Seeing what I held in my hands, Adriel floated closer and peered over my shoulder, reading along with me.

P.S. There is one other rumor about the saltmarsh dungeon that bears consideration. Most scholars dismiss it as mere fancy, but I thought it might pique your interest.

Sometimes, when the saltmarsh dungeon is brought up in recent histories—those chronicling the rise of the new Powers—mention is also made of an 'ancient adversary.'

The relationship between adversary and dungeon is unclear, though. Some texts imply the dungeon is the adversary's prison; others, their refuge. Who or what the adversary is, is also never described. Details on he/she/it are scantier than on the dungeon itself.

Perhaps this will help you on your quest. —Cyren.

"The lost Prime," I gasped. "She is the ancient adversary!"

"*That seems likely,*" Adriel murmured.

"You've figured out the Prime's location?" the guardian asked, his expression softening for the first time since I rejected his 'advice.'

"Yes, *she* must be the one hiding in Sickening Ooze," I replied before going on to explain what I'd learned from the gnomes.

"Hmm," Draven mused, tugging at his beard. His anger seemed to have dissipated entirely now. "I did not sense her when I scanned the dungeon just now—but that means nothing. Sickening Ooze is not under my control, and I can search it less thoroughly than Kolath can. If a Prime is there, she will undoubtedly be capable of hiding from all but Nexus' guardian."

The guardian's words prompted another Game alert.

Your task: <u>Locate the Lost Prime</u> has been updated. You have received unverified information that the Lost Prime is trapped in Sickening Ooze, the dungeon in the saltmarsh district of Nexus. Your objective remains unchanged: confirm her whereabouts and report back to Draven.

I dismissed the message almost as soon as it appeared and just in time to catch Adriel's next words.

"*...that she is in Sickening Ooze is interesting,*" the lich said.

Frowning, I glanced at Adriel. Her expression bore none of my own excitement. "What do you mean by that?"

"*The dungeon was ever the domain of Pestilence.*"

"It still is," I grumbled, thinking of all the diseases I'd acquired in the saltmarsh district and the unwelcome trait I'd earned as a result.

"*You mistake my meaning,*" Adriel corrected. "*I refer to House Pestilence, not the pestilence they leave in their wake.*"

"*House* Pestilence?" I repeated.

She nodded. "*The bloodline was always a little... odd. Unlike the other Houses, Pestilence didn't establish their Nexus chapterhouse in the city proper but in one of its dungeons.*" Her look turned thoughtful. "*It could explain how their Prime survived the new Powers' purge during the war.*"

Another memory popped into my head—Anriq's mention of the marshmen the werewolves were tasked with holding at bay on behalf of the Triumvirate. Knowing what I now knew, it sounded like the lost Prime and the marshmen were related. In fact, I would be surprised if they weren't.

Both had to spring from House Pestilence.

And both were likely using the saltmarsh dungeon as their base.

"That's great news!" I exclaimed, rubbing my hands in glee. "If Pestilence's Prime survived, perhaps some of its players did too. House Wolf isn't alone in this fight. We have allies. Better yet, they're entrenched in Nexus, on the very doorstep of our foes!" I looked at Adriel, expecting her to share in my delight.

But the lich was not smiling.

My grin faded. "It *is* good news, right?"

Adriel threw me an indecipherable look. "*There is one other thing you should know about Pestilence.*"

"Go on," I said, already knowing I wasn't going to like whatever came next.

"*House Wolf had no greater rival than Pestilence. In the entire history of the Game, the two never set aside their differences.*"

My newborn hope withered. "Really?"

Adriel nodded. "*Really. Many amongst House Death believed the entire reason your Primes based their lycan guard where they did was so that they could keep an eye on their foes.*"

"I see," I said, not knowing what else to say.

"It does not matter," Draven interjected, re-entering the conversation. "None of the old rivalries do. They all died the day the new Powers took over.

Whether it is Pestilence Prime in the saltmarsh dungeon or not, you will find her," he declared.

Not wanting to give birth to another argument, I didn't contradict him. Instead, I changed the topic. "It seems I was mistaken about Ceruvax's location, but my desire remains unchanged. Will you find the Wolf envoy and teleport him here?"

Draven looked at me in surprise but, thankfully, without anger. "Given this new information, will you not consider entering Sickening Ooze to find the lost Prime?"

I shook my head. "I told you, I will not re-enter another dungeon just yet." Especially one that could very well contain a den of new enemies and enmity born of ancient entanglements. Before I went anywhere near the saltmarsh dungeon, I would have to speak to Anriq and find out everything he knew about the marshmen. "First, I must see to my allies," I said, refocusing on Draven. "Will you honor your boon, guardian?"

Draven nodded slowly. "I will." He sighed. "But I don't know where your envoy is. Finding him will take time."

I frowned. "How much time?"

The centaur shrugged. "Hours? Days? I cannot say. I will have to scan every dungeon in the guardian network individually."

My lips turned down. That was far from ideal, but I couldn't think of any way to rush Draven. If he said it would take days, I had no choice but to give him that time.

"There is something else to consider," the guardian said abruptly.

I glanced at him. "Oh?"

"Your envoy may be in one of the broken dungeons, on the other side of the destroyed nodes." He stared at me expressionlessly. "In which case, I will not be able to fulfill your favor."

I grimaced, then waved aside the guardian's concern. "It's a risk I'm willing to take."

Draven nodded curtly. "So be it." He spun about, turning his back to me. "But do not fail me, Wolf. Do not fail my brethren. Too much depends on you."

I bowed my head. "I will not," I vowed.

"Good," he said, striding away without turning around. "I will begin searching the Endless Dungeon for your envoy. Return in five days. If your envoy is within reach, I will have found him by then. And if he isn't, then he is lost forever."

Not waiting for an answer, the centaur galloped away.

"Five days," I muttered.

"Can you wait that long?" Adriel asked quietly.

I shrugged. "It seems I have no choice but to."

"Where is he going anyway?" Ghost asked, watching Draven recede into the distance.

"Away from us, I suspect," Adriel replied. She turned back to me. *"What will you do now?"*

"Finish my Class advancement for starters." I glanced upward at the unchanging violet sky. "Then rest and recover." I threw her a wry smile. "It's been a long day."

She replied with a fleeting smile of her own. *"And after that?"*

My smile faded, and I glanced northwards. *Five days,* I mused to myself. That would be enough time to visit New Haven and return. I hadn't planned on visiting the city before leaving the dungeon, but if Draven was going to keep me at loose ends for five days...

"I will visit New Haven," I said.

Adriel nodded. *"I thought you might. In that case, I'll return to the court and reclothe myself."* She grimaced. *"I can't remember the last time I stayed in spiritform for this long."* She glanced at Ghost. *"I'm not sure how you managed it for all those years."*

The pyre wolf's eyes grew mournful. *"It was... difficult."*

Adriel ruffled her coat. *"That's all behind you now,"* she said soothingly. *"And soon, you will have even less to fear,"* she added, shooting me a meaningful glance.

I nodded, signifying my agreement with Adriel's unvoiced suggestion. The journey north would also give me the opportunity to acquire the Class ability point I needed to finally make Ghost my familiar. "That reminds me... what happens when I become an elite?"

Adriel's brows rose in surprise. *"You don't know?"*

"I don't," I confessed. "I know that whatever the Game has in store for me at level two hundred, it will include a significant boost to my power. And I won't lie, I'm looking forward to—"

I broke off. Adriel was shaking her head. "What's wrong?"

"I hate to be the one to tell you this, Michael," the spirit said, *"but little beyond the norm awaits you at your next level advancement."*

I stared at her. "You can't be serious!"

Adriel winced. *"I am, unfortunately."*

I threw up my hands. "But what about all the tales of powerful elites I've heard about?" Not waiting for her to answer, I went on. "The entire time I was in Nexus, other players kept filling my ears about the differences between regular players and elites, how elites were so much stronger, and how hard it was to become one. You can't seriously be telling me all those stories were false?"

"I'm not."

Consternation flickered across my face. "Then what *are* you telling me?"

Adriel sighed. *"Everything you heard was true—"*

"Then why—"

"—for Forcesworn players," she finished, speaking over me.

I groaned, realizing where this was going. "You mean Darksworn, Lightsworn, and Shadowsworn, don't you?"

She nodded. *"If that's what they're calling themselves these days."*

I closed my eyes. "And I don't belong to any of the Forces."

"You don't," she agreed. *"You are a scion. As a Housebound player, your progression path is different."*

I rubbed at my temples. "Go on, tell me how."

Adriel shrugged. *"There is not much to tell. You already know half of it. Scions awaken blood memories. Most can do so even as lowly rank one players. As they advance in rank, the number of blood memories they can hold increases. Players who bind themselves to the Forces are different. In the place of blood memories, they gain Force abilities but only start acquiring them at level two hundred."*

I opened my eyes. "Force abilities. You're saying that's what makes elites so strong?"

Adriel nodded. *"Yes. Many argue Force abilities are just as powerful as blood memories—that's nonsense, though."* She waved her hand dismissively. *"But that is a whole other topic."*

I chewed over her words, focusing on what was of immediate import. "How do elites earn these abilities?"

Adriel smiled humorlessly. *"That's the thing. Unlike blood memories, Force abilities are gained directly from the Game and are progressively awarded to Forcesworn players from tier five onwards."*

"But that's, that's..." I stared at her, at a loss for words.

"... so simple? Unfair?" Adriel chuckled darkly. *"I know what you're thinking, and you're right. In many ways, it is significantly easier for the Forcesworn to gather power."* Her lips twisted sourly. *"It is one of the many reasons their rebellion was successful."*

I frowned, not following this latest tangent. "What does *that* mean?"

Adriel sighed as she met my gaze. *"You already know how hard it is to acquire blood memories, right?"*

I nodded.

"Forcesworn don't have the same problem. What's more, the nature of the Forces makes bloodline strength less relevant. Couple those two things together, and what do you have? A whole bunch of players who felt—and rightly so, I may add—that they could advance higher and further outside their Houses than they could within them."

I rubbed my chin. "So... you're saying players are attracted to the Force because it is the easier path to power?"

"Yes," Adriel replied, nodding emphatically. *"Binding oneself to the Forces became so popular that it wasn't long before the Forcesworn outnumbered the Houses. From there, it was only a short step to believing it should be they who ruled—and not the Primes."* She shrugged. *"And the rest, you know."*

I nodded slowly. I did, indeed.

Adriel floated away. *"I see I have given you a lot to think about. I will leave you now. See to your progression and rest. We'll talk further in the morning."*

I glanced up. "What will you do in the meantime?" In spiritform, Adriel had little need for sleep.

The lich looked in the direction of the guardian. *"Perhaps I will go pester him for answers,"* she said with a smile.

I watched Adriel's retreat for a moment, then turned my attention inwards. It was time to complete my Class advancement.

✻   ✻   ✻

Choose your ascendant Class benefit now.

I stared at the Game alert hanging in front of my eyes while I pondered the three choices on offer: were's bite, wolf howl, and bloodlust.

Two of the options—bloodlust and wolf's howl—were combat-oriented. Bloodlust would give me a permanent aura, whereas the effects of wolf's howl were only temporary. As such, I expected the buffs provided by bloodlust to be weaker than the debuffs induced by wolf's howl. But, as ascendant abilities, I nevertheless expected both to be powerful.

Still, I felt little inducement to acquire either ability.

Wolf's howl only did what I already could with slaysight and charm, and even if its effects were more wide-ranging, the ability felt... redundant.

Bloodlust, on the other hand, was only beneficial when I had allies nearby, which, even though I'd adopted the commander Class, I didn't always expect to be the case. I still foresaw fighting many of my future battles alone.

That left were's bite.

It was the most intriguing of the three benefits the Game offered. Calling up its description, I studied it avidly again.

<u>Were's bite</u>: this trait activates the lycanthropy mutation in your blood. While it does not make you a werewolf, there is a small chance that your bite will permanently transform another player into one.

Admittedly, the reference to 'small chance' made the trait less appealing, but the promise of a *permanent* transformation more than made up for that lack.

From my discussions with Anriq, I knew werewolves were powerful. Besides the physical boost their were-forms gave them—which even a caster would find handy—a werewolf's health regeneration skills were nearly unmatched in the Game.

It would make my followers hardy fighters—with or without me close by to lead them. And that, more than anything else, made the trait attractive.

There were also other benefits. Anriq had strongly implied that a werewolf's Wolf Mark would, of its own volition, deepen with time in a similar manner that a Forcesworn's Mark did. It meant my followers would have an easier time evolving than I did.

Of course, I expected the trait would have limitations, too. Given what I knew of werewolves, I did not anticipate the bite would work on anyone who didn't bear *some* measure of Wolf blood. Hopefully, though, the restriction would not be too onerous.

Reviewing the options, I realized I'd already made my choice and, without further ado, willed my intent to the Adjudicator.

Ascendant Class upgrade complete.

You have gained the trait: <u>were's bite</u>. This trait gives your bite a 10% chance of granting another player the werewolf trait. Depending on the strength of the bitten player's blood and the Marks they bear, this probability will increase to a maximum of 20% or decrease down to 0%.

Note, were's bite is not a combat ability and cannot transform an unwilling subject, and in the event that the bitten player accepts your bite but fails to acquire the werewolf trait, their body will be fatally overrun with lycanthropy.

My lips turned down as I read the last bit again. "Fatally overrun," I murmured. That meant death. The repercussions of a failed bite were greater than I expected, leaving me less enthused about trying it out.

Still, at least it doesn't cause final death.

Despite the limitations, I would make the trait work—somehow. But that was a problem for another day. Sighing, I turned my mind to the next matter requiring attention: spending my new attribute points.

Here, at least, there were no pitfalls to avoid. The Game had granted me a whole twenty points for acquiring an ascendant Class, and I already knew how to spend them.

Your Dexterity has increased to rank 71. Other modifiers: +24 from items.

Your Perception has increased to rank 49. Other modifiers: +4 from items.

I invested seven points in Dexterity, gaining the fifteen slots I needed for the fade ability when it was ready for advancement, and the rest I dumped into Perception.

My new Power Mark had left me vulnerable, and given that I would soon be amongst players again, improving my deception skill and its abilities had become a top priority again. Loken had shown me often enough that it was possible to so completely change one's identity that not even another Power could penetrate the disguise.

And if Loken could do it, so could I.

With my player progression seen to, that left only two more matters to address before I could lay down and rest. Opening my eyes, I looked at the pyre wolf lounging silently by my side. "*Ghost,*" I said softly.

She glanced up at me. "*It's time?*"

I nodded.

Neither Ghost nor I could risk her being free while I slept—not yet. Knowing this as well as I did, the pyre wolf did not protest. Rising to her feet, she leaped at me. Her stygian form unraveling faster than it had formed, Ghost disappeared entirely before she could crash into me.

Ghost has cast unmanifest.

"I don't like this," Ghost grumbled from within the Cloak of the Reach.
"I know, but you won't have to endure it much longer. Just another day."
Ghost said nothing, but I felt her mindglow settle into the state that betokened sleep. My own chores done, I lay down and closed my eyes.

It was also time for me to rest and ponder what the new day would bring.

Chapter 389: Heading North

I set off early the next morning, traveling northwest along the mountaintop plateau. The journey passed without incident, and by late afternoon, when I broke for lunch, I was halfway to New Haven.

My rest the previous night had gone undisturbed. After I'd awakened, I'd found Adriel waiting for me. Unfortunately, she'd had no luck with Draven. The guardian, perhaps vexed by our choices, had refused to update her on his search for Ceruvax. Nor, for that matter, did he even acknowledge her presence.

Would Draven find Ceruvax?

Was the five-day estimate he'd provided accurate?

I didn't know. And as much as Adriel and I would have liked greater certainty, we had no choice but to set our rendezvous for five days hence at the lich's court. By then, I was sure matters with New Haven would be resolved—one way or the other.

I rose to my feet, my rest stop done. Striding forward, I peered nonchalantly over the plateau's edge and into the canyon below. The two lizard-like basilisks inhabiting it hadn't moved and were still positioned near the canyon's only exit.

"Will you fight them now?" Ghost asked eagerly.

I pursed my lips as I considered the question. Throughout the day, I'd periodically paused to search the dungeon's chasms for an easy battle—a 'quick' win.

Sadly, I hadn't found one yet.

I'd stopped here, hoping the giant basilisks would separate while I ate. I judged I could handily defeat one of the elite creatures, but two? Taking on both simultaneously would be risky.

Still, given the other elites I'd already passed by, I didn't think I was going to find an easier encounter before I reached New Haven. Letting my gaze drift eastwards, I studied the canyon's other inhabitants—a dozen stygians, all huddled together.

They were the only void creatures I'd encountered since I'd left the guardian's canyon. And they were also the other reason I was contemplating fighting.

I didn't think the stygians were a match for the basilisks, but if I handled things right, they might even the odds enough in my favor to kill the elites 'risk-free.'

I snorted derisively. As if there were any such thing.

"I suppose I've kept you waiting long enough," I said, finally in response to Ghost's question. Equipping my cat claws, I dropped over the edge of the plateau.

"Let's go bag us some lizards."

✳   ✳   ✳

You have cast heightened reflexes, load controller, fade, and trigger-cast quick mend.

You have cast facial disguise, assuming the visage of Taim, a level 247 human explorer. Duration: 3 hours.

You are hidden.

With my buffs cast and wrapped in illusion, I crept across the canyon toward my foes. There was no reason for me to employ facial disguise, of course, but improving my deception had become a priority, and while I wasn't sure if fighting as 'Taim' would advance the skill, I reckoned it was worth a try.

In the center of the canyon, I drew to a halt. The twelve stygians were clumped together on my left, right up against the east cliff wall. Six were hydras, while the other six were serpents.

Ahead of me, the two basilisks lazed. I wasn't sure whether it was by design or not, but the pair had the stygians bottled up in the canyon.

Narrowing my gaze, I studied the elites. Like most of the dungeon's denizens, the pair were large, as big as houses. In many ways, they resembled lizards, but from the few lumbering steps I'd observed them take, it was apparent the basilisks lacked those creatures' agility. I suspected the two would be slow, just like the stone golems I'd faced early on in the dungeon.

But that did not mean they weren't dangerous.

My gaze fixed on the basilisks' most prominent feature: their bulging pupil-less eyes. A dust cloud hung around those lethal orbs, partially obscuring them from view—for which I was more than thankful.

I didn't know much about basilisks, but I knew crossing gazes with one was ill-advised, and the dust swirling lazily about their eyes—and nowhere else—was definitely not natural.

Let's see if the Game can tell me anything. Reaching out with my will, I inspected both elites.

The target is a level 213 basilisk.

The target is a level 210 basilisk.

Basilisks are infamous for their petrifying gazes and can transform any foe foolish enough to approach them into living stone. The creatures, while flesh and blood creatures themselves, have no trouble consuming their petrified victims after drenching them with a saliva that slowly liquefies the statues back into flesh.

I sighed. *Bite and gaze.*

Those were two dangers I would have to avoid. But other than that, the Adjudicator had not told me anything I hadn't already suspected.

I guess I will have to figure out the rest. Looking to the left again, I drew in psi and flung it at the unsuspecting stygians.

You have cast mass charm.

8 stygians have failed a mental resistance check!

You have charmed 8 of 8 targets for 20 seconds.

Swamped by my will, the nether creatures fell under my spell without resistance. *"Attack,"* I ordered, tugging at the leash I'd wrapped around their minds.

Moving in tandem with each other, the bespelled creatures charged toward the basilisks. For a moment, the remaining four stygians stayed unmoving, looking confused by their companions' sudden attack, but before I could intervene further, instinct pushed them to follow their fellows.

Smiling thinly, I settled back on my heels to observe the approaching confrontation.

For all their seeming indifference towards the nether creatures, the basilisks stirred the moment the stygians moved. Lumbering around, they faced the charging beasts.

Multiple hostile entities have failed to detect you! You are hidden.

The stygian pack rushed past me, oblivious of my presence despite me sitting in the open. Hands on the hilts of my blades, I watched intently. The dust clouds around the basilisks' eyes were clearing, sucked into their flaring nostrils.

A moment later, twin beams of red rushed out.

Seeing death racing down upon them, the nether pack scattered. But they were too slow. The burning lances struck the two leading stygians, leaving tendrils of smoke in their wake.

Light flashed. Air screamed.

And when the dust settled, the hapless victims were gone. In their stead, two life-like statues remained.

Your minion has been petrified. A stygian serpent has died.
Your minion has been petrified. A stygian serpent has died.

My eyes narrowed. *Interesting.*

Howling and hissing in outrage, the remaining nether creatures surged forward. Staying stock-still as only lizards could, the basilisks watched their approaching foes.

No further beams lashed out.

They couldn't. The basilisks' eyes were obscured once more and this time the plumes of smoke were thicker and denser. But moment and moment, they were thinning.

Observing closely, I kept careful count.

One second. Two. Three. Four.

The smoke cloud occluding the basilisks' sight vanished anew, sucked into their nostrils again. A heartbeat later, two more burning lances lashed out.

Your minion has been petrified. A stygian hydra has died.
A stygian serpent has been petrified. A stygian serpent has died.

Five seconds, I mused. That's how long the basilisks had to wait between uses of their petrifying gazes. I could work with that. My gaze flickered back to the charging nether creatures.

Eight stygians remained. And now, they were in striking range. Surging forward, they slashed and snapped at the basilisks in vengeful fury.

Your minion has grazed a basilisk.
A level 165 stygian hydra has grazed a basilisk.
...

...

The elites bore the assault stoically, neither retreating nor responding in kind—not that the nether creatures appeared to be having much success; none of their attacks had done more than graze the big lizards.

A second ticked by, then another, while the stygians swarmed the elites. I frowned. Were the basilisks going to depend solely on their petrifying gazes?

A tail—heavy and as thick as a ram—whipped sideways.

A basilisk has failed to harm its target. A stygian serpent is immune to physical damage.

Jaws snapped, crunching down on a hydra's neck.

A basilisk has critically injured a stygian hydra.

Where the first basilisk's tail failed to do any damage, the jaws of the second nearly ripped through the neck of its foe in a single bite. *Right,* I thought, *whatever passes for basilisk saliva, it is clearly magical in nature and potent.*

And while the stygians might be immune to a tail whip, I wasn't. *That's another danger to beware of.*

✳ ✳ ✳

A few minutes later, all the stygians were dead, and ten new statues decorated the canyon. In the end, only two of the nether creatures had fallen victim to the basilisks' jaws; the rest had been petrified.

Safe in the shadows, I watched the elites. The hides of both basilisks were heavily scarred, but neither bore any significant injury. Seeking confirmation from the Game, I reached out and analyzed the pair.

The target is a level 213 basilisk. It is barely injured.
The target is a level 210 basilisk. It is barely injured.

It was time for me to launch my assault, and the best way to do that was from afar, using my telepathic abilities. Still, I couldn't forget the basilisks were elites with powerful ranged attacks of their own.

If my opening assault failed, or worse yet, if I were revealed, the tables would turn quickly. It was an eventuality I had to be ready for—which was why I had used the dying moments of the basilisks' skirmish with the stygians to prepare the battlefield to my liking.

And now my first target was nearly in position.

Through eyes narrowed to slits, I watch one of the basilisks slip ponderously closer to a trapped statue. Both elites had separated after the battle, each heading towards a different petrified victim. I had anticipated this. Knowing the creatures would want to feed, I had laid my traps around the newly made statues. So far, it looked like it had been a smart move.

"Is your plan going to work?" Ghost asked.

"I don't see why not," I murmured back. My gaze slid to the second elite. Unfortunately, it hadn't reached its chosen meal yet. I would have to wait a little longer. Sitting back, I renewed my buffs.

The first basilisk reached its target and, lowering its head, began to gnaw on the petrified stygian serpent. My brows furrowed in concern. I'd placed the trap crystal at the statue's base and could only hope that the copious amounts of saliva dripping from the basilisk's mouth did not destroy it. My gaze darted to the second elite. It was almost at its statue.

Good enough.

Pressing down on two of the remote triggers clenched in my hands, I activated their traps.

A blot of darkness trap has been activated.
A blot of darkness trap has been activated.

Ebon clouds mushroomed out from beneath the statues, enveloping the nearby basilisks. They could no longer see me, but I could see them perfectly. With my foes' deadliest weapon neutralized, I hurtled towards the closest one.

The creature appeared oblivious.

Despite the inky darkness shrouding it, the elite had not stopped feeding. I risked a glance behind and saw that the second basilisk was likewise unfazed.

I grunted. My foes' disdain did not matter. Soon enough, I would teach them fear. Drawing psi, I reached into the mind of the basilisk behind me.

You have cast slaysight.
An unknown entity has passed a mental resistance check! You have failed to induce your target to sleep.
Your mental intrusion has been detected!

I grimaced. The failure was not unexpected, yet I was still disappointed that my foe had felt my touch. Checking its advance to the statue, the basilisk behind me swung its head from left to right in search of its attacker. But fortunately, the black cloud I had wrapped around the creature did its job admirably.

A hostile entity has failed to detect you! You are still hidden.

Leaving off further thought of my failed assault, I faced forward again and gave my intended target my full attention. The elite's back was turned to me. Drawing nearer, I leaped onto its stout tail and dashed deftly up its torso.

I crossed nearly the entirety of the basilisk's length before it registered my presence, and by then, it was too late. Springing forward, I cleared the final distance to my objective—my foe's triangular head—in a single bound. Landing lightly, I thrust my raised blades downwards and straight into the basilisk's bulging orbs.

A second before the swords made contact, the creature's eyelids snapped close.

You have backstabbed your target for 2.5x more damage!
You have backstabbed your target for 2.5x more damage!

Both sword points penetrated the elite's thick hide half an inch deep, but no further. *Damn*, I muttered. Whipping out both blades, I raised them high while at the same time empowering my arms with renewed strength and speed.

You have cast whirlwind and piercing strike.
A hostile entity has failed to detect you!

I smiled in satisfaction at the Game message. Although my foe was aware of my presence, my fade ability, coupled with the blot of darkness trap, sufficed to keep it from finding me.

I rammed my swords downward again.

You have backstabbed a basilisk for 5x more damage!
You have backstabbed a basilisk for 5x more damage!
You have critically injured your target.

This time, my blades penetrated deeper, almost to the vulnerable orbs beneath. *One more time*, I thought. *That should do it.*

Withdrawing my swords, I prepared them for another strike even as the basilisk swayed beneath me, but despite the creature's frantic movements, I maintained my footing. *Here goes.*

A level 210 basilisk's penetrating gaze has missed you!

A red beam flashed through the darkness, missing me by less than a foot. Startled, I whipped my head around. The second elite had attempted to come to its fellow's aid by firing blindly in my direction. Clearly, it didn't need to see me utilize the deadly spell.

Thinking quickly, I drew on my will and wove a spell, releasing it as soon as it was ready.

You have cast ventro.

"I'm over here!" I screamed, projecting my voice to originate from a spot twenty yards to the right. Both basilisks' heads jerked in that direction. Windmilling my arms, I kept my balance, and once my foe stopped moving, I hacked downwards again.

You have backstabbed a basilisk for 5x more damage!
You have backstabbed a basilisk for 5x more damage!

I found my marks with pinpoint accuracy and struck the same spots I had before. The hardened hide of the basilisk's eyelids gave way, and leaning into the blows, I buried my blades hilt-deep into the soft tissue beneath.

You have crippled your target!
A level 213 basilisk has been permanently blinded and can no longer cast petrifying gaze.

I grinned broadly. *One down.* Opening my mindsight, I focused on the second elite. *One to go.*
Then, I shadow blinked.

Chapter 390: A Familiar Companion

It took only a handful of seconds to reduce the second elite to the same state as the first.

You have crippled your target!
A level 210 basilisk has been permanently blinded and can no longer cast petrifying gaze.

My work done, I somersaulted off the creature and backed away. There was no further reason to stay in close proximity to the big lizards and risk grievous injury from a lucky blow. Now that I had disabled their only ranged attack, it was much better to kill them from afar.

Drawing psi, I manifested a pair of astral blades in my hands and flung them at the closer basilisk.

Both daggers hit their mark, striking the elite's snout dead center.

You have injured your target, inflicting psi damage.
You have injured your target, inflicting psi damage.

I laughed. *It worked!* I hadn't been sure it would, especially given the spectacular failure of my slaysight spell.

"What's happening?" Ghost asked for what felt like the hundredth time. Understandably, she was eager for the battle to end and for her promised freedom, and I didn't judge her harshly for it.

"It's the beginning of the end," I replied. *"The astral blades have worked, and now I need only wear the elites down—cut by cut."*

Forming another pair of violet psi daggers in my hands, I cocked back my arms, took aim, and threw.

✳ ✳ ✳

The giant lizards were more stubborn than I expected.

While at no point had the battle's outcome been in doubt, that didn't stop the basilisks from obstinately pursuing me around the canyon. Three times, I had been forced to break off from the fight and renew my psi, and it was only around evening that the two creatures finally perished.

You have killed a level 213 basilisk.
You have killed a level 210 basilisk.

Exhausted but elated, I sank down in the middle of the canyon.
"Is it done?"
"Yes, Ghost," I replied wearily. *"It's done."*
"Finally!"
"I feel the same way," I said, flopping back to rest with my back pressed against the ground.

A drawn-out moment of nervous silence followed.

"And?" Ghost finally blurted. *"Did you get the levels you need?"*

I chuckled. The question was not unexpected. *"Let me check,"* I murmured. Turning my focus inward, I queried the waiting Game messages.

You have reached level 201!

Bold blood activated. You have been awarded 2 additional attribute points.

Your dodging and telekinesis have reached rank 17, your two weapon fighting rank 16, and your thieving rank 12.

Congratulations, Michael. You are now a tier 5 player and have joined the ranks of the Game's elite! For achieving rank 20, you have been awarded 1 additional attribute point and 1 Class point. Furthermore, your experience gains have decreased, and the time you require to resurrect has increased to 16 hours. The level cap on your skills has also been removed, and you may now learn tier 5 abilities.

My amusement faded as I read the Adjudicator's message.

Most of it was nothing out of the ordinary, but the increased time between respawns was troubling. It would give any halfway knowledgeable foe ample time to prepare for my resurrection, which made dying an even more unappealing proposition. Nothing could be done about it, though, so I stopped worrying.

Turning my attention to my skill gains, I felt my smile return. Four of my skills had ranked up, and even deception had advanced, if not enough to reach the next rank.

That clinches it, I decided. *From now on, I travel everywhere as Taim.* If I was fortunate, I could get the skill to rank twenty before I left Draven's Reach.

"Prime?" Ghost prompted.

"Sorry," I muttered. *"I got sidetracked. But yes, I gained a Class point."*

"At last," she whispered.

A pause. *"Will you do it now?"*

"I will," I replied firmly, determined not to keep her waiting longer. Heaving myself upright, I dropped into a cross-legged stance and called up the Class upgrade interface.

Assessing player's suitability for a Class upgrade...

Class points available: 1.

Player rank: 20.

Upgrade requirements met.

You may advance your Class to rank 11 by improving an existing Class benefit or selecting a new one. Do you wish to proceed?

I willed my intent to do so, then waited as breathlessly as I sensed Ghost to be for the offered list of benefits to appear.

Commencing Class upgrade...

Seconds ticked by. Then, sure enough, the trait Adriel had mentioned appeared. Ignoring everything else, my eyes fastened on it.

New benefit: <u>spirit familiar</u>. This trait allows a mage to form a familiar Pact with an entity housed inside a spirit vessel. Note, the spirit in question must accede to the binding, and once the Pact has been enacted, it cannot be renounced.

I read the trait's description twice to ensure I understood it, then aloud once more for Ghost's benefit. When I was certain she had digested the implications, I asked, *"Last chance, Ghost. Are you sure you want to go ahead? There will be no turning back after this."*
"I am," she replied without hesitation.
I inhaled slowly. There was no need for further discussion. Ghost was certain about her decision, as was I. *"Alright, here goes."* Closing my eyes, I willed my choice to the Game.

You have gained the trait: <u>spirit familiar</u>. This trait allows you to co-opt a spirit as an ally. Familiars can serve multiple roles, from that of a meat shield to a healer, and are often viewed as indispensable by their hosts. Beware, though, once bound, your familiar's spirit will become permanently intertwined with your own.

Upgrade complete. Class points remaining: 0.
Congratulations, Michael! Your voidstealer Class has advanced to rank 11!

Spirit vessels detected: 1, Cloak of the Reach.
Contained spirit: stygian pyre wolf named Ghost.
Do you wish to make Ghost your familiar?
If she accepts your offer, the stygian pyre wolf will become your spirit familiar forevermore. Her spirit will become irrevocably bound to yours, allowing her to acquire Game-gifted knowledge through you. Note, too, that as a result of the spirit binding, the item, Cloak of the Reach, will become soulbound if it is not already so.

"I do," I said, both for the Game's benefit and Ghost's, then holding myself still, waited for her response.
It was not long in coming.
Trails of smoke surged out of the Cloak of the Reach until they fully encompassed me. I held out my arms, sensing Ghost in the cloud. She bubbled with excitement and joy, and I knew if she had feet, she'd be dancing. This was her long-awaited moment.
Bright weaves of fire appeared.
Darting out from the stygian thundercloud, they slipped towards me, and instinctively, I reached for them.
Flesh met fiery weaves, and a connection was forged. A second later, the bonds deepened, surpassing the physical.
Our spirits touched.
Then merged.

Creating a familiar bond between the player, Michael, and the stygian pyre wolf, Ghost...

...

...

Tendrils of spirit broke free from the greater whole that was me. And from Ghost, too.

They mixed. Roiled. Meshed.

I felt her change. And myself as well. Its part played out, the errant tendril returned to me. Then another split off. And the process began anew.

I wasn't sure how long it went on for. Minutes at least, perhaps hours, but finally, I felt the ritual draw to a close, and our spirits separated for the last time. The binding was at end.

Familiar bond created.
Ghost has been successfully transformed into your spirit familiar.

I exhaled. The bond with Ghost was nothing like the one I'd formed with Gnat. That long-ago binding had been fleeting and had left me unchanged. This was *different*. Some small part of me had changed. Ghost had as well, but I suspected the changes the Game had wrought in her were larger.

Lifting my gaze, I studied the black smoke hovering about me. It was moving again. Surging inwards, the cloud imploded soundlessly, and when it was gone, a wolf stood in its place.

Ghost. My familiar.

I examined the pyre wolf closely. Her form was nearly identical to the one she had assumed before our binding.

But only nearly.

Squinting, I tried to pinpoint the differences. Ghost looked more... present. Her form was denser. *Solid*. Her eyes glinted acutely and with greater awareness. Her muscles rippled with new strength. And all about her, weaves of magic slipped into and out of existence.

The pyre wolf before me was, at one time, stronger, faster, wiser, and more formidable than she had been previously. Whatever Ghost was now, I *knew* she was no longer a lowly level one creature.

As if in confirmation, a Game message unfurled in my mind.

Ghost has cast manifest and has taken the form of a level 201 stygian pyre wolf.

My eyes grew round. Ghost was level *two hundred and one?* That was the exact same level as me, and I didn't think that was by coincidence.

Before I could pursue this surprising revelation further, Ghost spun into motion, twirling on the spot so fast I could barely follow her movements. Then, with startling suddenness, she froze to face me.

Ghost's lower jaw dropped open, and her tongue lolled out. *"Wow,"* she exclaimed in my mind. *"I feel... different. Powerful!"* Her eyes glinted mischievously. *"And strong enough to defeat even Duggar!"*

I smiled, the trepidation I hadn't even been aware I was feeling easing in an instant. No matter how much my companion had changed, she was still the same old exuberant Ghost, and that gladdened me no end.

I opened my mouth, a reply on the tip of my tongue, but before I could get the words out, I was interrupted by a veritable wall of text from the Game.

You have gained the trait: <u>mage-host</u>. As a result of your spirit familiar's nature, your Mind and Magic have each increased by +10 ranks.

You have gained a <u>stygian pyre wolf</u> for a familiar.

Unlike companions, familiars are not separate Game participants. They do not level independently or accumulate attribute points, nor can they absorb Game knowledge through skillbooks and ability tomes.

Instead, courtesy of their familiar bonds with their hosts, familiars will advance in level when their host does. They mirror their host's attributes and share their ability slots as well. It is only a familiar's energy pools, skills, traits, Class, and abilities that are separate from their hosts.

Depending on their innate nature—or Class—every familiar has a set of skills and abilities they may learn. These can be unlocked or improved by spending their Class points. A familiar gains Class points in the same manner a player does, at a rate of 1 every 20 levels.

Beware, though, all familiars have finite lives. In the event Ghost that loses her last life, or her spirit vessel is destroyed, she will suffer final death. Ghost's lives may be increased by expending Class points to acquire the trait: <u>born again</u>.

Note, your familiar's spirit vessel is more than a simple housing for her spirit when she is unmanifested. It is also a refuge she may use to rest and recuperate. While in the Cloak of the Reach, Ghost's health and energy pools will slowly recover over time.

Ghost has gained the trait: <u>free spirit</u>. Due to the excessive time your familiar spent as an unbound spirit, she is not limited as other familiars are in the distance she may travel from her mage-host or spirit vessel. She must, however, always remain in the same sector as the Cloak of the Reach.

Ghost has gained the trait: <u>psionic being</u>. Your familiar was once a dire wolf, creatures renowned for their psionic abilities. This knowledge has carried over to her new form, granting her the <u>telepathy</u> skill and 3 advanced telepathic abilities: <u>diresight</u>, <u>astral bite</u>, and <u>direshield</u>.

<u>Astral bite</u> is similar to astral blades and allows Ghost to buff her melee bite attacks so that they also deal psi damage.

<u>Diresight</u> is a variation of the mindsight ability and allows Ghost to sense, communicate, and even read the thoughts of any nearby unshielded mind. This is a Class ability and does not occupy any ability slots.

<u>Direshield</u> is telepathy-based ability that allows Ghost to both detect and repel unwanted mental intrusions. This is a Class ability and does not occupy any ability slots.

Courtesy of her new Class, stygian pyre wolf, Ghost has gained 3 master skills: <u>magma maw</u>, <u>stygian claws</u>, and <u>ash armor</u>.

<u>Magma maw</u> is a unique skill that only Ghost possesses. Nowhere else has the essence of the phoenix, Sunfury, been more deeply ingrained in Ghost's being than in her jaws. As such, unlike ordinary gorge and bite attacks, your familiar's maw attacks are magical in origin and deal fire

damage. Additionally, this skill allows Ghost to cast touch-based fire magic spells through her mouth.

Stygian claws is a unique skill that only Ghost possesses. Your familiar's claws have been formed from the fragments of dead stygian seeds, making her paws potent weapons for dealing both physical and necrotic damage.

Ash armor is a unique skill that only Ghost possesses. The natural armor of most creatures increases their physical damage resistance. Not so with your familiar. Due to her innate nature, as Ghost's ash armor skill increases, so does her ability to resist nether, fire, and physical damage.

Familiar Profile: Ghost

Level: 201. Rank: 20. Class: stygian pyre wolf (unique).
Lives Remaining: 1. Available Class points: 11.
Familiars only have a single pre-defined Class.

Attributes *(mirrors hosts)*

Strength: 21 (13)*. Constitution: 27 (19)*. Dexterity: 95 (71)*. Perception: 53 (49)*. Mind: 129 (117)*. Magic: 58 (38)*. Faith: 0.

Traits

spirit familiar: mirrors player attributes and level and shares ability slots with them.
psionic being: retains telepathic skills and abilities from her former incarnation as a dire wolf.
free spirit: can roam an unlimited distance from her host, but only within the same sector.

Skills

A familiar can only gain skills through Class upgrades.

magma maw (current: 1. max: 380. Magic, master).
stygian claws (current: 1. max: 130. Strength, master).
ash armor (current: 1. max: 190. Constitution, master).
telepathy (current: 50. max: 1170. Mind, advanced).

Abilities

A familiar can only gain abilities through Class upgrades.

Mind ability slots used: 71 / 117.
astral bite (5 Mind, advanced, telepathy).

Other abilities:
manifest (Class, basic).
diresight (Class, advanced, telepathy).
direshield (Class, advanced, telepathy).

"Yikes," I muttered. The Adjudicator had dumped a mountain of information on me, and I had a feeling it was going to take me a good while to digest it all.

"Keep watch for me, Ghost," I murmured as I sank back to the ground. "We'll talk in a bit, but in the meantime, I've got to review your Game data."

"Alright, Prime. Is it okay if I explore?"

"Don't go too far," I cautioned. "You still only have one life."

Receiving her nod of assent, I squeezed my eyes shut and began scanning through the Game messages a second time.

This is definitely not like my binding with Gnat.

This realization struck me again. By comparison, that had felt like a cheap parlor trick—and likely had been one crafted by Erebus through the use of a Pact to fool the lowly newbies he'd trapped in his web.

The next thing that occurred to me after reviewing Ghost's profile was her potential. While the pyre wolf lacked my versatility, employed correctly, she would effectively double our combat strength. Yes, Ghost wouldn't have her own attributes, and yes, it was disappointing that she would share my ability slots, but these deficiencies were offset by her Class skills—they were *unique*.

They complemented my own nicely. Even better, magma maw would give my familiar access to magic—something I lacked myself—and it didn't matter that it was only touched-base fire magic, adding any sort of magic to the mix could be game-changing.

Then, there were her ash armor and stygian claws skills—both would make her a formidable tank. Ghost's armor gave her *three* types of damage reduction, making it superior to my leather armor skill. More importantly, I expected her own attacks would bypass her foes' defenses. There couldn't be many fighters—or mages, for that matter—who were armored against necrotic damage.

Her telepathy, I was less certain about.

Not because I doubted the power of the skill but because its abilities would eat away at my own much-prized Mind ability slots. If Ghost and I both specialized in Mind, we would quickly run out of slots.

But things were different when it came to Ghost's Magic and Strength abilities and, to a lesser extent, her Constitution ones. I had little use for those slots, and my first instinct was to have Ghost focus her development in those areas.

Still, I hesitated.

There was another consideration to keep in mind: Ghost's Class points. They, more than our shared ability slots, would limit her advancement, especially seeing as how she would only gain one Class point every twenty levels. The other complication, of course, was that Ghost's Class points were also necessary to increase her remaining lives.

This all boiled down to one simple fact: Ghost could not acquire as many abilities as I did. At most, she would be able to specialize in two or perhaps three, abilities.

But there's no need to decide what those should be right now.

In fact, given how precious my familiar's Class points were, it made more sense to wait and see how she performed in combat before making a decision about her abilities. Really, the only thing Ghost desperately needed was more lives.

And for now, that's what I should focus on.

Ghost already had three skills and three abilities, all of which were currently usable, and until she advanced her skills a bit more, there was little point in investing further in her abilities.

It had also not escaped my attention that Ghost's telepathy was at rank five and not rank zero like the rest of her skills. Additionally, her telepathic abilities were already at *tier two*. It didn't make Ghost combat effective, not by a long shot, but it did give her a solid means of dealing damage, especially if she combined her astral bite with magma maw.

Rubbing my chin, I pondered my reasoning a bit further. Increasing Ghost's lives and saving the rest of her Class points for later seemed to be the smart choice. I nodded decisively.

That's what we'll do—my eyes drifted to the left, where Ghost was sniffing the basilisks' corpses—*assuming she agrees.*

"Ghost," I called out aloud, "come here, please. We have much to talk about."

✻　✻　✻

Ghost had no objections to my plan.

After discussing her profile with her, I got the impression that all the Game 'stuff' left her feeling overwhelmed, and she was more than content to focus on the abilities she already had rather than acquiring more.

Which was fair enough, I supposed.

Turning my focus inward, I called up Ghost's Class upgrade interface.

Your familiar may advance her Class to rank 2 at this time. Class points available: 11. Do you wish to proceed?

I signaled my intent to do so, and a list of benefits appeared. Amongst them was the one I was looking for.

New benefit: <u>born again</u>. This trait grants your familiar 1 additional life. Unlike players, familiars are not reborn in a safe zone, but in their spirit vessels. Their resurrection time is the same as their hosts.

Seems simple enough, I thought, and selected the trait twice on Ghost's behalf.

Your familiar has been awarded 2 additional lives. Total lives remaining: 3.

Upgrade complete. Class points remaining: 9.

Ghost's Class has advanced to rank 3.

"It's done," I said, opening my eyes.

Ghost wagged her tail. *"That means I don't have to go back into the Cloak, right?"*

My lips twitched upwards. "Correct," I murmured.

"Perfect!" she barked.

"One more thing... your diresight ability, I see it gives you the ability to read minds. How does that work?"

"Like it always did, I suppose. When I was a spirit being, whenever I wanted to see what someone was thinking, I would draw close to them and delve into their minds." I sensed her mental shrug. *"Sometimes it let me see their thoughts, other times it didn't."*

I rubbed my chin. "How close did you need to get?"

"Close enough that if I had physical form, I could've stretched out a paw and touched them."

"Touching distance then," I said, disappointed by the range of the ability. Then, something else occurred to me. "What about when you're unmanifested? Can you use diresight then?"

Ghost pondered the question for a moment. *"I don't think so. When I'm in the Cloak, I'm also cut off from my abilities."* She tilted her head. *"Why do you ask?"*

"Oh, just an idle thought," I said. "If you *could* use diresight while in the cloak, then you could read my mind and know what's happening around us. That way, you'd feel less disconnected from the world."

"Oh, I don't need diresight for that," Ghost replied easily. *"Since you completed the spirit binding, I can sense your thoughts like I used to before."*

I blinked. "So, you can see and hear what I see while unmanifested?"

"Yes," she replied happily.

"Ah. That's alright then."

Turning about in a circle, Ghost dashed off to the left. *"Oh, I almost forgot! I found something."*

Shaking my head ruefully—Ghost had moved on from her transformation and its implications quicker than I had—I followed the excited pyre wolf.

Ghost didn't lead me far, just around the corpse of the nearest basilisk.

Concealed behind it was a silver box.

A loot chest, I thought. Quickening my pace, I strode forward and flipped the lid open without ceremony. The loot box was only silver, the lowest value chest I'd yet found in the dungeon, but that was to be expected considering I was now of the same tier as its denizens and was an apt reminder of how far I'd come since entering Draven's Reach.

Peering into the chest, I inspected my rewards.

The target is a piece of <u>enchanted mosaic</u>.

The target is a <u>greater attribute gem</u>. It grants you 3 attribute points.

The target is the rank 4 familiar's collar: <u>shadow's friend</u>. This item has been enchanted to increase your familiar's stealth skill by +4 ranks and requires a minimum Dexterity of 16 to use.

I sighed. Silver chest notwithstanding, I'd really been hoping to find another upgrade gem. My sneaking was nearly at elite rank, which meant gaining a true invisibility ability was almost within my grasp. Sadly, it was not to be—not yet, anyway.

But who knows, maybe I'll find something else to fight soon. I was not hopeful, though. Shaking my head, I turned my attention to the rest of the chest's contents.

The mosaic piece, I eyed thoughtfully but left it where it was. I could only assume from its appearance that the dungeon had begun resetting, and it got me wondering.

How long until a new sector boss appears?

Draven's Reach had an exceptionally slow respawn rate, so it could be days yet or even weeks.

Not my problem, though, I thought, shrugging away the matter. I was sure Farren and Adriel would have worked out the implications for themselves. The pair likely already had the lich's court on alert and were more than capable of dealing with any new 'boss' that appeared.

Picking up the attribute gem, I activated it.

Greater attribute gem used. You have gained 3 attribute points.

Finally, I turned my gaze to the last item. "A familiar collar," I murmured, retrieving the jewel-studded metal ring. The collar was interesting, not for its characteristics—they weren't of much benefit to Ghost; she lacked the sneaking skill to begin with—but for what its existence implied.

Familiars could have their own gear.

I couldn't help wondering, though, what would happen to the equipment Ghost wore when she unmanifested. Would the gear accompany her into the Cloak of the Reach, or would it fall off?

Only one way to find out. "Come here, Ghost."

Padding forward, the pyre wolf looked curiously at the object in my hand. *"What is it?"*

"A collar for you," I said and explained further. Reaching forward, I clasped it around her neck.

Ghost has equipped <u>shadow's friend</u>, gaining +4 ranks in stealth.

"Do I unmanifest now?" she asked, looking at me with big, sorrowful eyes.

I chuckled at her exaggerated pretense at disappointment. "No need. We'll find out soon enough when the time comes."

The spark of delight in the pyre wolf's eyes returned. *"What do we do now, then? Continue to New Haven?"*

"No," I said, stifling a yawn. "We break for the night. I need rest, and I imagine in your new form, you are going to need sleep, too. We'll keep watch in shifts."

✳ ✳ ✳

I woke early the next morning and immediately went about finishing my remaining chores. Extracting the alchemy stone from my backpack, I placed it inside one of the basilisk's bodies, and while I waited for it to collect the corpses' reagents, I saw to my newly acquired attribute points.

Your Perception has increased to rank 56. Other modifiers: +4 from items.

Your Strength has increased to rank 14. Other modifiers: +8 from items.

When I was done, I had twenty free Perception ability slots—enough to advance my facial disguise ability to rank five, not that it was ready for that, but it was good to be prepared. The last attribute point I added to Strength, more for Ghost's sake than my own; the additional Strength would help with her claw attacks.

After the alchemy stone finished, I picked it up and stored it away.

New ingredients acquired: 4 x orbs of petrification.

I turned to Ghost. "Ready?"

She bobbed her head vigorously. *"Always."*

"Then, let's be on our way." Facing northward, I began walking.

✳ ✳ ✳

A few hours later, we reached the northwestern rim of Draven's Reach and the isolated gorge containing New Haven.

Pausing at the edge of the sheer cliff enclosing the city, I studied the scene before me. As expected, the nether fogbanks were gone. Nor were there any lurking stygians.

I frowned. *So why are the surrounding farmlands empty?*

I would have expected them to be bursting with farmers trying to salvage what they could from the fields. But I spotted no one outside the city walls. Not a single soul.

Perhaps it's the city's night-cycle.

I wasn't convinced, though.

"Is something wrong?" Ghost asked.

"Perhaps," I murmured. "I guess we'll find out soon enough." I glanced at her. "It's time."

The pyre wolf lowered her head. *"Do I have to?"*

I nodded. "The last time Taim was in the city, he was unaccompanied. Your presence will raise eyebrows, and we don't want that."

Ghost sighed but didn't object. We'd discussed the matter already, and she'd agreed she couldn't openly accompany me in the city. I knew how much she hated returning to the Cloak, though, so I didn't rush her.

The issue wasn't just Ghost's new form—one most would consider disturbing and frightening. It was also the pyre wolf's level. I'd analyzed her after disguising myself as Taim. Unfortunately, facial disguise did nothing to conceal her level—just my own—and my inspection had revealed her true rank.

Which was a problem since Taim was supposedly level two-hundred and forty-seven.

I could, of course, explain her away as my companion or ally since analyze had not revealed her to be a familiar, but doing that was unnecessarily complicated when there was a much simpler solution at hand.

Hiding her away was not a long-term solution, though, and I would have to consider more deeply how to disguise her in the future.

Ghost has cast unmanifest.

80

At the arrival of the Game alert, I glanced at the spot the pyre wolf had recently occupied and caught a glimpse of a few trailing wisps of smoke.

"*Thanks, Ghost,*" I murmured, studying the ground intently. No familiar collar lay there. *I guess that answers that.* I turned back to New Haven. *Time to find out what's been happening while I was away.*

Equipping my cat claws, I dropped down into the gorge.

CHAPTER 392: HAVEN COMPROMISED

I approached the city walls openly.

There was no need to hide. The guards on the wall were the marshal's men and, for all intents and purposes, my allies, yet... the faces my sharp-eyed gaze picked out from a distance were uniformly grim and unhappy.

Of its own accord, my right hand drifted closer to the hilt of ebonheart. To maintain my guise as Taim, I had stowed away my second blade. My eyes scanned the walls again.

Something had happened.

It must have. And whatever it was, my intuition was telling me it wasn't good. Drawing to a halt in front of the still-barred city gates, I raised my head to hail the guards on the parapets.

Multiple unknown entities have failed to pierce your disguise.

"Go away!" a thick-set soldier snarled. "City's closed."

My eyes rested on him. "Closed?" I repeated mildly.

"Yeah," he sniffed disdainfully. "No riff-raff allowed."

The insult did not perturb me. "Don't you recognize me? I'm Taim, the—
"

"The marshal's pet. Yeah, we know who you are," another guard added.

My gaze drifted in his direction. The second speaker was a dark elf and, by the insignia on his arm, a captain. "But the thing is, Elron is no longer in charge," he continued. "And *you* are definitely not welcome."

Outwardly, I stayed calm, but inwardly, my thoughts raced. What was happening in New Haven?

Elron had been ousted? How? And, more importantly, why?

When I'd left the city, the marshal's position had been secure. I'd been the fugitive, not him. Either Elron had overestimated his influence, or something had happened to trigger his downfall.

Leaning over the rampant, dark elf glared at me. "I said: get lost!"

"If you know who I am, you know *what* I am," I replied. "Your threats don't scare me."

"Oh, I know what you are," he sneered. Lifting his hands from where they had been concealed below the rampant, he drew a heavy warbow and pointed it unerringly at my heart. "But not even a player can outrun a hundred arrows." Raising his head, the captain yelled, "Draw!"

In response, more bows appeared, all pointed my way.

I didn't move.

Folding my arms across my chest, I studied the soldiers lining the city walls. Every face was grim, every gaze was stony, and while some refused to meet my eyes, no one looked scared. If I pushed them, it would come to a fight. And then I would have to kill a few.

Perhaps more than a few, I amended as I measured their resolve.

Something is not right here.

Ever so slowly, so as not to trigger a hasty response from the archers, I raised my right hand as if to rub at my chin, but in reality, tugged on one very particular chink in the sorcerer's coif.

Unlike the spectacles of ward seeing, the coif's enchantments were not always active—that would drain its magic too quickly—and it had to be enabled. Aside from that small drawback, the coif was superior to the spectacles—in every way. Not only did it let me perceive spelled wards, but it *also* identified the castings they contained.

You have activated a sorcerer's coif.

Glowing lines of magic appeared in my sight. Glancing left and right, I saw that the spell weaves covered the entirety of the city's walls in both directions.

You have detected a hostile spell!
The target is a tier 2 ward spell: <u>shrieking vines</u>.

My eyes tightened fractionally. Just as I suspected, the city was warded. *Shrieking vines.* I didn't recognize the spell but could guess what it did.

Lifting my head, I scanned the faces staring down at me anew. There were no youths amongst them. Every soldier on the wall was a veteran. And that, I suspected, wasn't happenstance either. My arrival had been expected.

And prepared for.

"What's wrong?" the dark elf jeered, mistaking my silence for fear. "Don't tell me the big bad player is afraid of a few proles?"

I didn't respond, unsure what to make of the dark elf's obvious animosity. I'd never met him before, and he had no cause to dislike me, yet clearly he did.

"Come on," the captain said, egging me on. "Step forward. *Give* me an excuse to kill you."

Why do you need an excuse? I wondered but kept the thought to myself.

A nearby sergeant threw his superior a sharp glance—cautioning him maybe?—but didn't otherwise intervene. Had the soldiers been ordered to turn me away, but *only* to turn me away? If so, the dark elf officer was skirting the edge of those orders. "What's your name, captain?" I asked finally.

"And why would I tell you that?" he scoffed.

I shrugged. "It's only your name. Where's the harm in sharing it?"

The captain grew tight-lipped, saying nothing.

I didn't need the elf to tell me his name, of course. I could analyze him and find out that way, but I didn't bother. Tilting my head to the side, I studied the officer curiously. "Now, who's afraid?" I asked softly.

The captain's hands tightened around his bow. Yet, even so, he did not release the arrow he'd knocked.

I stepped back. I'd learned all I was going to, I decided. *Time to de-escalate.* "Alright, you win," I said, raising my hands, palms out. "Don't shoot, and I'll go—peacefully."

The dark elf's lips curved upward in a triumphant grin. "Then get! And don't you dare come back!"

Now that I can't promise.

Bowing deeply—and with more than a hint of mockery—I retreated from the gate.

✳   ✳   ✳

Your deception has reached rank 16.
Multiple hostile entities have failed to detect you! You are hidden.

I didn't go far, just far enough to wrap myself in shadow and ponder my next move. The encounter at the city gates had been disturbing and less enlightening than I'd hoped. Central in my thoughts was the question: why had the council closed New Haven?

It could only be the council who were responsible; no one else had the power to remove Elron from office. Well, the possessed did, but they should be long gone from the city by now.

I'd discussed the problem of Castor with Adriel before we'd parted ways, and she had assured me Farren would recall the city's possessed contingent. And given what I'd seen of New Haven's wards, Farren appeared to have already made good on that promise. No way would Castor or any of his cohorts use such lower tiered spells to keep me out.

And keeping me out appeared to be the city's primary intent.

There had to be more to it, though, surely. The city wouldn't risk leaving their fields unattended solely to bar me from entering. Would they?

I bit my lip, thinking. I wasn't certain what game New Haven's council played, but it didn't appear well thought out. Closing the city and leaving the fields fallow—and not just the southern fields but the northern ones—was not smart.

Soon, the city's populace would starve—if they weren't already. After which, the people would riot. And then, the council would lose their grip on the city, and I could stroll in. All I had to do was camp outside the city and wait for that to happen.

But I couldn't do that.

For one, I didn't have the luxury of time, and for another, Elron might need help. It had not escaped my notice that the captain had not reported the marshal as dead. And if Elron were alive, I would not abandon him.

So, I had to enter the city. The only question was how I went about that.

The wards on the walls were an... inconvenience. Still, they had me wondering what role New Haven mages played in matters.

"What about the north gate?" Ghost suggested.

Setting aside my wandering thoughts, I focused on her. The two of us had been discussing potential strategies for infiltrating the city. *"What do you mean?"*

"You said the south gate was the same one we used the last time," the pyre wolf pointed out. *"If the city was expecting you to return, maybe that's why it's so heavily guarded. The other city entrances might be... less so."*

"Hmm, you may be onto something there." Rising to my feet, I studied the city. I was more than one hundred yards outside the walls, far enough that the guards could not spot me lurking in the shadows but close enough for my own sight to remain unimpaired by the distance. *"Let's see if you're right."*

Slipping quietly through the abandoned fields, I circled the city. From what Elron had told me, I knew New Haven had four entrances, one at each point of the compass.

It didn't take me long to draw even with the east gate. Pausing, I scanned the walls.

The city's eastern perimeter was almost as well-guarded as the southern one, but that didn't negate Ghost's theory. Given New Haven's geographical location in the dungeon, the southern and eastern entrances were the ones I was most likely to use when approaching the city. *"The east gate is a no-go, too,"* I reported.

Continuing onward, I angled past the east perimeter and made for the north wall.

It, too, was warded, and its gate was also closed, but less than fifty soldiers lined the ramparts. *"You were right, Ghost,"* I murmured. *"The northern entrance is poorly guarded."* But were the defenses lacking enough that I could teleport into the city *without* alerting the guards?

Only one way to find out.

Veering left, I made for the city.

✳   ✳   ✳

Cloaked in shadows, I crept closer to the walls. So far, the soldiers atop the parapets were oblivious to my presence.

At the fifty-yard line, I paused.

I was within shadow blink range. Teleporting past the shrieking vines would be easy from here, but that still left the problem of remaining unseen once I was on the ramparts, although I could *probably* escape detection by the soldiers long enough to teleport out again.

But why take that risk?

Blinking past the wards and the soldiers on the wall would be simpler—and safer. For that, though, I would need to find a teleportation target. Sending psi rippling outwards, I activated my mindsight.

Tendrils of my will flooded the space around me, revealing every consciousness within a hundred yards. There were fewer than I expected. Still, there were enough to give me options. Disregarding the mindglows on the ramparts, I focused on the ones beyond.

Thirty yards past the wall, I spotted a cluster of mindglows, which by the subdued nature, I judged to be the dreaming minds of a company of soldiers. Given the barracks I'd spied next to the city's outer walls during my previous visit, that was the most likely scenario, anyway.

Reaching out with my will, I inspected each consciousness until I found what I sought.

The target is...

The target is...
The target is Egan, a level 93 human.

A human was perfect for what I planned, especially one who was likely a soldier. *I aim for him,* I decided. Rising to my haunches, I padded forward.

Forty yards separated me from the wall. Thirty.

Multiple hostile entities have failed to detect you!

Drawing to a halt, I recast fade, then resumed my silent stalk through the field of overripe crops. From the ramparts, the sounds of the guards' chatter floated downwards. They were relaxed and at ease, no threat.

Twenty yards from the wall, I stopped. My target was within range. *This is it.* Spinning together weaves of psi, I stepped out of the real and into the aether.

You have cast shadow blink.

✷   ✷   ✷

You have teleported 50 yards. You are hidden.

I was in a bedroom.

Utilitarian and small, it housed only a bed, a wardrobe, a table, and a chair. Glancing up from where I was crouched on the floor, I took in the snoring shape stretched out on the bed.

He was garbed in the same uniform as the other city soldiers and bore the insignia of a lieutenant. I'd found an officer. Even better, I wasn't in a barracks dormitory, and the room was empty except for Egan and me.

For a moment, I was tempted to explore the building I was in further but decided against it. Sleeping or not, I could trust soldiers to be more alert than the average citizen, and there were easier ways of finding out what was happening in the city.

Unbending, I rose to my full height and studied the oblivious figure on the bed more carefully. When I was certain I had memorized his features, I slipped towards the wardrobe and opened it.

Three pairs of uniforms were stacked neatly on the shelves within. I smiled broadly. *Perfect.* Swiping the first set, I redressed and adjusted my disguise.

You have cast facial disguise, assuming the visage of Egan, a level 93 human. Duration: 3 hours.

Time to go. Directing my mindsight into the city, I searched for another teleportation target.

It didn't take me long to find one.

Forty yards away was a solitary individual. She was moving quickly, angling away from me, and I had to act fast if I was going to use her to teleport. Drawing psi, I shadow blinked.

You have teleported into Noli's shadow. You are hidden.

I emerged from the aether behind the dwarf, who was in far too much of a rush to notice the new shadow at her rear. Staying still, I took in my surroundings.

I was in a city street, out in the open and exposed.

A side street—narrow and overshadowed by the buildings bordering it—was close by. I jogged towards it, my footfalls silent, and before Noli or anyone else could spot me, I ducked within its sheltering embrace.

"*I'm in,*" I reported to Ghost.

"*Good job.*" She paused. "*What now?*"

With my back pressed up against a wall, I peeked out of the alley. Noli had disappeared around a corner, and the streets were empty. My arrival in the city had gone unnoticed.

"*Now, we find Gamil,*" I replied. Trusting in my disguise, I slipped out of hiding and strode boldly down the street.

Gamil's shop hadn't changed in the intervening weeks. The same could not be said for the rest of the city, though.

Squads of soldiers patrolled the streets, and what few civilians moved about, did so quickly and furtively. I drew the attention of more than one passing patrol, but my uniform and officer's insignia were enough to ward them off, and I reached my destination unmolested.

Sitting in the shadows of an alleyway, I studied the building on the opposite side of the street. There were no customers, only a lone figure pottering in the backroom. Gamil. The old shopkeeper was Elron's friend and had helped me find the marshal once. I was hoping he would do so again.

Activating the sorcerer's coif, I re-inspected the surroundings but failed to spot any wards. I had no reason to suspect a trap, but the changes in the city had me on edge. Something was wrong in New Haven, and as yet, I wasn't sure what.

I glanced down both directions of the street. No one was in sight. Kicking off from the wall I rested against, I marched purposely toward the shop. Anyone watching would think me just another soldier going about his orders. At the entrance of the antique bazaar, I paused again and altered my face.

You have cast facial disguise, assuming the visage of Taim.

Then, turning the doorknob, I slipped into the shop. "Gamil?" I called softly.

The shuffling in the back room stopped. "Who is it?" the shopkeeper asked, his voice thin and wavering.

"Taim."

Silence followed as Gamil processed my response. My answer had no doubt startled him. It was not every day a hunted fugitive openly announced his presence, after all.

Making no move to advance further into the room, I watched the shopkeeper with my mindsight, wondering if he would bolt. If he did, I would make my escape, but I was gambling Gamil wouldn't.

The last time I'd seen the old man, I had been open about my run-ins with the city council and the possessed, and it hadn't seemed to bother him any. With any luck, his attitude hadn't changed.

Footsteps shuffled closer, and a moment later, a hunched-over shape yanked back on the curtains separating the backroom from the main floor. "So," Gamil mused, studying me through watery eyes. "It is you."

I nodded.

"That explains it, then."

My brows crinkled. "Explains what?"

The old man gestured at the door. "The new madness infecting New Haven. It's all your doing."

"I've only just arrived in the city," I objected.

"So?" Gamil sniffed. "What does that have to do with anything?" Before I could respond, he went on, "Didn't you cause enough mischief the last time?"

"What happened wasn't my fault," I protested. "At least not entirely. The possessed were as much to blame. If they hadn't tried to capture me—"

"You're right, of course," Gamil interjected. He sighed. "Forgive me. I'm just irritable and tired. My words were uncalled for. But this latest nonsense... it's upsetting." Turning around, he ambled back the way he came. "Follow me," he called over his shoulder. "I'm guessing you're not here to shop. Let's talk in the back."

Wordlessly, I trailed after the shopkeeper and caught up to him just as he was lowering himself into a chair. "Sit," he said, pointing to another chair with his cane.

I sat.

Resting his hands on top of the cane, Gamil studied me. "Tell me why you have come."

"I want your help," I said quietly.

One corner of his lips twitched. "I gathered as much. What do you need?"

"Information, primarily," I replied. "What's going on in the city?"

Gamil sat back, one eyebrow lifting. "You don't know?"

I shrugged. "I don't. I wasn't exaggerating when I said I just arrived, you know."

The shopkeeper grunted. "Well, it's nothing good. Martial law has been declared. New Haven has been in lockdown since two days ago."

Two days? That was interesting timing. "But why lock down the city?"

It was Gamil's turn to shrug. "I have no idea."

I frowned, hardly able to credit that.

Seeing my look, the shopkeeper added, "I saw the decree myself. It bore the council's seal and was signed by Cilia, but no reasons for the orders were given."

"And you still accepted them?" I asked skeptically. "The populace, too? A city full of people just upped and locked themselves away on the council's say-so?"

Gamil snorted. "You seem to have forgotten where we are, boy. We *live* in a dungeon. Attacks are a regular occurrence, and sometimes, the only way to stay alive is to hide. So, when the council *orders* you to stay home and lock your doors, you do."

"Hmm." I wasn't entirely convinced, but I conceded Gamil had a point. After centuries, it wouldn't be hard to train a scared populace into unquestioning obedience. "So, people believe the order is for their own safety?"

Gamil nodded.

I rubbed my chin in thought. "You said Cilia signed the decree. What about the rest of the council? Were their names on it, too?"

"No. Only *her* name was on the decree—which was strange, admittedly. As for why the rest of the council didn't cosign the order, I don't know. There's been no news from the fortresses since all this began."

It was another ominous sign, especially since both Elron and I considered the dark elf, Cilia, to be our biggest enemy on the city council. I leaned forward. "And what about the marshal? Where is he?"

"Under house arrest."

I blinked. "What? Why?"

Again, Gamil shrugged. "I can't say, I'm afraid. Elron's arrest is not common knowledge, and I only managed to find out that much because... well, let's just say I know people. But as to the reason for his arrest, I haven't managed to uncover that."

"But why house arrest?" If the council—or Cilia—were going to imprison Elron, I would've thought they would want him secured in New Haven's deepest, darkest dungeon.

Gamil chuckled. "This is the high marshal we're talking about, son. *His* soldiers may be willing to do the council's bidding, but only up to a point. I suspect if it became common knowledge that their commander had been thrown in jail, the council would have a revolt on their hands."

"I see." I bit my lip. "I assume they're holding Elron in his house in the southern part of the city?"

"That's right."

I rose to my feet. "Then, I guess it's about time I rescued him."

✳   ✳   ✳

I didn't leave Gamil's shop immediately.

According to the old man, the daily curfew was about to be lifted, and the city's citizens allowed to walk the streets again, if only for a short period, and under the watchful eye of the patrolling soldiers.

Better to wait, I decided. *I will be less conspicuous in a crowd.*

"What will you do when you find Elron?" Ghost asked.

It was a pertinent question, and I wasn't sure of the answer myself yet. *"I don't know. Help him take over New Haven, maybe. Or flee."* I sighed, then conceded. *"Or I might do nothing. Time will be the deciding factor."*

Three days. That was how long I was willing to remain in the city. If Elron's problems required more time to resolve, they would have to wait. I only hoped that if it came to that, I could make the marshal understand I wasn't abandoning him. I would return when time permitted—*after* I'd seen to the wellbeing of my other allies.

Reminded of my timetable, I looked out of the antique shop's glass-paned windows. People had begun to trickle onto the streets. None appeared at ease, though, and even as they hurried about their business, many cast uneasy glances at the hovering soldiers.

"If you're waiting for it to get busier, I should warn you—it doesn't," Gamil said.

I glanced over my shoulder at the old man. "It doesn't?" I asked, slightly disbelievingly. While there were a few people on the streets, the crowds I had observed on my first visit to the city were absent.

He shook his head. "It doesn't." Seeing my expression, he added, "People are afraid. Most can sense trouble in the air, and no one wants to get caught up in that, not if they can help it."

I nodded slowly. It looked like my waiting was over. Turning around, I shook his hand. "Thank you again."

Gamil shrugged. "Thank me by saving Elron."

"I'll do that," I said and slipped out of the shop.

Imitating the other stragglers on the street, I bowed my head and shoved my hands in my pocket. Then I hurried southward as if on important business.

Two streets away from the old man's shop and out of sight of the closest squad of soldiers, I reset the illusion wrapped about me.

You have cast facial disguise, assuming the visage of Egan.
Your deception has reached rank 17.

Keeping to the shadows, I made my way through the city. The crowds never thickened, but the guard patrols certainly did. New Haven's southern districts were especially fraught with soldiers, leading me to believe that this region of this city was more problematic than others.

Still, despite the heavy military presence, I reached my destination unhindered. The marshal's house was dead ahead, only a hundred yards away. Slowing my steps, I lifted my head and ran my gaze across the surroundings.

The place swarmed with soldiers.

Squads stood guard at every intersection, with soldiers looking both inwards and outwards as they searched for threats. More than one gaze fell upon me, and despite my officer's badge and soldier's uniform, suspicion clouded the face of some sergeants.

Multiple unknown entities have failed to pierce your disguise.

This won't do, I thought.

It was only a matter of time before one of the soldiers took it upon themselves to wonder why a lieutenant was wandering the streets alone and decided to question me.

Reaching the next crossroads, I turned left and out of sight of the marshal's jailors. My disguise wasn't going to get me through Elron's door.

I would have to find another way to reach him.

✳　✳　✳

Twenty minutes later, I was sitting in the shadows of a narrow alleyway one street over from the marshal's house. I was not alone, however.

Multiple hostile entities have failed to detect you! You are hidden.

Two squads of guards occupied the alley with me, one on either end of the street. Together, they effectively blocked off entry or exit from the alley. I had no intention of trying to slip past them, though.

I entered the street by climbing down from the roof of one of the adjacent buildings, and my planned exit would be just as unconventional.

Unfurling my mindsight, I inspected the surroundings. While the street I was on did not border the marshal's house, it was close enough to put every consciousness inside within easy reach of shadow blink.

There were only a few people in the building, though. Reaching out with my will, I inspected them one by one.

The target is Algar, a level 120 human.
The target is Tymen, a level 103 human.
The target is Elron, a level 151 dark elf.
The target is Lanna, a level 110 half-elf.

I frowned. Elron's jailors hadn't just been posted outside, three were inside with him, and by the feel of their minds, they were awake and alert. Even worse, the guards were close to the marshal, likely in the very same room, and showed no sign of leaving.

I could get to Elron and his jailors—no doubt about it—but could I kill the three before they raised the alarm and the patrols from outside rushed in?

Not without doing some prep work first.

Of course, acting before I teleported into the marshal's house was dangerous, too. Mindsight only revealed unshielded minds, which meant there was a chance that my count was off.

If I tried bespelling the guards from afar and missed one... I would still end up being discovered. However, it was the least risky option open to me.

So, which will it be? Charm or sleep?

Sleep, I decided. If I charmed the trio, I would likely be forced to kill them once the spell expired, and I wanted to avoid that if I could help it. Slaying Elron's soldiers—and in front of him, no less—would not sit well with the marshal, even if those very same soldiers were currently serving as his jailers.

My course decided, I gathered psi and swamped the area around Elron with my will, not bothering to avoid the marshal himself.

You have cast slaysight.
You have induced 4 of 4 targets to sleep for 40 seconds.

So far so good. Tense with anticipation, I waited.

A heartbeat passed, then another, but no cry of alarm rose.

I relaxed slightly. There was still no guarantee I wasn't walking into a trap, but the chances of a mind-shielded guard not shouting for help after witnessing his fellows fall to the floor were vanishingly small.

Drawing more psi, I shadow blinked.

You have teleported 30 yards.

I stepped out of the aether with my sword drawn and ready for anything. Whirling around, I swept my gaze across my surroundings.

I was in the marshal's lounge.

Two crumpled forms lay at the door—the soldiers Lanna and Tymen—
another was slumped in a chair—Algar, he looked vaguely familiar—and a
fourth figure snored on the couch opposite him.

Elron.

Except for the four sleeping shapes, the room was empty, and the last of
my tension dissipated. Sheathing my blades, I strode over to the unconscious
marshal. I didn't have much time. Leaning over, I shook Elron roughly.

**You have taken hostile action against your bespelled target!
Enchantment broken. Elron is no longer asleep.**

The marshal awoke with a start, his hands automatically searching for
the sword at his side. I slapped his arm away before he could more than half-
draw the blade. "Stop. It's me. Taim."

Elron froze, and his head jerked upwards. "Taim?" he asked, eyes
widening. "You're back."

I nodded, even though that was self-evident.

The marshal smiled. "Then all is not lost," he said—too loudly for my
liking.

"Shhh," I hissed. "We don't want to alert the guards outside."

Elron's brows furrowed.

I jerked my chin in the direction of his sword. "Your jailors may have let
you keep that, but I don't think they would take too kindly to me dropping
by to visit."

Elron's expression cleared. "Ah, I understand now. But you got it wrong.
They're not my jailors."

It was my turn to frown. "What?"

The marshal did not answer immediately. His gaze darting about the
room, he picked out the slumped forms of the three soldiers. "You did that,
I presume?"

I nodded curtly, still waiting to hear what he meant.

"Are they hurt?"

I shook my head brusquely. "No. Just asleep."

He exhaled in relief. "That's good," he murmured.

"Elron," I hissed through clenched teeth. "You still haven't told me
what's going on. If those three aren't your jailors, what are they, and why
are they here?"

The marshal met my gaze. "They're my guards, and they're here for my
protection."

I stared at him blankly for a second, then sat beside him. "Alright, I guess
you better start at the beginning."

"How long until they wake up?" Elron asked.

I shrugged. "Any second now." Right on queue, a Game alert opened in my mind.

Your enchantment has lapsed. Your targets are no longer asleep.

The two soldiers at the door moaned while the one sitting down jerked upright suddenly, his eyes widening. He bore a captain's insignia on his arm, I noted. "Sir!" he exclaimed, hands fumbling for his sword.

"It's alright, Algar," Elron soothed. "I'm fine."

Algar has failed to pierce your disguise.

The captain's gaze shot sideways to me. "But–but what about…"

I recognized him now. The officer in question was the one on duty when I'd first arrived in the city. At the time, he and Elron had seemed well-acquainted, which made sense in light of what the marshal had just told me. "Algar, isn't it?" I asked. "You remember me, don't you?"

In the face of my obvious lack of hostility, the captain calmed. "You're that… player."

"That's right," Elron replied before I could answer myself. Standing up, he swung to face the two guards at the door. "And he is my friend, too. I trust you three will keep his visit a secret?"

The trio saluted smartly. "Yes, sir!" they echoed in unison.

"Thank you," Elron replied. "Now, leave us, please."

The two soldiers at the door hurried out, followed more slowly by Algar.

"Oh, and Captain," the marshal said, stopping him, "make sure we aren't disturbed."

"As you wish, sir," Algar said and closed the door on his way out.

Seating himself, Elron faced me, his expression one of quiet intensity as he leaned forward. "Now. Tell me everything. Did you succeed? Did you find the exile?"

I waved aside the marshal's question. "We'll get to that in a bit. I'm more concerned about what's happening in the city. Matters in New Haven are not what I expected. What's gone wrong?"

Elron's face fell, his only sign of disappointment at being made to wait. "What *hasn't* gone wrong?" he muttered as he sat back.

"Gamil told me the city is under lockdown," I said. "And the guards on the wall wouldn't let me enter when I approached."

"That's Cilia's doing," Elron said grimly.

"Gamil said so," Leaning forward, I planted my elbows on my knees. "We had a plan for getting rid of her. *You* had a plan. Did it fail?"

"It did—and spectacularly, too," the marshal replied bluntly.

I winced. "What happened?"

"The possessed happened," Elron answered. "It seems I underestimated how close Cilia and Castor were. My plan to unseat her from the council was going perfectly—I had the votes I needed and the dark elf patriarchs behind me—then Castor found out." He fell silent.

"And?" I prompted.

"And," Elron continued bitterly, "he wouldn't let his mistress be removed. He even went so far as to threaten to kill the other councilors if they attempted to oust her again."

I blinked in astonishment. "Mistress? You mean Castor and Cilia...?"

Elron nodded. "Believe me, I was even more surprised." He shook his head. "Anyway, after my failed attempt to usurp Cilia, she knew I was an enemy, and slowly but surely, she has been tightening the noose around me. I've been under house arrest for more than two weeks now."

I glanced meaningfully at the door. "Those three didn't look like any jailors I've run across before."

A bitter-sweet smile flickered across Elron's face. "Cilia may have won the main contest between us, but I've not capitulated, and the battle is far from over. Even now, most of the army remains loyal to me." He sighed. "But enough have chosen to side with her that if I contest her orders, it will come to open fighting in the streets—and I can't risk that." He lowered his head in shame. "I'm sorry to say, but I failed to complete my part of the plan."

"So, to be clear... the whole house arrest is a façade, and the soldiers on the street outside are yours?"

"Not entirely," the marshal replied. "*Most* of the soldiers in the district are mine. Even so, Cilia has spies amongst them. If I left, they will get word to her." He shrugged. "I've been biding my time and waiting for the right opportunity to strike."

For a moment, I didn't say anything while I tried to figure out what the new dynamic in the city and the army's divided loyalties meant for my own plans. "I bet the soldiers on the south wall belong to Cilia," I muttered, recalling the dark elf captain I'd spoken with at the gate. "And probably those on the east wall too."

The marshal studied me curiously. "What makes you say that?"

I relayed my conversation with the captain on the south wall, and Elron's face twisted in distaste. "That's Minakawa. I should have kicked him out of the army long ago."

I couldn't agree more but didn't pursue the matter further as something else occurred to me. "Wait... did you say you've been under house arrest for two weeks?"

Elron nodded.

My brows furrowed. "Then why the citywide lockdown? Gamil said the curfew only began two days ago."

"He's right about that," Elron confirmed. "As for why..." The marshal shook his head. "That's what my informants have been working overtime to discover. But all I've managed to find out thus far is that the order was Castor's idea."

I inhaled sharply. "Castor? You mean he's still in the city?"

Elron's brows furrowed. "Of course. Where else would he be? Since the lockdown began, he and the other possessed have been holed up in the lower levels of Cilia's fortress. I haven't managed to figure out what they've been doing there either."

Rising to my feet, I began pacing. I'd been wrong. Castor and the others had not been recalled. Either Adriel had failed to get her message through to Farren or...

Or the liches had betrayed me.

I shook my head. *Don't be a fool, Michael. The very notion is ridiculous!* There was no way Adriel and Farren would do that, not after all we'd been through.

No, the answer had to lie elsewhere.

Two days, I mused, reflecting on the timeline again.

Two days ago was when we'd killed the archlich. It could not be coincidence that this was also when Cilia and Castor had locked down the city. Avery, I remembered, was in the lich's court and, by his own admission, able to speak to Castor across the dungeon.

Is that it?

Had Avery told Castor about Loskin's death? *Probably.* But even if he had, so what? The possessed's existence depended on a lich's goodwill, which bound them—willingly or unwillingly—to Farren and Adriel.

Unless...

Was Castor attempting a rebellion? Was he making some sort of play against Farren and Adriel?

But that idea was nearly as ludicrous as the notion the lichs had betrayed me. Without Farren and Adriel, there were no more possessed. Castor's continued immortality depended on a lich rehoming him when he died. That fact alone would ensure the failure of any attempted coup.

Unless Castor thinks he has a bargaining chip.

I froze, considering that startling possibility. *What sort of—?*

I swung back to the marshal. "You said Castor and the possessed are in Cilia's castle, correct?"

He nodded.

"Have you managed to get a precise fix on their location?" Before he could answer, I went on, "Could it be that they are not in the fortress itself but in the underground tunnel between New Haven and the lich's court?"

The marshal's eyebrows rose. "They are, in fact, holed up in the fortress' lowest level, the one leading directly to the tunnel. How did you guess?"

Things were starting to make sense. Not answering Elron, I continued to ponder the slowly unraveling mystery.

"You know what Castor is up to," Elron cut in, his word less statement than question. "Tell me," he demanded.

I met his gaze. "I do. Castor is holding the city hostage."

✳   ✳   ✳

The marshal's face scrunched up. "Hostage? But against who—"

"The archlich—the new archlich, I should say." I resumed pacing. "This is a power play."

Bowing my head, I thought it through. The last time we'd discussed the tunnel, Elron had told me it was easily defended, that a small group could hold it against an entire army if needed. That being the case, it was not inconceivable that Castor might try to cut off Farren from the possessed's only source of new bodies.

He had miscalculated, though.

The new archlich was nothing like the old one. Farren wasn't interested in new bodies. That era was over. From here on out, the possessed were going to be as mortal as everyone else. But Castor didn't know that. Not yet.

"New archlich," Elron said abruptly, interrupting my musings again. "You said *new* archlich." When I swung around to face him, he added, "Does that mean what I think it means?"

I smiled. "If you're asking, did I succeed in finding the exile, then yes. If you're asking if the old possessed leader is dead, then also yes."

Resting his arms on the side of his chair, Elron pressed his hands tightly together until the white of his knuckles showed. "There's more. I can tell," he said, his eyes shining.

I laughed. "You're right. There is. Both the exile and the new archlich—who are siblings, by the way—have allied with me. I won't go into all the details right now, but suffice it to say there will be no more 'bodies' harvested from New Haven. The city's populace is free to exit the dungeon whenever it wishes."

Awe suffused Elron's face. "You did it," he whispered.

I nodded mutely, giving him time to savor the moment, then added, "There's more."

"More?" he echoed.

"The breach in the dungeon's barrier has been repaired, the harbinger has been defeated, and the void tree has fled."

The marshal's face went blank as he struggled to comprehend the enormity of what I was telling him.

"In simple terms, what all this means is the void is no longer a threat. New Haven need not fear the nether anymore. I can't tell you everything, but I'm certain that, for the next few centuries at least, the void will not return to Draven's Reach. The city is safe."

"Safe," Elron repeated.

I nodded solemnly. "Stay or leave. The choice is now entirely in your people's hands."

The blank look left Elron's gaze, and he slowly lifted his eyes to mine. "This is all your doing?"

I grinned. "I had help. Lots of it."

The marshal uncoiled and, skipping forward jerkily, gripped my hands in his. "Thank you," he said fervently. "On behalf of—"

"No thanks are necessary," I said, cutting him off. My smile faded. "And truthfully, my actions were not purely altruistic."

Elron did not back away. "You want something."

"I do," I replied. "It's a big ask. And dangerous, too." I held up my hand, stopping him from speaking. "But it is an *ask* only. New Haven will be free to deny me if it so wishes."

"What do you need?"

Breaking free of Elron, I stepped back. "We'll get to that in good time. Right now, we have a more immediate matter to attend to—figuring out how to deal with Cilia and Castor."

CHAPTER 395: A DARING SCHEME

"I have a few ideas on how to go about that," Elron said.

I studied him curiously. "You do?"

Elron laughed. "Of course. Before today, my hands were tied. But now... now, I know there aren't any external threats. That leaves me free to concentrate my forces."

My eyes narrowed. "You're thinking about launching a direct assault."

"I am," the marshal agreed. Stepping away, he yanked open the door and shouted, "Algar! Get in here." Turning back to me, he explained, "Algar isn't just any officer. He is also my aide and right-hand man."

The human captain—broad-shouldered, squat, and built like a fighter—stepped back into the room, his eyes darting curiously from Elron's jubilant grin to me. It was not hard to read the question in his eyes. *What did you do to my commander?* they seemed to ask.

"Taim has brought great news," the marshal said.

"Sir?"

"The archlich has been defeated, the way out of the dungeon lies open, and for good measure, he's sent the void packing too!" Elron rocked back and forth on his heels. "You know what that means, Algar, don't you?"

To his credit, the captain did not doubt his commander. "Yes, sir," he replied, the light in his eyes brightening until they matched Elron's. "When do we begin the assault?"

"Soon," Elron said, reseating himself. "But first, bring Taim up to speed on our plans."

The captain swiveled around to face me. "We have companies loyal to the marshal encamped all over the city. Of course, the greatest concentration of our forces is here in the southern district, but we also have men ready to move in the eastern, northern, and western districts. The plan is to smash Cilia's loyalists in those quadrants before moving on her stronghold."

"What sort of numbers are we talking about?" I asked.

"Ignoring the councilors' personal guards, city militia, and other household outfits that usually supplement the city's defenses during emergencies, the New Haven regular army numbers thirty thousand soldiers, and ordinarily, they all report to the marshal, but..." Algar's gaze darted sideways to Elron as if fielding the question to him.

"But these, of course, are not ordinary times," the marshal finished for him. "Not every company commander has openly declared their allegiance—for Cilia or against. Some, rightly or wrongly, fear repercussions from whoever emerges victorious out of this and have chosen to play their cards close." He grimaced. "Unfortunately, it makes getting a firm count problematic. However, I've received assurances from enough men whose word I trust to believe we will outnumber the enemy."

Algar nodded in agreement with his superior's assessment. "We expect minimal resistance in the districts. With both surprise and numbers on our side, we will roll over the enemy quickly, no question. Once we've secured the outer city, we will converge on the city center and lay siege to the councilors' fortresses."

I pursed my lips. "Won't delaying the assault on Cilia's stronghold give her and Castor time to prepare?"

"It can't be helped," Algar replied. "We must clear the city first or risk exposing our flanks. And given what the possessed are capable of, we can't afford to be distracted at an ill-opportune moment."

That much I understood. Still...

"The situation is even worse than that," Elron interjected. "As you know already, each councilor has their own stronghold. We will have to divide our forces to lay siege to their fortresses. If one—or worse yet, *all*—chooses to sally forth, we will face simultaneous attacks from multiple fronts. On their own, the four fortresses make capturing the city center a strategic nightmare. We can't risk making a bad situation worse by giving Cilia and Castor additional avenues from which to counterattack." He shook his head. "As much as I hate to admit it, moving on the central district before the rest of the city is secured will be a mistake."

My brows rose. "Then you believe it is not just the Cilia we face but the entire council?"

Elron shrugged. "I don't know. The information coming out of the fortresses is sketchy." He glanced at Algar. "Tell him."

"The dwarves have locked down their stronghold. Word is that Thane Stormhammer is missing, but the dwarves won't speak to anyone and are unwilling to confirm or deny the rumors. The situation with the orcs is similar. Chief Lorn is refusing to grant audiences, and not even the servants are being let out. As for the human contingent..."

Pausing, Algar eyed me sideways—was that because I was a human or because he was? "High Lord Sienna has accepted the marshal's overtures," he continued, "and has secretly pledged her support for our cause even while she freely comes and goes from Cilia's fortress."

"Needless to say," Elron added, "I don't trust anything coming from the high lord's mouth."

"I wouldn't either," I said, remembering how Sienna appeared to hang on to Cilia's words during our previous meetings.

"Given the situation, we have no choice but to assume that all the other councilors are allied with Cilia," Elron concluded.

I inclined my head, agreeing with him on that point.

"That then is the plan," Algar said. "Or its broad strokes anyway." He glanced at the marshal, who nodded.

"What do you think?" Elron asked.

"I think..." I said, articulating my thoughts slowly, "I think... it will take too long."

The marshal frowned. "What does that matter?"

"I'm on a timetable," I replied quietly. "I have to leave New Haven in three days. A siege, I fear, will take longer."

"Three days," Algar exclaimed. "That's not nearly enough time!"

I agreed and glanced at Elron to see what he made of my response. The marshal's face had gone blank. "Then we can't count on your support?" he asked stiffly.

I shook my head. "On the contrary, you can. But we will have to amend the plan."

✳   ✳   ✳

"Amend how?" Elron asked, his eyes narrowing.

"We cut off the head of the snake," I replied promptly. "Castor and Cilia. With them dead, there's no reason for your arrest or further conflict. The rest of the council will fall in line afterward."

"Don't bet on it," Algar muttered under his breath, low enough that I didn't think he meant me to hear.

Ignoring the captain, I addressed Elron, "How many possessed does Castor have with him?

"Fifty," the marshal replied. "All of them will fight tooth and nail to protect Castor, too." He rubbed his chin. "You're talking about a surprise attack, I presume?"

"I am."

He shook his head. "It won't work. Taking on fifty possessed will require the entire army, and there is no way we can conceal the movements of that many soldiers. Cilia's spies will warn her when we begin our march, and by the time we reach her fortress, the First and her allies will be ready and waiting."

"You're right, of course," I said mildly. "Which is why I'm not suggesting we use the army."

"Then how do you propose we deal with the possessed?" a confused Algar asked.

Saying nothing, I kept my gaze locked on the marshal, who, from the thoughtful frown on his face, was beginning to realize my plan. "You intend on killing them yourself," Elron replied softly. "Don't you?"

I nodded mutely.

Algar's eyes widened. "That's preposterous!" When only silence greeted him, he asked in a smaller voice, "Isn't it?"

Elron studied me searchingly. "I don't know. Tell us, Taim, is it?"

I didn't shy from the marshal's gaze or the silent accusation they contained. If this was a feat I was capable of, he seemed to ask, why hadn't I dealt with the possessed more directly before?

"I'm *not* powerful enough to take on fifty possessed, not in an open fight." I snorted. "That would be suicide. But I *am* a moderately good sneak, and I believe I can reach Castor and Cilia without sounding the alarm—" I paused—"and kill them."

"You're an assassin!" Algar cursed.

I shrugged. "I can be."

Elron looked less perturbed by the revelation. "Have you forgotten Castor is an elite, and you fell afoul of his wards before? He will not leave himself unprotected in Cilia's stronghold."

It didn't surprise me that the marshal had heard of my misadventure in the Mages' Guild. "I've come some way since my last clash with Castor," I answered vaguely. "He will not catch me unawares again."

Still looking doubtful, Elron stayed silent for a drawn-out moment. "You're sure you can do this?" he asked finally.

I smiled. "There are never any guarantees. You and I both know that." I exhaled. "But I am confident enough of my chances to try. And don't forget I will have surprise on my side. Only Gamil, Algar, your two guards, and yourself know I'm in the city. Castor and Cilia won't be expecting me."

The marshal nodded slowly. "Very well. If you think it can be done, we'll try it your way. What do you need from us?"

"Information for starters," I replied. "Floor plans for Cilia's fortress, the location of her chambers, and that of the underground tunnel entrance."

Elron glanced at Algar.

"We have all that," he confirmed.

"Good," the marshal said, turning back to me. "Anything else?"

"The names and descriptions of Cilia's most trusted people, especially those who frequent the fortress often." I pursed my lips, thinking. "Also, it might be helpful if..."

✳   ✳   ✳

Hours later, just as midnight was approaching, Elron, Algar, and I finished our scheming.

The plan was simple. I would kill Castor and Cilia. After which, a small force under Algar's command would sweep into the fortress and overrun the councilor's remaining adherents. Elron, meanwhile, would stay in the southern district so as not to arouse the suspicions of any watching spies.

The marshal would not, however, be idle. While Algar and I were dealing with the more immediate threat, he would correspond with the other New Haven leaders and make sure the city was ready for a smooth transition of power from the old regime to the new.

First, though, I had to accomplish my part.

Which, while doable, might not be as easy as I'd made out to be. Much would depend on me retaining the element of surprise. If Castor and his cronies learned I was coming, things would get complicated fast. Practically, I knew I would only get one chance. If I failed, there would be no going back to the drawing board; we would have to fall back on Elron's plan.

And that I can't afford.

Glancing up, I saw my destination up ahead: the large central square at the heart of the city. It was time to set things in motion. Turning my head fractionally, my eyes found Algar on the opposite side of the street. Making a fist, I gave him the pre-arranged signal.

The captain, who'd been discreetly tailing me as I made my way across the city, nodded, acknowledging the order, before disappearing into a nearby building. He and the squads he brought along would wait there for the signal to move in.

Veering left, I turned off the main road and into a side street and inspected the surroundings with my mindsight. No one else was about. For the moment, at least, I was the street's only occupant.

Excellent.

Closing my eyes, I drew on my stamina.

You have cast lesser imitate, assuming the visage of Minakawa. Duration: 1 hour.

Your facial disguise enchantment has been dispelled.

My visage changed from Egan's to Minakawa's between one step and the next. It was not just my face that changed, though. This time, the illusion that settled on me was more complete, causing even the appearance of my limbs and torso to match that of my dark elf subject.

It turned out the captain I'd traded words with on the south wall was one of Cilia's most trusted soldiers and was often spotted frequenting her fortress. Minakawa was currently asleep in one of the city's southern barracks, but no one at the fortress was likely to know that.

Relying on a tier two spell—lesser imitate—for such a crucial mission was not ideal. I would have much rather preferred using the higher-tiered spell, facial disguise. However, it was not up to the task in this instance. Only lesser imitate could so completely transform my appearance as to make me look like a dark elf. And unfortunately, of all the subjects Algar had suggested, Minakawa was the best fit and, whether by happenstance or not, the one I was most familiar with.

Still, I didn't intend to impersonate the dark elf captain for long. Once I was through the fortress' outer gates, any number of other guises would lend themselves to use.

Running my hands across my shoulders, I casually swapped out Egan's lieutenant's badge for Minakawa's captain tabs. My disguise complete, I turned right at the next intersection and strolled boldly into the central square sitting at the heart of the city.

Four fortresses bordered the open space. Cilia's to the north, Sienna's to the south, Stormhammer's to the west, and Lorn's to the east.

Orienting on the northern castle, I made directly for it.

As I drew closer to the fortress, recognition crossed the faces of the two guards on gate duty. "Min," the first greeted. "What are you doing here?"

Min?

My pulse quickened. The familiarity of the soldier's greeting suggested the pair knew the dark elf captain well. *How well?* I wondered, my thoughts racing. Would my disguise hold up to scrutiny?

I didn't know, and that worried me. But there was no turning back now; I'd passed the point of no return.

Firming my steps, I walked up to the gate.

CHAPTER 396: STRIKING BACK

Multiple unknown entities have failed to pierce your disguise.

The Game message reassured me, as did the soldiers' open expressions. Neither was suspicious—yet.

"Duty calls, as always," I replied with an easy smile as I drew to a halt before the guards.

"You have come with news about that player, haven't you?" the second guard guessed shrewdly.

I let my eyebrows rise.

Both soldiers chuckled in response. "You shouldn't be surprised, Min," the first said. "News travels fast in this city."

I nodded agreeably. "Don't I know it."

"You will be wanting to see the First, then," the second guard said, moving to unbar the gate.

"If she has time to spare," I replied.

For some reason, that made the two laugh uproariously. "Who do you think you're kidding?" one said between guffaws. "Everyone knows the First *always* has time for you."

The other guard smirked knowingly. "You must be quite something."

With difficulty, I kept my face impassive—*are the guards implying what I think they are?*—then on second thoughts, forced a scowl onto my face. "I don't know what you mean," I muttered.

"Of course, you don't," the first said smoothly as he swung back the gate and waved me inside.

Keeping up my pretense of anger, I hurried wordlessly past.

"Don't let Castor catch you," one of them called after me.

"I hear he has quite the temper," the second added.

Saying nothing, I stomped harder, which only made them laugh more.

✳   ✳   ✳

As I rushed through the fortress' bailey, I worried over the guards' parting words but, after a moment, realized it would make my job easier—not harder.

I'd planned on changing faces as soon as I got into the fortress proper, but now I had cause to reconsider. If the guards' innuendo was more than fanciful thinking on their part, then no one in the fortress would question Minakawa's presence in Cilia's bedchamber.

I could get in *and* out without arousing suspicion. *It's worth a try,* I reflected and slipped into the main keep.

Multiple unknown entities have failed to pierce your disguise.

Even at this late hour, the place was busy. Countless servants, guards, and courtiers hurried about on some business or the other. But despite my unannounced presence, no one thought to challenge me or even bothered to give me a second glance.

Security seems lax. Well, that's all for the better.

Wading through the crowd, I casually scanned the passing figures, trying to discern if any were possessed. I spotted no scarred faces, though, nor anyone wearing the distinctive blue robes of the Mages Guild. It added further weight to Algar's information.

Perhaps Elron's aide is right. Perhaps all the possessed really are holed up in the fortress' lower levels. If so, it would make completing the first half of my mission that much easier.

Recalling the floor plans I had memorized, I mapped a path to the First's rooms. They were on the topmost floor, and since the city was currently in the midst of its night cycle, there was a good chance I would find her there.

Walking slowly—but with purpose—I made my way through the fortress. As I ascended through the levels, the flow of people through the corridors subsided, so much so that it was almost down to nil by the time I reached the final floor.

I slowed my steps.

My target was close—or so I hoped, anyway. Unfurling my mindsight, I let my awareness expand outwards.

There were less than a dozen mindglows within a hundred yards of me, and none were in my immediate line of sight. Keeping my mindsight open, I advanced further along the floor.

A few minutes later, I came to a halt. Up ahead and to the left was a long, opulently furnished corridor. Cilia's suite lay at its end—nearly within reach *if* I could get past the two vigilant sentinels standing watch at the entrance.

Those must be the bodyguards Algar warned me about.

Leaning casually against a passage wall—and still out of sight of the pair—I reached out with my will and analyzed both.

The target is Jasmayne, a level 106 dark elf.
The target is Redpaw, a level 117 dark elf.

Analyze confirmed my suspicions—the two *were* Cilia's bodyguards. But where was the First herself? According to my mindsight, the rooms beyond the pair were empty.

I frowned. Was Cilia shielded? It was certainly a possibility if not a pleasant one. If that were the case, the only way I would find my target would be by setting eyes on her.

Which meant getting past the guards.

No turning back now. Turning my head from left to right, I scanned the corridor I stood in. There were plenty of vacant rooms around. Drawing up to the door of the closest, I turned the handle.

Locked.

Not a problem. Inserting a dagger into the keyhole, I jiggled the small blade until the simple mechanism sprang open.

You have successfully picked a lock.

Slipping into the room, I closed the door behind me and examined my surroundings. Judging from the uniforms lining the wardrobe, I was in a maid's chamber. *Hmm, not ideal,* I thought, hesitating. *Should I find another room?*

No.

Even though my disguise appeared to be holding up, I couldn't waste time unnecessarily. Here would have to do. Reaching into my bag of holding, I extracted the Cloak of the Reach and spread it on the floor. Unfortunately, due to the necessity of maintaining my disguise, I'd been forced to unequip most of my usual gear.

"*Come out, Ghost,*" I murmured.

"*Finally!*" she exclaimed, streaming out of the garment.

Ghost has cast manifest and has taken the form of a level 201 stygian pyre wolf.

Filled with my familiar's inky-dark presence, the room suddenly looked too small. "*It's time to get to work,*" I said. "*You remember what to do?*"

"*Keep watch and warn you if anyone approaches,*" she replied, bobbing her head vigorously. "*But are you sure you don't want me accompanying you?*"

I shook my head. "*Better you don't. If I can, I want to do this without drawing needless attention—or spilling unnecessary blood.*"

"*Alright,*" Ghost grumbled, her head sagging in disappointment. Stretching out on the floor, she yawned, "*I'm ready whenever you are.*"

I smiled, not for a moment deceived by her play at disinterest; Ghost was pleased to be out. "*Be back soon,*" I said in farewell.

Slipping into the corridor again, I rounded the corner and stepped into view of the bodyguards.

✳ ✳ ✳

**Two hostile entities have failed to pierce your disguise.
Your deception has reached rank 18.**

My disguise held.

Letting no sign of my delight at that fact show, I continued my lazy stroll up the corridor. The senior guard, Redpaw, nodded impassively as he spied me—a damn sight more professional response than the one I'd received from the pair at the gate.

"She is sleeping," the other—Jasmayne—remarked when I drew up before them.

Thinking the comment was a refusal, I opened my mouth, arguments at the ready to wheedle my way past, but before I could voice any of them, Redpaw slid the door open in silent invitation.

Containing my surprise, I snapped my mouth closed.

Minakawa, it seemed, really was one of Cilia's favorites. Not trusting myself to do more than nod imperiously, I slid past the bodyguards and into the room beyond.

Behind me, the door closed quietly.

Remaining in place, I took stock. From Algar's floor plans, I knew I was in the entrance chamber of the First's living quarters.

The room was small and contained almost no furniture, just a single desk, and chair—meant for an assistant or secretary, I guessed. A rug covered the floor, and paintings decorated the walls. More importantly, though, there were three exits to choose from—all presently hidden behind closed doors.

Expanding my awareness, I searched the rooms beyond but found no mindglows. Jasmayne's comment had settled my doubts, though. Cilia was near. I was sure of it.

Only two questions remained. Which room was the First in? And had she shielded herself or the room? The First was a mage, I recalled, so either possibility could hold true.

Moving soundlessly, lest the bodyguards outside hear, I unbuttoned my soldier's uniform and extracted the bag of holding I'd concealed within. Opening the bag, I peered inside.

It did not take me long to find the item I sought.

You have equipped and activated a sorcerer's coif.

The response was instantaneous. Threads of magic snapped into view, all concentrated on the antechamber's leftmost door—Cilia had to be in the room beyond.

You have detected a hostile spell!
The target is a tier 2 ward spell: <u>slumber's sentinel</u>.

I frowned. The ward's name was... cryptic. Would it keep me out, hurt me, or simply awaken its caster? I didn't know, but I couldn't imagine the spell was dangerous. The bodyguards had let me in without hesitation, after all.

It's a detection ward, I thought. *Has to be.*

Creeping up the door in question, I studied the spell wrapped around it more closely. The weaves had been thickly laid, especially around the keyhole and the door handle—which left me in a bit of a quandary. Even with the most agile hands, opening the door without triggering the ward would be impossible.

I'll have to risk it, I decided.

Extending my right arm, I let my hand hover over the handle. Ghost was an attentive presence at the edge of my mind, and I focused on her for a second. *"Status?"* I asked.

"All clear," she reported. *"No one has approached since you left."* She paused. *"How are things going on your end?"*

"No problems yet. But I'm about to enter a warded room."

Concern filtered across the link. *"Isn't that dangerous?"*

"Possibly," I conceded reluctantly. *"It's the only way to get to the First, though. I'm not sure what will happen when I trigger the ward. Probably nothing, but stay alert—in case, you know."*

"Of course, Prime."

Closing our mind link, I returned my attention to my surroundings. It was time. Screwing up my courage, I closed my hand around the door handle.

You have triggered a ward!

CHAPTER 397: THE FIRST VICTIM

Slumber's sentinel activated. Caster awakened.

My first response was relief. The ward had activated. And it had not harmed me.

Trepidation followed on its heels. Things were going *too* well. Was this a trap?

It isn't. It's just nerves. Brushing aside the feeling, I pushed open the door and stepped across the threshold.

The room was dark, but I had no trouble picking out its contents. Curtains draped the walls to the left and right, a chandelier hung from the ceiling, and in front of me stood an oversized bed. Amongst its ruffled sheets, I spotted my target. The First.

Cilia has failed to pierce your disguise.

The dark elf councilor was sitting up in the bed, her eyes still clouded by sleep. "Min?" she asked groggily.

Closing the door quietly behind me, I stepped closer. "It is, dear," I murmured.

Cilia patted an empty spot beside her on the bed. "I didn't know you were visiting today. Come—" She broke off, eyes clearing. "'Dear.' You called me 'dear.'"

I cursed. I'd betrayed myself, I realized. Dropping my right hand to the sheathed blade around my waist, I quickened my stride.

"Since when am I 'dear?'" Cilia demanded, her voice rising.

The First had not grasped the truth yet, but she would—and soon. Any moment now, she was going to cast, or worse yet, shout for help. I couldn't let that happen. Drawing psi, I rushed through the aether.

You have teleported 4 yards.

I blinked back into existence, blade drawn and poised to strike. Cilia's gaze whipped in my direction, dawning realization and fear in her eyes. Her mouth opened, a scream bubbling in her throat.

I was quicker. Striking fast, I buried ebonheart hilt-deep in her neck.

You have killed Cilia with a fatal blow.

The dark elf councilor sagged listlessly, only the black blade keeping her upright. For an interminable second, I stared at the corpse. It was done. My first target was eliminated, the job done.

So, why do I feel unclean?

I had killed before. Numerous times. Defenseless targets, too. But this was the first time I'd deliberately sought and hunted down a target—one who, while opposed to me, *hadn't* actively been trying to do me harm. I had not hesitated to act, to do what was necessary. But now that the deed was done, I felt... unsettled.

The First had to have been killed, I didn't doubt that. She might not have been as vile as Castor, but she had allied herself with him and his followers, knowingly allowing the possessed to steal away her people's lives, and for that, she deserved death.

I don't regret killing her, I told myself. *I don't.*

But the First hadn't been a combatant. She was a victim, and this hadn't been a battle, it was an execution—an assassination, plain and simple. It was a fine line I tread, I realized, one easy to cross. Murder was but a step away, and it would be oh-so-easy to stray onto that path.

Am I becoming what I—

"*Prime?*" Ghost barked through the mind link, intruding on my black thoughts. "*What are you doing?*"

Shaking free of my reverie, I gently lowered Cilia's corpse back onto the bed. "*The First is dead. Mission accomplished.*"

Even though I didn't share my doubts about what I'd done, I knew Ghost sensed them. "*Good,*" she said, uncomplicated satisfaction filling her voice. "*She needed to die. Time to move onto the second?*"

Straightening, I surveyed the room. I should search it, I knew, but I felt little desire to linger. "*Yes,*" I replied. "*Coming to you.*"

Turning my back on the dead body and blood-spattered sheets, I left the room without a backward glance.

✳ ✳ ✳

I exited the First's bedroom as swiftly as I'd entered. After re-entering the antechamber, I closed the door behind me and then proceeded to lock it.

Cilia's death had gone unnoticed by her bodyguards, and I wanted to keep it that way as long as possible. The locked door would not fool them for long, but it would buy me some time, and every minute I delayed the alarm being raised increased my chances of success with my second target: Castor.

Him, I had no compunctions about killing any way I could. In fact, I found myself looking forward to the deed.

Turning around in a slow circle, I examined the antechamber. Everything was just as it had been when I got here. *Good.* Closing my eyes, I gathered psi, and shadow blinked.

You have teleported to Ghost.

I stepped out of the aether in the maid's quarters to find the pyre wolf on her feet, her tail wagging impatiently.

"Keep watch, I need a second," I murmured, then began to undress. Removing the soldier's uniform I'd been wearing, I re-equipped my old gear.

You have cast facial disguise, assuming the visage of Bron.

Your lesser imitate enchantment has been dispelled.

You have activated the simple mode enchantment of the belt of the chameleon. Your armor and weapons are now hidden.

I was done wearing Minakawa's face. From this point on, it was better to walk around the citadel as a faceless servant than as the more notable dark elf captain.

As far as the First's bodyguards were concerned—or anyone else in the citadel, for that matter—Minakawa was still in Cilia's chambers. If the alarm were raised before I'd completed the second half of my mission, it would be *him* that the guards would be searching for. No one would suspect my involvement until much later—if ever—and that meant Castor wouldn't be alerted to the fact that a player hunted him.

I didn't plan on letting things go wrong, of course, but it was always nice to have a contingency in place. Redressed and re-armed, I put on my final piece of clothing: the Cloak of the Reach.

Ghost's expression fell at the sight of the garment. *"I'm going to have to go back into it, aren't I?"* she asked sadly.

I nodded. "Unfortunately, yes."

With a sigh to express her distaste—just in case I'd failed to mark it before—the pyre wolf let her form dissipate.

Ghost has cast unmanifest.

"You'll get your chance to fight soon enough," I said soothingly. *"I suspect things with Castor will not go as smoothly."*

Ghost did not reply, but I felt her interest quicken. Smiling, I edged up to the closed door and checked the corridor beyond with my mindsight. It was still empty.

Time to find and kill Castor, I thought and stepped out of the room.

✳   ✳   ✳

I made my way back to the ground floor without mishap. According to Algar, the fortress had two subterranean levels. The first held the castle's storerooms, and the second its prisons. Unfortunately, access to both was tightly controlled. Consequently, Elron's captain had only been able to provide me limited information as to their layout.

I knew, though, that the entrance to the underground tunnel was located at the far end of the prison, which ordinarily would have left it well protected. To reach the tunnel, most intruders would have to traverse the entirety of both subterranean levels—navigating whatever safeguards lay between.

Not me, though.

With mindsight and teleport, I could bypass all the possessed's protections and reach my destination in an eye blink. Or I *could have* if not for another unexpected wrinkle, something I only discovered after I unfurled my mindsight while on the ground floor.

The levels beneath were opaque to me.

According to my mindsight, the subterranean floors were empty of life. I did not for a second believe that, though. In all likelihood, the possessed had magically shielded the area.

Frowning, I contemplated what this meant for the plan. *"Trouble?"* Ghost asked, sensing the direction of my thoughts.

"Maybe," I said. *"I can't see into the floors below."*

"Oh. Does that mean we will have to make our way through the lower floors on foot?"

"It does," I agreed. *"But there is more to it than that."* Not explaining further, I waited for Ghost to figure out the problem herself.

She fell silent for a moment, thinking. *"You're worried about how we will find Castor?"*

I nodded imperceptibly. *"I am."*

Unfortunately, the possessed leader's location was more of a mystery than Cilia's had been. Knowing he was somewhere in the fortress' lower levels was one thing. Finding him was another—especially since I was now on the clock.

Sooner or later, the First's body would be discovered and the alarm raised, and while the precautions I'd taken should buy me some time, it would not be enough to search three whole levels thoroughly.

It was a good guess that Castor would be in the tunnel itself, but that was all it was: a guess. If he wasn't there, or if the tunnel itself was a vast complex—I still knew nothing of its layout—things could go pear-shaped quickly. I'd been counting on using my mindsight to narrow down the search area and teleport to get me to my target once I located him. Now, though...

Now, I had to face the possibility of not finding Castor in time.

"We should change the plan," Ghost asserted.

A smile flickered across my face. *"We should,"* I agreed, having come to the same conclusion myself. Adjusting my stride, I turned left—towards the fortress' kitchens. It was where Algar's spy worked.

The original plan called for me only to contact the spy *after* I'd killed Castor, but that had been on the assumption I could quickly locate and eliminate the possessed leader. Now, I was faced with the stark possibility of being unable to do that.

But the genie was already out of the bottle. The rebellion had started, and there was no halting it now. Algar and his men would assault the fortress— whether I was successful or not—and I could not leave them in the lurch. I had to give them as much chance to succeed as possible—even if I failed.

Which meant launching the assault early, before I tried taking out Castor.

If Algar attacked the fortress before the possessed were alerted, the rebellion could still succeed. It would undoubtedly be bloody. Castor and the others would not go down easily, but it would be *less* bloody than if Algar and his men assaulted a primed and ready fortress of possessed.

A hostile entity has failed to pierce your disguise.

"Hey! Who are you?" a voice demanded. "And what are you doing here? The kitchens are a restricted area."

I looked up to find a severe-looking woman glaring at me. She stood on the threshold of the door to the kitchen as if she meant to physically bar me from entering. "I'm Bron," I replied easily, stopping three feet away. "I'm looking for Eclarie."

"The head cook?" she asked. "Why?"

I shrugged as if it was a matter of no consequence. "I have a message for him."

She held out a hand. "Give it to me. I'll see that he gets it."

I shook my head. "Oh no, I can't do that. It's from one of the high and mighties. You know how they are. They insisted I deliver it *personally* into Eclarie's hands."

The woman scowled.

"Sorry," I said unapologetically. "Just doing my job."

"Wait here, then. I'll fetch him."

Smiling, I gave her a half-bow. "Of course."

✳   ✳   ✳

Eclarie did not look like a cook, much less the master of an entire keep's kitchens. Rail-thin, he seemed more than a little malnourished. Coming to a stop before me, he blinked owlishly. "Who're you? I don't know you."

Mindful of the woman who'd gone to fetch Eclarie still hovering in the background, I said, "Alest sent me." Alest was the code word Algar had given me.

The cook's eyes tightened fractionally. "Maeve," he called over his shoulder without looking back, "you can go. I'll take care of this."

The severe woman's lips thinned, but she didn't protest as she flounced off. After I was certain she was gone, I moved closer to Eclarie. "It's time," I whispered.

His brows rose. "They're both dead?"

I shook my head. "Cilia is. Castor isn't. I'm heading down to the lower levels to take care of him now, but there are... complications." I hesitated. "I might not succeed," I admitted.

The spy did not react to my words as I expected. His eyes roving over my form, he studied my face and garb carefully. "You're... him? *You're* the player?"

I nodded.

"You don't fit the description Algar gave me," he said with open disbelief.

"I'm wearing a disguise," I said curtly.

Eclarie's interest sharpened. "A disguise?" He gestured to my face. "What sort of disguise can do that?" he asked with genuine interest. "Your features are completely different!"

I held tight to my impatience. I wanted to deliver my message and get gone, not waste my time in idle chatter with Algar's spy. "It's an illusion," I replied in a manner that didn't brook further comment. "Did you hear what I said?"

"I did," Eclarie replied absently, still staring at my face with avid interest.

"*And?*" I asked sharply.

His gaze darted back to mine. "And I will inform Algar. Do you still want him to go ahead with the attack?"

I relaxed. So, Eclarie had been listening, after all. "Yes. Tell him to wait four hours, though."

The spy frowned. "Why?"

"I think the First's death will go unnoticed for at least that long, and I still want to try for Castor. Four hours should be sufficient to get the deed done." *If I can find him.* "But if it isn't, I'll try to get him during the chaos ensuing after Algar's attack." *Assuming I'm still alive.* "Either way, Algar should prepare for the worst."

Eclarie nodded slowly. "I'll make sure he is warned. Anything else?"

I shook my head. "No, that's it."

"Then I best get back before anyone starts asking questions." Turning around, the cook headed toward the kitchen. On the threshold, he paused. "Oh, and good luck."

"Thanks," I muttered, hurrying away in the opposite direction. *I think I'm going to need it.*

The stairs leading down to the fortress' storerooms were guarded, at least in principle. The two soldiers on duty were slovenly and their uniforms unkempt. The door beyond them hung open, and both held mugs of ale in their hands.

Getting past would be easy, and for a moment, I was tempted to simply stroll past, but prudence won out in the end. Slowing down, I checked my surroundings. The adjacent corridors were busy, but no one was watching me or the guards.

It was time to act. Drawing psi, I spun the weaves of a familiar spell and reached into the two soldiers' minds.

You have cast slaysight.
You have hidden your presence from 2 of 2 targets for 40 seconds.

The spell went off without a hitch, blinding the guards to me. Maintaining my unhurried pace, I ducked past their sloshing mugs and windmilling arms and slipped through the door.

Beyond, I found a wide staircase spiraling downwards.

It was empty, which was all to the good. I was now in an area off-limits to the castle servants. No disguise would serve to protect me here. I suspected whatever face I wore, a lone figure, would be looked on with suspicion by the passing patrols. And the sub-levels were heavily patrolled. That much, at least, Algar had been able to tell me.

It was time to forgo deception in favor of stealth.

I glanced upwards. Magelights dotted the ceiling, but their light was subdued, a gentle glow instead of a harsh glare, leaving shadows aplenty along the staircase's edges. Bracing my back against the closest wall, I enfolded myself in darkness.

You are hidden.

I was ready. With my senses extended, I tiptoed down the stairs. My mindsight was still disturbingly blank, which was a surprise. I'd expected the shield protecting the sub-levels to begin at the threshold I'd just crossed, but it obviously didn't—I'd received no warning from the Game.

Perhaps it begins at the base of the stairs. Which I supposed would serve just as well. Shrugging away the mystery, I continued onwards.

The staircase was a short one, and after what I judged to be a full revolution, it exited onto the lower level. As the floor came into sight, I drew to a halt, my feet firmly planted on the last step.

There was no matching door on the storeroom level—nor guards, only empty corridors. Peeking around the wall, I studied the passages to my left and right. Both were empty, as was the one dead ahead.

Hmm.

The lack of a second guard post was curious. Perhaps they'd been deemed unnecessary, given the teams rumored to patrol the level. It mattered little, but I needed to perform one more check before entering the level proper.

Raising my right hand, I rubbed the side of my helm.

You have activated a sorcerer's coif.
You have detected a hostile spell! The target is a tier 5 dampening field: <u>scryer's bane</u>.

My eyes narrowed. The protections the possessed had woven about the lower levels were more extensive than expected.

A dampening field was more akin to a debuff than it was to a ward. I would endure its effects the entire time I remained in the area it encompassed—and I had the feeling that included the entirety of both lower levels.

What this particular damping field did was debatable, though. At the very least, I expected it would disable my mindsight. Beyond that, I couldn't say.

There was no point delaying further, though. If I wanted to get to Castor, I had to enter the field, and it was best I did that when no one was around to observe me. On that thought, I stepped off the staircase and onto the storeroom floor.

You are <u>scry-locked</u>. While scry-locked, you are prevented from using any remote observation ability of tier 4 and below. This includes both psionic abilities and mana-based spells.
Duration: infinite. The debuff will remain in effect as long as you stay within the dampening field.

The Game alert came as no surprise.

Still, I remained motionless while I took stock. As expected, my mindsight had forcibly closed, restricting me to only what I could perceive with my physical senses.

My other abilities remained unaffected, though, and the scry-locked debuff didn't appear to be causing me any physical harm, which was a relief. *"Ghost, can you hear me?"*

"Of course, Prime," came the immediate response. *"Is something wrong?"*

"No. My mindsight has been blocked. I was checking if we could still communicate."

"You are in the lower levels?"

"I am."

"Do you need me to manifest?"

"Not yet. Let me find Castor first. Until then, I don't want to—"

I broke off, my gaze turning left, drawn by the sound of tramping feet.

An infantry squad had just turned a distant corner and had come into sight. This group of soldiers was nothing like the pair above. Their hauberks and weapons were impeccable, and their eyes were hard as they roved over the surroundings.

"We'll speak later, Ghost. I've got company." My eyes darted between the central and right passages. Both were empty, and for a moment, I hesitated in deciding which corridor to enter.

I didn't have a layout for this floor. All Algar had been able to tell me was that the prison entrance was at the far end of the level. For now, I would have to guess which path offered the shortest route to my objective.

The central passage it is, I decided and crept forward.

✳   ✳   ✳

Multiple hostile entities have failed to detect you!
Multiple hostile entities have failed to detect you!

The storeroom level was a maze of corridors and large rooms, all helpfully labeled to identify their contents. The patrols were as common as I feared, but thankfully, the many side passages and rooms provided me with numerous hiding spots, and I was able to avoid detection.

Unfortunately, the floor's architecture worked against me, too, confounding my sense of direction—even with the help of the pioneer's compass to guide me—and it was only after a good thirty minutes spent wandering the maze that I finally located the exit to the next level.

Sitting on my haunches in the T-junction, I considered the downward spiraling staircase. There was no door barring my way, nor guards for that matter. So far, the lower levels were not living up to their reputation. Except for the roving patrols, security had been lax. Would the prison level be any different?

I shrugged. *Only one way to find out.*

Rising into a half-crouch, I padded down the stairs and, shortly, came to its end. This time, a door blocked my progress. Coming to a halt, I studied the obstacle.

The door was unwarded but stoutly constructed from steel and wood and looked like it had been made to repel heavy assault. There was no lock, but a small grille window was on the upper half of the door. And from beyond, I could hear voices.

Guards.

Inching forward, I crept up to the door, and the voices grew louder.

"... I win!"

"By hell, you do. That's only a pair of Jacks you're holding."

"Yeah? And what do you have that can beat that, sarge?"

"How about trip-aces?"

I reached the door just as muted groans and loud cheers erupted from beyond. Listening carefully, I counted. There were five distinct voices—more guards than I cared to try dealing with silently. They were still making a racket, though, so setting aside my disappointment, I checked the door by pushing gently against it.

It didn't budge.

Given that there was no lock, it had to mean the door was barred from the inside. My lips twisted sourly. It was another complication I didn't need.

How am I going to raise the bar from this side?

I could charm the guards and force them to open it that way, but I would be compelled to kill them thereafter, and leaving dead bodies in my wake was a good way of making sure the alarm was raised.

So, no killing—and no charming. What other options did I have?

Not a helluva lot. Glancing up, I studied the grille window. At a guess, it was for the guards to eyeball the prison's visitors before they let them in. Could I bluff my way past?

I rubbed my lips, contemplating the idea. Trying to do so would be risky. I didn't know who exactly was allowed access to the prisons, and while there were a few faces I could try—Cilia's or Avery's, for instance—the possibility that the guards would require a code word made me hesitate. If they became suspicious and decided to sound the alarm, I could do little to stop them from this side of the door.

Trying to bluff my way through is too complicated, I decided.

What did that leave?

I could teleport past the door—the grille window would give me a line of sight to a suitable target—but if my stealth failed, and the chances that it would in a room full of guards were high, I would have to kill them all.

Right, I don't like any of those options. What else was there?

I slowly unbent. There was one other possibility. It required using a mix of deception and mental trickery. It might not work either, but if it didn't, at least I would be no worse off than with any of the other options I considered. First, though, I needed to determine the room's layout.

With my back braced against the door and as much of my face and head shielded from view, I peeked around the grille window and into the room.

Five hostile entities have failed to detect you!

The guards came into view. They were gathered around a small table on the right side of the chamber, laughing and backslapping each other as they studied the cards arrayed on it.

I leaned over further.

Five hostile entities have failed to detect you!

More of the chamber came into focus. Two magelights were bolted onto the ceiling—their light harsh and bright. Weapon racks lined the left wall, and directly opposite me was another door—presently open. There was one last thing to check.

Activating my sorcerer's coif, I reinspected the room.

Five hostile entities have failed to detect you!

The scryer's bane spell from the storeroom level was also active in the prison guardroom, but there were no additional wards. *Perfect.* My gaze darting back to the guards, I analyzed each in turn.

The target is Lushiel, a level 63 dark elf.
The target is Manir, a level 72 dark elf.
The target is Hase, a level 56 dark elf.
The target is Torne, a level 60 dark elf.
The target is Kol, a level 61 dark elf.

Hmm. Judging by their levels, the prison guards were not the best of Cilia's household guards. Overrunning their minds should be simple. My gaze found the highest leveled dark elf. Manir. By the stripes on his shoulder, he was the group's sergeant. There was no ale on the table, but from the sergeant's big, toothy grin and dull eyes, he was neither alert nor all that bright.

My plan can work, I thought, sitting back down. Drawing psi, I began my preparations.

CHAPTER 399: PASSING UNSEEN

You have cast heightened reflexes, load controller, fade, and trigger-cast quick mend.

With my buffs in place, I rose to my feet and peered through the small window.

Five hostile entities have failed to detect you!

The guards had resumed their card game, and no one was looking my way. It was time to act. Drawing psi, I flooded their minds with my will.

You have cast slaysight.
You have induced 5 of 5 targets to sleep for 40 seconds.
Your mental intrusion has gone undetected!

Almost simultaneously, the guards fell asleep. Four of them simply sagged in their chairs, their heads drooping until their chins rested on the chests while their cards fell from deadened hands. The fifth, though, slumped forward fully, his head hitting the table so hard I couldn't help but wince in sympathy.

That's going to leave a bruise.

Fortunately, the accidental bump did not disrupt my spell, and the guard in question stayed asleep. Still, I waited a heartbeat longer to make certain. When none of the guards stirred, I moved on to the next stage of my plan.

Drawing psi, I shadow blinked.

You have teleported into Manir's shadow. You are hidden.

I stepped out of the aether in the guardroom. Adroitly avoiding waking any of the sleeping dark elves, I tiptoed to the inner door and peered out. A wide, poorly lit corridor stretched out before me. More importantly, it was empty.

Good, I won't be disturbed. I turned back to the guards—and, for a moment, was tempted to leave them as they were.

Unfortunately, I couldn't rely on the elves not figuring out they'd fallen foul of a hostile spell. Even though none of the prison guards had detected my mental intrusion during the casting itself, even the most thick-witted would realize something was amiss when they all woke simultaneously.

Somehow, I had to stop that from happening.

And the only way I could think of was to distract them. Hurrying back to the table, I gently pulled the sergeant's chair two feet away and lowered the remaining guards' heads onto the table one by one. My movements were careful enough that my sleep spell remained undisturbed.

Stepping back, I inspected my handiwork. Manir was out of harm's way, and the others were in position. I was ready. Backing away from the table, I measured the distance to the inner door. Two quick steps were all it would take to slip into the corridor and out of sight.

Good enough. Inhaling deeply, I kicked out sharply.

The toe of my right boot drove into the underside of the table, toppling it over—and not so incidentally striking the four sleeping guards whose heads rested on it.

Spinning on my heel, I dashed out of the room, not waiting to observe the outcome of my actions. The Adjudicator would tell me soon enough. Sure enough, just as I dived into the corridor and pulled the shadows around me, a Game message flashed into my mind.

You have taken hostile action against 4 of 5 sleeping targets. Lushiel, Hase, Torne, and Kol have awoken!
You are hidden.

A small smile stole across my face. My ploy had gone just as I'd hoped, but my work was far from done, and success was not yet guaranteed. Drawing on my will, I readied my next spell while the four very-much-awake guards lumbered to their feet.

"Urgh... wha...?"

"...did something happen?"

"I could've sworn we were..."

"Sarge? Where's sarge?"

"There he is."

"Is he... sleeping?"

My spell completed—and not a moment too soon either. Without hesitation, I released it.

You have cast ventro.

"Open up, you louts!" I bellowed, projecting my voice to originate from somewhere on the staircase. "In the name of the First, I demand entry!"

The confused muttering of the four ran aground, their attention captured by the 'visitor.'

"Who's dat?" one hissed—Lushiel, I thought.

"A visitor?" Kol hazarded.

"Now? But isn't it nighttime up there?" Hase protested.

"Does anyone know what happened?" Torne asked. "Weren't we in the middle of a—"

"Imbeciles!" I shouted. "Did you not hear me? I said open up!"

The visitor's strident demand drew the guards' attention again. Then, as I had hoped, one headed towards the outer door. Listening to his footsteps, I pictured him peering through the grille window.

"Who's there?" Kol called out.

"Impertinent buffoon!" I shot back in an affronted tone. "Where are your manners? You shall address me as milord!"

Momentary silence.

"Who is this clown?" Lushiel muttered.

"Sarge should be dealing with this," Hase added.

"How did the table topple over?" Torne asked in a bewildered tone. "Does anyone know?"

"Who cares," Kol snapped. "Wake the sarge." His voice dropping into a more respectful tone, he asked, "Where are you, milord? I can't see you."

I smiled. *That's because you're looking in the wrong direction.* "Did you not hear me the first time," I demanded in pretended annoyance. "I told you — the First doesn't want my identity revealed. I *cannot* show myself."

"Uh-huh, of course..." Kol mumbled, clearly at a loss on how to proceed. "Wha, urgh— uh..."

Your slaysight spell has expired.

"Oww! That hurts." That was the sergeant, awake once more. I couldn't see him, but I guessed that he was rubbing furiously at his forehead right now.

"Who hit me?" he demanded.

"You there!" I interjected before anyone could think to answer him. "Are you the one in charge?"

Another long pause.

"Who in the devils is that?" Sergeant Manir demanded eventually.

"A visitor," Kol replied, then added in a low undertone, "a *highborn* visitor."

"One with a bone stuck up his ass," Lushiel muttered just as softly.

"I heard that!" I snapped.

"A visitor?" the sergeant asked, studiously ignoring Lushiel and my interjections. "No one informed me we would be receiving any today."

"That's because this is an unscheduled visit," I declared airily. "No one will ever know it happened. That's the way the First wants it, and that's the way it will stay. Now, let me in, god dammit!"

Footsteps. The sergeant, I imagined, had gone to peer out the outer door himself. "Can you see him?" he whispered.

"No," Kol replied.

Manir chewed over this for a moment. "Do you have a letter of authorization, milord?" he asked tentatively.

"Of course not!" I replied in an offended tone. "That would make this visit official, wouldn't it? And we can't have that!"

"Then I'm afraid I can't let you through, sir," Manir said. Was that a smile I heard in his voice? Did it please the sergeant to deny the highborn twat?

I let the silence draw out. "Is that what you want me to tell the First?" I hissed. "That you, a mere sergeant, *refused* me, her agent, entry?"

"If you must," Manir replied stiffly, but this time, there was no mistaking the underlying glee in his voice. "I have my orders, too, milord, and without the necessary paperwork, I can't let you in. I'm sorry," he finished, sounding not at all sorry.

"I see," I said thinly. "Goodbye, sergeant."

I ended the conversation there, letting it hang abruptly. I'd done what I could to redirect the prison guards' attention away from the events of a minute ago. Now, it was time to find out if I'd done enough. Sitting still, I listened intently.

Quiet still reigned in the guardroom, the five elves no doubt somewhat perplexed by their highborn visitor's sudden departure.

"Is he gone?" Torne asked finally.

"I think so," Kol said.

"Good riddance," Lushiel scoffed.

"Should we inform the captain?" Hase asked.

The others fell silent, waiting for the sergeant's response. I did, too, my hands wrapped tightly about my blades. Whether he knew it or not, what Manir said next would determine the fate of the five.

"No," Manir said at last.

"But sarge," Hase protested. "Orders require us to report—"

"Report what? That we had a visitor we never saw?" Manir sneered. "What do I say when the captain asks his name?"

No one answered.

"How about, 'Sorry, cap, never got it,'" Manir continued, answering himself. "Knowing the captain, he won't let the matter lie there. He'll ask: 'What's he look like then?' Then what do I say?"

Once more, the others stayed silent.

"How about: 'Oops, sorry cap, we never got a look at him,'" Manir said, shouting now. "'Have you been drinking, sarge?' he'll ask next. 'Of course not,' I'll reply. 'Then what were you doing when the visitor arrived?' And what should I say to that? Hmm? Anyone?"

I winced. The sergeant's voice had gone up more than a few decibels, and he was clearly worked up. From the palpable silence of the other four, I guessed they were as much in awe of their sergeant's outburst as I was.

"Should I tell him I was asleep?" Manir asked, resuming his tirade. "What do you think the captain will do then? He'll come down on us like a ton of bricks, that's what. He'll send his bully boys to search this room from end to end because clearly, we must have been drunk to have been so derelict in our duties that we failed to gather so much as a single useful detail about our visitor! In fact, I have an idea," he hissed. "Why don't you be the one to report to cap, Hase? Would you like that?"

"Nah, sarge," he replied weakly.

"Then shut the hell up and forget about that highborn idiot!" Manir yelled. "I don't know what you four did to me, and I don't care, but I'm not about to endure a chewing out from the captain over any of this."

"But sarge," Kol protested. "I swear, we did nothing to—"

"I don't want to hear it," Manir snapped. "Torne, Lushiel, get that table back up. Hase, deal the cards. Enough of this shit. Let's play!"

✳   ✳   ✳

Grinning happily, I crept away from the guardroom. My gambit had proved even more successful than I could've imagined. Even better, I'd reached another significant milestone in my player development in the process.

Your sneaking has increased to level 200 and reached rank 20, allowing you to learn tier 5 abilities.
Your insight has increased to level 201 and your deception to level 185.

My smile broadened. At long last, I'd achieved the necessary skill level to upgrade my fade ability. All that was left was to acquire another upgrade gem.

Which will happen soon enough, I promised myself. After all, I was in a tier five dungeon. Now, though, was not the time to be thinking of that. I had an elite to kill.

Returning my attention to my surroundings, I studied the corridor. Steel doors lined the left and right walls—all closed. From the lack of sound emanating from beyond, I suspected the rooms they led to were deserted.

Pausing at one of the doors, I peered through the tiny cut-out in its center. A tiny chamber lay beyond. The room was barely eight feet across, and its contents—a dirty mattress and bucket—were equally sparse.

It's a prison cell, I concluded. *Unoccupied too.* Frowning thoughtfully, I resumed my passage down the corridor.

For the next minute, I journeyed in silence, passing more empty cells but encountering no branches, side passages, or turns in the corridor. Finally, though, just as the first guardroom passed out of view, the passage's end came into sight. Drawing to a halt, I dropped to my haunches.

A door was up ahead—a half-open door.

Little light escaped from beyond, and if not for my keen dark vision, I doubted I would've noticed the door, much less that it was open. The room's contents were still too far to discern, though. Without my mindsight, I was half-blind and less in control than I was used to being—an unhappy state of affairs that I found myself enjoying less and less—and until I got closer, I wasn't going to learn anything. Sighing, I resumed my advance.

"..."

"...tired?"

"...long... can... morning."

At the sound of the voices, I paused again. The room was occupied. But not by prisoners, I decided. The door was open and the entrance unwarded— I'd checked already.

Who then? Possessed?

Possibly. If it *was* possessed up ahead, though, they were about to pay for their carelessness. Gripping the hilt of my blades in readiness, I padded onward.

"you... what... did?"

"...disgusting!"

"... blood... I... he likes it."

"Ssh, not so loud. You'll wake the cap!"

They're prison guards, I decided, my shoulders sagging. I'd been hopeful the chamber would prove to be the start of the possessed's domain, but alas, it seemed I'd have to search a while longer. *It must be just another guardroom.*

Sliding up to the door and bracing myself against the adjacent stone wall, I peeked into the room.

Multiple hostile entities have failed to detect you!

The chamber was larger than the guardroom I'd just passed through and was lined with bunks from one end to the other. *Not a guardroom, then. A barracks.*

Only half the bunks were occupied, which I guessed meant the other half belonged to guards still on duty. Running my eyes over the still forms on each bed, I took count.

There were twenty guards in the barracks, eighteen of whom were sleeping. My eyes drifted to the pair lying on adjacent bunks in the right corner of the room. They were still whispering furiously to each other, and even though I was less than a dozen yards away, they were ignorant of my watching presence.

A closed door caught my attention. It was not far from the pair. The sign affixed on it read: "Captain's Quarters. Do NOT Enter." My gaze flickered to the left side of the room. Three doors stood there, respectively labeled: "Wardroom," "Mess," and "Officer's Quarters."

Finally, I turned my gaze to the far wall and its single open door. No sign graced its surface.

That's my exit.

Pursing my lips, I considered how to get there. There was a clearly demarcated aisle between me and the door, but it passed straight through the neat lines of bunks. Still, I didn't think the snoring guards were much of a threat. Nor, for that matter, the two sleepless ones in the right corner of the room.

Retreating a few steps, I dropped flat onto the ground. *I'll crawl my way through,* I decided.

CHAPTER 400: CONFINEMENT

Multiple hostile entities have failed to detect you!
Multiple hostile entities have failed to detect you!

In the end, navigating the barracks proved as easy as I expected.

My biggest fear had been being interrupted by a change of watch or a chance-waking guard, but thankfully, neither of those eventualities materialized.

Dragging myself past the door at the far end of the barracks, I found another corridor. This one was also lined with closed steel doors.

More prison cells? I wondered.

It seemed likely. Sighing, I rose to my haunches and scanned the empty corridor stretching away into the distance. Where in hells were Castor and his people?

Not here, I decided morosely.

I was running out of time, I knew, and while it did not press down urgently yet, it would soon. Still, there was nothing for it but to keep searching.

On that cheerful thought, I crept forward silently.

✳ ✳ ✳

The corridor fed into a crossroad.

Choosing a direction at random, I pressed on, but after multiple twists and turns, the passage came to an abrupt end. Ruing the wasted time, I returned to the crossroad and tried the next fork.

Unfortunately, the outcome was no different the second time around. *Another dead end,* I cursed, staring down the blank walls enclosing me. My lips thinning, I retraced my steps and entered the last unexplored passage.

Surely, I will find Castor at the end of this one.

My optimism proved unwarranted.

A half dozen intersections later—and no few dead ends—and with my frustration mounting by the minute, I was still no closer to finding the possessed. Thus far, except for the guards in the two rooms, I'd encountered no one. All I had to show for my efforts were silent passages and empty prison cells.

Maybe sneaking through was a mistake, I reflected. Maybe it was time to backtrack to the start of the level and question the prison guard captain. *Or perhaps Sergeant Manir.*

I chuckled darkly. The thought had a certain appeal. *Certainly, it would be better than—*

"Goti... is... that... you...?"

An unknown entity has failed to detect you!

I froze. The thready voice was barely audible—even in the hushed silence of the corridor. Tilting my head to the side, I tried to pinpoint the speaker's location.

"You... still... alive...?"

There, I thought, gaze fixating on a prison cell a few dozen yards ahead. *He is in there.* Cautiously, I stalked closer.

"...talk... to... me... damn... you."

It had to be a prisoner, I decided, slipping up to the steel door in question.

"He's gone, Wostil," another voice said tiredly.

About to peer through the small window in the prison door, I paused. The second speaker was in the adjacent cell and, by the sounds of it, in better condition than the first.

"... that, you... Megtir?"

"Yes..."

"When... he... go?"

"I don't know," Megtir replied sadly.

"Two days ago, I think," a third voice interjected.

"Surlin?"

"Yes."

"I thought you were dead."

A weary laugh. "It takes a lot more than a bunch of damn dark elves to kill me."

"Who... else lives...?"

"Me."

"I do."

"Me too, but not for much longer, I fear."

"I am—"

"Shut up, everyone!" a harsh voice ordered.

Silence descended. I stilled, too, recognizing the speaker. The last time we'd met had been during Castor's ambush in the council chamber.

I'd found the missing dwarven thane.

"I thought I told you all: no talking," Stormhammer continued. "We need to conserve our strength for..." He paused, taking a ragged breath. "For when—"

"For when what, milord?" the one called Megtir asked woodenly. "For when we're rescued? There is no chance of that happening anymore."

"You don't know that," Stormhammer growled.

"I do," Megtir said wearily. "It's been too long."

Another silence. Then, Stormhammer spoke again. "Wostil, why did you call out?" he asked, choosing to ignore the despondent Megtir. "My orders were clear."

"I'm... sorry, thane," Wostil rasped. "I... I... thought... heard something,"

Megtir snorted. "You're hallucinating again. The guards haven't come in days. The possessed must be done with their tests."

My ears perked up at that. *Tests? What tests?*

"Do you think they've succeeded?" another asked, fear lacing his tone.

"No," Stormhammer said firmly before Megtir could answer. "If they had, none of us would be alive, and our bodies no longer our own." He grunted. "No, it's much more likely they've given up."

No one contradicted him, not even Megtir.

"Now everyone shut up and go back to sleep," the thane ordered.

As quiet descended in the corridor again, I eased myself against an adjacent wall and pondered the situation. I'd found the dwarven thane and what, by the sounds of it, were the remnants of his personal guard. By my count, there were at least eight prisoners in the nearby cells—not counting those souls too far gone to speak—which left me in a bit of a quandary.

Did I rescue them?

Doing that meant revealing my presence—to both prisoners and possessed. There was no way I was going to sneak through the remainder of the level with eight injured and weary dwarves in tow. I could ask Stormhammer's men to stay put, of course, but there was no telling if they'd agree. And even if they did, a guard patrol might spot them and sound the alarm which, while admittedly unlikely given what Megtir had said, might still happen.

On the other hand, the dwarves had information—about the possessed's whereabouts and what they were doing—information I desperately needed.

So, to speak to the dwarves or not?

I bit the inside of my cheek. *Not*, I decided reluctantly after a moment's consideration. Once I revealed my presence, there was no going back. And truthfully, until I killed Castor, the dwarves would be safer in their cells. And if I failed in the process, well, there was no harm done either. The prisoners would not manage to escape unaided.

They're better off in their cells for now.

Kicking off the wall, I resumed my silent stalk down the corridor.

✳   ✳   ✳

It turned out I didn't need help finding the possessed. Less than five minutes after I left the thane and his men behind, the corridor I was following spilled out into an immense hall.

A hall that was very much occupied.

Hugging the nearby wall and cloaked in shadows, I surveyed the scene before me through widened eyes, more than a little horrified by what I beheld.

No prison guards were in sight, but the hall practically crawled with possessed. There had to be at least twenty of them moving about in the room. Yet, it was not the possessed's scarred and ruined bodies that I found appalling, but the rest of the hall's contents.

Assorted wooden and metal structures filled the space—unusually thin and elongated tables, thick chains hanging down from the rafters, steel cages, open pits of steaming liquids, spiked chairs, and many more accouterments whose workings I failed to grasp but whose purpose was abundantly clear.

They were instruments of torture.

Bloodied instruments, all. And currently in use.

A piercing wail rose above the background noise. My gaze darted left—to the source of the scream and the gruesome device from which it arose. A large orc had been squashed inside the tiny coffin, and it was getting smaller by the second as the possessed attending to it turned the lever at the bottom.

The orc shrieked again, his voice raw with agony. I wrenched my gaze away, unable to bear the sight. No one else in the room was similarly affected. None of the possessed so much as flinched at the sound, and the room's other occupants—another dozen orcs—were too absorbed in their own pain to give their companion's plight much thought.

I bared my teeth in anger. Wolves were killers but never needlessly cruel. What the possessed were doing was disgusting. Revolting. And I wanted to charge into the room and put an end to it—immediately.

But I couldn't do that.

Castor wasn't among the possessed in the room, and I couldn't afford to forewarn the elite I was coming. A cool head was needed; whatever I did next had to be done carefully, with precision and forethought.

Don't lose sight of the mission.

I surveyed the room again, seeking more information. *How long has this been going on for?* I wondered, swallowing my distaste as I inspected each torture victim minutely. *And more to the point, why?* The possessed were a lot of things—callous, self-centered, greedy—but gratuitously cruel? They had never struck me as such, so why were they torturing the orcs?

Not torturing, I corrected, recalling Stormhammer's words. *Conducting tests.*

But what sort of tests are these?

An irregularly shaped mound in the far-right corner of the room caught my attention. It was hidden in shadow, but that made little difference to me. Narrowing my eyes, I studied the mound.

It was a pile of bodies. Discarded and heaped atop one another like so much offal. My anger quickened. And not only mine.

"We have to put a stop to this," Ghost growled.

"I agree," I said, already revising my plans. I could no more ignore the atrocities in this room than Ghost could. My gaze drifted over the corpses. They all appeared to be of dwarven or orcish origin. Judging by the size of the mound, the possessed had performed their 'tests' on scores of prisoners.

Another tortured scream cut through the air.

"Do something, Prime!" Ghost urged.

"Rest assured, I will," I murmured, eyes sweeping the room again. *"But before I act, I need more information."*

"What are you looking for?"

"The tunnel entrance," I replied absently.

The torture chamber was the only area I'd not fully explored on the level yet. I'd followed every other passage to its natural end but hadn't found the way down to the underground tunnel. I was sure Castor wouldn't leave its entrance unguarded, and considering the number of possessed in the hall, I was betting the way down was in this very room.

But I couldn't see it.

In fact, other than the open archway through which I'd entered, the hall appeared to have no other exits — I'd reached the end of the prison level and, for all intents and purposes, had hit a dead end.

"Hansen," a possessed yelled. "Get Dirk!"

Ignoring him, I kept searching the room. The possessed operating the coffin device looked up. "What? Why?"

The first possessed gestured to the orc gasping for breath beneath him on a torture rack. "This bugger is about to die."

"So?" Hansen asked callously.

"*So* he is one of the proles' head honchos."

Hansen blinked. "You mean Lorn?"

That caught my interest. Leaving off my examination of the chamber, I fixed my gaze on the victim in question. The orc was a bloody mess, his face all but unrecognizable. Reaching out with my will, I analyzed him.

The target is Lorn, a level 47 orc. He is near death.

"*Ah,*" I breathed.

"*What?*" Ghost asked.

"*It's not only Stormhammer the possessed captured. They're holding Chief Lorn prisoner, too. That's why the orcs refused Elron's overtures. They didn't want to admit they lost their leader.*"

"That's the one. This is him," the first possessed replied after a too-long silence.

"Jorge, you fool! I told you to leave him alone. What were you thinking?"

Jorge shrugged. "Yeah, yeah. I know. We can't let him die."

Hansen laughed. "There's no 'we' here. This is your mess. Clean it up yourself!"

Jorge's mouth dropped open. "But Castor left you in charge. If the prole dies—"

"If he dies, I'll let Castor know *you* failed to follow orders," Hansen interrupted. "The boss' wrath will fall on you, not me. I'll make sure of that."

Jorge stared at his companion in horror, much to the amusement of the other possessed looking on.

"Now, stop standing there like a gaping idiot!" Hansen roared. "Can't you see he is dying? Go and fetch Dirk."

Jorge still didn't move.

"Quickly!" Hansen snapped.

Coming out of his stupor, Jorge dashed into motion. I followed his progress with interest. There was no one named Dirk in the hall. I'd already analyzed everyone and confirmed as much.

And Jorge didn't head towards me and the room's only apparent exit, but to the left side of the room. Crouching down, he fidgeted with something on the floor.

An illusion has been lifted. You have found a hidden hatch!

"*Well, well,*" I murmured, a smile spreading across my face as Jorge disappeared down the hatch. "*There you are.*"

CHAPTER 401: BLOODED

"You've found the tunnel entrance?" Ghost guessed.

"I have," I replied, turning back to Lorn. The New Haven councilor was in a bad way, but I could do nothing for him.

I had three health potions left, having given the rest to Adriel and Farren in preparation for the fight against the harbinger, but trying to get one to Lorn meant revealing myself, and I couldn't do that—not yet. Whoever Dirk was, I hoped he could help the orc. Once he did, I would act.

In preparation for the upcoming encounter, I studied my foes. Now that the entertainment Jorge had provided was over, most of the possessed had gone back to work—torturing prisoners—but not Hansen. No longer feigning disinterest, he'd strode over to the hapless orc and studied him with as much concern as I felt.

At level one hundred and forty-two, Hansen was the biggest threat in the room. All the others were below rank thirteen, which was a relief. Given the disparity in numbers I was facing, that went a long way to balancing the odds. Still, more than half the possessed were casters—adding an element of unpredictability I disliked—and I knew I couldn't count on a quick or easy victory.

But I had surprise on my side. And Ghost.

The chances were good, I thought, of not only defeating the torturers but also preventing them from alerting the rest of their companions in the tunnel below.

"What's the plan?" Ghost asked.

"Nothing complicated," I replied with a shrug. *"We defeat the possessed in this hall while stopping them from being reinforced from below."*

A pause. *"How do we do that?"*

My gaze drifted to the hatch. Jorge and another possessed—Dirk presumably—were climbing out. *"We make sure the trapdoor stays closed."*

"You said 'we' again," Ghost observed with barely suppressed eagerness. *"Does that mean...?"*

I smiled. *"It does. It's time you joined in the fight."*

✳   ✳   ✳

Before hurrying off to join Hansen, Jorge and Dirk resealed the hatch and renewed the illusion concealing it, but I had already marked its location in my mind and didn't doubt I'd be able to find it again.

As the pair made their way across the hall, I began moving, too, sliding along the wall at my back.

Multiple hostile entities have failed to detect you!

None of the possessed even glanced my way. The shadows around the room's edges were thick, and my stealth was too high for them to spot me.

It was slow going, but eventually, I reached my target destination—an alcove less than three yards from the hatch. Drawing to a halt, I turned my attention back to the possessed huddled around Lorn.

The orc's wounds had disappeared.

While Lorn's face was no less bloodied, his bruises had faded, and the dazed, senseless look from his eyes had vanished. In fact, given the murderous snarl on the orc's face, he was fighting fit once more.

I rubbed my chin thoughtfully. *So, Dirk is a healer,* I thought, studying the still-chanting possessed. *Useful that.*

"Are we ready to begin?" Ghost asked.

"Just about," I replied. Closing my eyes, I saw to my buffs.

You have renewed your facial disguise, cast heightened reflexes, load controller, fade, and trigger-cast quick mend.

Opening my eyes, I studied the hatch again. I'd already inspected the room with my sorcerer's coif but had uncovered no wards. The forthcoming battle would be a straight-up fight—as much as any fight was one, anyway. I *did* need to protect the hatch, though.

And for that, I needed to get closer.

Glancing up, I scanned the room. No one was looking my way. Still, it paid to be careful. Dropping down flat, I crawled toward the hidden trapdoor.

Multiple hostile entities have failed to detect you!

Stretched out on the floor and obscured by the torture devices, there was little chance of me being spotted. Reaching the hatch, I rubbed my thumb across the blue rune on my wristband.

You have passed a thieving skill check!
You have removed 24 trap-making crystals from your trapper's wristband. Remaining trap-making crystals: 100 of 200.

Thus far, I had been nursing my traps, but with my time in Draven's Reach coming to an end, I could afford to be a bit more expansive in my use of them. Maneuvering carefully around the spot I knew the hatch to occupy, I set my traps.

You have connected 10 bear clamp elements to 10 pressure plate triggers and 2 darkness elements to 2 motion pins.
12 tier 3 traps have been successfully configured!

Not wanting to risk any damage to the hatch itself—who knew what alarms would be set off?—I forwent using the more destructive toys in my arsenal. Besides, I didn't need the traps to kill my foes. I could do that well enough on my own; I only needed to stop the possessed from going down the hatch.

The trapdoor seen to, I rose into a crouch and peered over the adjacent table.

Dirk, Hansen, and Jorge were still clustered around the strapped-down orc, and from the looks of it, the healer was berating the pair. The other seventeen possessed were unhelpfully spread about the room, leaving me with no group to target with my area of effect spells. *Oh well.* I would just have to make do.

"*What now?*" Ghost asked.

"*You manifest.*"

A pause. "*As in right now?*"

"*Yes, as in right now,*" I said, smiling at her disbelieving tone. Leaving her to it, I drew psi and began my assault.

You have cast slaysight.
You have induced 4 of 4 targets to sleep for 40 seconds.

As one, Jorge, Hansen, Dirk, and Lorn's eyes closed, the former three slumping to the floor while the orc sagged back against his restraints. *Perfect.*

The four were now out of the fight. Hopefully, by the time they woke up, Ghost and I would have dealt with the rest of the possessed. Ignoring the surprised murmurs in the room at the collapse of their trio, I glanced at the burgeoning cloud of darkness next to me. "*You remember the plan?*"

Ghost nodded, her predatory gaze not shifting from her chosen target—a lanky possessed eight yards away.

"*Then go do your worst,*" I ordered lightly.

Ghost has taken the form of a level 201 stygian pyre wolf.

Not needing a second invitation, the pyre wolf bounded forward. As yet, her appearance had gone unnoticed, but that wouldn't last. Still, I judged Ghost would manage her first kill unimpeded.

A splotch of fast-moving blackness, the pyre wolf blurred across the room. Three yards from the possessed, she sprang. A pleased grin stretched across my face. Ghost had timed her leap perfectly.

Unfortunately, her target chose just then to turn.

Perhaps the mage had spotted the streak of orange and black at his back. Or perhaps some inbred instinct had warned him. Whatever the case, as the possessed swung around, he raised his arm to ward off the incoming attack.

Your familiar has injured Cedric.

The mage's maneuver foiled Ghost's attack, turning a killing strike into a glancing blow. Still, he would've done better to dodge. As the heavier and much larger pyre wolf crashed into her foe, he toppled backward, borne down by her weight.

Ghost has activated astral bite.
Your familiar has knocked down her target.

Yelping in surprise—and fear—Cedric tried to fend off Ghost's searching jaws, but the pyre wolf was having none of it. Lowering her head, she savaged the mage's arm with teeth that dripped with fire and psi and gouged his torso with paws tipped by gleaming bits of darkness.

Ghost's magma maw has increased to level 2.
Ghost's stygian claws has increased to level 2.
Ghost's telepathy has increased to level 51.
Ghost's magma maw has increased to level 3.

...

It would not be a clean kill nor a quick one, but I had no doubt my companion would triumph—given enough time, of course. However, the fracas was not overlooked.

Cedric's screams were noticed. Shouting and yelling, the remaining possessed turned and reached for their weapons. Ghost sensed the change in the room, too. Pausing her frenzied assault, she raised glowing eyes to glare at our foes.

"Stay on the mage," I instructed before she could break off entirely. *"I'll buy you some time."* Scanning the chamber, I picked out the most immediate threat—a female possessed.

Reacting faster than her fellows, the woman already had her right arm raised and pointed at Ghost. It was not an innocent gesture. Undoubtedly, she was about to unleash a casting on my familiar.

If I let her.

Diving into the aether, I rushed toward her.

You have teleported 8 yards.

I emerged back in the real, crouched and hidden in my target's shadow. Killing her would be easy, but I intended something more elaborate. Swift as thought, I unbent and wrapped my arm around the woman's neck, jerking her up until her feet dangled off the ground.

You have interrupted your target's casting. Jacilyn's fire ray spell was disrupted!
A hostile entity has detected you! You are no longer hidden.

Jacilyn shrieked—loudly—and heads whipped in our direction.

"Shut up!" I roared—equally loud—and placed the tip of ebonheart against her neck.

"W-w-ho... are ... you?" she asked, swallowing fearfully.

Ignoring her, I craned my neck from left to right and surveyed the room. In the process, I gave the other possessed a good look at my face. Baring my teeth, I waited for the inevitable moment of recognition.

It was not long in coming.

You have passed a mental resistance check! A hostile entity has failed to pierce your disguise and has been fed false analyze data.

"It's him! He's back!"

"Who?"

"The player. Taim! The one the boss is after!"

I concealed a smile. I'd captured the attention of every able-bodied possessed in the room, meaning that, for the moment at least, Ghost and her foe were forgotten.

"What about the thing that's got Cedric?"

"Forget the devil dog! Get Taim!"

"But Castor said—"

"The bastard killed Avery! He's mine!"

"No, stop! We can't take him alone. We need the others."

Spells were released, bows were drawn, fighters began their charges, and shields popped into existence. The last was unfortunate but couldn't be helped.

Your familiar has killed Cedric.

It was the moment I'd been waiting for.

Not hesitating, I thrust ebonheart downward, ending my captive's life in a single violent stroke. Flinging away the corpse, I tossed the stone vials I'd been holding ready.

You have ignited 3 smoke bombs.

Plumes of gray exploded in the room, partially obscuring me from view. They did nothing to stop the avalanche of projectiles heading my way, though.

"Move, Ghost!" I ordered. Doing the same myself, I dove to the side and out of the center of the approaching onslaught.

You have evaded 4 of 11 attacks, and your void armor has repelled 2 hostile spells.
A cold missile has hit you.
A wilting ray has grazed you.
A sunburst dart has struck you.
A swarm of insects have bitten you.
Void armor charge remaining: 75%. Your health has decreased to 87%.

The storm descended—and passed—leaving me only a little worse for wear. I was chilled, stung, partially blinded, and weakened, but for all that, the rain of spells was ineffective.

If that's the best they've got, I thought as I bounced back to my feet, *this will be a short fight.*

A gloom bolt has struck you.

No sooner had I finished the thought than a heavy quarrel found me, punching a hole through my gut.

Liga Tor has critically injured you!
Quick mend triggered!

Suddenly weak-limbed, I dropped back to one knee. *Damn, where did that come from?* I hadn't even seen the crossbow bolt. Either the archer had uncannily good aim, or I had abysmal luck.

"Prime!" Ghost cried.

"I'll be alright," I gasped through gritted teeth. *"Don't come to—"*

Movement at the edge of my vision drew my eye.

A warrior was charging toward me through the smoke. I'd survived the first spate of attacks, but the next wave was already incoming. However, I was in no condition to face it.

Grasping the bolt in my gut to prevent it from dealing more damage, I rolled awkwardly across the ground and into the nearest smoke plume.

You are hidden.

Chapter 402: Murder and Mayhem

You have evaded Arcla's attack.
Multiple hostile entities have failed to detect you!

Heavy, hobnailed boots skidded past, missing me by only inches. I exhaled noiselessly. *That was too close,* I thought.

Ghost thought so, too, and through the familiar bond, I felt her sudden alarm.

"I'm alright," I projected, heading her off before she could rush to my rescue. *"Continue attacking. That'll keep them distracted while I heal."*

The pyre wolf wasn't convinced but didn't demur. Padding through the gray haze, she stalked her next victim.

"Where is he?" the lizardman warrior demanded abruptly. I couldn't see him through the smoke, but it sounded like he was nearly atop me.

"What do you mean?" someone shouted from across the room. "He was right there. You should've—"

"I missed," the lizardman—Arcla—hissed. "One second, he was there, the next, he vanished." A pause. "He must've teleported out."

"Don't be too sure," the second speaker warned. "The bastard is a sneak, too. He could still be close."

"Find him!" a third ordered querulously.

Good luck with that, I thought, smiling toothily despite my pain. Even injured as I was, I knew the chances of any of the possessed finding me were minimal. Still, I dared not see to my healing until I put more space between me and the warrior.

"How about you do something about this smoke first?" Arcla retorted sourly. "I can't see shit in all this—"

Another shriek tore through the hall.

My grin widened. That was Ghost savaging a second victim. Clenching the hilt of ebonheart, I waited to see what the lizardman would do.

Would he continue to search for me?

I had my answer a moment later when Arcla whirled around and rushed toward the source of the cry. I relaxed. Ghost had done well to draw the possessed away from me, but now *she* would be the focus of their attacks. I would have to hurry. Dragging myself across the floor, I ducked under one of the tables I'd spotted earlier.

It was time to recuperate and get back into the fight.

✻ ✻ ✻

Your familiar has killed Liga Tor.
Your familiar has killed Drusula.
Your familiar has killed Hakin.
Your familiar has killed Neefalar.

You have restored yourself with quick mend. Your health is at 100%.

It took me a few minutes to tend to my wounds.

By that time, Ghost had managed to kill four more spellcasters and, amazingly, had avoided being hit by anything more serious than a glancing blow herself.

Although that was perhaps more on account of the possessed's wariness of her than anything else. None of them seemed quite sure what she was, and that had made both their warriors and mages hesitate. Admittedly, the pyre wolf made for a fearsome sight. Still, the possessed's lack of confidence had cost them.

Where they hesitated, Ghost did not. Time and again, she had rushed in, bowled down her target, and savaged him, then retreated before the enemy could retaliate. It had proven to be a remarkably successful tactic—while it had lasted, anyway.

Eventually, the possessed had wised up and concentrated their fire, forcing Ghost to prowl menacingly—but also impotently—around the room's edges. The tide had shifted against my familiar.

But now it was time for me to re-enter the game.

My original plan was in tatters, of course. I'd been hoping to slay the twenty possessed quickly with a combination of mayhem, stealth, and mental trickery. Unfortunately, the fifteen survivors—including Dirk, Hansen, and Jorge—were now alert, armed, and gathered in a close-knit group in the center of the room with their every defense up.

Not every element of my plan had failed, though.

The traps I'd planted around the hatch had served to keep my foes from calling for help. After the hapless Arcla—now limping—had twice triggered the bear clamps, the possessed had retreated en masse from the trapdoor.

Unfortunately, it didn't look like they intended on staying away forever.

From the shifty glances Hansen and Dirk were casting in the hatch's direction, I suspected they'd devised a plan to destroy my defenses and were getting ready to act.

Do they have a thief amongst them? I wondered.

That didn't seem likely, though. Otherwise, my traps wouldn't have lasted as long as they had. Still, they intended *something*. Rising to my haunches, I snuck out from beneath the table.

Multiple hostile entities have failed to detect you!

The possessed had given up searching for me, but they *had* managed to dissipate the smoke and light the hall brighter than a meadow under a noonday sun. I remained concealed, but the moment I attacked, I knew I would be revealed.

Hansen's hand twitched and, in response, four heavily armored possessed advanced toward the hatch. Sliding out from behind the chest at the far end of the room where she'd taken shelter, Ghost moved to intercept them.

"*Wait,*" I instructed. "*Let's see what they do.*"

"*Why?*" she asked, retreating behind the chest again.

"All huddled together like that, they are going to be difficult to take down," I explained. I could force the possessed to spread out myself—using either charm or terrify—but if they did so on their own, so much the better.

Alas, a moment later, the rest of the possessed followed on the heels of the first four and marched toward the hatch in a double column.

Hmm, not good. I rubbed my chin.

"What do we do now?" Ghost asked, anticipating my next thought.

"What else?" I rejoined, my lips quirking up in a smile. *"We wait."* Drawing psi in readiness, I did just that.

The possessed drew closer to the hatch, their weapons pointed outwards, and their eyes scanning the hall—especially the area around the chest where they knew Ghost stalked. My own eyes narrowed, I watched them in turn. Hansen surely didn't intend on walking the group straight through my traps, did he?

I snorted quietly. I could only hope he would be so foolish.

"Prime, you see that?" Ghost asked abruptly.

"See what?" I asked, not taking my eyes off the possessed column.

"The orc. He's escaping."

Huh? Wrenching my gaze away from the possessed, I glanced over my shoulder, and sure enough, saw a bruised and battered orc hunched over and limping toward the room's main entrance. It wasn't Lorn but one of the others who'd been less securely fastened.

The enterprising fellow was using the possessed's distraction to make his escape. Still, I didn't rate his chances. In as poor condition as the orc was, he wouldn't make it past the first guard he encountered, and surely he knew that as well as I did. I frowned. *What does he think he is doing?*

The tread of marching footsteps came to a stop.

Dismissing the orc from my mind—dealing with him would have to wait until later—I turned back to the possessed. Hansen had brought the column to a halt five yards from the hatch, a safe—if barely so—distance from the nearest trap.

"Now," Hansen barked.

In response, one of the possessed waved his arms.

Urog has cast Aziman's dust of revelation.

Lazy streams of luminescent powder wafted from the mages' hands toward the hatch. After hovering midair for a second, the glowing specks descended, settling around each trap I'd so painstakingly seeded earlier.

Ah, so that is what they are about.

Smiling victoriously, Hansen pointed at the closest trap. "Destroy that!" he crowed. Obediently, Urog lowered his wand and fired.

A hostile entity has triggered a trap!

As the mage's fire dart struck the trap, a bear clamp—the trap element in this instance—materialized and snapped closed, its jagged metal teeth closing on empty air.

A bear clamp has been activated. No target found.

My lips turned down sourly, knowing what was coming next.

"Excellent!" Hansen exclaimed, rubbing his hands together gleefully. "Now, the next."

A hostile entity has triggered a trap!
A hostile entity has triggered a trap!

...

My expression growing progressively more unhappy, I watched my traps being destroyed. But still, I didn't act. The time was not yet right.

My gaze darting left to right, I scanned the surroundings anew, mapping obstacles and potential hiding spots. Whether by happenstance or not, the immediate area around the hatch was devoid of torture devices — leaving me with few options for cover.

But it also meant there were no innocent prisoners nearby, which suited me just fine. Removing a handful of vials from my belt, I calculated trajectories.

"Prime, why are we doing nothing?" Ghost cried. *"We should attack!"*

"Not yet," I replied, tight-lipped.

"But they are destroying your traps," she growled.

"I know," I replied grimly.

Another bear clamp was destroyed—that made six—then another. And another. I bit my lip. *Maybe Ghost has the right of it. Maybe I should—*

A hostile entity has triggered a trap! A blot of darkness trap has been activated.

Ebon clouds mushroomed out to swallow the leading quarter of the possessed column in darkness. I jerked erect. It was what I'd been waiting for. Finally, the possessed had triggered the wrong trap—or the right one, from my perspective.

Winding back my arm, I flung away the vials I'd been holding ready.

You have ignited 2 acid bombs and 2 firebombs!

The resulting conflagration was predictably apocalyptic—if contained. Drenched in acid and fire, warriors screamed while the mages, safe behind their shields, chanted furiously, no doubt casting spells to douse the flames.

No one died. But more than one grievous injury was sustained, and just as importantly, the protective shields of the spellcasters dulled and weakened, and some were even destroyed altogether.

Hansen and Dirk staggered out of the cloud of darkness, their faces stunned as they beheld the chaos behind them. Not wanting to injure the possessed healer, I'd been careful to target the rear of their column with my bombs.

Hansen's mouth opened, but before he could issue whatever command he intended, I released the psicasting I'd prepared.

You have cast slaysight.

Between one heartbeat and the next, tendrils of my will bathed the entire possessed column, and psi surged into the minds of six random targets.

You have terrified 4 of 6 targets for 40 seconds.

You have failed to terrify 2 of 6 targets. Note, targets protected by magic shields are immune to mental manipulation.

The spell succeeded, inciting the fear centers of four possessed to a fever pitch. Their eyes bulging and their chest heaving, the afflicted possessed shrieked and burst into motion—adding to the already considerable mayhem in the enemy's formation.

I wasn't done yet, though. Drawing more psi, I wove a second spell.

"Stop running, you fools!" Hansen yelled. Reaching out, he attempted to grab one of the fleeing warriors, but the man evaded his grasp. "Stand your ground and fight, dammit!"

Predictably, he was ignored.

"It's that player," Dirk shouted. "He did this!" Which was obvious enough but did nothing to restore order.

"Spread out and find him!" Hansen barked.

It was too late for that, though. My spell was ready, and without hesitation, I released it into the enemy's midst.

You have cast mass charm.

You have charmed 4 of 10 targets for 20 seconds.

You have failed to charm 6 of 10 targets. Note, targets protected by magic shields are immune to mental manipulation.

I smiled grimly. My two spells had bespelled just over half of the remaining possessed—fewer than I liked, but still enough for what I intended next. Drawing my blades, I rose to my feet.

"Let's finish this, Ghost," I said and blinked into battle.

You have killed 10 hostile entities.
Ghost has killed 4 hostile entities.
You and Ghost have reached level 202!

It did not take long for Ghost and me to mop up. When we were done, fourteen more corpses littered the chamber, including all of the original possessed torturers. We kept only Dirk alive.

Deliberately so.

Striding over to the healer, I knelt by his side. Dirk was still knocked out cold, but other than for the large lump on the back of his head where I'd struck him earlier, he was uninjured. *He will come to soon,* I thought.

"Watch him," I ordered.

Padding up to me, Ghost lay down on all fours and rested her snout inches from the unconscious possessed. *"My pleasure, Prime."*

Rising to my feet, I began to turn away, then paused. *"You did well today,"* I said.

"Thank you," she said, beaming with pride at the praise.

It was well-deserved, too. Ghost had killed nearly as many possessed as I had, and she'd coped admirably on her own when I'd been forced to withdraw from the fight.

Her performance allayed many of my fears about her abilities. Ghost *was* combat-effective, and from here on out, she would only get better. I had no doubt her skills had advanced immensely during the battle. To see just how far she'd progressed, I called up the relevant Game messages.

Your thieving has reached rank 13, and your channeling rank 19.

Ghost's magma maw and ash armor have reached rank 2, her stygian claws rank 3, and her telepathy rank 6.

My eyebrows rose in mild surprise.

Ghost had profited even more from the battle than I'd imagined. *All* her skills had leveled up. Her stygian claws skill alone had gained three ranks. Of course, this was primarily due to how low the skill had been to begin with. Nevertheless, her rapid progress was encouraging.

At this rate, her skills will reach tier two in no time.

On that note, I invested my new attribute points in Magic and Strength. Ghost would need the ability slots—and soon.

Your Strength has increased to rank 15. Other modifiers: +8 from items.
Your Magic has increased to rank 39. Other modifiers: +20 from items.

"Do we head down the hatch now?" Ghost asked.

"Not yet." I let my gaze drift to the room's other occupants—the bruised and battered orcs. Except for the one who had chosen to flee, the rest had remained motionless during the battle, watching the possessed die with burning gazes and silent hope. *"First, we tend to the prisoners."*

✳　✳　✳

I approached Lorn first.

As I walked up to him, I felt the gazes of the other orcs following me. Their eyes were hard and cold, but whether it was fear or anger that lurked within, I couldn't tell just yet.

I'd already analyzed each of the orcish prisoners, and while some were in a bad way, and all sported one injury or another, none of their wounds were life-threatening. It seemed the other possessed torturers had taken better care of their subjects than Jorge had—for which I was more than a little grateful. It made what I had to do next a little easier.

My attention shifted back to the orc chief.

He, too, watched me, observing my advance in eerie silence and looking as composed as the day we'd first met despite his restraints and recent torture.

"So. You have returned," Lorn remarked as I drew to a halt a yard from him.

"I have," I replied, studying the chieftain.

Even though Jorge was no longer hurting Lorn, and Dirk had healed him, the torture device restraining the orc was too small for his large frame, and he had to be in all sorts of discomfort. In fact, it was safe to assume Lorn was in agony. In spite of this, no flicker of pain crossed his face.

The chief arched one eyebrow delicately. "You did not find what you were searching for?"

He was referring to the exit portal, I knew. "I did, actually."

Surprise flickered across the orc's face. "Then why come back?"

I shrugged. "I have unfinished business in New Haven."

Lorn blinked slowly as if his fears had been realized. "You have come to kill me then."

I tilted my head to the side. "Why would you think that?"

"Isn't it obvious?" he asked, holding my gaze. "We betrayed you."

I stared at him blankly.

"You would make me speak my shame?" he asked bitterly.

I said nothing.

"Very well," he said, his face tightening fractionally. "When we summoned you to the council hall, we *knew* Castor and his fellows were waiting to ambush you. You must've suspected as much already." He hung his head. "We were complicit in the attack. *I* was complicit."

"Ah, that," I said, having nearly forgotten the incident.

Lorn raised his head, an incredulous look on his face. "You forgot?" he asked, correctly interpreting my tone.

My lips twitched upward. "Forgive me. I've had a lot on my plate recently."

Lorn continued to stare at me disbelievingly. "So, if not to kill, why have you come?" he demanded.

"Ah, but I *have* come to kill," I said softly. "Just not you."

The orc fell silent. "Castor," he guessed finally. "It's him you're after."

"Correct. He is the true architect of New Haven's ills."

The first glimmer of hope—and eagerness—entered Lorn's gaze. "Then free me. Free all of us, and we will help you!"

"Oh, I intend to," I replied. "But first, we must discuss terms."

It was Lorn's turn to stare blankly. "Terms?"

I opened my mouth to reply, but before I could, another intervened.

"Terms? What bloody terms!"

✳   ✳   ✳

I turned around, recognizing the speaker. A band of dwarves—and a single orc—crowded the entrance to the hall. All of them were ragged, unarmed, and filthy, but despite this, their eyes shone with steely determination. This was one lot of prisoners that were not going to be recaptured.

"Welcome, Stormhammer," I greeted. "I was wondering how long you would take to get here."

The dwarven thane's brows drew down.

"Where are the rest of your companions?" I asked mildly. There were far fewer dwarves with thane than I'd heard earlier.

Stormhammer's eyes narrowed to slits. "You knew we were trapped in those damnable cells," he accused.

"Yes."

"And you left us to rot anyway?" he growled, a dangerous edge to his voice.

"I did."

"Why?" Stormhammer bellowed. "By all that is holy, why?"

Folding my arms, I stared down at the angry dwarf. "Softly," I warned as the echoes of his shout died down. "We don't want Castor's cronies to hear you."

The thane's empty hands curled into fists, but he saw the sense of my words and reined in his temper. "Why?" he hissed again.

"Because you were safer there," I answered evenly.

"Safer!" Stormhammer sputtered, his face going purple with rage again. "Who in hells do you think—"

"Enough!" Lorn barked.

The thane swung around to glare at the still-restrained orc.

"We owe Taim," Lorn said before he could speak. "Not just for saving the city from the nether, but for today's rescue also." He glanced at the orc standing behind the dwarven thane. "Zorgulg would never have been able to free you if not for what Taim did here." Lorn met Stormhammer's gaze again. "And we owe him, too, for our betrayal," he finished softly.

The thane looked away. "That was not my choice," he spat.

"It wasn't," Lorn agreed. "But you went along with the rest of us, anyway."

"And look where it has got us," Stormhammer ground out harshly. "The council disbanded, New Haven under Castor's thumb, and Cilia ruling as his puppet! How is any of—"

"No longer," I interjected, interrupting him mid-rant.

"What?" Stormhammer asked, staring at me in confusion.

"Cilia no longer rules," I clarified. "She's dead."

My words set the thane's guards whispering, and even the orcs shifted restlessly. What was that in their eyes? Happiness? Approval? *Both,* I thought.

Stormhammer himself strove to appear indifferent, but despite his best efforts, I saw the hungry gleam in his eyes. "You killed her?" he asked.

"Yes," I replied bluntly, "and when we're done here, I will go below and kill Castor too."

The whispers died down, and the intensity in the gazes of the watching dwarves and orcs grew until the air seemed to burn with anticipation. *They want this,* I thought. *More than anything else, they want Castor dead.*

"I will do it alone," I added prudently a moment later. "I do not want or need help." Vengeance was a heady brew but a dangerous one, too. If I was not careful, the prisoners' desire for revenge could get the better of them—upsetting my own plans.

"What about the archlich?" Lorn asked, his brows pinching in worry. He at least seemed to be thinking further ahead. "Won't he retaliate?"

"He's already dead," I replied offhandedly.

"What?" Stormhammer scoffed. "You kill him too?"

I chuckled. "Actually, I did."

The thane opened his mouth, no doubt to ridicule my claim, but something in my expression stopped him. Yanking on his beard, he shifted uncomfortably.

My amusement faded. "Unlike your council, I knew better than to place New Haven's fate in the hands of the possessed. Nor was I alone in my distrust of them. Someone in your city saw matters like I did and allied with me."

"Who?" Stormhammer demanded.

"It was Elron, of course," Lorn guessed.

"Correct," I replied. "Together, the marshal and I formulated a plan to rid the city of the possessed, open the way out of Draven's Reach for your people, and rid this sector of the nether." The last was stretching the truth a bit. Elron and I hadn't *planned* on killing the harbinger, but I doubted anyone would complain now that the deed was done.

"Are you saying you... succeeded?" Lorn asked slowly.

I swung to face him. "Mostly. Right this minute, Elron and his men are preparing to sweep aside the remainder of Cilia's force." I raised my voice, speaking to the room at large. "New Haven will be free again. You have my word."

The murmurs in the room rose again, and I sensed the mood lift, but this time, it wasn't vengeance that drove it. The prisoners were thinking of the future, not just their own, but their families. They were imagining a life beyond the dungeon, seeing a lifetime of hope coming to fruition.

"That sounds nice," Stormhammer said abruptly, slashing his hand down to silence the others. "But there is a cost, isn't there?"

I hadn't given the dwarven thane enough credit, I realized. Despite his temperamental nature, he was no fool. Like Lorn, he was looking beyond, seeing more than what was immediately in front of him.

"There is always a cost," I said softly.

"You want something," Lorn guessed shrewdly. "You aren't helping New Haven simply out of the goodness of your heart. You need something from us."

"Those terms you mentioned," Stormhammer added. "What are they?"

I fell silent, considering.

In hindsight, I realized it had been a mistake to mention 'terms' earlier. I hadn't wanted to broach the matter this way, nor did I think we had time to deal with all the details right now. Time was short, and I still had to get to Castor, but I suspected neither the thane nor the chief would let the matter rest until they had an answer.

There's nothing for it but to move forward.

Taking a deep breath, I plunged on. "Let me free the others first. Then we can talk."

Freeing Lorn and the other orcs was only the work of a few minutes. Healing them all was beyond me, however—which was why I had spared Dirk in the first place.

"What is that thing?" I heard one of the newly freed orcs mumble.

"Some sort of devil dog," the dwarf helping him muttered.

"If you ask me, it looks like a stygian," another said. A pause. "We should kill it."

That's just about enough of that, I thought. Striding back to the hatch, I stopped at Ghost's side.

"Listen up, everyone," I said, clapping loudly to capture their attention. "This here is Ghost. She is a pyre wolf and my partner." I deliberately left out the part about her being my familiar. Perhaps I was being paranoid, but the less anyone knew about Ghost and me, the better. "She can also hear and understand everything you say," I warned. "So be polite and show some respect. She is half the reason you lot are alive, after all."

For a drawn-out moment, no one said anything, then a surly-looking dwarf asked, "Is it going to eat him?"

"*She.* Not it," I growled. "And eat who?"

"Him," the dwarf said, pointing at Dirk.

I rolled my eyes. "No. The possessed is alive. Ghost is guarding him."

"*Maybe I should eat* him," Ghost said, glaring at the dwarf who'd insulted her.

"Alive?" another asked. I recognized his voice from the prison cells. Megtir was his name. "Why is he alive?"

"Dirk is a healer," I explained. The significance of this seemed to fly over the heads of most of the orcs and dwarves.

"Fools!" Lorn snorted. "Taim spared the possessed so he could heal you ingrates. Isn't that right?" he asked, looking at me.

"Correct. When Dirk regains consciousness, we'll put him to work."

"Will he cooperate?" Megtir asked doubtfully.

"He will if he wants to live," I replied grimly.

"We can always feed him to the devil dog otherwise," another chipped in helpfully.

Before I could respond to that, Stormhammer shoved his way to the fore of the crowd of orcs and dwarves. "Enough questions. Have you lot forgotten where we are?"

Sheepish looks were his only answer.

"Grab some weapons—there are plenty lying about—and guard the entrance." The thane glanced in Ghost's direction. "And the hatch." Lorn must have told him about it, I realized.

"Don't go too close," I warned. "Some of the traps I laid about it are still active."

Stormhammer nodded curtly. "Now, if you're all done here, it's time we finished our talk."

$$*\quad*\quad*$$

Delaying only to relay some final instructions to Ghost—I trusted her more than the prisoners to guard the hatch and warn me of any incoming danger—I followed Lorn and Stormhammer to an empty corner of the room. None of the other orcs and dwarves were close by, giving us at least the illusion of privacy.

"Begin," Stormhammer demanded without preamble. "Tell us your terms."

"One thousand soldiers," I replied, equally curtly.

The thane's bushy eyebrows drew down. "What?"

"In exchange for freeing you and Lorn and killing Castor, I want New Haven to loan me a company of one thousand of its finest soldiers."

The two councilors exchanged glances. "For how long?"

That was a little trickier to answer. The soldiers were for claiming the dire wolves' former home valley, of course. In order to take control of the sector, I needed a faction and a force of one thousand loyal to said faction to hold its safe zone for a limited duration.

Unfortunately, I still didn't know what that duration was. *Something else I must remember to ask Adriel about.*

"A month," I said finally.

"And that's all you want?" Lorn asked. "Those are the sum of your terms?"

"Yes," I replied.

Originally, I'd intended on forming a Pact with one of the Game's more mercenary Powers, buying the use of their faction, and employing actual mercenaries—from the bounty hunters guild—to form the requisite company of soldiers.

But since becoming an ascendant player, I had acquired the ability to form a faction myself—even though I was still fuzzy on how to go about doing that—and New Haven had plenty of soldiers to spare. It would be much simpler to have the New Haveners fight under my own banner and secure the sector that way.

Mercenaries were *expensive,* after all.

Stormhammer's expression, meanwhile, had turned sour. "Damnable players," he muttered.

My proposal was not going down well, I suspected. Still, I kept my own face impassive. "If it's too much to ask, we can negotiate the time period they will serve. But I will not budge on the number. I need one thousand soldiers, no less."

Once more, the thane's reaction caught me by surprise.

"Too much to ask, he says," Stormhammer fumed. "Bloody imbecile!" Throwing up his arms, the dwarf stomped off in disgust.

Perplexed, I watched him go. Was I really asking for too much? I didn't think so. But perhaps under the circumstances, the thane didn't believe the city could spare the soldiers.

Lorn chuckled, drawing my attention.

"It's not that you ask too much," the orc explained, "but too little."

I blinked. "Too little?"

The orc nodded. "The thane is a proud man. What he does not say—and I agree with him—is that he finds your offer insulting." Lorn paused. "Do you truly value the lives of our people so little?"

"I don't," I protested. "And I meant no insult, but I also have no desire to extort—"

"If you asked for five thousand men, we'd given them to you," Lorn said, his humor fading. "Twice that if need be."

"I don't need so many," I objected. Never mind that I had no way to feed and house an army of that size—yet.

"Then we will have to come up with a reward of equitable value," the orc replied, undaunted. "I will discuss the matter further with Stormhammer. But in the meantime, you have my word we will provide the soldiers you requested." He winced. "I know it is a bit much asking you to trust one who has already betrayed you, but will you?"

"I will," I replied gravely. "The situation is different this time around, and I'm willing to overlook the council's previous... errors in judgment." I met his eyes. "But there will be no second chances after this."

"Understood," Lorn said, the smile returning to his face. "Now that that is settled, you best return to your companion. Your prisoner looks to be stirring."

Glancing over my shoulder, I saw Lorn was right. Dirk was awakening.

✴   ✴   ✴

I was back at Ghost's side before the possessed could open his eyes, and when he did, the first thing he saw was me kneeling over him.

"You!" he exclaimed, his eyes going wide with shock.

"Me," I agreed, placing the tip of ebonheart beneath his chin. "Don't do anything stupid now."

Dirk jerked back from the black blade, then promptly winced as the back of his head rubbed against the hard ground. "What did you do to me?" he whined.

"Don't be a baby. It's only a little bump." I glanced to the left. "Your companions fared much worse."

Following my gaze, the possessed blanched. "You killed them!" he whispered, aghast. "All of them!"

"I did," I said, smiling agreeably.

"Castor will kill you for this!"

"Not if I kill him first," I retorted.

The healer stared at me speechlessly for a moment before he realized I was serious. "You're mad!"

I laughed. "Maybe." My smile faded. "Now, as pleasant as this conversation is, I'm afraid we don't have much time. Do you *know* why you are still alive?"

Confusion flashed across the possessed's face, only to be chased away by fear a second later. "You want me to tell you how to get to Castor. But I won't. No matter what you do to me, I won't tell you a thing!"

I pushed ebonheart deeper into soft flesh. "You will," I promised. "And you're right, I want you to tell me where Castor is. But if I only wanted that, I could've picked any of your companions instead. But I didn't. I chose you. Do you know why?"

Consternation flickered across Dirk's face.

Reaching down, I turned his face to the left. "What do you see?"

The healer said nothing.

I smacked him across the head. "What do you see?" I repeated.

"Proles?" he ventured.

"People," I growled. "*Injured* people. You will heal them."

"But they're just dumb proles," he whined. "Why would I bother to—"

I smacked him again—harder. "Because if you don't," I hissed coldly, "you will join your friends. And this time, there will be no archlich to bring you back."

The blood drained from Dirk's face as he went white as a sheet. I laughed cruelly. "I see you know of Loskin's fate. Do you think I'm incapable of doing the same to Castor?"

Dirk shook his head dumbly.

"Good. Then you will cooperate?"

He nodded.

I glanced over Dirk's head at Ghost. She was sitting so still her presence had gone unnoticed by the healer—hard as that was to imagine. "Is he being sincere?" I asked.

"*He is,*" she replied.

Dirk craned his head back to see who I was talking to and, when he spotted Ghost, tried to scramble away, but I was holding him too firmly for that.

"What are you doing with a stygian?" he cried. "Get it away from me!"

"Relax," I said. "Ghost is no stygian. What she is doesn't matter, but as far you're concerned, she is a truthsayer. She can read your every thought." Which, while not true, was a close enough approximation that under the circumstances, it didn't matter.

Ghost was using her diresight, which she'd activated the moment Dirk had awakened. The ability was in many ways similar to my own mindsight, but there were a few subtle differences.

For one, Ghost could read minds.

Not perfectly, not against a strong-willed person, and not without adequate preparation or being nearly on top of her subject, but she could do it. And well enough to sense if Dirk was lying.

"You understand what that means?" I asked, focusing on the healer again.

"If I lie to you," he said haltingly, "I die."

I smiled. "Good, I see that you do." I sat back. "Now, start talking. Where can I find Castor?"

Dirk told me everything I wanted to know and more.

The possessed described the layout of the next level, the location of Castor's personal chamber, and even the elite's daily routine. So eager was the healer to please that he described in minute detail every trap and ward between me and my target.

"Do you think he told you the truth?" Lorn asked when the possessed was done.

"I know he did," I replied, glancing towards the center of the room where Dirk was healing the injured orcs while under the watchful eyes of a pair of dwarves. "My companion verified everything."

Lorn shot the pyre wolf a speculative look but forbore comment. "What will you do now?"

"Go down, of course," I said. "And kill Castor."

"What about the wards and defenses the healer described?" Stormhammer asked.

"I've ways of getting around them," I said evasively.

The thane grunted noncommittally. "And what do we do with *him* when he is done?"

He meant Dirk, I guessed. "That is for you and Lorn to decide," I said firmly. "I promised the possessed his life, and I won't kill him. But whether you choose to honor my word..." I shrugged. "It's your choice."

"Then we will endeavor to make the right one," Lorn said before Stormhammer could respond.

The thane yanked on his beard, a gesture I was becoming familiar with. "I know which way I will be voting," he growled. "After the possessed's damnable experiments, none of my people will suffer one to live."

I looked at the dwarf curiously. "I never did ask..." I waved vaguely in the direction of the torture devices. "What was the purpose of all that?"

The torture the orcs and dwarves had undergone was undoubtedly a painful subject—for which reason I'd avoided it up to now—but the thane's statement was too intriguing to let pass unquestioned.

"It was Castor's attempt at repossession," Lorn replied shortly.

"A piss poor one," Stormhammer grumbled.

I blinked. "Repossession through torture? How would that work?"

"I have no idea," Lorne said, "but the possessed seemed to think that if they took us to the brink of death, they could somehow extract our spirits without killing the body, thus leaving the way open for their own spirits to enter."

"Huh, I see," I said, having no idea if such was possible. It was yet another thing I would have to speak to Adriel about. But I was less concerned by the end goal of Castor's experiments than that they'd occurred at all. The elite should not have had free reign to do what he'd done.

The entire incident was a reminder I still had to decide what to do about the possessed, not just those here, but those in the archlich's court. Granted, the ones under Castor's command were likely the very worst of the group, but I knew for a fact that there was some equally bad back at the court — Avery, for instance.

Could I let them go unpunished?

I'd been hoping to wash my hands of the matter and leave it in Farren's capable hands.

Now, I was no longer sure that was wise.

I shook my head, dismissing my musings. Deciding the possessed's future was a dilemma but not one I was going to solve now. I turned back to the hatch. "Well, I guess I better get going."

Stepping forward, Lorn clasped my hand, and a moment later, so did Stormhammer. "Good luck, Taim."

I shook their hands and glanced at Ghost.

"Do I really have to unmanifest again?" she asked forlornly.

I shrugged. *"You could always stay behind and help the orcs and dwarves guard our rear."*

Not bothering to dignify that with a comment, the pyre wolf rose to her feet and began unraveling.

Concealing a smile, I strode up to the hatch and opened it. It was time to finish what I'd started.

✳ ✳ ✳

The four hours I'd given myself to find and kill Castor were nearly up. Soon, Eclarie would pass on my message to Algar, and Elron's men would begin their assault.

I had to get to Castor quickly.

Still, I didn't plan on rushing. Thanks to Dirk, I knew the probable location of the thirty remaining possessed, and I fully intended to kill as many of them as I could before I got to Castor.

I'd maintained a confident façade before Lorn and Stormhammer, but the truth was that the defenses the elite had emplaced around his personal quarters were beyond my means to penetrate. He'd employed wards similar to those I'd encountered in the Mages' Guild tower, and even being able to see the castings with the sorcerer's coif would not let me bypass them.

Given that, I determined I was unlikely to get into Castor's chambers undetected. Which left the next best thing.

Making him come to me.

And ensuring that when he did, he had no allies to turn to for help. Thankfully, the other possessed were less protected than the elite himself, hence step one of my revised plan: *search and destroy.*

And I was about ready to begin.

Soft-footed, I climbed down the ladder from the hatch. As Dirk had predicted, the corridor it exited onto was empty. Stepping off the last rung, I dropped into a crouch.

You are hidden.

There was only one way forward. Behind me was a dead end, and some ten yards ahead was the open doorway of a guardroom beyond which the rest of the complex waited.

Contrary to my original expectations, the fortress' third subterranean level was not one long tunnel. Instead, it housed a multitude of rooms, corridors, and halls that contained everything the possessed needed to live comfortably.

Creeping forward, I made my way to the open door and peered into the room beyond. Just like Dirk had said, two possessed lounged inside. They were supposedly guarding the level's entrance, but according to the healer, none of the possessed ever took their sentry duties seriously.

Which perhaps explained why the two were asleep.

Drawing ebonheart, I inched up to the pair. They snored on, oblivious. Shaking my head at their foolishness, I slipped the black blade through the back of the first, then across the throat of the second.

You have killed Tvar.
You have killed Jeeharim.

I moved on, not bothering to hide the blood pooling on the sofa or disguise the corpses.

Because, of course, I didn't plan on leaving anyone alive to witness any of it.

✳ ✳ ✳

The next room contained four possessed playing cards and drinking beer. Like the first pair, they were none the wiser when I crept into the room.

Still, I didn't take any chances.

You have induced 4 of 4 targets to sleep for 40 seconds.
You have backstabbed Horn!
You have backstabbed Amylia!
You have backstabbed Cein May!
You have backstabbed Tomas!
You have killed 4 hostile entities.

Gently, I rested the head of my last victim back onto the table. It was almost too easy killing the possessed this way, but I wasn't about to complain.

Six down. Twenty-four to go.

✳ ✳ ✳

My next target almost surprised me.

I was creeping down a narrow corridor, stalking the possessed coming down the other way. With the heavy shadows lining the passage and my fade active, I didn't expect her to see me until too late, but somehow, I must have given myself away.

A hostile entity has detected you! You are no longer hidden.

The possessed jerked to a stop, her eyes widening as I materialized out of the shadows less than ten yards away. Her mouth opened, a scream on the tip of her tongue.

Bursting into motion, I drew ebonheart while simultaneously weaving psi.

You have teleported into Coril's shadow.

I emerged from the aether, and without pause to regain my bearings, I lunged forward, thrusting ebonheart into the possessed's defenseless back.

My blade struck true, and I found my foe's heart.

You have killed Coril with a fatal blow.

The corpse collapsed at my feet with no greater protest than a quiet sigh. I glanced up and down the corridor. No outcry followed; the kill had gone unnoticed.

Sheathing ebonheart, I moved on.

✳ ✳ ✳

Five rooms later, five more possessed lay dead.

All had been sleeping and in the exact rooms Dirk had told me to search. According to the healer, the possessed routinely slept in shifts, twelve at a time.

Unfortunately, the rest of Dirk's information proved less accurate, and I failed to find the other seven sleepers. Either Dirk had lied—which I doubted—or the seven were not following their usual routines.

Exiting the last empty room, I accepted the inevitable. I wasn't going to find the missing sleepers. *This calls for a change of plan,* I decided. If the seven were wandering around, they could stumble across the corpses I'd left in my wake, and I wasn't ready for the alarm to be raised.

There were still eighteen possessed alive—including Castor.

Time to head to the great hall.

According to Dirk, the great hall was where the possessed usually congregated, and even at the oddest hours, I could expect it to be busy. It was for this reason I'd originally opted to leave it for last.

I reached the chamber in question without incident. From the sounds of merriment coming from within, I could tell the hall was occupied. There had to be at least a dozen possessed inside. Five yards from the entrance, I melted into the shadows.

"It's time, Ghost."

Wordlessly, the pyre wolf took form behind me. *"How do we do this?"* she asked.

"I go in first," I said. *"You wait until the shouting starts, then you rush in and start killing."*

Ghost's mouth dropped open in a doggy smile. *"Simple. I like it."* She paused. *"But what if someone escapes?"*

I shrugged. *"At this point, it doesn't matter. We can kill as many as we can, then we wait for Castor to arrive."*

"You're sure he will come."

"Oh, I have no doubt," I said grimly. Reaching within, I drew on my stores of energy and altered my face.

You have cast facial disguise, assuming the visage of Dirk.

Stepping out of the shadows, I glanced back. *"Ready,"* Ghost said in response to my look.

Nodding curtly, I strode into the possessed's great hall.

✳   ✳   ✳

The room was as busy as Dirk warned. As I stepped across the threshold, curious gazes glanced my way, but on seeing my face, the onlookers turned away disinterestedly.

Multiple unknown entities have failed to pierce your disguise.

Maintaining a relaxed stride, I advanced into the hall even as I surveyed its occupants. My disguise was holding, but it wouldn't last long. Sooner or later, someone would notice the discrepancy in size between me and the healer, and before that happened, I had to act.

The room was laid out as a typical mess hall, with long rows of tables running the length of the room. It was large enough to host as many as a hundred people, but at present, only fifteen possessed were in attendance.

And much to my relief, Castor was not amongst them.

That'll make things easier, I thought, angling towards the left side of the hall. The possessed had gathered in two groups, one on either side of the room.

The group on the right was larger and easier to deal with indirectly. Weaving psi, I flung a casting into their midst.

You have cast mass charm.
6 hostile entities have failed a mental resistance check!
3 hostile entities are immune to mental attacks!
You have charmed 6 of 9 targets for 20 seconds.

Six of the possessed seated at the table I'd targeted froze, and even from half the room away, I saw the perplexed expressions of the trio not bewitched. *"Attack,"* I commanded, relaying the order to my minions before the three could make sense of what they were seeing.

As one, my new allies rose and descended on their former comrades. I kept walking, my gaze fixed on the other table and the six possessed gathered there.

"What the hell has gotten into you, Gerrad?" someone shouted behind me.

"Hey! Stop—" another yelled.

"They're bewitched!" the third cried. "Help!"

The screams were Ghost's cue, and through our bond, I sensed her flow into motion. *"Deal with the possessed at the right side of the room first,"* I told her.

"Got it, Prime."

At the table ahead, heads rose, eyes drawn to the ruckus behind me. One possessed, though, glanced in my direction. His gaze skipped over me, then jerked back as something caught his attention.

You have failed a mental resistance check! Songbird has pierced your disguise.

I didn't hesitate. Drawing psi, I blinked.

You have teleported into Songbird's shadow.

Ebonheart flashed out, decapitating the gnome in one smooth motion. A shriek erupted from my right. Ignoring the woman, I turned to my left and the warrior surging to his feet. Fumbling for the axe at his side, he swung at me.

I ducked beneath the blow, then thrust upward with both blades, burying them in my foe's chest.

You have killed Zurice.

Something blurred toward me from the right. Yanking free my swords, I wrenched myself out of the way.

You have evaded Tomsin's attack.

Backstepping, I found myself facing four possessed—an archer, a caster, and two warriors. Beyond them, I spotted Ghost's dark form rushing in. Trusting her to take care of the possessed in the other side of the room, I turned back to my opponents.

Four hostile entities have failed to pierce your disguise.

"Dirk, what's wrong with you?" the caster asked.

"It's not Dirk," Tomsin replied grimly. "Dirk can't fight like that."

"Then who—?"

"Can't you guess?" I asked lightly. "It's Taim." Not waiting for a response, I dashed forward.

You have cast windborne.

I manifested the windslide directly beneath my feet and mapped a dizzying path around the four facing me. The archer's bow was drawn, and he fired after only a split-second's hesitation, as did the mage.

But the pair's hesitation cost them, and both projectiles sailed harmlessly past me. Before they could target me again, I reached the two warriors, borne forward on wings of air.

The one on the right—an elf—slashed at me with his longsword. I parried the blow with ebonheart. The windslide jinked right, taking me with it and leaving the javelin thrust of the second warrior snapping at nothing but empty air.

Finding himself suddenly flanked, the elf swung around to face me again. Too late, though. Faithful was already snaking out, and before the warrior could parry the blow, carved a line of red across his neck.

You have killed Haiken with a fatal blow.

The windslide bore me on and away from the spurting blood. Dismissing the remaining warrior from consideration—I was already out of his reach—my gaze locked on my next targets—the archer and the caster.

Still in the midst of preparing their next attacks, the pair's eyes widened as they saw me barreling toward them. The archer fired—prematurely, it turned out—and the bolt went wide. Wiser than his fellow, the mage dropped his staff and turned to flee.

But it availed him little.

In a flash, I was between the two. Faithful cut left, and ebonheart chopped down.

You have killed Tomsin with a fatal blow.
You have killed Merrick with a fatal blow.

The windslide ran aground and I somersaulted off. Whirling around, I turned to face my last foe.

The warrior's face was pale with shock as his gaze skittered between the corpses of his former companions—it had only been an eyeblink earlier that they had been alive and hearty.

Raising my blades, I took a step forward. The warrior's eyes jerked back to me. I smiled menacingly.

It was enough.

Dropping his javelin, he turned and fled.

Smiling, I let him go.

Chapter 406: Don't Toy with an Elite

Ghost had as little trouble with her half of the skirmish as I had. She, though, did not suffer any of the possessed to live.

Your familiar has killed 9 hostile entities.
Your deception has reached rank 19.
Ghost's magma maw has reached rank 3, and her stygian claws rank 4.

"Should I chase him?" the pyre wolf asked, eyeing the corridor down which the warrior had fled.

"No," I replied absently, surveying the room again. *"I need him to warn Castor."*

"Oh. So you mean to lure him here?"

"That's right, and before he arrives, we need to prepare the ground."

"Prepare how?"

"Well, by laying some traps for one," I said, rushing to the center of the room.

Castor knew I had good stealth, which would make him wary of the room's shadows and edges. This being the case, he would mostly likely stay in the hall's center—making it the perfect place to lay my traps. Raising my left arm, I tapped the blue rune on my trapper's wristband.

"Won't he suspect an ambush?"

"He might," I replied. *"But I doubt that will stop him from coming after me anyway."*

"But surely he isn't so foolish as not to search for traps first?" Ghost persisted. *"You've used them against him before, after all."*

I lowered my arm. *"You're right,"* I said in dawning realization. I'd employed my traps to escape Castor's ambush in the council hall, and that incident was memorable enough that the elite would expect something similar this time around.

"So, no traps then?" Ghost asked, watching me carefully.

I bit my lip, thinking. *"Oh, I still think traps are warranted,"* I said at last, *"but perhaps a bit more creativity is required."*

✻　✻　✻

A little later, Ghost and I were ready.

I had no idea how long Castor would take to respond and, as a result, had to rush my initial placement of the traps, but as time ticked away, and the elite didn't appear, I expanded my ambush, until ten minutes later, I had set all the traps I needed—and more.

But still, the elite didn't show.

"What's keeping him?" I muttered from where I lay, nestled in shadows filling the southwest corner of the room.

"Maybe he is not coming," Ghost suggested. She, lacking my stealth, had been forced to return to the Cloak of the Reach.

"Oh, he is coming," I said, but I was no longer as certain as before. Saying nothing else, I turned my attention back to the doorway I'd spent the last few minutes watching.

The hall had two entrances. The south one through which Ghost and I had first entered, and the north one, down which the warrior had fled. Given what I knew of the level's layout, I expected Castor and the remaining possessed under his command, numbering a whole three—assuming the elite hadn't killed the warrior for his cowardice—to arrive through the north entrance.

But maybe Castor was being clever. Maybe he was circling around to the south entrance—or had decided to bypass the great hall altogether.

Damn, I hope not. Both possibilities would certainly complicate matters.

Another ten minutes passed, forcing me to contemplate abandoning my ambush. It didn't look like Castor was coming. But just as I was giving the idea of retreat serious consideration, a Game message dropped into my mind.

You have passed a Perception check! You have detected two hostile entities.
Macklin is no longer hidden!
Amber is no longer hidden!

I tensed, ready to burst into motion. Ghost and I were no longer the great hall's only occupants. Outlined in the open doorway of the north entrance were two slim figures. Crouched low and with only their heads moving, they scanned the room, each movement slow and deliberate.

Which, for a second, puzzled me.

Didn't the pair realize they'd been uncovered? But it looked like they hadn't. *Huh, fancy that,* I thought with a small smile. It seemed non-players, even those of the possessed variant, didn't receive helpful messages warning them they'd been uncovered.

A second later, one of the figure's gazes crossed over my hiding spot—

A hostile entity has failed to detect you! You are still hidden.

—and continued on without pause.

My grin widened. I clearly outclassed the pair when it came to Perception and sneaking. The question now, though, was what next?

Castor still hadn't shown himself, but I had no doubt that Amber and Macklin were *his.* The elite had obviously sent the pair to scout the way forward—a move I hadn't anticipated. Still, seeing as the two had failed to uncover me, there was no reason to alter my plans.

Easing back into the shadows, I waited to see what they would do next.

The pair crept into the room, not all the way, just a few feet, and swept the hall again with their eyes. Once more, they didn't find me.

A third scan, then a fourth—both of which came up negative. Finally, seemingly reassured, the pair unbent from their crouches. Glancing over his shoulder, Macklin whispered, "It's clear, boss."

A pause. "You're sure?"

I stilled my excitement. I recognized the voice. It was Castor, and from the sounds of it, he was somewhere in the corridor beyond the north entrance and showing more caution than I'd expected. Could the elite be nervous?

It certainly seemed so. *Now, now, Castor, don't be shy. Come on in.*

"Yes," Amber replied. "He isn't here."

"Our people?" Castor asked, not budging from wherever he waited.

"Dead," Macklin said flatly.

"What about traps? Have you found any?"

The pair exchanged glances, and Amber rolled her eyes. Macklin's response was more measured. "We're just about to look," he said.

"Well, get on with it, then," Castor snapped testily.

The scouts closed their eyes, no doubt activating some sort of trap detection ability. I watched on, curious to see if they would fare any better this time around. My thieving skill was significantly lower than my sneaking. Just how good were these scouts?

A second later, I had my answer.

Amber has spotted your traps!
Macklin has spotted your traps!

Huh, I grunted disappointedly. I clearly needed to work on my thieving skill more.

Both scouts' eyes snapped open, and even though they were nowhere near the closest trigger, they both jumped back in shock. "Damn," Amber exclaimed.

"What's wrong?" Castor demanded.

"There's at least twenty traps here," Macklin answered. "Enough to blow us all into nothingness." His eyes narrowed as he studied the glowing flecks of red only he could see. "We might be able to disable them," he added—somewhat reluctantly, I thought.

"Don't," Castor ordered. "I have a better idea. I'm coming in."

Macklin's eyes widened. "You're sure, boss?"

"Yes," Castor said, his voice growing louder as he drew closer. "If that bastard went to all the trouble of laying that many traps, you can bet your ass he is hiding somewhere close by, watching."

The elite's voice was filled with a confidence that set me on edge. *What is he planning now?* I wondered. I didn't know, but I suspected things were about to come to a head soon and set about renewing my buffs.

Your Dexterity has increased by +8 ranks for 20 minutes.
You have gained an encumbrance aura for 10 minutes.
You have blurred your form, making yourself 50% harder to see for 2 minutes.
You have trigger-cast quick mend.

A moment later, Castor appeared in the doorway with two figures in tow. My attention fixed on the elite. Even in the dimly lit great hall, he sparkled, covered from head to toe in an array of spelled defenses. Clearly, Castor was taking no chances.

"If it's a show he wants, let's give him one," he went on. "Let's see how he likes watching his friends burn."

My gaze shifted to the two men behind the possessed.

It was Lorn and Stormhammer.

✳   ✳   ✳

For a moment, I froze.

What were Lorn and Stormhammer doing here? A myriad of possibilities flashed through my mind, including the worst ones.

The pair had betrayed me again. Their torture had been a ploy. I'd been deceived.

Then, a third figure walked in—the warrior who'd fled earlier. In his hands were a pair of heavy chains. My thoughts still reeling, I followed the thick iron links to the other end, where they wrapped around the orc's and dwarf's hands.

They're prisoners.

The realization only made things worse. Now, my plan really was in shambles. If Lorn and Stormhammer were victims, I couldn't in good conscience let them die. I would have to save them.

Damn. Damn. And damn.

"You hear me, Taim?" Castor called out suddenly. "I'm holding the councilors hostage. If you don't do as I say, I'll walk them through the very traps you set for me. How does that sound?"

"Don't listen to—" Lorn began but got no further as the warrior cuffed him across the back of the head.

"Kill the bastard, Taim!" Stormhammer growled before he, too, was similarly silenced.

Castor laughed, but there was an edge to it. "I hold all the cards, Taim. Show yourself! Or your friends will pay!"

"Prime, what do we do?" Ghost asked.

I had no answer for her, lost for a moment in a sense of déjà vu. This situation was similar in many ways to the one I'd found myself in with the goblin goliath and the dire wolves.

The Fangtooths had held Aira's pups captive, and it was only through the dint of luck and carelessness on the part of the goblins that I'd been able to save them.

Somehow, I didn't think Castor would be nearly as careless.

But then, I thought, the fog of indecisiveness around my mind clearing, *I'm no longer the same player I was then.* A plan coalescing, I began casting.

"ANSWER ME, TAIM!" Castor screamed, the whites of his eyes filling with light—a golden, hot, hungry light. Was that a spell he was casting?

Macklin eyed his superior uneasily. "You're sure he is here, boss?"

"I am," Castor spat, specks of saliva flying from his mouth. "Last chance, Taim," he growled. "If you don't reveal yourself this instant, I'll—"

You have cast ventro.

"I'm here," I replied, projecting my voice so it floated out of the south entrance corridor. The four possess spun in that direction. Castor's hands clenched and unclenched, and I could see he itched to throw his magic at me. But he had no target—yet. "What do you want, Castor?" I asked.

"You!" he retorted. "Give yourself up and that unholy nether creature you've summoned."

"Hear that, Ghost? You're an unholy nether creature now."

"It's a step up from devil dog, I suppose," she said, sounding amused.

"And why should I do that," I replied, making no effort to conceal my incredulity. "You'll only kill me and the councilors after I do." While I spoke, I began a second casting.

"Oh, I will definitely kill you," he hissed. "Them, I will spare."

"I don't believe you."

"That's too bad because if you want them to live, you have no choice but to trust me," Castor spat.

"You're wrong, actually," I said and released the casting I held ready.

You have cast mass charm.
You have charmed 5 of 6 targets for 20 seconds.
You have failed to charm 1 of 6 targets. Note, targets protected by magic shields are immune to mental manipulation.

Not unexpectedly, I failed to charm Castor, but it was not him I had intended on bewitching anyway.

"*Attack,*" I barked, tugging on the mental leash I'd wrapped around the minds of the warrior and two scouts. Lorn and Stormhammer, I gave an altogether different command. "*Flee,*" I instructed the moment their chains fell free from the warrior's hands.

My five enthralled subjects burst into motion. In the meantime, I kept casting.

You have cast piercing strike, doubling the damage dealt on the next attack. You have cast whirlwind, increasing your attack speed by 100% for 3 seconds.

Drawing their weapons, the three possessed rushed toward Castor while the prisoners bolted out the north entrance. Castor didn't immediately notice—not until three steel blades clanged against his spelled defenses.

Your minions have failed to injure Castor. The target's shield has blocked their attacks.

"What are you imbeciles doing?" the elite roared, spinning around to glare at the trio.

The three, of course, remained mute. Thrusting his javelin forward, the warrior prodded at the elite's shield again.

"Stop that, you—" Castor began, then broke off.

He'd noticed the fleeing councilors, I suspected—which was my cue to enter the fray. Drawing psi, I shadow blinked.

You have teleported into Castor's shadow.

I emerged from the aether, cloaked in shadow and within striking distance of my target. Lunging forward, I struck simultaneously with ebonheart and faithful.

You have backstabbed Castor for 5x more damage! Piercing strike deactivated. You have backstabbed Castor for 2.5x more damage!
Your target's shield has blocked your attacks.
A hostile entity has detected you! You are no longer hidden.

My blades struck the magic dome surrounding the elite with the force of twin sledgehammers, but for all that, they barely seemed to dim its glow. Still, I succeeded in my intent—drawing Castor's attention away from the two fleeing figures.

"You *will* die!" he barked as he turned to face me. Flinging his arms upwards—and not toward me as I half-expected—Castor barked a single, guttural command. Suspecting nothing good would come from the elite's spell, I threw myself backward.

Unnecessarily, it turned out.

It was not an attack that launched from Castor's hands but a casting of an altogether different kind.

Castor has cast Light's Wrath.

The ceiling above the elite rippled as if it were a carpet. A hole formed, not to the prison level above, but to somewhere *other*, a place filled with Light— Light so thick and dense it manifested as roiling banks of clouds. The hole— a tear in reality, really—expanded rapidly until the entire hall was bathed in its harsh glare.

Then, the Light began condensing.

A level 208 Archon of Light has answered your foe's call!

I cursed softly, realizing what Castor was about. He was summoning a supernatural creature, one that was an elite in its own right.

One elite I could face, two I wasn't so sure.

Time to reevaluate, I decided. Racing to the far end of the room, I spared a moment to glance over my shoulder and check the north entrance. There was no sight of Lorn and Stormhammer—some good had come from my assault on Castor, then.

The pair would keep running right up until they regained control of their minds, and perhaps even then, they wouldn't stop. I'd done what I could to keep them safe. Their fates were now in their hands.

Ducking beneath a table, I turned back to face Castor. He was still lost in his casting with his arms spread and his gaze fixed upward. But it was the portal of Light that drew my attention.

It had contracted sharply, returning the hall to much of its former gloominess. From within, a figure descended.

A pair of feet appeared—cat-like, taloned, and with golden fur that yet retained the Light's luminescent cast. More of the summoned entity emerged. Two muscled thighs, a sculptured torso, clawed hands, and finally, a maned and squashed face reminiscent of a lion.

So that's an Archon of Light, I thought, staring at the lion-man. The creature's glowing eyes pulsed in time with Castor's, hinting at the summoner's bond with his pet.

Finished with his casting, Castor turned to survey the hall. Not seeing me, he gestured at the three possessed. "Get rid of these!" he ordered irritably.

The archon swung to face my minions. All this time, they had kept up their relentless attacks on Castor's shield, and even now, they did not turn to face the lion-man looming over them. The archon, easily twice the height of even the warrior, came to a halt behind the scouts.

One massive paw rose, then fell.

Your minion has died.

The lion-man's clawed hand tore through Amber, burning through her leather armor with frightening ease and rendering the flesh from her bones. Watching from the shadows, my eyes narrowed. The blow had not been purely physical. There had been an element of light damage accompanying it.

The archon struck again, claiming Macklin's life as easily as he had Amber's.

"Should we not help them?" Ghost asked.

I shook my head. *"No. As harsh as it sounds, it serves us better if they die. Let Castor kill them off. He'll have to face us alone then."*

The archon advanced on the last possessed. Sweeping both his arms downward, the lion-man clapped his hands against the side of the warrior's head with a resounding smack.

It split as easily as a melon.

I winced. *Damn, that thing is strong.*

Not a flicker of remorse graced Castor's face. Swinging around, he addressed the seemingly empty room. "You see that, Taim?" he sneered. "That's the death that awaits you. Now, will you keep lurking in the shadows, or will you show your face?"

I said nothing.

"Your ploy with the councilors was clever. What was that ability you used? Some sort of charm spell?" Turning about, he paced the length of the room, the archon following silently in his wake. "It seems I underestimated you. You're more than a simple thief." Spinning on his heel, Castor swept his gaze over the room.

A hostile entity has failed to detect you!

"But your parlor tricks will not save you," he continued. "Your *traps* will not save you. Did you think I forgot about them?" Raising his arm, Castor pointed at the center of the room—and the trapped area identified by Macklin and Amber.

Forked tongues of lightning, so bright I had to shield my eyes, arced across the hall from the elite's hands to the spot in question.

Castor has triggered a trap!
Castor has triggered a trap!
...
...

The twenty traps I'd laid in the center of the hall activated simultaneously. Poison clouds mushroomed. Bombs exploded. Lightning struck.

All without effect. Castor was too far away to feel their fury.

"Oh, what a lovely show," the elite snickered. "Primitive, though. Did you really think you could defeat me with such simple devices?"

"They worked well enough against Loskin," I said, again using ventro again to project my words so they emerged from the south corridor.

"You lie!" Castor said, whirling to face me—or the direction he thought me to be. "That was the hellspawn's doing!" I assumed he meant Adriel. "A worm like you could never expect to defeat the archlich."

Lowering his right arm behind his back, Castor discreetly waved his hand, a silent signal—and what should've been an unseen one, too—for the archon to advance into the corridor.

Safe on Castor's right flank, I smiled. He'd taken the bait. Perhaps I could still salvage some part of my plan. *"Get ready to manifest,"* I murmured to Ghost.

"Just say the word, Prime," she replied, her voice dripping with eagerness.

"Who told you?" I asked, playing for time. "Avery?" It couldn't be Avery, though. The last I'd seen him, he was dead in Regus' house, and I was sure Farren would never have resurrected him.

"Who told me doesn't matter," Castor said scornfully.

The archon passed through the hall's southern entrance, and I tensed, getting ready. *"Now, Ghost. It's time. Come out."*

"What matters is that I know you for what you are," Castor ranted. "A sniveling, conniving worm, incapable of facing a true opponent. When I'm done with—"

An archon has triggered a trap!

I grinned broadly as Castor's creature unwittingly walked into the *real* ambush. The traps I'd set in the great hall had been a decoy and only large enough to convince my foe of their authenticity.

In the south corridor, all forty or so trap elements activated near simultaneously, raining down an avalanche of destruction on the hapless archon. I'd been hoping to use the traps on Castor himself, of course, but the elite creature would do just as well.

An archon has died.

My gaze flickered back to Castor. The possessed was standing with his mouth agape, staring at the south entrance. For once, he'd been rendered speechless.

Ghost has taken the form of a level 202 stygian pyre wolf.

Glancing to my right, I exchanged nods with my familiar. We were ready. Rising to my feet, I shadow blinked.

It was time to put an end to Castor.

✳   ✳   ✳

You have teleported into Castor's shadow.

Emerging from the aether on Castor's left flank, I repeated my previous maneuver, striking at him first with ebonheart, then faithful.

Your target's shield has blocked your attacks.

My attacks were no more successful than they had been the first time around. This time, though, I did not break off. Empowering my blades with stamina, I dug in and kept bashing away at the elite.

You have cast whirlwind and piercing strike.
Your target's shield has blocked your attacks.

A snarl of outrage on his face, Castor swung to face me. I didn't let my eyes wander, but through the familiar bond, I sensed Ghost begin her charge. The elite had placed his back to her and wouldn't see her coming until too late. All I had to do was hold his attention until then.

Castor raised his arms.

I steeled myself for the expectant attack but didn't slow the tempo of my own assault. How long would it take to burn through Castor's shield? Too long if the brightness of the dome around him was any indication.

Electricity sparked in the elite's hands.

Castor has cast seeking storm.

I dodged left.

The maneuver was perfectly timed, but it didn't matter—the lightning followed me, arcing from Castor's hands to my chest.

You have been hit by a lightning bolt.
Your void armor has reduced the elemental damage incurred by 45%.
You have passed a magical resistance check! Castor has failed to stun you!
Void armor charge remaining: 92%.

I flew backward with the force of the blow but, thankfully, was not rendered immobile. Castor's brows drew down. "Why aren't you dead?" he demanded. "Or stunned?"

Not deigning to reply, I rose smoothly back to my feet and charged him anew.

Unfortunately, my attack did not perturb the elite at all. Shooing me away like I was some sort of fly, he unleashed a second lightning bolt.

I ducked beneath the projectile.

But once again, it didn't matter. The jagged bolt still found me.

You have been hit by a lightning bolt.
You have failed a magical resistance check! Castor has <u>stunned</u> you. Duration: 3 seconds.
Void armor charge remaining: 84%.

I fell face forward, my cheek smacking the ground. Electricity surged through me, setting my teeth chattering and my limbs trembling. I couldn't move, but I could still see—and out of the corner of my eye, I spotted Ghost.

The pyre wolf was crouched down on her haunches, ready to leap onto an unsuspecting Castor.

"No," I rasped.

Ghost stilled, her burning gaze flickering towards me. *"Why?"*

"Must... wait," I replied, not having the energy to explain further. If Ghost attacked Castor alone, he would only disable her the way he had me.

Unaware of the threat at his rear, the elite strolled toward me, electricity still sparking in his hands.

His booted feet came to a stop inches from my face. "Look at you," he scorned. "Pathetic."

Give me another second. Then we'll see who is—

A third bolt tore through me.

**You have been hit by a lightning bolt. Castor has <u>stunned</u> you.
Void armor charge remaining: 76%.**

Castor chuckled. "I like you this way, I think. Something about this position…" He laughed again. "I don't know. It just suits you, don't you think?"

"*Prime,*" Ghost growled. "*Let me attack!*"

"*No!*"

Castor squatted down. "I was going to kill you quickly, you know," he said lightly, "but now I think I will make you grovel first."

I still couldn't move, but I did my best to glare back at the elite with as much venom as I could muster.

"Ah, I see you still have some fight in you. But don't worry, that won't last." Reaching out, Castor let the palm of his hand hover above my face.

Knowing what was coming, I tensed.

It made no difference, though, as the bolt dove down into me at point-blank range.

**You have been hit by a lightning bolt. Castor has <u>stunned</u> you.
Void armor charge remaining: 68%.**

**Void thief triggered!
You have acquired the channeled spell <u>seeking storm (stolen)</u> from the possessed, Castor, and will retain memory of it for the next 12 hours. Seeking storm (stolen) is a tier 5 spell that allows you to unleash 10 lightning bolts at your chosen target. The projectiles can be released all at once or individually and can in no way be evaded or dodged.
Void siphon and negate activated!**

If I hadn't been stunned, I would've laughed. Castor had just made me immune to his spell, and he didn't even know it!

The elite frowned, perhaps seeing something in my gaze. "Find that funny, do you?" he growled.

"*Get ready, Ghost,*" I whispered. "*When I move, you do too.*"

"Well, you will learn, I promise," Castor continued as he rose to his feet. Pointing downward with both hands, the elite fired another round of bolts.

**You have been hit by a lightning bolt.
You have been hit by a lightning bolt.**

The projectiles passed through me, neither harming nor stunning me further. Castor didn't know that, though.

"I'm sorry. Did I hurt you?" he mocked. "When I'm done…"

I tuned him out.

The elite's words no longer mattered. Turning my focus inwards, I listened attentively to my body instead, waiting for the previous stun to wear off. Any moment now…

You are no longer stunned.

"*Now!*" I yelled. Closing my hands around the hilt of my blades, I surged upward. At the same time, Ghost bounded forward.

Castor's eyes rounded with shock. "How did you—"

I didn't let him finish. My swords flying faster than thought, I pounded on him.

Your target's shield has blocked your attacks.

My attacks didn't get through, of course. Castor's defenses were far from crippled, but the momentum of the battle had shifted, and the elite was on the back foot. Now, I only had to make sure he stayed that way.

Weaving psi and stamina, I kicked up the speed of my attacks a notch.

You have cast windborne, whirlwind, and piercing strike.
Your target's shield has blocked your attacks.
Your target's shield has blocked your attacks.
Your target's shield has...

...

Looking somewhat bewildered, the elite raised his hands, but before he could unleash whatever spell he prepared, Ghost bowled into him.

Your familiar has knocked down Castor.

The elite flew forward, thrown off his feet by the force of Ghost's assault. Having anticipated the attack, I neatly sidestepped as Castor's shield bubble rolled past.

Then, I pounced.

As did Ghost. Working in tandem, we rained down blows on the elite lying face down on the ground.

Your target's shield has blocked your attacks.
Your target's shield has blocked your attacks.
Your target's shield has...

...

It took longer than it should have for Castor to flip himself around and face us, and even then, he still appeared befuddled. Raising a hesitant hand, he unleashed a spell at me.

Castor has failed to harm you. You are immune to lightning bolts.

I didn't even blink or slow my assault as the spell fizzled against me. Castor would have done better to target Ghost. But now it was too late.

Your target's shield has been destroyed!

My lips twitched upward in a satisfied grin. I'd done it. The elite was done for. "Goodbye, Castor," I whispered and plunged ebonheart straight through his heart.

You have killed Castor with a fatal blow.

CHAPTER 408: MOPPING UP

I sagged down onto the corpse. "Well, that wasn't too hard, was it?" I murmured.

Ghost looked at me askance, unable to tell if I was joking.

Chuckling, I labored back to my feet and checked the waiting Game messages.

You and Ghost have reached level 204!
Your shortswords has reached rank 19, and your chi rank 17.

My skills had improved only minimally during the battle, but that was to be expected at this stage. Sadly, none of Ghost's skills had ranked up. She had gained a few levels in each, though. Sticking with my previous strategy, I invested in an attribute that would benefit us equally.

Your Magic has increased to rank 43. Other modifiers: +20 from items.

The additional magic would improve Ghost's maw attacks while strengthening my void armor at the same time. For now, it was a nice compromise, but I knew, sooner or later, I would have to switch my focus back to Mind and Dexterity.

"Prime, incoming."

Looking up, I saw the pyre wolf sitting erect and staring at the north entrance. Glancing that way myself, I frowned.

The archway was empty. *"What is it?"* I asked.

"Listen," she replied.

Trusting her—Ghost's senses were as keen as mine—I strained my ears. At first, I heard nothing. Then, I caught the sound of soft footfalls.

Someone was trying to sneak up on us.

Moving as quietly, if not quieter, I edged up to the archway and peered around the edge.

Two figures were advancing on the great hall, their movements comically slow. *Lorn and Stormhammer.* I relaxed. "There's no need for that, councilors," I said, stepping out in the open.

The pair froze.

Smiling broadly, I waved them forward. "Come on in. Castor's dead."

✳   ✳   ✳

Stormhammer didn't believe me, not until he saw the corpse himself, and then he could barely contain his glee. "You did it!" he chortled. "I can't believe you actually did it!"

"Thanks," I said with a lopsided grin. "Your confidence is inspiring."

Oblivious to my tone, Stormhammer nodded. "It would've been a tough ask for anyone," he added sagely. "Well done."

Deciding to change the subject, I eyed the weapons the pair were carrying. "What were you going to do with those?"

Lorn looked down at his hands and only then seemed to realize what was in them. "Oh. We were coming to help."

I could have said a dozen different things at the moment—about how foolish that would've been, not to mention counterproductive, I'd just freed them, after all—but looking at Lorn's flushed face, I saw that he knew all that already. "I appreciate the thought," I said finally, then gestured toward the north corridor. "Did you run across anyone else back there?"

Lorn shook his head, still looking uncommonly flustered.

"Good." It wasn't a guarantee that the level was clear, but it did reinforce my belief that all the possessed were dead, and unfortunately, I didn't have time to conduct a thorough search just yet. "How did Castor capture you two, anyway?"

"He came through the hatch not long after you left," Stormhammer answered. "I'm not sure who was more surprised—him or us. But before the bastard could attack, he fell afoul of your traps." The dwarf grinned. "Our people cleared out in a hurry after that."

"What about Dirk?" I asked.

"We killed him before we ran from Castor," Lorn said, rejoining the conversation. He reflected for a moment. "Although now that I think about it, I'm not convinced the elite was all that interested in us."

Stormhammer scowled at him. "Oh, yeah? Then what do you think he was there for? To hand out flowers, maybe?"

"Of course not," Lorn said coldly. "It could be—"

"You said your people cleared out," I interjected. "How did Castor get you two, then?"

The pair exchanged glances, and this time, even Stormhammer had the grace to look sheepish. "We stayed behind to face the bastard," the dwarf mumbled. "It was my idea."

I winced.

He reddened. "I'll admit it was foolish."

Sighing inwardly, I turned back to Lorn. "Why do you think Castor entered the prison level?"

The orc rubbed his chin. "Honestly? I'm not sure. But the moment the elite came up the hatch, he only had eyes for the dead possessed." He paused. "Seeing their corpses seemed to scare him."

Stormhammer snorted. "You think he was running?" he scoffed. "Castor was a right smug bastard. He'd never run!"

Ignoring the thane, Lorn went on, "It was only after we killed Dirk that Castor turned on us, and then it was only to question us. After which, he brought us here. The rest you know."

"Reinforcements," I concluded. "Castor was looking for reinforcements."

The idea that the elite—'a right smug bastard' as the thane labeled him— might go seeking help before facing me had not occurred to me, and it should have. If it had, I could've laid deadlier traps around the hatch and ended all this sooner.

"Sorry, I should have realized he might do that," I muttered.

Lorn shrugged. "No one is blaming you, and everything turned out well in the end."

Stormhammer clamped a hand on my shoulder. "You did well, Taim. No doubt about it. Thanks to you, New Haven is free again."

"Not entirely," I replied. "Not yet, anyway. Elron's men still have to —"

"Mere mopping up," Stormhammer said, stopping me. "I have no doubt the marshal is up to the task."

"Still, we should return to the fortress and reveal ourselves," Lorn added. "It may reduce the loss of life up there."

"Agreed," I said. Turning around, I led the way. "Let's go."

✳   ✳   ✳

I'd been hoping to explore the possessed complex further after killing Castor—finding the underground tunnel to the archlich's court was high on my list of priorities—but Lorn was right. The sooner he and Stormhammer returned to the city above, the fewer lives would be lost restoring New Haven to their rule.

On our way to the hatch, we ran across the rest of the prisoners. Having banded together, they had decided to storm the possessed's lair and rescue their recaptured leaders. Whatever foolishness had afflicted Stormhammer and Lorn was obviously catching.

While the councilors restored order amongst their men, I took stock of our new 'company.' All told, we numbered more than fifty. Dirk had done his job well, and every single one of the former prisoners was hale and hearty.

Even better, according to Stormhammer and Lorn, their fellow prisoners were all members of their elite personal guards. And while no one was fully kitted out, everyone had a weapon to hand.

In short order, we got going again and spilled out onto the prison level. Then began the laborious task of fighting our way out.

I let Ghost take point.

She needed the training and experience more than I did. Hanging back, I fell into the role of observer, only intervening with my mental tricks when necessary. One after the other, the pyre wolf, orcs, and dwarves stormed the chain of guardrooms protecting the exit.

Under my watchful gaze, we lost no one.

Tackling the storeroom level went equally well. None of the roving infantry patrols were a match for the company—now fully outfitted in the dead guards' armor and weapons—not to mention Ghost, and to no one's surprise, we emerged on the ground floor of Cilia's fortress brimming with confidence and with no casualties to speak of.

There, we found a force, one thousand strong, waiting.

✳   ✳   ✳

Ghost's magma maw and ash armor have reached rank 6, and her stygian claws and telepathy rank 7.

The sight of the enemy did not daunt the company. The men's blood was up, and despite the numberless rows of soldiers arrayed against them, they were eager to charge.

"We should attack," Stormhammer urged, gripping the hilt of his axe tightly. The weapon was slick with blood, having fed deeply in the subterranean levels.

"We don't know who they are," Lorn countered.

"They're dark elf soldiers!" Stormhammer growled. "That's enough for me."

"They could be Elron's men," Lorn pointed out.

"Ha! Here so quickly? Not likely," Stormhammer scoffed. "Besides, if the marshal was here, he would be at the front of that lot. He always did fancy leading from the fore."

"That's true," Lorn conceded. "Maybe we should—"

"Wait," I ordered, pushing my way to the front from where I'd been guarding the company's rear.

Breaking off, the two councilors turned to face me. "What do you think, Taim?" Lorn asked quietly.

I didn't answer immediately. Drawing to a halt beside Ghost, I turned to study the force waiting ahead. The enemy—if that's what they were—were all dark elves. They occupied the entirety of the corridor, an unbreachable barrier. There would be no getting around them, I realized. The only way past would be *through*, and despite his brash words, I doubted even Stormhammer relished the prospect.

My gaze fell on the first row of soldiers. They stood braced to attention some twenty yards away, making no move to attack, and seemed just as confused as we were.

Are they friend or foe? I could almost see them thinking.

Many of the dark elves' gazes rested on Stormhammer and Lorn—clearly recognizing them—and no few on me. Unfortunately, what they made of our presence here was less certain.

Friends or foes, I wondered.

"Do either of you recognize anyone?" I asked out of the side of my mouth while I searched for an officer.

Lorn and Stormhammer shook their heads.

"Damn," I muttered. There was no officer in attendance either, not that I could see, anyway.

"Wasn't Algar the name of the marshal's aide?" Ghost asked suddenly.

I glanced at her curiously. The pyre wolf had not met the human captain, I recalled, but I'd mentioned him more than once to her. *"That's right. Why do you ask?"*

"There's someone going by that name a hundred rows back."

I stared at her blankly for a moment, then realization hit. *Of course.* We were out of the dampening field; Ghost had used her mindsight. But still... to have searched nearly a thousand minds and to have pinpointed Algar's exact location in such a short span of time was a remarkable feat.

"Nicely spotted," I murmured. "I think they're friends," I said to the councilors. I began to turn away, then paused. "Don't do anything rash," I warned, looking pointedly at Stormhammer.

Not waiting for the thane's response, I swung around to face the dark elves. "You there!" I said, gesturing to the senior-most looking soldier, "Fetch Algar. Tell him Taim is here."

The soldier stared at me blankly.

"Move, man! Or do you want this rebellion to be for nothing?"

The dark elf still didn't move.

I sighed. "Tell Algar Castor is dead. Tell him that *all* the possessed are dead."

That finally got the soldier moving.

✳　✳　✳

Matters resolved quickly after that.

In what must have been record time, the soldier shoved his way through the rear of the column and returned just as quickly with Captain Algar in tow.

"Taim!" the human exclaimed on seeing me. His gaze darted to my companions, and he bowed hastily. "Thane Stormhammer. Chief Lorn." He fell silent for a second, seemingly at a loss for words, before blurting, "How?"

I smiled. "I found them in the prison cells below," I replied, assuming his oh-so-succinct question pertained to Lorn and Stormhammer's presence.

"But what were—" the captain began.

"We can discuss all of that later in the comfort of the council chamber," Stormhammer interjected. He glanced pointedly at the soldiers still blockading the corridor. "In the meantime...?"

Algar inclined his head. "Of course. My apologies, thane." He spun on his heel. "Follow me if you please. The marshal will be anxious to hear what you have to say.

Word of our victory traveled fast, and a host of orcish and dwarven dignitaries waylaid us en route to the council hall. Before the chief, thane, or myself had a chance to exchange more than curt farewells, the pair were swept away.

"We must talk later," Lorn called over his shoulder. "The council will meet in the morning. Make sure you are there."

"I'll be there," I shouted back before he disappeared from sight.

"Still creating a stir wherever you go, I see," a quiet voice said from behind.

I turned around. Despite the crowds filling the corridor, everyone was giving me—or rather Ghost—a wide berth, and I picked Elron out easily. He was the only one who'd dared the empty space around us. "Elron," I greeted.

"And what's this?" the marshal asked, sizing up Ghost.

"*She* is my... companion. And *she* can understand everything you say." In an aside to Ghost, I added, *"Perhaps it's time I put a chain on you. I'm getting drearily tired of explaining all that."*

Not unsurprisingly, Ghost didn't dignify my comment with a response.

"Ah. I see," Elron said, walking closer. "And what *is* she?"

"A pyre wolf," I replied blandly, knowing full well the term would mean little to him.

Elron's lips curved upward. "Still keeping your cards close, Taim?"

"Always," I said with a grin.

Striding forward, the marshal knelt before Ghost, showing an impressive lack of fear. "Does she have a name?"

"You can call her Ghost."

Elron stretched out his arm. "It's a pleasure to meet you, Ghost."

For a moment, I was afraid the pyre wolf was going to lick him—Ghost huffed disdainfully as she caught the stray thought—but instead, she stuck out her paw and placed it in Elron's waiting hand.

The marshal shook the paw gravely, his sharp intake of breath the only sign he'd noticed what I half-hoped he wouldn't. Sighing, I waited for the inevitable question.

"She is of stygian descent?" Elron asked as he rose to his feet.

"Only partly," I hedged.

A troubled look crossed Elron's face.

"Ghost can be trusted," I added. "As much as I can be."

The marshal pursed his lips and then nodded sharply, dismissing the matter. "I will take your word for it." He leaned forward. "Is it true, then? Is Castor really dead?"

I smiled. I had been wondering when he'd get around to asking. "He is— as are the other fifty possessed under his command."

The marshal stepped back, his eyes dancing with joy. "Then it's done," he breathed. "We've won."

I clasped his hand. "Yes, we have, my friend. New Haven is free at last."

✴   ✴   ✴

I was ushered away then, and tired from the day's exertions, I did not protest as the marshal escorted me to one of the many vacant rooms in the fortress.

"How did things go on your end?" I asked as we passed through one of the quieter fortress corridors.

"As well as could be expected," Elron replied. "There were some casualties, but once the First's people realized no help was forthcoming, many of her officers surrendered without a fight. I've regained full control of the army."

"Good. What about the Cilia's supporters? Do you have them all in custody?"

He hesitated. "Only some," he admitted. "Many died during the fighting. And others are... problematic."

"Problematic?" I asked sharply. "Problematic, how?"

"They come from prominent families and with no clear evidence of wrongdoing on their part—" he shrugged—"their fate will be for the council to decide."

I frowned but nodded, understanding his predicament. "What about Sienna?"

"*Her*, we have," he said with satisfaction as we came to a stop before an ornate door. "This is yours."

"Fancy," I remarked.

He smiled. "Nothing but the best for the savior of New Haven."

I grunted. "I'll see you in the morning?"

He nodded. "First thing. The council meets then." He pushed open the door. "Good night, Taim."

"Good night, Marshal," I replied and entered the room with Ghost in tow. Turning around, I studied my new quarters. Fancy was an understatement. It was downright sumptuous.

"Well, Ghost," I said, stifling a yawn. "I'd say we've earned it." I turned to face her. "Wouldn't you?"

But the pyre wolf was already asleep, stretched out across the full length of the bed.

I shook my head ruefully—it seemed my snide comments from earlier were not going to go unpunished. I was as tired as my familiar, but before I could rest, there was one thing that needed doing: casting spellhold.

My void armor still retained memory of Castor's spell, seeking storm, though it would not keep for much longer, and as powerful as the spell had proved, I was sure it would come in handy at some future point.

Letting my magic form the weaves of the seeking storm spell, I directed the casting into the ring on my finger.

Spellhold enchantment activated.
You have successfully stored the <u>seeking storm</u> spell in the ring, mage's surprise. This spell may now be trigger-cast when required.

Unrolling a sleep sack, I lay down on the floor. It had been a long day, and while much of it had not turned out as I'd anticipated, Ghost and I could be proud of what we had achieved.

Smiling contentedly, I drifted off to sleep.

✳ ✳ ✳

I awoke to a stinging sensation on my cheek. Opening my eyes, I glared at my companion. She'd licked me.

"Oow," I complained, rubbing furiously at the burned patch of skin. "That hurt."

Ghost was unrepentant. *"Morning, Prime,"* she said brightly. *"It's time we got going."*

"It's too early," I objected. "Let me sleep for another—"

"It's past noon," Ghost interjected.

I blinked. "It can't be. Elron would've—"

"The marshal has come and gone twice already."

I sat up. "Twice? Why didn't you wake me?"

She shook her shoulders in a lupine version of a shrug. *"You were exhausted and needed sleep."*

"Then why wake me now?"

"Because you've slept enough," she retorted, and before I could protest, added, *"And because the marshal is back again."*

Right on cue, a knock sounded on the door. "Taim? Are you awake? It's Elron. We need to get going."

Sighing, I rose to my feet. "Coming," I called. "Be there in a minute."

A pause. "You better hurry. The council is already in session."

✳ ✳ ✳

Thirty minutes later, Elron and I were outside the council chamber and staring at its new doors—doors that had been conspicuously reinforced after my last memorable visit.

"Are you ready?" the marshal asked, looking me over.

I nodded. My disguise as Taim was back in place and my thoughts fresh and sharp. Ghost had been right; I'd needed to sleep.

Elron glanced to my left and shifted uncomfortably. "It might be better if..."

"She's coming with me," I said firmly before he could complete the thought. Ghost had spent long enough as a disembodied spirit and now that the New Haveners knew about her, I saw no reason to hide her existence from them.

"Alright," Elron conceded. "But some on the council may not take kindly to her presence." He turned to the guards. "Let us through."

Wordlessly, the pair swept aside the doors and gestured us forward. Following on the marshal's heels, Ghost and I entered the chamber.

175

The council hall itself had not changed in the intervening period. Magelights hung from the rafters and guards lined the walls, and once more I found myself facing the council across a large oak table.

This time, though, only three of the four seats were occupied.

Lorn and Stormhammer rose at my entrance, the third figure—a human—did not. It was not Sienna, which did not surprise me. I had expected the high lord—or was that former high lord?—to lose her place on the council.

This must be the new human representative, I thought, studying the heavy-set man curiously. There was no warmth in his gaze and his clothes were even more ornate than Sienna's had been.

"Welcome, Taim," Lorn greeted warmly. "I trust you slept well?"

"I did, and my apologies for arriving late. I overslept."

Stormhammer grunted. "You missed nothing. Just a whole lot of hot air and pointless arguments," he said with a glare in the direction of the seated human.

The man ignored him, his eyes fixed on Ghost. "What is that animal doing here?" Waving a jewel-ladened hand, he gestured the guards forward. "Get it out!"

"Who is that fool?" Ghost asked, baring her teeth.

My attention on the soldiers, I didn't answer. Many shifted uncertainly and a few fingered their weapons, but before any could try fulfilling the new councilor's order, Elron waved them back and they settled down.

"Ghost stays," Stormhammer growled.

The human stared at him incredulously. "Ghost? It has a *name?*"

"The pyre wolf is a friend," Lorn said. "If not for her and Taim, we'd still be imprisoned by the possessed."

The human's lips compressed, and I got the distinct impression he thought that would've been a good thing.

"Do we need to put the matter to a vote?" Lorn asked coldly, perhaps sensing the same thing.

"You'll lose," Stormhammer added—somewhat gleefully, I thought.

The human's mouth twisted sourly. "Very well. It can stay."

My eyes narrowed, having had about enough of the man's insults but before I could say anything, Elron spoke up. "Perhaps some introductions are in order, high lord? I don't believe you and Taim have met."

"Yes, yes, that's true," the human said. Leaning back in his chair, he offered what was patently a false smile. "I'm High Lord Carnien, the new human councilor and successor of our dearly departed Sienna."

I didn't return the greeting. "What happened to Sienna?" I asked bluntly.

"She was killed last night," Elron said.

"*Murdered,* Marshal, not killed," Carnien said, stressing the word. "Are you finally ready to deliver your report on the investigation?"

Placing his arms behind his back, Elron pressed his hands together. "The findings are... inconclusive."

"Inconclusive," Carnien crowed. "How predictable!"

My gaze flitted between the two men. "What investigation and why is there one?" I asked.

"Sienna died while in the custody of my men," Elron answered.

Carnien slapped the palm of his hand down on the table. "Again, with the euphemisms, Marshal. She didn't just die, she was murdered. And right now, the list of suspects isn't all that long."

Elron stiffened. "It wasn't any of my men."

"Well, *someone* killed her," Carnien retorted. "If it was a mysterious third party that did the deed—as you've been insisting all along—why have we seen no evidence of them? Is it because you haven't been able to find them or because there is no one to be found? One makes you incompetent, the other complicit."

For a rare moment, the marshal's control slipped and unbridled rage shone in his eyes.

"That's enough, Carnien," Lorn said sharply. "No one here is accusing the marshal."

"Well, someone should," the high lord spat. "Like I said before, he is unfit for Cilia's seat. The position should go to Minakawa!"

It took me a moment to parse Carnien's words and when I did, I turned to Elron. "*You* are going to be the new First?" I asked in a tone too low to carry to the councilors. Not that they would have noticed anyway. Carnien's words had sparked another argument between the three.

"Not by choice," Elron replied. "And not if Carnien has any say in the matter." He glanced at me sideways. "After some of the dark elf families nominated Minakawa, I had no choice but to put forward my own name as well. There is no way that snake can be allowed onto the council."

I couldn't agree more. "But I don't understand. Why is Minakawa *even* alive?"

Elron snorted. "The coward was one of the first to surrender. He switched allegiance the moment he heard Cilia was dead."

My lips turned down. I'd woken up this morning, reinvigorated, and expecting to spend the day in tough—but fair—negotiations with the council. I'd already secured Lorn's and Stormhammer's commitment when it came to the one thousand soldiers, but there was so much more New Haven had to offer House Wolf—and I, them—and I'd been looking forward to the opportunity of discussing matters with the council.

Instead, I'd turned up to witness another power struggle.

Because that was all this was—a gambit by Carnien, Minakawa, and their allies to take over the council.

"And him!" Carnien suddenly shouted. Glancing up, I saw the councilor's venomous gaze was fixed on me. "By your precious marshal's own admission, he assassinated the First. What is he doing free? He should be languishing in a cell, not walking these hallowed halls!"

I laughed.

I couldn't help it. *He can't be serious, can he?* Surely, not even the human high lord was daft enough to believe he had any chance of throwing me in prison?

Stormhammer pounded the table with two closed fists. "Enough!" he roared. "We've listened to enough of your damnable nonsense for one day, Carnien. No one is imprisoning Taim. Nor will Lorn or I disallow the marshal's nomination. His candidacy stays. Now, I'll ask you for the last time, will you accede to Elron's confirmation as First?"

The high lord stared at the thane, drawing out the moment. "No," he said succinctly.

The dwarf's face grew red, and he flexed his hands. "Why, you miserable, no-good, misbegotten..." The thane continued to spew insults, but he did no more than that and despite his clear desire to throttle the life out of the other councilor, he made no move toward him.

Carnien jumped to his feet. "I will not be spoken to like that, you pompous fool!"

Sighing, I turned back to Elron as the councilors became embroiled in another argument. "Why do Lorn and Stormhammer need him to agree? Can't they overrule him and confirm you as First anyway?"

The marshal shook his head. "When it comes to the appointment of new councilors, the vote must be unanimous. I can't be made First without the support of *all* the existing councilors. What's more, until the council is complete again, no other matter can be brought before it."

"Then why in hells did Lorn and Stormhammer confirm *him* as the new high lord?" I asked in frustration.

Elron's expression grew pained. "Because while it is up to the council to confirm a councilor, it is the city's families that decides the candidates. The human families put only one candidate forward—Carnien. In this case, both tradition and law dictate the council adhere to their decision." He shrugged. "Lorn and Stormhammer had no choice but to confirm Carnien."

"I see," I muttered. "And I'm guessing both Carnien and Minakawa are cut from the same cloth?

"If you mean, are they both fools who would do anything for power, including going to bed with the possessed, then, yes, they are."

"Hmm." Bowing my head, I rubbed at my temples, finally understanding the full scope of the predicament facing the council.

"In fact," Elron mused, "I'm fairly certain it was Carnien who had Sienna killed. He always wanted her seat. His impatience must've got the better of him. He shook his head. "The fool. If he only waited, the seat would've been his anyway after she was convicted and deposed."

I looked up. "How sure are you of that?" I asked sharply.

Elron glanced at me. "Of what?"

"That Carnien killed Sienna."

"As sure as I can be without proof. Why?"

I ignored the question. "Are you willing to bet your council seat on it?"

The marshal hesitated, then nodded curtly. "I am."

"Good," I murmured. "Don't let the guards interfere."

He frowned. "Interfere with what?"

I didn't answer. He would find out soon enough. Striding forward, I wrapped my right hand around ebonheart's hilt, and even through the councilor's heated conversation, the hiss of steel was unmistakable.

Day Thirty in Draven's Reach

All eyes in the room were on me, and along the edges, I sensed the guards jerk into belated movement.

"Back," the marshal snapped. "Hold your positions."

Thank you, Elron. Once more, the marshal was showing me more trust than warranted. *"Ready Ghost?"*

"I am," she replied serenely, keeping pace beside me.

"What is the meaning of this?" Carnien demanded shrilly as I advanced on the councilors with naked blade in hand. Lorn and Stormhammer, perhaps knowing me better, said nothing, but they, too, looked concerned.

Reaching the oak council table, I didn't stop and instead leaped atop it while Ghost flowed around. "I've had just enough of this nonsense," I said, strolling leisurely across the table. "Elron and I didn't work so hard just to replace one tinpot dictator with another."

Stopping in front of Carnien, I held the tip of ebonheart at his throat.

"What are you doing?" he cried stridently. "You can't threaten me, it's illegal!"

"Of course I can," I replied lightly. "In case you haven't noticed, I'm not from New Haven, nor am I bound by its laws." Ghost completed her half-circuit around the table, and coming to a halt behind the councilor, rested her head atop his shoulder.

Carnien shrieked. "Lorn! Stormhammer!" he gasped. "You can't let him do this. Help me!"

Orc and dwarf stayed silent.

I smiled. "No one is coming to rescue you, Carnien. It's just you and me." Leaning forward, I rested an elbow on one knee. "The marshal told me something quite interesting just now. Do you want to know what?"

"No!" he screamed.

"He tells me he thinks you had Sienna killed," I said, paying him no mind. "And you know what?" I asked, my expression growing colder, "I believe him. Tell me, Carnien, did you murder the high lord?"

"No!" he yelped. "There's no proof. The marshal himself told you so."

Ignoring the councilor once more, I turned to Ghost. "Is he telling the truth?" I asked loud enough that even the most hard-of-hearing guard couldn't fail to hear me.

In an unmistakable gesture of denial, Ghost sat on her haunches and shook her massive head.

"Well, there you go," I said, turning back to Carnien. "Ghost just read your mind, and she thinks you're lying."

"What? No! Impossible," he sputtered.

I pressed the black blade deeper into his throat. "I want every last detail. Or I promise you, you won't live to see tomorrow."

✳   ✳   ✳

Where Ghost's word alone might not have been enough to convince the skeptics, I knew a confession from Carnien's own mouth might, which is why I pushed him for the details.

It took some time and a few more salacious revelations of Carnien's thoughts by Ghost before the new high lord finally cracked and spilled everything.

It made for a gory tale, but in the end, it turned out to be a story as old as time.

Carnien had wanted power for himself and, seeing an opportunity, had grasped it, not caring what happened in the process or who got hurt. There was no conspiracy, nor were any possessed involved—as I half-feared there might be—and no treachery beyond his own.

In fact, the only remarkable thing about Carnien's tale was the assassin he'd employed. He or she was unusually gifted. To sneak into a room full of guards, kill Sienna, and slip back out, all unseen, well... that was no small feat.

I withdrew my blade when the big man finally sputtered to a stop. "You've got enough?" I asked the marshal.

"Every man here heard the high lord confess to his misdeeds," Elron said, raising his voice and playing to the audience as I had. "Didn't you?"

The soldiers nodded and yelled in affirmation.

The marshal turned back to me. "We have enough," he confirmed.

"Take him away," Stormhammer said, throwing Carnien a look of disgust.

Rushing to do the thane's bidding, two guards dragged the high lord— former high lord now, I expected—away. Jumping off the table, I faced the councilors. "Now what?"

Lorn sighed. "Now, we have a new headache."

I opened my mouth to protest, but Lorn raised a hand, stopping me. "I'm not saying I disapprove of what you've done, but sometimes I wish your methods were... less direct."

Stormhammer chuckled. "Oh, I don't know. I quite enjoyed the way Taim handled that buffoon."

Lorn threw him a look. "You would. But the human families might not once they hear what's gone on here." He glanced back at me. "They will have to be informed and another candidate for high lord put forward. And under the circumstances, that might take time."

I pursed my lips. "Speak plainly, Lorn. What are you saying?"

He sucked in a breath. "Until the council is fully reconstituted, New Haven can't honor the pledge Stormhammer and I made to you, nor can we discuss any other matters of significance. We will have to wait for the new high lord to be appointed."

"I see," I muttered. "And how long will that take?"

He shrugged eloquently. "A day? Two? No more than that, I hope. But it really depends on the human families."

I bowed my head, thinking. Two days I could manage, but no longer than that. Draven would be awaiting me and besides, I was also anxious to return to the Pack. "I'll wait," I said finally.

"Thank you," Lorn said, breathing easier.

"Are you two not forgetting something?" Stormhammer interjected.

Lorn and I turned to him questioningly.

"We may have to await on the human families for the new high lord, but in the meantime—" the thane gestured to Elron—"we have a new First to appoint."

✳   ✳   ✳

The ceremony confirming Elron as the dark elves' First was blessedly short. Immediately thereafter, all three councilors were bombarded with queries from the city's families, and I was left to my own devices.

Not quite ready to return to my room, I took to the streets.

I had no particular destination in mind and instead, with Ghost by my side, wandered aimlessly for hours. We were recognized, of course—at least Ghost was—and to my surprise, we received more grateful nods and smiles than we did glares and muttered oaths.

Elron's soldiers were everywhere, mostly on cleaning duty, clearing debris, and restoring broken structures. The marshal had made light of the opposition they'd face, but judging from the amount of wreckage I witnessed, the fighting in the streets had been intense.

It was the sight of New Haven's citizens on the streets again that I found the most satisfying, though.

Now that the curfew had been lifted, the ordinary people of the city were enjoying their restored freedom. Meandering through the crowds, I smiled in true pleasure. No matter what came of the upcoming negotiations with the city's council, it did not take away from what Ghost and I had achieved. We'd left New Haven a better place.

And that's about all I can truly hope for these days.

"Deep thoughts, mister?"

Coming to a halt, I glanced over my shoulder. A young human girl—she couldn't be older than sixteen—was addressing me. Her hands and face were ingrained with enough dirt that I suspected she rarely, if ever, bathed. Her clothes were tattered, and her limbs were undernourished.

A street kid, I thought. Her eyes, though, were bright and gleamed with cunning. *A smart one.*

"Dangerous that," the waif continued, a hint of menace underscoring her tone. "Especially on these streets."

At the girl's not-so-subtle prompting, I glanced around. Lost in thought, I'd turned down a dark alley. To my eyes, the street was as brightly lit as any other, but to most, it would appear full of shadows, which was why the alley was empty—other than for Ghost, myself, and the girl, of course.

Am I about to be mugged?

I blinked, finding the notion hard to credit. *Perhaps I've overestimated this one's intelligence.* Even if the waif *could* take me, there was still Ghost to consider, not to mention the dozens of soldiers within easy shouting distance. She would not succeed, not on her own.

"She's alone," Ghost said, anticipating me.

I nodded imperceptibly. "Not today, kid," I said with a weary smile. "And not me. Find someone else to rob."

The girl laughed. "I thought players were more perceptive than that. I'm no robber."

"She's armed," Ghost said.

My eyes narrowed, spotting the dagger sheathed along the inside of the girl's forearm. The shirt she wore covered it, but it could not disguise the telltale bulge entirely. And now that I looked carefully, I saw the girl's clothes weren't as worn out as I'd originally assumed.

They'd only been made to look that way. The dirt under her fingers was real though, as was her malnourishment.

"Minakawa sent me," she added when I didn't immediately respond.

Not a thief. Armed. And disguised to look innocuous.

"You're an assassin," I said, connecting the dots.

She beamed. "Bingo."

Snarling, Ghost stepped forward, placing herself between me and the girl.

"Whoa. Hold on a minute. I'm not here to kill you. Tell your dog to back down."

Baring her fangs, the pyre wolf let droplets of flaming saliva drip onto the ground.

The assassin gulped. "Really. I'm not," she protested, her eyes fixed on the sizzling stone underfoot.

"Ease up, Ghost."

"Why?" she growled back.

"Well, for one, she didn't refer to you as 'it,'" I said lightly, then added more seriously, *"I don't think she means us any harm. Not yet."*

Ghost huffed in disdain but did as I asked. Sitting down, she rested her head on her forepaws and watched the girl through an unblinking stare.

I addressed the girl again. "Aren't you a little too young to be an assassin?"

"I'm twenty," she replied stiffly.

"Huh. Not young at all." I folded my arms, making further connections. "I take it you're also the one Carnien hired to murder Sienna?"

"I am," she replied matter-of-factly.

"How did you do it?"

Her eyes narrowed. *"That's* the first thing you want to ask me? Not, why am I here, or why I haven't killed you yet?"

I snorted. "You couldn't kill me even if I decided to let you try."

She grinned. "You're probably right."

I frowned. "Then why are you here?"

Her grin broadened. "Oh, so now you want to know?"

My frown deepened. The girl was beginning to get on my nerves. "Talk," I growled. "Last chance."

Her grin faded. "Minakawa paid me to kill you." Ghost's ears flickered up. Not missing the wolf's reaction, the assassin added hastily, "But I'm not going to. Players are too dangerous to tangle with."

"So, you *didn't* take his money?" I asked skeptically.

Her smile returned. "Oh, I did, but I'm not going through with the job."

"So you said already. But you still haven't told me why you're here." I paused, a thought occurring. "Please don't tell me you've gone through all the trouble of tracking me down in the hopes of extorting more money?" I threw her a pained look. "Did you think I'd pay you *not* to kill me?"

She blushed, giving herself away.

I sighed. "I see. Well, you're not going to get anything from me, so you best run along."

Ghost lifted her head. *"You're letting her go?"*

"I am."

"But she's a threat!" she exclaimed indignantly. *"The girl's admitted to being paid to kill you."*

"She's hardly a threat, Ghost."

"But what if she comes back when you're asleep? She's a self-confessed assassin!"

I rolled my eyes. *"If it's escaped your attention, so am I at times."*

"What you do is different," she protested.

"Sometimes, I'm not at all certain it is," I murmured. *"Besides, you're forgetting I met Sienna. She was about as nice a person as Cilia. I won't hold her murder against the girl. And if she has committed any other crimes, really, I don't want to know about them."*

No matter what the assassin claimed her age to be, she looked entirely too young for me to want her blood on my conscience.

"You're too soft," Ghost accused.

I laughed. *"I doubt many will agree with you there, Ghost."* Turning my back on the girl—*young woman*, I corrected—I strode away.

"Wait!" she called suddenly.

Sighing, I swung back around. "What is it now?"

"There's another reason I sought you out..."

I gestured impatiently with my hand. "Yes? And what is it? Spit it out."

She shifted uncomfortably and was silent for so long I didn't think she was going to answer, but just as I thought about leaving again, she spoke.

"The Adjudicator said I should find you."

I froze.

I hadn't heard right. I *couldn't* have. "Say that again," I whispered.

"The Adjudicator, he asked me to—"

You have teleported 4 yards.

I blurred into motion, moving so quickly the young assassin didn't realize what was going on until she felt ebonheart digging into her skin.

"The Adjudicator?" I growled, yanking her head back with my left hand. "Who told you to use that name?"

"What?" she sputtered, her eyes growing wide with fear. But it was only pretend-fear, I realized as I spotted her right hand inch closer to the dagger concealed along the inside of her left arm.

"Don't," I warned. "I know about the blade. If you draw it, you're dead."

Still, she scowled. "What do you want?"

I pressed ebonheart into her neck. "Tell me who told you about the Adjudicator."

"No one!"

"You're lying," I hissed.

"I'm not," she protested. "No one told me. The Game spoke in my mind. It told me to find you. It said if I did, I'd be rewarded."

The Game?

"I thought it meant money. Look, just let me go, please. If I knew you were this batshit crazy, I never would've—"

"Shut up," I ordered. No sooner than she did so, I reached out with my will and analyzed her.

The target is Nyra, a human.

That Adjudicator's response left me no less baffled.

The Game had not defined the young woman's level, and ordinarily, I would have taken that to mean that she was a civilian. But I believed her when she said she was an assassin.

And that patently made her *not*-civilian.

The Game also hadn't labeled Nyra a player, which it should have if she was one of the Game's rare civilians. And anyway, she couldn't be a player. She had to be lying about that. But why? What could she hope to gain? There were *no* players in Draven's Reach other than me. I knew this for a fact. The Adjudicator himself had told me so when I'd entered the dungeon.

Unless...

"You say the Adjudicator spoke to you in your mind?" I asked softly.

"Yes," Nyra replied.

"For how long has this been going on?"

She stayed silent.

I shook her. "For how long?"

"Years," she replied in a clipped tone.

"Be precise," I growled.

Nyra hesitated, then said, "I first heard him when I turned eighteen." Tilting her head back further, she met my gaze defiantly. "Right around the time I should have."

Spinning the young assassin around, I stepped back and stared at her in surprise. "Then you know what you are?"

She nodded mutely.

"I don't," Ghost declared. *"What is she?"*

"She is one of the Game's rarities," I answered aloud. "A native of the Forever Kingdom born with the potential to become a player. Isn't that right, Nyra?"

The young woman evinced no surprise at my use of her name. "That's right."

I sensed Ghost's confusion. *"So, she is a player?"*

"Not yet," I said, still speaking aloud. "Unlike those of us summoned from other worlds—who become players on entering the Game—the natives of this world are given a choice in the matter. If Nyra doesn't adopt a Class, she will remain a non-player."

I'd learned all this from Captain Talon during one of our more interesting discussions about players after I rescued his son, Sturm.

"You mean prole," Nyra interjected.

I shook my head. "I don't like that word. Don't use it."

"What does that make her?" Ghost asked. *"Friend or foe?"*

I pursed my lips. "I'm not sure."

Nyra frowned. "Do you always talk to yourself like that?"

"Sometimes, I do," I replied blandly. "But this time around, I'm speaking to my companion, Ghost."

She stared at me blankly. "Who?"

"The wolf sitting at my feet and ready to tear out your throat on my say so," I said, figuring it wouldn't hurt to instill some fear in the self-styled assassin.

Nyra's gaze dropped lower. "That's a wolf? I've never seen one before."

I smiled faintly. "Ghost is no ordinary wolf. Ordinary wolves don't spit fire."

"Or speak to people mind-to-mind?" she guessed.

"You figured that out, did you? Good. Watch what you say around her. Ghost isn't as tolerant as I am."

Nyra inched back. "Right, I take it we're done. I'll just be on my way, then." Turning around, she began to slip away.

"Stop!" I barked.

For an instant, Nyra kept moving, and I could see she was contemplating escape.

"Ghost will only run you down," I called.

That stopped her in her tracks. "What do you want?" she demanded, turning around.

I smiled. "I thought that was my question to ask."

She was not amused.

I chuckled. "For starters, I want to know everything the Adjudicator has said to you."

"Then, you believe me?"

I shrugged noncommittally.

"And after that, you will let me go?"

"If everything you say pans out," I said, ignoring the question, "I have a choice to offer you."

Her eyes narrowed. "What choice?"

"We'll get to that. But for now—"

"There he is!"

I broke off, my gaze darting to the three soldiers entering the alley. "Told you I saw him come this way," one said.

"Well spotted, Zot," the sergeant accompanying him congratulated.

"Sir," the third said, stepping around Nyra as if she wasn't there. "I'm glad I found you!"

I studied the young soldier as he drew to a halt before me. Despite the army uniform he wore, he bore no weapons, and his face was flushed from running.

Not a soldier, I amended. *A messenger.* "Is something wrong?"

He shrugged. "I don't know, sir. I only know that the marshal—pardon me, the First—ordered me to escort you back to the council. And *with all due haste.*"

"Call me Taim," I said absently. Had something happened?

Something must have. Elron wasn't one to panic, and whatever it was, it sounded urgent. "Alright, let's go."

The messenger spun on his heels, already hurrying away.

"What about her?" Ghost asked.

I glanced in Nyra's direction. She was pressed up against the wall, looking for all the world as if she were trying to disappear into the brickwork. The young assassin was a complication but an opportunity, too, and I couldn't let her go just yet.

"She comes with us."

✳   ✳   ✳

Nyra, of course, protested. But I was having none of it.

"I'm telling you, this is a mistake," she said for what must have been the fourth time.

"And why is that?" I asked, watching in amusement as she tried to yank free from the sergeant who held her right arm in an iron grip. Nyra's weapon had been confiscated, which was the only reason he hadn't been stabbed yet.

As usual, she refused to answer.

Shrugging, I kept walking. We had already crossed the city, and the fortress' main doors were in sight.

"They'll recognize me," Nyra blurted suddenly.

I studied her curiously. "Who will?"

"The councilors. The nobles. Someone."

There was a tremor in Nyra's voice that bespoke fear—real fear if I was any judge—but I already knew she was a practiced liar, leaving me to doubt my observations. She would make for an excellent deception player, that was for sure.

"Is this because—" my gaze darted to the soldiers escorting us—"of your recent exploits?"

"Of course not!" she scoffed. "I do better work than that."

I raised one eyebrow. "Then why would anyone recognize you? Or even care if they did?"

"They just will," she replied weakly.

"Whatever you're afraid of, don't worry. You're under my protection. No one will touch you."

"'Under your protection?' Is that what you call forcibly dragging me somewhere I don't want to be? Ha! What a joke."

I closed my eyes, striving for patience.

"This one seems to be more trouble than she is worth," Ghost observed.

"Maybe," I conceded. *"But keep an eye on her anyway while I deal with the council. Until I say otherwise, she is to be treated like Pack."*

"Understood, Prime."

We passed through the doors of the fortress and made our way to the council hall. Nyra struggled all the way, attracting curious stares from the keep's occupants. I watched closely, but despite the attention she received, I saw no spark of recognition in any of the watchers.

We reached the council hall in short order and found Captain Algar waiting for us at the doors. "Taim," he exclaimed. "Finally! What kept you?"

I opened my mouth to explain, then shook my head. "Never mind. What's going on?"

"No time to explain," he said, tugging me forward. "They're already antsy enough in there. Let's get—" He broke off, noticing Nyra for the first time. "Who's this?"

"An assassin-in-training," I replied with a straight face.

"Funny," he said, making a face at me before shooting Nyra a second look. His brows furrowed. "Do I know you?"

"No," she replied harshly.

Algar scratched his head, then shrugged. "It doesn't matter. She will have to wait here."

I hesitated.

"I don't know who the girl is to you, Taim, but matters in the city are uncertain enough as they are." Algar pointed to the council hall. "Believe me, creating any more of a stir than you have already will not help you. It will only hurt your cause."

I sighed, not really understanding but willing to trust his judgment in the matter. "Alright, she can remain here, but Ghost will stay with her."

Algar smiled, looking relieved. "Perfect." He threw the pyre wolf an apologetic look. "The First told me about her, and I don't mean this disparagingly, but she will cause more alarm than we can afford right now. It's better if she stayed outside, too."

Ghost flopped down beside Nyra. She didn't look offended. If anything, Algar's words seemed to have pleased her.

I turned back to Algar. "Why do I get the feeling I'm not going to like whatever is going on in there?"

"We have it under control," he said firmly. He began turning away, then paused. "Just try to be diplomatic."

Diplomatic? When was I not diplomatic?

I didn't voice the question aloud, though. Algar likely had a vastly different opinion from me on the subject. I glanced at Nyra. "Behave. And don't try anything. Ghost is more than your match."

Glaring back at me, she said nothing.

Sighing, I waved Algar forward. "Alright, let's get this over with."

Not needing to be told twice, the captain pushed open the doors to the council hall and led the way in.

✳   ✳   ✳

Things inside were not what I expected.

The council chamber was busier than I'd ever seen it. Richly dressed dark elves, dwarfs, orcs, and humans lined the walls, outnumbering the guards many times over. They were clumped together in isolated groups and, one and all, seemed to be involved in animated discussions with their fellows.

"What's going on?" I asked Algar over the clamor of noise filling the hall. "Who are all these people?"

Algar's lips thinned. "The city's finest," he replied as we cut a path down the center of the chamber. "It's founding families. They all insisted they be there for this."

I blinked. "Be here for what?"

He threw me an unreadable look. "You'll find out soon enough." Coming to a halt in front of the council table, he raised his voice, "Lords, I have brought the player Taim as requested."

The murmur of conversation died as all eyes in the room turned toward us—me specifically. Feeling as if I'd been ambushed, I held myself still as I surveyed the table.

The three councilors—Stormhammer, Lorn, and now Elron—occupied pride of place at the center, but they were not alone. Crowding the rest of the table were a host of other dark elves, dwarves, orcs—and humans. I gave the humans a second look, wondering which one was the new high lord.

I paused as I picked out a familiar face. *What is Gamil doing here?*

Lorn rose to his feet. A hush had descended on the chamber, and I could feel the anticipation build. "Lords, ladies, we're gathered here this evening for an unprecedented event. Our human cousins have settled on their choice of candidate. However, there are some in his hall who have questioned the validity of their choice. Ordinarily, these questions would be ignored. It is, after all, the right of each tribe's first families to select their representative and for the council to approve it."

Turning around, Lorn swept the hall with a stern gaze. "However, given the recent and... untimely deaths of two council members, concerns—*frivolous* concerns, I might add—have also been raised about the council's neutrality and its ability to judge the new candidate on merit alone." The orc chief's voice had turned distinctly frosty toward the end, I noted.

Finally having an inkling of what was going on, I followed Lorn's gaze as he picked out individual faces in the crowd. *So, those are the troublemakers.*

Not missing what I was about, Elron threw me a warning look. Was that a silent message not to interfere? If so, why had they brought me here?

"Then, too," Lorn continued, "we must consider the recent upheavals in the city and the uncertain future New Haven faces. The council must be whole again, but the council must also have the unquestioning support of the people. Given all this, I and my fellow councilors are unanimous in our view that this matter cannot be allowed to drag on or for resentment to simmer."

Lorn glanced at Elron and Stormhammer, who both nodded decisively to indicate their support of his words.

"As such," Lorn went on, "for the good of the city, the council has decided that the matter will be decided tonight, once and for all, and in an open hearing with all parties present."

He sat back down, and Elron rose to his feet. "Will the nominated speaker for the objectors step forward," the First instructed, his voice studiedly neutral.

A figure separated itself from the crowd.

My mouth twisted as I saw who it was. *Minakawa.*

"I'm here," the dark elf captain said, but not before throwing me a venomous look.

"Step forward and take your seat," Elron said coldly when Minakawa continued to glare at me.

Throwing the First a scornful look, the dark elf made his way to the table and sat down. Elron sat back down, and all eyes turned to Stormhammer.

"Bah, what a circus," the dwarf muttered, looking even more disgusted than usual by proceedings. "Gamil," he barked.

"Yes, thane," the old shopkeeper replied.

"Present your case," Stormhammer ordered curtly.

CHAPTER 412: MAKING THE COUNCIL WHOLE

At Stormhammer's words, I felt my shoulders relax.

Gamil was someone I knew and trusted. For a moment, I'd feared having to deal with another Carnien. And while I did not know the old man well enough to claim we were friends, I knew him to be fair. Certainly, he was no Carnien, and I had no doubt that New Haven would benefit with him as the new human high lord.

Using the cane at his side, Gamil pushed himself erect. "Thank you, thane," he said. "But before I begin—" he glanced in my direction—"Taim, Algar, take your seats, please."

There were only two empty chairs left at the table, and Gamil's words made it obvious that they had been reserved for Algar and me. Feeling the eyes of the room on me, I followed the captain to the table.

Before I could sit, though, Minakawa shot to his feet. "This is absurd! Why is this player being given a seat at the council's table? He is not even a citizen of the city!"

"Sit down," Lorn said mildly. "Taim has done more than enough for New Haven to warrant a voice at this council." His eyes grew lidded. "More, I dare say, than some charged with the city's protection."

The dark elf flushed at the orc chief's thinly veiled insult, but he didn't back down.

"Don't overstep, *Captain*," Stormhammer warned before the elf could resume his protest. "You are only here to present the dissenting case and have no say on whom the council chooses to give a voice to. Try our patience, and you *will* be evicted."

Minakawa glared at Stormhammer, but whatever he saw in the thane's eyes must have convinced him the threat was not an idle one because he sat down abruptly.

Stormhammer grunted, not having the grace to hide his disappointment. Had he been hoping to kick Minakawa out? "Sit, Taim," he said, irritably waving me to my seat.

Hiding my smile, I took my seat, but in passing, I noted no one had questioned Algar's right to a place at the table.

"My case is simple," Gamil said, continuing as if there'd been no interruption, "my family was amongst this city's first settlers, and though my ancestors may have opted for a humbler existence than most in this room, I have as much right to a place on this council as anyone else."

He sat back down, and for a moment, no one said anything. The abruptness of Gamil's argument seemed to have caught many flatfooted. However, it was not long before Minakawa was up again.

"That may be," the dark elf said, "but it is not your family's past that anyone is questioning. It is the dubious choices of its present-day descendant."

Elron rolled his eyes. "Enough with the insinuations, Captain. Spit it out. Say what you mean."

"Very well, Marshal, I will," Minakawa said, throwing Elron a disdainful look. "Everyone knows the only reason the humans nominated Gamil is because of his ties with *him*." The last was said with a pointed glare my way.

"That's Master Gamil to you," Lorn said. "And what you say is not news to anyone. The human families have made clear that Gamil's association with Taim is the main reason they put him forward as a candidate."

It was news to me. "Is that true?" I asked Algar in a whispered aside.

"It is," he replied just as softly and without looking in my direction. "Some even suggested *I* become the human councilor. Thankfully, I remembered Gamil in time and put to rest any such notions."

"I see," I murmured, rubbing my chin. "And since when did I become so important?"

Algar glanced at me sideways. "Times are changing, Taim. You are a valuable commodity these days. Your associates will be looked on as favorably as those tied to Castor once were."

I winced, not liking the comparison at all.

Minakawa, meanwhile, was rambling on. "... cannot be allowed to interfere! He has no standing in..."

"Stop!" Stormhammer barked, finally having enough of the elf's theatrics. "Your point is well understood. Gamil *knows* Taim. The council acknowledges this as fact."

Amused murmurs rippled through the hall, a fact not missed by Minakawa, whose face only darkened further.

"Now, is that the sum total of your arguments?" the thane asked. "Or is there another reason why you object to the good Master's candidacy?"

"There is also the matter of Carnien's removal," Minakawa said frostily.

"What of it?" Lorn asked sharply.

"And Elron's appointment," Minakawa went on, ignoring the orc's question.

Elron rubbed at his temples. "Make your point, Minakawa. We are fast losing patience." He gestured to the attending families' representatives lining the walls, many of them as old as Gamil. "And you are not making any friends here by dragging things out."

"Very well," the captain said, his mouth twisting sourly. "I find it more than passing strange that Carnien and myself—both men known to disfavor the player—were removed from the council and replaced by two who are patently under his thumb."

Stormhammer snorted. "You were never on the council to begin with, boy."

"We also know," Minakawa said, raising his voice to speak over the thane, "that Taim is a telepath of considerable skill."

A hush descended on the chamber as people began to make the connections the dark elf intended, and once again, I felt myself the center of attention. Ignoring the fearful glances cast my way, I kept my face impassive as I locked eyes with Minakawa.

He had surprised me with his cleverness.

What he suggested was nearly impossible to prove... or disprove. But the fact that I was a player, one who'd done nearly impossible things, no less, would count against me. If I could do all that, how hard would it be for me to twist the minds of a few non-players?

Not hard. Not hard at all—or so most would believe. And already, I could see the idea taking root.

The three councilors read the room as well as I did. "What you are suggesting is impossible," Lorn said grimly.

"Is it?" Minakawa smirked. "After all, we *know* Taim used a truth spell on Carnien. We *know* he's played tricks on the minds of the former First's guards and the possessed. And by all accounts, he even bewitched you and the thane during your rescue. Didn't he?"

Tightlipped, Lorn said nothing.

The thane was too forthright for that, though. "Only to save us, you little bastard," he growled. "Don't impugn Taim's name."

"There you have it!" Smiling triumphantly, Minakawa spun around to survey the hall. He had them, he knew. "Stormhammer admits that the player toyed with his mind! If Taim could do that once, what's to stop him from doing it again?"

Across the table, Elron met my eyes. *Things aren't going well,* his expression seemed to say. My lips quirked. That was an understatement. People were shying from my gaze, and the woman to my left actually shifted her chair away.

Well played, Minakawa.

With a few carefully worded statements, he had transformed me from hero to villain. Shaking my head in bemusement, I rose to my feet.

Still basking in the attention of the room, the captain remained oblivious. The families noticed, though, and the murmurs circulating the chamber began to die down.

"What are you doing?" Algar hissed. "Sit down."

I shook my head minutely. "The only way to put a stop to this is to face it head-on."

"Don't!" Algar exclaimed, his alarm growing. "You'll only make things worse. Minakawa's insinuations are little more than hot air. He has no proof. Once he's had his say, the council will confirm Gamil, and this will all be over."

"No, Algar, it won't," I murmured. "Minakawa's words will fester in the minds of the families, and sooner or later, it will boil over, and there will be blood in the streets again."

Not waiting for Algar's response, I turned to face my accuser. Minakawa was staring at me. As was the rest of the chamber. The silence had deepened, with everyone waiting on my words.

One way or the other, New Haven's future would be determined in this room today.

"You have something to say, Taim?" Minakawa asked smugly.

"Nothing," I said softly.

"Well, I think that settles—" Minakawa began, confident in his victory now.

"Nothing," I said loudly. "There is nothing to stop me."

"What?" Minakawa asked, consternation flickering across his face.

I met his gaze impassively. "You asked what's to stop me from toying with the council's minds, didn't you?"

He nodded, still looking confused.

"The answer is nothing. Nothing stops me. If I wished, I could tear you from limb to limb right here, and no one and nothing could stop me. If I wished, I could turn your mind into a puddle, and nothing could stop me."

I stared coldly at Minakawa.

"Nothing except my conscience."

I swept the room with my gaze, my eyes hard. "Each of you in this hall has some measure of power. What stops you? What stops you from hurting any man, woman, or child you care to?" My gaze flickered back to Minakawa. "What stops you from sending assassins after those you fear?"

The dark elf tried not to react, but the fear in his eyes betrayed him. *Yes, I know,* I told him, my gaze boring into his.

I turned back to the room. "What stops any of us from doing the things we know we can get away with? Nothing... except our conscience." A smile touched my face. "Or so I hope."

Sporadic bouts of nervous laughter broke out across the room.

I inhaled deeply. Now came the hard part—revealing my identity or at least the parts more widely known. "Minakawa is not wholly wrong, though. I have deceived New Haven. I have deceived its people, its councilors, and its marshal."

The laughter died away, replaced by sharp, brittle silence.

Lorn's face had blanked, and he watched me stone-faced. Stormhammer wore a look of confusion, and even Elron was frowning.

Prudence dictated I not bring this up now, but prudence also required I come clean. My identity as Taim had never been meant to serve as a permanent deception and if, as I hoped, the New Haveners and I remained allied beyond my time in the dungeon, then sooner or later, they would discover who I was. When that happened, it would make them doubt everything else about me.

Unless they heard the truth from me first.

"I have deceived you," I said quietly, "but not in the way Minakawa means. When I first entered the city, I concealed my true identity to protect myself, and ever since, I have walked around the city wearing the persona of Taim. But that is not who I am." Raising my chin, I let the illusion wrapped around my face unravel.

Your facial disguise spell has dissipated.

"My name is Michael, and I'm a level two hundred and four voidstalker."

Gasps and whispers sounded around the hall, but I assumed that was more as a result of the changes to my appearance than the disclosure about my level. The councilors' faces had settled into polite masks. They would need time to digest my revelation, I sensed. Minakawa, though... he was openly gloating.

Ignoring the dark elf, I went on. "Lastly, consider this. Assuming I had this power Minakawa claims, and assuming I am as unscrupulous as he believes, I could've wrenched control of his mind and stopped him short before he even spoke. Yet I didn't." I paused, letting the thought settle in their minds. "If you wish to judge me," I finished softly, "then judge me by my actions. Not your fears."

"Well said... Michael," Gamil murmured.

I inclined my head to him, then turned to the councilors. "I've said my piece. Whatever decision New Haven makes, I will respect it. When you are ready, call for me. I will be in my rooms."

Lorn nodded solemnly.

Pushing back my chair, I strode out of the hall without a backward glance.

CHAPTER 413: THE SURROGATE

I didn't quite slam the door behind me.

Matters were not proceeding as I had hoped, and instead of a grateful council, I was staring down the possibility of Stormhammer and Lorn reneging on our deal.

The die was cast, though, and I'd done what I could to mend the damage, both that inflicted by Minakawa and my own prior deceit. *"Let's go,"* I said to Ghost the moment I barged into the entry foyer. Not stopping, I made for the exit into the corridor beyond.

"Is everything all right?" she asked.

"Not really," I growled. *"But it is out of our hands now. Let's get some rest. We have a long day of traveling ahead of us tomorrow."*

If the council—whoever sat on it—didn't have a positive answer for me by then, I would begin my journey back to the guardian immediately. While I understood the difficult position I'd put Stormhammer and Lorn in—and Elron now, too, I supposed—I tired of the city's politicking. Either the New Haveners saw through Minakawa's lies and understood the reasons for my own deception—or they didn't.

Either way, Farren and his people would see to the city's evacuation. Meanwhile, I would have to begin searching for the thousand mercenaries I required elsewhere.

"Where are we going?" Ghost asked.

"To our rooms," I replied.

"What about the girl?" Ghost asked.

I stopped short.

I'd completely forgotten about Nyra. Lifting my head. I spotted her standing in the same corner I'd left her with a quizzical look on her face.

Of course. She didn't recognize me.

But that didn't stop her from identifying me. "Taim?" she hazarded after a moment.

My clothes and gear had given me away, I guessed. Still, the girl was unusually perceptive to have made the connection so quickly. "Yes," I grunted, waving her over. "Or, more correctly, Michael. Taim is one of my aliases."

"More than a mere alias," she objected. "Your entire face is different!"

I waved aside her words. "An illusion, no more."

"Fascinating," Nyra remarked, her eyes glinting. "How did you do it? Can you show me?"

I began to shake my head, then paused, sensing an opening to resume our previous conversation. "I can't, but the Game can."

She blinked, instantly understanding what I meant. "You used a player ability, then."

I nodded.

"I could show you how to obtain similar abilities of your own," I offered.

She turned away. "Forget it. I'm not interested."

I tilted my head to the side. "Why not?"

She turned back to me. "Was this the choice you were going to offer me? The opportunity to become a player?"

"Something like that." I paused, sensing her resistance to the notion. "Why? Don't tell me you *don't* want to become a player?"

"I don't."

I arched one eyebrow. "Whyever not?"

She scowled. "How can you ask that? You must know what the possessed are. You've killed enough of them, or so I've heard!"

"Ah, you're afraid of the possessed, is that it?"

Her scowl deepened. "I'm not afraid of them. But only a—"

The council doors opened, interrupting her. Someone rushed out. Algar. Turning around, I faced him as he came to a stop before me.

"Captain," I greeted, my tone noticeably cooler. Right now, I was not feeling all that charitable towards New Haven's officials.

"Taim..." he began stiffly. "Or do you prefer Michael?" he asked, with more than a hint of a bite to his words. Clearly, Algar was also unhappy about my deception.

"Michael will do," I replied evenly. "Has the council finished its deliberations already?" If it had, I doubted it boded anything good for me.

Algar shook his head. "No. The First sent me. He said he would've come himself, but what with his new position..." He shrugged. "He can't leave while the council is in sitting."

"Understandable," I murmured. "And what message did Elron ask you to deliver? Not a warning to leave the city, I hope?"

"What?" Algar's eyes widened. "No! The First thinks too highly of you for that. In fact, he sent me to make sure *you* didn't leave the city."

"Why would he do that?" Nyra asked. "And what did you do to make leaving the city necessary?"

Algar shot her a curious glance but ignored her question. As did I. "You can tell Elron I will give him until tomorrow," I said. "If the council doesn't have an answer to my request by then, I will begin my search for allies elsewhere."

"What request?" Nyra probed, but once more, she went unanswered.

The captain nodded. "I'll tell him. What will you do until then?"

That was a good question and was something I'd been wondering myself. Initially, I'd thought of sleeping, but I couldn't do that until I'd dealt with Nyra.

"You should train her," Ghost said, speaking up abruptly.

My gaze slid to the pyre wolf. *"Train her? I got the feeling you didn't like her."*

"I've reconsidered. You need allies, Prime. Strong ones, preferably." Ghost shrugged. *"But even half-starved pups can become dangerous one day— especially player pups."*

Smiling, I turned back to Algar. "Tell me, captain. How did New Haven go about turning its citizens into players?"

✳   ✳   ✳

Algar's brows furrowed. "Why would you—"

Breaking off abruptly, he spun to face Nyra. Reacting almost as quickly, the young woman leaped back, her hand falling to her empty sheath.

But the captain made no aggressive move towards her. "With all that dirt and grime, I didn't recognize you. But now I remember where I've seen your face before. You're that surrogate!"

I frowned. "Surrogate?"

Algar glanced at me, shock still written across his face. "How did you find her?"

"I didn't. She found me."

The captain shook his head. "I can't believe it. We've been searching for her for two years, and the minute you show up, she falls into your lap."

It didn't quite happen that way, but I didn't contradict him.

"Anyway," Algar went on, "you can leave her with me. I'll take her into custody."

My frown deepened. "Custody? What did she—"

"Look out, she's about to bolt," Ghost warned.

"Stop, Nyra!" I said sharply, without turning around. "You won't get far."

The young assassin stilled.

"Come here," I ordered.

Reluctantly, she stepped up beside me, and I turned back to Algar. "Now, as I was asking, what did she do?"

Algar's gaze flitted from Nyra to me. "You don't know?"

"I don't know why *you* want her," I corrected. "Explain, please."

"She is a surrogate," Algar replied as if that clarified everything. But after a lengthy pause when he saw I remained no more enlightened, he went on. "Two years ago, Nyra underwent her player identification tests. The mages put her through the divining rings, and she was marked as a potential player. We lost her shortly thereafter, though, and have been searching for her ever since."

"Lost her!" Nyra muttered. "You mean, I escaped."

I glanced at her. "I take it that the testing was not voluntary?"

She snorted. "Of course not."

"Forced testing," I murmured. "Does everyone in New Haven go through it?"

"Yes," Algar replied, shifting uncomfortably. "It's mandatory for every New Haven citizen upon maturity."

I could tell from the captain's queasy expression how distasteful he found the whole notion, yet he'd not answered my original question. "But what is a surrogate?"

It was Nyra who answered. "It's what New Haven calls those of us *lucky* enough to be chosen as hosts for the possessed," she said, her voice dripping with sarcasm.

Algar winced at her tone but did not disagree with her statement.

"Are there any more surrogates in the city at the moment?" I asked softly.

The captain shook his head. "There has never been more than one born every few generations."

"Much to the council's dismay," Nyra added bitingly.

Ignoring her, I stayed focused on Algar. "I take it then, running away when one is a surrogate is a crime?"

He nodded. "The possessed see to it that the city is punished if we lose a surrogate."

My lips thinned. I could only imagine how the archlich's people would have reacted to the loss of their 'fresh bodies.' It was not a subject I wanted to dwell on, though. "But that is all in the past now, isn't it, Algar? With Castor and Loskin dead, there is no further need for the tests *or* for the city's players to give themselves up."

The captain opened his mouth, then frowned, and closed it again. "The council hasn't passed any decrees on the matter yet," he said finally, "but I suppose the tests' banning is... inevitable."

"I think so, too," I murmured.

"Wait! What?" Nyra blurted.

I turned to her. "You didn't know?" I asked, feigning surprise. "The archlich is dead, and the possessed's forced culling of New Haven's players is over—for good."

✳   ✳   ✳

It took even longer than I expected for me to convince Nyra that the possessed were no longer to be feared. By that time, the young assassin, Algar, and myself were sitting down at supper in one of the fortress' many dining halls—an empty one—while Ghost crunched her way through her own food on the floor beside me.

Nyra ate with the typical enthusiasm of someone half-starved, wolfing down portion after portion without pause. Finishing my own plate, I turned to Algar. "Now that we've established being a surrogate isn't a crime, or rather, shouldn't be one, I presume there will be no more talk of taking Nyra in custody?"

"There won't be," he agreed. "I will also pass on word to the city watch. "No one will try to arrest her."

I smiled. "Thank you."

"Does that mean I can get my dagger back?" Nyra asked between mouthfuls of food.

"No," I replied without even turning to look at her. "Incidentally, Algar," I continued casually, "Is Nyra here wanted for any other crimes?"

The young assassin stopped chewing.

Algar's brows creased. "Not that I know of. Why?"

"Oh, nothing. Just an idle query, nothing of import," I replied.

Nyra's mouth resumed moving.

"That, though, does bring me back to my original question," I said.

"Which was?" Algar asked.

"How did New Haven turn its potential players into players? After all, before a surrogate could become, well, a surrogate, they would have needed to be turned into fully-fledged players first."

Algar leaned back. "Ah, I see where you're going with this. The mages keep a cache of artifacts in their tower for just this purpose. I'm not sure what they are—" he shrugged—"but they work."

Pushing away from the table, I rose to my feet. "Then let's go have a look, shall we?"

Now that Nyra understood becoming a player wasn't an automatic death sentence, she looked on the notion more favorably. In fact, if the eager glint in her eye was anything to go by, the prospect excited her.

"You know," I said as we strode through the city, "you're going to be New Haven's first player and probably the only one for some time."

She nodded absently, not looking away from the thin, tall spire of the Mages' Guild peeking over the city's horizon.

"It may prove a hefty burden to bear," I mused.

This captured her attention. "What do you mean by that?"

"Once we reenter the Kingdom, you will be the only player we have to protect us," Algar said. "Assuming you don't run away again, that is."

Nyra glared at him. "What about him?" she asked, jerking her thumb at me.

"Oh, I'd help," I replied cheerfully, "*assuming* the council wants anything to do with me after today. I suspect, though, that they won't."

"You don't know that," Algar protested. "Elron believes in you, and his words still carry weight with the families."

I shrugged, not as optimistic as Algar.

To my surprise, the captain had remained by my side after leaving the fortress. Apparently, he was under instructions by the new First to chaperone me until the council concluded its meeting.

Still, I was grateful for his presence. Algar would prove useful in gaining access to the mages' store of artifacts.

Each of us lost in our thoughts, we made the rest of the trip in silence. At the entrance of the guild, I waved Algar forward, and he strode into the foyer.

There were two blue-robed apprentices at the front desk, both of whom I recognized from my previous visit. *Noel and Corin.* The pair fixated on Ghost the moment she walked in, barely noticing the rest of us.

"Is that... a stygian?" Noel whispered.

"No, haven't you heard? It's that player's pet," Corin replied.

"Pet? As in a familiar?"

"I don't think so, he isn't a mage. Now, shush," Corin said. "They'll hear you."

Algar stepped in front of Ghost. "We're here to see Horlick," he announced.

Corin shook himself and refocused on the soldier. "The archmage is busy," he replied. "Will you prefer to wait or come back—"

"Tell him it's Captain Algar," he interjected. "I'm here on council business and at the behest of the First himself. Horlick will make himself available—immediately—and escort us to the vault."

The apprentices' eyes widened at the mention of the First and the council. "Of course," Noel squeaked and hurried away.

Wordlessly, the captain rejoined us where we waited near the door.

"At the First's behest?" I murmured. "Really?"

"No, not really," Algar replied, seemingly untroubled by the falsehood he'd just uttered. "But if Elron knew the nature of your request, I'm sure he would not deny it."

I grinned. "Of course."

✳   ✳   ✳

Not long after that, we were escorted to the seventh floor. I looked around curiously. This level and the one below were the only two I'd not explored during my previous visit to the Mages' Guild.

"Looks different, doesn't it?" I remarked, studying the sparkling array of wards through the sorcerer's coif. They covered nearly every door we passed.

"I don't like it," Ghost replied, wrinkling her nose. *"It stinks of magic and the possessed."*

Her comment gave me pause. *"Are there any around?"* The wards curtailed my mindsight, limiting me to only what I could perceive with my physical senses.

"No. It's an old smell. The possessed left here long ago."

I nodded, relieved. Just then, our escort came to a stop before a large stone door. A single figure stood waiting before it. He, too, I recognized. It was Horlick, the city mage who'd angered Avery on my last visit. He'd clearly been promoted in the interim.

The archmage focused on Algar. "Captain," he greeted. "I am surprised to see you here." His gaze flickered over the rest of us, pausing the longest on Ghost. "And with guests."

"It is the guests that bring me," the captain replied. "This is the player, Michael, and his companions, Ghost and Nyra."

Horlick frowned. "Michael? I thought the player was named Taim."

"An alias," I replied before Algar could. "A precaution, you understand."

"Wise of you," Horlick said, nodding slowly. "But what brings you here? It's surely not in the hope of finding Game artifacts. Our guild keeps no items that would be suitable for a player of your level." He glanced at Algar reproachfully. "As the captain should've informed you already."

I shook my head. "It's not for me, but for—" I gestured to Nyra, "—my apprentice that we've come."

Horlick studied the young assassin for a moment, then his eyes widened. "The surrogate!"

I nodded, waiting patiently for the archmage to get over his alarm so I could explain the situation. He surprised me, though.

Smiling from ear to ear, Horlick stepped forward to grasp the startled woman's hands. "At long last! I had hoped you would have found your way here sooner. But now is as good a time as any, I suppose."

"You have?" Nyra asked, bewildered.

The archmage nodded. "What the possessed did to your kind—what they attempted to do to you—was disgusting, and I'm appalled that our city tolerated it for so long." He tugged her forward. "But come, I assume you are here for the Class stones?"

Nyra looked at me.

"She is," I replied, seeing the confusion in her gaze.

"Excellent," Horlick said. He waved his arm, and the stone door guarding the vault rolled back, revealing a cold, windowless room.

Following on the archmage and Nyra's heels, I inspected the chamber. There were a dozen tables spread across the room, neatly arranged in three rows. Most of them held an assortment of items, some partly deconstructed, and some in the process of being painstakingly rebuilt. Shelves lined the perimeter of the room, and these too, were cluttered, holding all sorts of magical components.

This is a workshop as much as it is a vault, I thought.

Horlick led us to the only table not overflowing with random bits of gear. It held three items: a trio of slate-thin jewelry cases. Opening them one by one, he revealed their contents.

Bronze stones.

"Ah," I breathed.

Nyra stepped back suddenly, a startled cry escaping her lips. "What's this?" she asked, waving her arms at the empty air in front of her.

"Easy," I soothed. "It's just the Adjudicator describing the Class stones."

"The Adjudicator?"

I nodded. "This is how Game artifacts will always appear in your mind's eye when you inspect them."

"I see," she said, turning back to the table with a calmer mien. "What do I do?"

"Nothing—yet," I replied. Inhaling deeply, I settled my thoughts. "First let me run you through the basics of the Game..."

✳   ✳   ✳

"So, I have to choose?" Nyra asked when I was done.

The young assassin, Algar, and Horlick had listened attentively—and with no little fascination—to my impromptu lecture on the Game. Only Ghost had evinced no interest. Flopping down on the floor, she'd gone promptly to sleep.

I nodded. "You are fortunate to have such a varied selection of Classes to choose from." I gestured to the hundred odd Class stones in the jewelry cases. "Most of us begin with a far more restricted set of options than these." I glanced at Horlick. "Where did these stones come from?"

"They've been here since the city's founding," he replied. "Brought by the first players accompanying the city's populace during the exodus. Of course, over the years the stockpile has grown considerably smaller."

"How did... how did the others before me choose?" Nyra asked.

Horlick winced. "None of the surrogates were given a choice. The possessed picked for them—randomly mind you." He shook his head sadly. "You see, it didn't matter what Class they took up. They were never going to retain their bodies long enough for it to matter."

A shadow passed over Algar and Nyra's faces.

Nyra turned back to me. "When you offered me a choice before..." She pointed to the Class stones. "Was this what you meant?"

I shook my head, surprising her. "No. That choice will come later—*after* you've become a player. But it is not something I will speak openly about yet."

Seeming to take this as a hint, Algar said, "We should leave you two then. Give Nyra space to make her choice, and you the privacy to explain whatever you need."

Inclining my head in thanks, I watched Horlick and Algar go before turning back to Nyra. She was still staring at the Class stones—struggling to hide her uncertainty, I thought. "If you wish, I can offer some advice."

Relief too sharp to hide flickered across her face. "Please do."

I stepped up beside her. "Before I do, tell me which Class attracts you the most."

Unhesitatingly, Nyra pointed out a stone.

Picking up the bronze marble in question, I inspected it.

This is a basic Class stone. It contains the path of a <u>spy</u>. This Class confers a player with three skills: daggers, deception, and insight. This Class also permanently boosts your Dexterity attribute by +1 and your Perception attribute by +1.

I chuckled. "I'm not surprised. It seems to suit your current skill set perfectly!"

Nyra's stiffness eased. "Then you think it's the right choice for me?"

I set the stone down on the table. "Actually, I don't."

She frowned. "I don't understand."

Reaching into my backpack, I drew out the dagger I had the sergeant confiscated from her earlier. "I'm assuming you're quite good with this already?"

She nodded.

I handed the blade back to her. "Then, you don't need the daggers skill from the Game, not to start off with, anyway. Your existing knowledge will serve you well enough for now. Although, after some time—presuming you want to master the weapon further, of course—you can still acquire the skill."

Nyra pursed her lips. "That makes sense. What do you advise then?"

Picking out three other stones from the jewelry cases, I set them down on the table. "I suggest acquiring one of these."

This is a basic Class stone. It contains the path of a <u>sniper</u>. This Class confers a player with three skills: longbows, sneaking, and focus. This Class also permanently boosts your Dexterity attribute by +1 and your Perception attribute by +1.

This is a basic Class stone. It contains the path of a <u>spellslinger</u>. This Class confers a player with three skills: wands, fire magic, and two weapon fighting. This Class also permanently boosts your Dexterity attribute by +1 and your Magic attribute by +1.

This is a basic Class stone. It contains the path of a <u>sharpshooter</u>. This Class confers a player with three skills: shortbows, chi, and telekinesis.

This Class also permanently boosts your Perception attribute by +1 and your Mind attribute by +1.

Nyra's eyes flitted from the stones to me. "Why shortlist those three?"

I smiled. "All of them have one thing in common: they offer you a ranged attack, and considering where we are now, that's to your advantage. There are no low-level foes in Draven's Reach for you to fight, and believe me, you don't want to go toe-to-toe with anything here."

I pointed to the sniper stone. "This will enable you to attack from so far away that most foes won't perceive you, even after you've hit them, and that's not even considering the added boost sneaking provides to your stealth. Sneaking will *also* allow you to inflict burst damage, while the focus skill will give you the ability to replenish your lost stamina."

I turned to the spellslinger stone. "This one is a little different. With it, you can dual wield wands, attacking rapidly from range. It does, however, lack any skills that allow you to retreat or escape—so there is that to consider. But magic is versatile, and once you hit level one hundred and gain a mage's shield, defense will not be something you have to worry about."

"And finally, there is the sharpshooter Class," I said, gesturing to the last stone. "Shortbows will give you a ranged attack, telekinesis will allow you to rapidly reposition, and with chi, you can buff yourself in various ways, depending on the situation."

"All three stones are good," I concluded. "And either one will serve as a solid foundation for the rest of your Class, but in the end, you should choose whatever appeals to you the most."

"Uhm..." Nyra said, shifting uncertainly. Reaching out, she let her hand hover over stones.

"Take your time," I said gently.

Retracting her hand, she swung around abruptly. "You still haven't told me why you're helping me. And don't tell me it's all from the goodness of your heart!"

I grinned. "Not entirely." I glanced in the direction of the vault's entrance. The stone door was closed, and Nyra and I were alone. Still, I hesitated. Telling her what I was about to, was a risk, especially if she rejected my offer, and I hadn't meant to go down this path until she took up her Class and became a player.

"You can trust her," Ghost said sleepily.

"I didn't realize you were awake," I replied.

She snorted. *"I've been trying, but the girl's thoughts are painfully loud."*

I threw the pyre wolf a sharp glance. *"Did you read her mind? Is that why you think I can trust her?"*

"I did," she admitted.

"When?"

"While you were in the council hall. I had occasion to lean against her."

"Ghost," I said despairingly, *"you should know better than to read her mind. It's invasive. We don't do that—not to friends and allies, anyway."*

"I know you said to treat her like Pack," Ghost replied contritely. *"But she was paid to kill you. I had to make certain she wasn't going to try."*

"What if she sensed what you were about?" Then, any goodwill I'd earned from Nyra would likely have vanished.

"But she didn't," Ghost replied stoutly.

I sighed, deciding not to belabor the point. *"Alright, done is done. But please don't do it again, not without speaking to me first."*

"Yes, Prime." A pause. *"Do you want to know what I learned?"*

"Go on."

"The girl is grateful to you, both for not killing her and shielding her from the city watch." Ghost sniffed. *"Not that she wants you to know that. Nyra has been on the run for two years and is tired of living on the streets, but she is also suspicious of those in power, especially after Carnien. He double-crossed her, refusing to pay her what he owed her for Sienna. Anyway, from everything I've sensed in her, the girl is not treacherous. If she gives you her word, she is not likely to break it."*

"Thank you, Ghost," I said, musing over her report. It was certainly comprehensive, and as much as I disliked the manner in which the pyre wolf had obtained her information, I couldn't deny it made my next decision easier.

Turning my focus outward, I found Nyra staring at me.

"Talking to... Ghost?" she guessed.

I nodded. "We were discussing how far we can trust you."

Nyra's eyes narrowed, but she said nothing as she waited for me to go on.

"Before I explain, I need you to give me your word."

"Word on what?" she asked warily.

"That you will not reveal what I am about to tell you to anyone."

She laughed. "I'm an assassin. I'm used to keeping secrets."

I studied her carefully. "Are you?"

Confusion flickered across Nyra's face. "Am I what?"

"An assassin," I clarified. "Sienna was your first kill, wasn't she?" Ghost hadn't told me so, but the pyre wolf's information had helped me complete the picture that was Nyra.

She was *not* the cool, confident, killer I had first marked her out to be. Her skittishness now made sense, and her fear was not completely feigned as I'd assumed. She had most likely spent the last two years sleeping on the streets and perpetually half-starved.

More than anything else, it was desperation that motivated Nyra. Desperation for a better life. This was something I could both understand and sympathize with.

Nyra, meanwhile, was scowling at me. "What makes you say that?"

"This is not the time to be defensive," I said mildly. "If you want me to share my secrets with you, you will have to be open with me too. Now, was Sienna your first kill?"

She hesitated, then nodded jerkily. "She was. What of it?"

"Was it hard?" I asked, ignoring her own question. "Killing someone?"

Discomfort flickered across her face. "Yes," she said shortly.

"Good, it should never be easy." I inhaled deeply. "Now, as to the choice I offer you: do you know what a follower is?"

"A follower..." Nyra mused, her brows crinkled. "I'm assuming you don't mean in the general sense of the word?"

My lips twitched. "No, I'm referring to what the Game terms followers." I paused. "A follower is a player who binds themselves to another... player."

Despite my resolve to be open with Nyra, I couldn't tell her everything. For one, if I told her I was a Power—even if only an Initiate one—she'd likely run screaming. And for another, I still didn't truly believe I was one myself. Not yet.

"And why would any player do such a thing?" Nyra asked. "Bind themselves to another, I mean."

I shrugged. "For many reasons. But in your case, I will offer you attribute points. You remember what I told you about them?"

She nodded.

"For context, a level one player begins the Game with only two attribute points. I will give you thirty."

Her eyes widened. "And what do you want in exchange?"

"Your pledge of loyalty," I said bluntly. "To me personally. If you agree to become my follower, the Game will enact a Pact between us." I'd explained what a Pact was to her earlier and didn't do so again. "The Pact will require you to follow my orders. In return, I will pledge to equip you, help you advance in the Game, and finally protect you from the Game's Powers—and if I can't do that, avenge you."

I held her gaze. "This next bit is important, so listen carefully. The Pact is *not* irrevocable. You retain your free will and can break it, but if you do so, the Adjudicator—not me—will exact a price, and I warn you, it will be steep."

Falling silent, I watched Nyra intently, waiting to see what she made of my offer.

She took her time, thinking it through. "I understand what I can get out of this... deal, but what is in it for you? Why take on a level one player as a follower—one ignorant of the Game, too! Surely, there are more suitable players out there?"

I chuckled, but my amusement was only fleeting. "Actually, there are not. Trust, you will learn, is a rare commodity in the Game. And there are not many I dare trust."

I paused, reflecting on how to phrase what I needed to. "You see, Nyra, I'm not just any player. What I am—and I will not explain fully what that is right now—is a player who is anathema to most of the Game's Powers. They will kill me and any who follow me just for what I represent. So, before making your decision, understand that tying your fate to mine will likely mean being hunted—ruthlessly."

Surprisingly, Nyra laughed. "That, at least, is something I'm already familiar with."

"You've convinced her," Ghost declared with a prodigious yawn.

I smiled. "Then, have you decided?"

Nyra inclined her head. "I have. I will become your follower... Michael."

✳   ✳   ✳

"Excellent," I said with a heartfelt smile. "Then the first step is to take up your Class."

Nyra turned back to the four stones awaiting her on the table, and I could almost see the question running through her mind: a spy, a sniper, a spellslinger, or a sharpshooter. Which was best?

This time, Nyra didn't deliberate over her options.

Reaching down, she plucked up one of the stones and glanced at me. "Now what?"

"Will your choice to the Adjudicator," I replied.

Her brows furrowed in consternation, but I knew she'd done what I asked because a second later, the bronze marble disappeared from her open palm.

Nothing about Nyra changed, not visually, anyway.

But I knew everything had. She was a player now, irrevocably and forevermore. Curious to learn her choice, I reached out and analyzed her.

The target is Nyra, a level 1 human sniper. She is a player and bears no Marks.

My eyebrows rose. "Well, well, a sniper. I admit I'm surprised. I really thought you'd go with the spellslinger or sharpshooter."

"Why's that?" she asked absently, her eyes turned inward as she read through the Game messages that were probably still unfurling in her mind.

I smiled. "Magic is hard to resist—in any form."

She focused on me. "They tempted me, I admit. But in the end, I found the idea of dealing death from afar while hidden more attractive."

I laughed. "I know what you mean."

She squinted at me. "You don't look any different, though. I thought..."

"You thought you'd be able to tell other players on sight?"

She nodded.

"You will. First, though, you'll need to obtain the trait, Marked—which you will soon enough." She opened her mouth, more questions on the tip of her tongue, no doubt, but I waved her to silence. "I'm sure there's much more you want to know, and I promise I'll tell you what I can. But later." I glanced at the door.

Algar and Horlick hadn't reappeared, but they had to be getting impatient. "Shall we finish up before we're interrupted?"

She nodded, knowing what I meant but looking only slightly anxious at the prospect.

"Good, then let's begin," I said, more than a little nervous myself.

I was about to take on my first follower. In some ways, doing so would be no different than becoming the alpha of the arctic wolves. Like I had with them, I would be pledging to protect and aid Nyra.

But in other ways, what I did today was different.

This time, the Game itself would be involved. And in a very real sense, this would be my first official act as a Power. Only Powers could form Pacts. And here I was about to create one.

There would be no denying what I was after this.

Seeming to feel the weight of the occasion as I did, Ghost rose to all fours and stood stiffly at attention. Inclining my head one last time to Nyra—whether the gesture was meant to reassure her or me, I wasn't quite sure—I closed my eyes and reached out to the Adjudicator.

Initiating a Pact between Wolf Lord Michael and the player Nyra...

✳　✳　✳

Finalizing the wording of the Pact took longer than expected.

The concept of a follower Pact was simple enough to understand, but the details were more difficult to iron out, especially since the Pact could be tailored differently for each follower.

It took several iterations, but eventually, Nyra and I reached consensus on a contract whose terms both us and the Adjudicator found agreeable.

You have formed a follower Pact with the player, Nyra.

She will unquestioningly obey all your commands in battle. Outside of combat, Nyra will retain greater autonomy but must still obey any directives you issue. These include a call to arms, truces, and any declaration of friends and foes.

In exchange, you pledge to protect and aid Nyra against other Powers and any enemies of your chosen faction. Additionally, you will grant Nyra a boon of 30 attribute points.

This Pact will terminate once Nyra reaches level 249.

Opening my eyes, I exhaled slowly. "There. It is done."

Nyra tugged at her hair doubtfully. "It is? I don't feel any different."

I shook my head. "You won't. As I said, the Pact will not impinge on your will. You may break it if you wish, so long as you are prepared to accept the Game's punishment."

Then, too, the commitments I'd asked Nyra to make were not onerous. Outside of a few carefully selected obligations, Nyra was free to play the Game as she desired. It was no less than I would've wanted had our positions been reversed.

Surprisingly, it was the Pact's termination clause that the Adjudicator had found most objectionable. I was not sure why that was the case, but perhaps it was because what I attempted was non-standard. I couldn't imagine many follower Pacts being created with one attached.

I'd tried wording the termination clause differently to account for Nyra's possible evolution at some point, but the Game would not accept any variation I put forward, and in the end, I had to define the termination point in the simplest way possible: by Nyra's level.

At level two-hundred and fifty, Nyra could potentially become a Powerful Initiate, and I was the last person who was going to rob her of the opportunity of doing so—assuming she got that far—hence the Pact's automatic termination at level two hundred and forty-nine.

I couldn't say for certain that being my follower *would* prevent Nyra from becoming a Power—after all, followers and Sworn were different, and technically, Nyra was still unSworn—but until I knew for certain the differences between the two, I wasn't going to risk compromising her.

"What's this bit about 'chosen faction?'" Nyra asked. She'd been intently reading the Pact while I'd been lost in thought, I noted—which was a good thing. I didn't want her to take her responsibilities lightly.

"I've yet to join or create one," I replied. "It is another matter we must discuss later."

"If you say so," she muttered, clearly overwhelmed. She glanced at the door. "Now what?"

"There are two more things we must do before we can rejoin the others." I paused. "Three, actually."

Saying nothing, she waited for me to go on.

"First, there is the matter of your attribute points. We must deal with that before the Pact can be fully sealed."

Turning my attention inward, I checked my player status and, specifically, my attribute ranks.

You have 0 attribute points available.
Strength: 15. Constitution: 19. Dexterity: 71. Perception: 56. Mind: 117. Magic: 43. Faith: 0.

Bequeathing three of my hard-earned attributes to another was going to hurt, but there was no doubt—given the conversion ratio—they would better serve Nyra than me. And I had come to the decision that if I was going to all the trouble of recruiting followers, it served my interest to make them as strong as possible.

And truly, thirty free attributes would be game-changing for a level one player like Nyra, whereas the loss of three attributes would hardly impact me at all.

So, what to cut? I wondered, studying my attributes.

Magic, I decided after a moment.

Of all my attributes, Magic was the area where I had the greatest surplus. Yes, it powered my void armor, and yes, Ghost would need it for her own abilities, but lowering Strength and Constitution would weaken the pyre wolf even more, and Dexterity, Perception, and Mind were too important to my own abilities to compromise.

It had to be Magic.

On that note, I willed my intent to the Game.

Your Magic has decreased to rank 40.

Commander ability triggered. 3 attributes have been transferred to Nyra in the form of 30 attribute points.

Your Pact with Nyra has been sealed, and she has been sworn into your service as a <u>follower</u>. Total followers: 1 / 100.

As a result of her new status, Nyra's spirit signature has been etched with a new Mark. She now bears the <u>Mark of Michael</u>!

Congratulations, Michael, you have bound your first follower and have accomplished the feat: <u>The First of Many</u>! Requirement: attain your first follower. As reward, you and your familiar have been awarded 1 Class point each.

I stared at the Adjudicator's messages with a half-strangled expression. The free Class points were certainly welcome. But Nyra's new Mark was... troubling.

Not to mention revealing.

I'd feared something like this, though. Now, I could only hope my plan for dealing with it would work.

"Wow," Nyra exclaimed. She, too, had no doubt been inundated with Game alerts. "What do I do with all these attribute points?" she whispered.

"If you want my advice, you will invest twenty in Perception, five in Strength, and five in Dexterity," I said.

She glanced at me. "Not that I'm disagreeing, but why so much in Perception?"

"Perception is the governing attribute of your longbow skill. The higher it is, the easier you will be able to pick out and hit your targets. And if we're going to stand any chance of leveling you up in Draven's Reach, you will need the added boost it provides you." Withdrawing an object from my backpack, I placed it on the table. "Also, there is this."

The target is the rank 5 longbow: <u>quaker</u>. It increases the damage you deal by 50%. Additionally, all arrows fired from this bow will bear the enchantment: <u>paralyzing touch</u>. Any target hit that fails a physical resistance check is stunned for 3 seconds. This item requires a minimum Perception of 20 to wield.

Nyra stared at the weapon in fascination. "Is that as nice a bow as I think it is?"

"Quaker is a bit more than nice." I smiled wryly. "Certainly, it's much better than anything I ever had when I started off. Invest in Perception, and you will be able to use it. The added Strength and Dexterity should also make drawing and firing the bow easier."

Nyra's hand moved hesitatingly to the weapon, then paused. "It's for me?" she asked incredulously.

I nodded. "I found the bow early on in Draven's Reach. Unfortunately, it's nearly the only piece of equipment I have that is suitable for you. It's yours now." I grinned. "But only if you want it." I had no doubt that she would, though.

"Thank you," she said fervently, closing her hands around the bow. "And I will do as you advise with my attributes."

"Good. That takes care of the second thing."

"What's the last thing?"

I inhaled. "Concealing your new Mark—if we can."

Her brows creased. "You mean this 'Mark of Michael' thing?"

I nodded.

"What is it?" she asked, still sounding confused.

"It's a spirit signature and will let every player you come in contact with know that you're my follower, which for many reasons is not ideal and not something I wish for."

She nodded slowly. "How do we hide it?"

"Like this," I said, laying a hand on her and willing my intent to the Game.

Commander ability triggered.
Do you wish to pass on your <u>secret blood</u> trait to your follower, Nyra?

"Yes," I said aloud.

Analyzing player...

Shifting impatiently, I waited.

"What's going on?" Nyra whispered.

"The Adjudicator is checking your bloodlines," I replied absently.

"My bloodlines?"

"It's your—" I began, then broke off as more alerts scrolled through my mind.

Analysis complete.
The player Nyra's blood is unawakened, and she is unbound to any House. She carries 27 bloodline strains, one of which is of Wolf. You may pass on the secret blood trait to your follower.

Note that doing so will not awaken her blood. In order for Nyra to acquire blood memories of her own, she will have to undergo a blood awakening.
Do you still wish to proceed?

My shoulders sagged in relief. I hadn't been certain that granting secret blood to Nyra would work, but after I had learned that the Adjudicator had told her to find me, I'd suspected that the odds were better than even that she had *some* measure of wolf blood. The Game didn't do anything without reason, and the Adjudicator's tasks, I'd long begun to suspect, were a subtle means of guiding players.

Still, I had gambled. Correctly, it turned out.

Now, to find out just how this works. Willing my answer to the Game's query, I waited.

Nyra has been awarded the trait: <u>secret blood (lesser)</u>. As a weaker variant of secret blood, this trait will only hide a single aspect of Nyra's ancient lineage—her Marks. Players and Powers alike will be deceived. The effects of this trait are untraceable and permanent. However, it will only apply to her Marks.

"It worked!" Laughing in delight, I glanced at Nyra. Her eyes were unfocused again.

"So many messages," she murmured.

"Don't worry about them," I said, still grinning. "They're only informing you that no one will be able to see your Mark of Michael anymore."

She frowned. "You're sure? What about this bit about becoming a 'wolf-friend?'"

My grin faded. "What?"

She glanced sideways at Ghost. "Is that because of her?" she asked doubtfully. "Because somehow I don't think we're friends yet."

Ghost's ears perked up. *"Prime, she's not lying! She has the Wolf Mark. I can see it."*

For a second, I could only stare at Nyra and Ghost in shock. Nothing I had done should have granted Nyra the Wolf Mark—so why had she received it? And it was not that I doubted Ghost, but I had to be certain. Reaching out with my will, I analyzed Nyra again.

The target is Nyra, a level 1 human sniper. She is a player and bears a Mark of Michael (hidden) and a Mark of Wolf (hidden).

Note that only you and others who follow you can see Nyra's Mark of Michael.

"You're right, Ghost," I murmured, "but I don't know why—"

The arrival of yet more Game messages interrupted me.

Your follower, Nyra, has completed the hidden task, <u>Join the Wolves</u>, and has received the Mark, Wolf-friend.

Your follower has accomplished the feat, <u>Play the Game</u>, and has received the trait, Marked.

"Ah," I exhaled.

It seemed Nyra was destined to be more firmly bound to House Wolf than even I had anticipated. Something we'd done must have triggered the completion of a hidden task for Nyra.

"You know what all this means?" she asked, correctly interpreting my reaction.

I nodded, then sighed. "I do, but explaining it is going to take a lot longer." I headed for the door. "Come on, I'll explain on the way."

"Where are we going?" she asked, hurrying to catch up.

"To find something to kill." I glanced over my shoulder at her. "Preferably without you dying in the process."

Chapter 416: A Night Out in the Gorge

It turned out that the gorge in which New Haven was located had a spawn point.

According to Algar, it was only a minor spawn point and one the city's soldiers regularly cleared out—before the advent of the stygian seeds, of course. Since the nether had fled the dungeon, the spawn had repopulated, but as a result of Cilia's decree of martial law, no one had revisited it.

Which was fortunate for Nyra and me.

I'd been planning on taking my new apprentice outside the gorge, but this was much better.

"Are you sure you want to do this?" Algar asked for what felt like the tenth time. "And now?"

The captain had insisted on accompanying us on our excursion. Not only that, but he'd also brought along two full squads of soldiers with him.

"Yes," I replied. "I have little else to do with my time while the council deliberates. And besides, it's best that Nyra's first encounter as a player is an easy one. This is perfect."

"Nothing in Draven's Reach is ever easy," Algar grumbled.

That was true enough.

I glanced at Nyra. The young woman had withdrawn into herself since we'd passed through the city's west gate, and I was sure she heard barely one word in ten that Algar and I spoke. From the constant twitch of her fingers and the way her eyes flitted suspiciously across the terrain, I guessed she was nervous.

"First time out of the city, Nyra?" I asked lightly.

She nodded jerkily but didn't stop scanning the horizon.

I rubbed my chin, wondering how to get her to relax. This was no way to be going into battle.

"It can be daunting," Algar said, breaking the silence before I could. "I know my first time out was."

That drew Nyra's attention. "It was?"

Algar nodded. "All the folds in the land, trees, rocks, and what-not. *Anything* can be hiding behind them, right?" He shook his head ruefully. "I tell you, that first day, I jumped at my own shadow more times than I care to admit."

Nyra's mouth curved in a half-smile. "How... how did you deal with it?"

"I put my faith in my sergeant," Algar said. He gestured to the twenty soldiers marching behind him, "And the men around me. They knew what they were about. They'd done it before. And in my gut, I *knew* they would get me through whatever we faced."

Nyra nodded slowly as she internalized the captain's words. Her shoulders straightened, and her eyes cleared. She was still nervous, but she no longer looked like she'd bolt at the first sign of trouble.

Glancing at Algar, I nodded approvingly.

He inclined his head in acknowledgment before his eyes darted forward again. "We're almost at the cave. How do you want to do this?"

I turned to Ghost, and she glided away. *"On it, Prime."*

"Ghost is going to the cave," I told Algar, who had observed the pyre wolf's departure with interest. "She'll keep an eye on the creatures while we get into position. Where's that ridge you mentioned?"

"It's this way," he said, breaking right.

Following on the captain's heels, I surveyed the newly dubbed sniper walking beside me. Algar had seen Nyra outfitted, and now she wore the standard garb of a New Haven archer: brown leather armor, arm bracers, and a hooded cloak. Quaker was strapped across her back along with a full quiver of the stygian arrows.

"Ready?" I asked quietly.

"I am," she replied, her voice shaking only a little.

Reaching into my backpack, I retrieved a brace of items and handed them to her. "These are for you."

You have lost a small bag of holding.
You have lost a slotted-potion belt and 1 full health potion.
You have lost an adept's ring (+6 Magic).

"More gifts?" she asked in wonder.

I shrugged. "Most are secondary gear that I have no use for any longer. The health potion is the most important item, though." It was one of only three I had left. "Keep it close. You remember what I told you about them?"

She nodded mutely.

While Algar had been getting things ready for our expedition, Nyra and I had had a much longer conversation about the Game and... about House Wolf. She now knew nearly everything and certainly more than enough to set Loken and his fellows hunting me to the ends of the Kingdom.

Still, her own fate was tied to mine, and I doubted very much that she would betray me. *But,* I conceded, *perhaps I did tell her too much.* I suspected knowing just how hunted I was—*we were*—was contributing to her nervousness.

"We're here," Algar said abruptly.

Glancing up, I saw that the trail we'd been following had come to an end at the summit of a small hill. I clamped a hand on Nyra's shoulder and waved her forward. "Come, let's do this."

✳   ✳   ✳

The cave in question was little more than a hole in one of the sheer walls surrounding the gorge and was likely one I never would've ventured into. From the lookout point Algar had led us to, we had a clear—if distant—view of the cave mouth.

I glanced at Nyra. "You think you can shoot that far?" It was about three-hundred yards to the cave mouth, not an easy shot even for an experienced archer, but Nyra had the Game to help her—and twenty bonus Perception attributes.

She bit her lip. "Let me see." Unhooking quaker, she drew and knocked an arrow. I stepped back, giving her some space.

"Wait," Algar instructed. Turning to the soldiers still waiting on the trail, he yelled, "Everard, come here!"

We both threw him questioning glances.

"Everard is a master archer, one of the best in the city. It's why I brought him. He can advise Nyra." He inclined his head. "If she wishes."

"Good idea," I said, once again, surprised by the captain's forethought.

Withdrawing farther, I watched as the master archer—a wiry but otherwise nondescript dark elf—stepped up to Nyra's side and wordlessly began correcting her stance. Then, he drew his own bow and began to demonstrate the correct way to nock, draw, and release. Eventually, seemingly content, he barked one word, "Release!"

Her brow creased in concentration, Nyra took aim and fired.

The arrow did not immediately fall to ground as I half-expected. Instead, it arced over the intervening distance—evidence of a good shot. *Impressive for a first try,* I thought.

Lowering her bow, Nyra watched with the rest of us as the stygian arrowhead struck the cliff wall some thirty feet above the cave. She winced. "I was aiming for the entrance," she muttered.

From where she crouched near the cave mouth, Ghost looked over her shoulder at me.

"Ranging shot," I explained.

Disdaining to reply, the pyre wolf turned back to watch the cave mouth. The two creatures inside had not yet emerged and wouldn't, according to Algar, until someone ventured within.

"Well?" the captain asked, staring at Everard.

The master archer grunted, looking surprised. "The bow has the range for it. But I warn you, it's going to be some time before the girl's going to be hitting anything from this far out."

"That's alright, we have time," I replied with a grin. "And I think you'll be surprised by how fast she learns."

✷   ✷   ✷

Leaving Nyra in the capable hands of Algar and Everard, I slipped down the hill and joined Ghost at the cave mouth. Neither the captain nor his soldiers would play any role in the upcoming battle.

My own role would be minimal, too. Assuming everything went according to plan, Nyra would do all the killing.

"Well?" I asked Ghost as I dropped down into a crouch beside her.

"It's exactly as the captain said," she reported. *"Two wisps wait inside. I can't tell their levels, though."*

"That's alright." Reaching out with my will, I inspected the two bright bubbles of awareness in the far depths of the cave.

The target is a level 201 shadow wisp lord.
The target is a level 203 shadow wisp lord.

I rubbed my chin thoughtfully. Both wisps were elites and of the shadow variant. According to Algar, the nature of the creatures that spawned in this cave sometimes changed, but there were always two, and they were always wisps.

Which was why Nyra was using stygian arrows.

Wisps were immune to physical damage. Ebonheart and faithful would be useless against the creatures, but then, I didn't plan on damaging them myself, only holding their attention.

"Will you be able to lure the wisps out one at a time?" Ghost asked.

"I hope so," I replied. *"You better go join the others,"* I added as I prepared my buffs.

She didn't budge. *"I should help you."*

"You can't," I said. *"Not against these two. You're not ready to face such foes."*

"But—"

"And then there are Nyra's arrows to consider," I went on inexorably. *"You know, the entire time I'm trying to tank the wisp lords, I'm going to have to dodge her missiles too?"* I shook my head. *"It's already complicated enough. Better I do this bit alone."*

The pyre wolf's shoulders sagged. *"Very well, Prime,"* she said, slinking off dejectedly.

I felt bad for Ghost, but I'd only spoken the truth. Without any magical defenses against Shadow, she'd be vulnerable against the wisps. As it was, I was concerned about my own ability to fend off the creatures.

With my null force skill only at rank three, my Shadow resistance was hardly worth much. Still, if things didn't pan out as I hoped, I had plenty of escape options—which my familiar didn't.

Your Dexterity has increased by +8 ranks for 20 minutes.
You have trigger-cast quick mend.

My buffs were in place, and I was ready. Neither fade nor load controller would be needed for the upcoming confrontation, so I hadn't bothered activating either ability.

Glancing over my shoulder, I saw Ghost was already out of range. The time to act had come. Weaving psi, I drove tendrils of my will into the mind of the farthest wisp.

You have cast slaysight.
You have induced a level 201 shadow wisp lord to sleep for 40 seconds.

Perfect, I thought. Swapping targets, I sent psi surging into the mind of the second elite.

You have charmed a level 203 shadow wisp lord for 20 seconds.

"Come," I ordered. Subservient to my will, the creature did as I bade. Rising to my feet, I backed away from the cave mouth.

The wisp came swiftly.

But it did not come unprepared. Darkness surrounded it, ephemeral weaves of shadow that sliced through the air in lazy circles around the wisp. There was nothing comforting about the shadows, either. They certainly weren't natural, and they certainly wouldn't hide me from the wisp.

It's an aura.

Steeling myself, I stretched out a finger and touched the leading edge of my minion's shadow cloak.

Warning: you are about to enter the <u>embrace of shades</u>!
This is not a spell that distinguishes allies from hostiles. As long as you remain within its field of effect, you will sustain shadow damage.

Grimacing, I jumped back and out of the range of the wisp's aura. I'd endured its cloying touch for less than a split-second, but even that was enough for me to know that staying close to the wisp was going to hurt.

But hopefully not for long.

Continuing my retreat, I drew my minion farther away from the cave. The wisp itself was an anomalous blob of darkness that floated on unseen currents. It lacked any sort of physical form or limbs and, without its aura, would have appeared innocuous to the casual observer.

But it was not harmless.

Far from it, and I had less than five seconds to get it positioned. Reaching the flat stone clearing we had designated as our killing ground, I strode to the center and glanced over my shoulder.

From high up on the hill, three hundred yards away, Everard gave me the thumbs up. Holding up my hand in the agreed signal of 'wait,' I turned back to face the wisp and summoned it closer.

The spell I'd wrapped about its mind would fail about... now.

You have lost control over a level 203 shadow wisp lord.

For a second, the creature stayed frozen in place. I could almost imagine the primitive thoughts running through its mind. Where was its companion? Why was it here? Should it attack or retreat?

Of course, it chose to attack.

Rushing through the small distance that separated us, the wisp descended on me in a furious storm of shadows.

I didn't react. Keeping my arms crossed across my chest, I waited.

You have entered the <u>embrace of shades</u>!
You have failed a magical resistance check! You have failed a mental resistance check!
You are <u>shadow-haunted.</u> While haunted, you will sustain ongoing shadow damage, and your mental acuity will be reduced by 90%. Duration: infinite. The debuff will remain in effect as long as the source spell is being channeled.

"*D-a-m-n,*" I swore.

But I had barely had time to finish the thought before the debilitating effects of the wisp's aura swamped my mind.

CHAPTER 417: BEFUDDLED

Between one instant and the next, my thoughts slowed, and even thinking became hard.

You have sustained shadow damage.
Your void armor has reduced the damage incurred by 15%.
Void armor charge remaining: 95%. Your health has decreased to 90%.

"Prime, are you okay? Your mind, it feels wrong."
Ghost's sending came through our link, bright and clear, but brushed by so fast I almost failed to catch it.

You have sustained shadow damage.
Void armor charge remaining: 90%. Your health has decreased to 80%.

"I'm... alright," I replied. I knew I was. Or at least I thought I was. This was all part of the plan. Wasn't it...?
Why was I here again?
The wisp.
Oh... right.

You have sustained shadow damage.
Void armor charge remaining: 85%. Your health has decreased to 70%.

The creature—it was my friend, wasn't it?—floated above me, less than three feet away, close enough for me to reach out and touch it.
A ball of condensed darkness took shape in the space between us. It roiled and churned with thick weaves of shadows so dense they looked almost solid. *That's... pretty,* I thought and began to stretch out an arm.
The darkness flashed, and the orb surged forward.

A shadow orb has injured you!
Void armor charge remaining: 74%. Your health has decreased to 44%.

I staggered backward, hurt more by the wisp's rejection than anything else. The pain from the orb's strike—little more than a distant sensation of numbness—was easily ignored.
"Heal!" Ghost screamed.
Heal? Could I heal?
Of course, I could. I had a potion bracelet on my arm that—
"Not that. Quick mend."
Oh, yes.
Summoning psi, I gathered the necessary weaves or tried to. Time and again, they slipped out of my grasp. *Disobedient things,* I scolded but persevered on. Ghost didn't sound happy, and I didn't want to anger her further.

You have sustained shadow damage.
Void armor charge remaining: 69%. Your health has decreased to 34%.

The wisp began forming a second orb.

I paused. It was as beautiful as the first. *Would it grow as large?* I wondered.

"Don't stop casting," Ghost ordered.

The command confused me. What was the hurry? But I couldn't disobey Ghost, not my familiar. *She knows best,* I thought sleepily and resumed my laborious casting.

You have sustained shadow damage.

Void armor charge remaining: 64%. Your health has decreased to 24%.

Quick mend triggered! Your health is at 44%.

I stopped again, surprised by the Game message. Had I cast quick mend already? I didn't recall doing so. *Hmm, should I continue?* Would Ghost be mad if I didn't?

But any concern I felt over the possibility faded as the orb before me reached full size. My attention swapped to it. *It will flash again soon,* I thought happily.

A shadow wisp lord has evaded Nyra's attack.

An arrow streaked through the air, missing my face by only inches. I blinked. What was that?

The projectile gave the wisp pause, too, and I saw the orb's churning slow as the creature's regard turned elsewhere. My shoulders sagged. *How disappointing. I thought I was—*

You have sustained shadow damage.

Void armor charge remaining: 59%. Your health has decreased to 14%.

Void thief triggered!

You have acquired the channeled spell, <u>embrace of shadows (stolen)</u>, from a shadow wisp lord and will retain memory of it for the next 12 hours.

Embrace of Shadows (stolen) is a tier 5 spell that surrounds the caster in a debilitating aura 6 yards in diameter. The aura's shades will haunt the mind of any creature—friend or foe—that enters the spell's field of effect, causing them to become <u>shadow-haunted</u>.

Entities afflicted by the debuff will find that their thoughts grow wayward or grind to a halt altogether. Note that the spell is only effective against sentient foes. Creatures lacking higher thought processes are largely unaffected.

The aura will remain manifested for as long as the caster channels the spell.

Void siphon activated!

A conduit has been forged between you and a shadow wisp lord, allowing you to steal mana from your foe whenever it casts a spell at you.

Void negate activated!

Your void armor has learned to completely resist the effects of the embrace of shadows, granting you effective immunity against the spell for

the next 12 hours. Note that your void armor must be operational in order for negate to function.

You are no longer shadow-haunted.

As quickly as it appeared, the fog around my mind vanished—and the direness of my straits hit me.

The orb flashed.

Letting instinct take over, I flung myself to the side.

You have evaded a shadow orb!

You have siphoned a portion of a shadow wisp lord's mana. Void armor charges remaining: 61%.

"Prime, you're back!" Ghost cried, unadulterated joy coloring her voice."

"All thanks to you," I sent back, spinning psi as I rolled back to my feet. *"Thanks for keeping me alive."*

"You're welcome," she said cheerfully. *"Do you need any help?"*

"Not anymore," I murmured as the wisp floated closer. Its aura enclosed me again, but of course, it no longer had any effect on me. Stopping two yards from me, the creature began summoning another shadow orb.

Keeping a wary eye on the growing ball, I kept casting.

I'd made a foolish mistake by starting the encounter without my mental shields raised. I had assumed—erroneously, it turned out—that as a creature of magic, the wisp would have no mind-affecting spells. I'd been wrong, and it had nearly cost me my life.

You have cast fortified mind, reserving half of your psi for your mental shields. Psi remaining for use: 50%.

Raising my mental defenses now was not strictly necessary—I could no longer be shadow-haunted—but who knew what other mental manipulations the wisp could perform?

It paid to be cautious.

My psi defenses in place, I began casting anew. Seconds later, the wisp's fully formed orb surged toward me, but with my mind free of the shades, I had no trouble sidestepping the attack.

You have evaded a shadow orb. Mana siphoned.

I circled my foe. Twice now, it had failed to hit me. Would it change tactics? But no, another ball of darkness was forming beneath it.

Motion at the periphery of my vision drew my attention.

It was Algar—waving frantically. No doubt, he was wondering if I needed help. The earlier hit I'd sustained must have worried him as much as it had Ghost. Raising my hand, I gave him a thumbs-up.

A second later, another arrow arced across the sky. Good, Nyra had resumed firing.

With one eye on the approaching projectile and another on the wisp, I kept weaving psi. Contrary to its name, quick mend was not a combat spell, and it had a long casting time, but after my time in the arctic tundra, I'd learned how to use it while on the move. Still, enacting the spell in battle required patience and time.

Nyra's arrow neared the end of its arc. My eyes narrowed. It looked on target. Watching intently, I waited.

The projectile screeched downward. Oblivious, my foe kept casting.

Nyra has grazed a shadow wisp lord.

There was no contact.

The sniper's arrow passed straight through our ethereal foe—but not before inflicting a small measure of damage on the way through.

"Well done, Nyra," I murmured, my gaze still on the wisp.

Despite the assault from above, the creature did not turn aside from me, seeming to have decided I was the greater threat—which, truthfully, I was. Giving the group on the hill another thumbs-up, I leaped over the next orb the wisp flung my way.

I suspected I would be spending the rest of the night dodging, healing, and channeling. And I didn't mind in the least. Given the strength of the wisp's Shadow magic, the encounter would benefit my null force skill as much as it did Nyra's archery.

An almost perfect training scenario, I thought with a smile.

✳ ✳ ✳

It took twelve long hours to kill both wisps.

I'd spent nearly the entirety of that time on my feet, dodging one orb after the other, while Nyra peppered the creatures with arrows, exhausting quiver after quiver—the ever-efficient Algar had brought spares.

Although, 'pepper' was perhaps not the right term.

During the initial few hours, my apprentice had missed nine times out of ten. But miss or hit, every draw of the bow improved her skill, and as the hours dragged on, her accuracy improved, and killing the second wisp took only half as long. In fact, Nyra not only managed to train her longbows skills, she also improved her focus skill, using it to regain her stamina between volleys.

The only downside to the encounter was that Ghost was unable to participate. While her direshield would likely protect her from the wisp's mental assault, she had no way to heal the damage she'd sustain from its aura, and in the end, thoroughly bored with the whole exercise, she went to sleep.

Nyra has killed a level 201 shadow wisp lord.
You and Ghost have reached level 205!
Your follower, Nyra, has reached level 21!
Your dodging has reached rank 18, your insight rank 21, and your null force rank 6.

Exhausted, I sagged to the ground as the second wisp finally died. It seemed that despite my best efforts to affect the battle's outcome only minimally, the Adjudicator had seen fit to award me a level—thereby reducing Nyra's own gains in the process.

The skill advancements, I didn't mind, at all. I'd gained three whole ranks in null force, improving my void armor's Light, Dark, and Shadow damage reduction by fifteen percent. *Not too shabby for a half day's work,* I thought, stifling another yawn.

My gaze dropped to the stone floor. Drained as I was, even its cold, hard surface looked inviting, but I couldn't sleep, not yet. *"Ghost, you're awake?"*

No response.

Sighing, and more than a little jealous of the sleeping familiar, I pushed myself back to my feet. There was work to be done. Striding over to the wisps, I set down the alchemy stone. While I waited for it to collect the reagents from the translucent corpses, I invested my newly acquired attribute point.

Your Magic has increased to rank 42. Other modifiers: +20 from items.

"What's that?"

Turning around, I saw Nyra, Algar, and the rest of the soldiers approaching. Ghost, still napping on the hill, was conspicuously absent.

"This," I said, picking up the small object, "is an alchemy stone, and it's the only way players like us can harvest our kills."

New ingredients acquired: 10 x shadow ectoplasm.

Nodding absently at my answer, Nyra surveyed the arrow-strewn clearing. "This was a lot more effort than I expected," she admitted, looking as exhausted as I felt.

I snorted. "Those wisp lords were elite creatures, and ordinarily, you wouldn't have scratched them." I held her gaze. "You did good."

She ducked her head, uncomfortable with the praise.

"More than good," Algar added. "The army would not have fared as well."

I looked at him curiously. "How *would* you have done it without any players to assist?"

The captain shrugged. "The marshal usually deployed two full companies—mostly archers—to deal with the wisps, but even with such a weight of numbers on our side, there were often casualties." He gestured to the empty clearing. "This took time, yes, but there are no fallen to mourn. A much better outcome."

"Much better," I agreed.

Nyra straightened, her confidence buoyed by Algar's words. "What now?" she asked eagerly.

"We return to the city and sleep," I said firmly.

"Oh," she said, looking somewhat disappointed.

I smiled. "But first, let's go find out how the Adjudicator has chosen to reward your efforts."

Chapter 418: No Good Deed Goes Unrewarded

While Algar and his men collected the spent arrows, Nyra and I investigated the wisp's cave. Just as I hoped, there was a chest.

Disappointingly, though, it was only bronze.

"Go ahead, open it," I said.

Not needing to be told twice, the young woman bent down and flipped open the chest's lid. Leaning over, I peered within.

The target is a <u>lesser attribute gem</u>. It grants you 1 attribute point.

The target is the basic ability tome: <u>hobbling shot</u>. Governing attribute: Perception. Tier: basic. Requirement: rank 3 in any archery skill. With this ability, an archer can slow his target for 3 seconds, reducing their movement speed by 50%. Hobbling shot can only be performed using a ranged weapon.

You cannot learn this ability.

The target is the advanced skillbook: <u>poisoning</u>. Governing attribute: Dexterity. Poisoning is the art of dealing slow-but-assured death. It is often dismissed as merely a sub-school of alchemy and thus not worth acquiring. Yet the discipline is much more than that. Not only can a poisoner mix his own deadly brews on the fly—with limited equipment, no less—he can also see them expertly applied to his weapons.

Some master poisoners have also been known to possess the ability to strengthen ordinary toxins, create antidotes, and even formulate their own specialized lethal concoctions.

You have no available skill slots and cannot learn this skill.

"Well," I murmured, chewing on my lower lip, "that is certainly an interesting box of loot."

Nyra nodded enthusiastically, not tearing her gaze away from the chest's contents.

I smiled, understanding her fascination. "Can you use the books?"

"Yes," she said softly.

"Then, they're yours. I would advise acquiring both skill and ability."

She looked at me then. "You don't want them?"

"No, they will suit you better." I glanced at the last item. "But I won't mind the attribute gem."

Wordlessly, she handed it to me, and without ado, I employed it.

Lesser attribute gem used. You have gained 1 attribute point.

Your Magic has increased to rank 43.

My smile widened. When I'd transferred three of my attributes to Nyra, I'd not anticipated recovering them so quickly. *No matter the outcome of the council's deliberations, this has been a fruitful day,* I thought in satisfaction.

Spinning on my heel, I headed for the exit. "Take your time, Nyra," I called over my shoulder. "And when you're ready, we'll head back to New Haven.

✳   ✳   ✳

Hours later, I awoke in my room in the fortress. Thanks to the night spent hunting, I slept through the morning and most of the afternoon.

Ghost and I had a long trip ahead of us. This was the fourth day of the five Draven had asked for, and I meant to begin my journey back to the guardian today—no matter how late the hour of our departure was.

I'd not spoken to Nyra about my plans yet, nor had I explicitly told her she needed to accompany me—which she didn't. Ultimately, the decision would be hers.

"Good afternoon, *Prime,"* Ghost greeted.

Opening my eyes, I found the pyre wolf sitting attentively at the foot of my bed. I glanced at her suspiciously. "Is that a note of scolding I detect in your tone, Ghost? Have I woken too late?"

"Not at all," she replied easily. *"There is still daylight left."*

"There is always daylight left in this place," I muttered, glancing out the window at the unchanging purple sky.

"Exactly," she replied with a twinkle in her eye.

I chuckled. "Alright, you've made your point." I rose from the bed. "Where's Nyra?" I'd left Ghost with the young woman last night to make sure nothing untoward happened to her. I'd not forgotten about Minakawa, after all.

"She's in her room next door and waiting just as impatiently to get going."

I nodded. "One second." Turning my focus inward for a moment, I spun psi.

Yesterday had taught me a valuable lesson, and I'd resolved to keep my mental defenses raised during my every waking hour from here on out, no matter how safe the surroundings appeared. I'd even tried to leave fortified mind active last night, but I knew from the Game's morning report that the spell had deactivated the moment I'd fallen asleep.

Sadly, it was not a passive spell.

You have cast fortified mind.

"Ready," I pronounced and strode out the door with Ghost on my heels.

Nyra must have been listening attentively for me because the moment my door opened, she emerged from her own room. "Finally up, I see," she said, her smirk reminiscent of the bravado she'd displayed during our first meeting in the alley.

I forbore comment, and she fell into step with me.

"Where are we going?" she asked after a moment.

"To the council chamber," I replied. "Hopefully, they have an answer ready for me by now."

"Oh, they do," she said.

I glanced at her in surprise.

"Captain Algar stopped by." She paused. "Several times, actually."

My eyes narrowed.

"He gave up finally," she said, a smile tugging at the corner of her mouth, "and told me to bring you whenever you awoke."

"I see." Frowning, I wondered how to interpret Algar's behavior. Was it a good sign? I shrugged. I would find out soon enough, anyway. I turned back to Nyra. "I'm leaving today."

She missed a step and almost fell, but I caught her in time. "When?" she asked after righting herself.

"As soon as the council meeting is done." I hesitated. "I know it's short notice, but I need to know if you'll be accompanying me. I won't force you to. It'll be dangerous, and I expect leaving your home will be—"

"I'll come."

I stared at her. "Just like that? You don't have to think about it?"

She grinned. "I *have* thought about it." Her smile faded. "Besides, there is nothing for me in New Haven anymore."

"Alright," I said. "I won't try to convince you otherwise. It's what is best for you, anyway. It'll be a long time before you can level up on your own in Draven's Reach. Once we're out, we can find a more suitable dungeon for you."

Excitement glinted in her eyes. "Then you plan on leaving the sector entirely?"

I nodded. "We'll be here a few more days further, but yes, before the week is out, I expect us to be gone."

✳   ✳   ✳

We found Captain Algar outside the doors to the council hall, his foot tapping impatiently.

"Tai—I mean, Michael. At last! What kept you?"

I rolled my eyes. Was everyone going to berate me today? "I'm here now," I pointed out. "What's going on?"

"The council is ready to address you," he replied.

I studied his face. "That doesn't sound good."

Algar looked away. "It's best if you hear the news from them. Come, I'll announce you." Before I could respond, he turned on his heels and entered the council hall.

I followed more slowly and reached the doors just as Algar reemerged a few seconds later. "You can go in," he said.

I glanced at my companions. "I hate to impose, but while I'm in there, will you escort Nyra and Ghost into the city? There are some supplies we need to purchase."

"Of course." He paused. "You're leaving today?"

"Yes, it's time I headed back on out."

To my surprise, Algar didn't try to stop me, nor did he attempt to convince my apprentice to stay behind. "I'll have them back before you're done," he promised.

"Thank you," I said. Handing Nyra fifty gold coins—the greater part of what I carried on my person—I rattled off the list of the items I thought we needed.

After the trio left, I turned back to the council hall and inhaled. "Right, let's find out what they have to say," I whispered.

Pushing open the doors, I strode forward to meet the council.

✳ ✳ ✳

Four familiar faces were waiting for me inside—Lorn, Stormhammer, Elron, and Gamil. The shopkeeper's presence was a good sign. Overshadowing it, though, was the councilors' unsmiling faces.

The news isn't good, I deduced with a sinking sensation.

"Sit, please," Lorn said as I drew to stop before the table.

Mutely, I did so.

For a moment, the council studied me, my face in particular. "There was much debate about your identity last night," Lorn began without preamble.

"It went on for longer than any of us hoped or expected," Elron added by way of apology, "but in the end, all the families agreed: whether you call yourself Taim or Michael is irrelevant."

I exhaled softly, sitting easier.

"Whatever your reasons for the deception, we understand your desire to protect yourself," Lorn said.

"However," Gamil continued, "addressing who you are was only one of the hurdles we had to cross last night." He grimaced. "My appointment to the council was another sticking point." He paused. "And while my nomination finally went through, it was not without... conditions."

I said nothing, but I had a sneaking suspicion I was not going to enjoy what came next.

"The families are... hesitant," Lorn said.

"About what?" I asked sharply.

The orc threw me a pained look, visibly searching for the right words, but before he could find them, Stormhammer intervened. "About leaving," the thane said bluntly.

I blinked. "I'm not sure I understand."

Elron rubbed at his temples. "It seems we—I—overestimated the families' enthusiasm for rejoining the surface world."

I gaped at him, finally realizing what they were driving at. "They want to stay *here?*"

"In short, yes," Stormhammer replied.

"Why the hell do they want that?" I demanded.

Gamil chuckled. "They're afraid," he said softly.

"Of me?" Planting my elbows on the table, I leaned forward. "Surely, we can convince them that—"

"No, not of you," Lorn interjected. "Of your *kind*."

I sat back, folding my arms.

Elron took up the explanation. "Minakawa may have failed to convince the families that Gamil's appointment—or my own for that matter—was the result of an elaborate manipulation on your part, but that does not mean they did not heed his words."

"Or that they failed to understand the implications of your own accomplishments," Lorn added.

I shook my head. "I have no idea what any of that means."

"Your actions have convinced the families that you players are a much bigger threat than the possessed ever were," Gamil said.

"Give it to him straight," Stormhammer grumbled. "In short, lad, the ease with which you defeated Castor, the archlich, *and* the harbinger has scared everyone witless."

"But I did nearly none of that on my own," I protested. "I had help."

"It's not only about fear," Elron said firmly. "It's also about power."

I turned his way.

"Here, in this isolated dungeon, away from the factions and their Powers and players, the families have a say in what happens," Elron pointed upward. "But up there?" He shook his head. "They're smart enough to realize they'll have little control."

Groaning, I put my head in my hands. What Elron said was true enough, and I had no counter-argument ready.

"Then, too, before last night, none of us truly realized the full scope of what you've achieved in Draven's Reach," Lorn said quietly.

Raising my head, I stared at him.

"You've made New Haven into a *true* haven," he pronounced.

Lifting one hand, Gamil ticked off points on his fingers. "You defeated the possessed. You killed the harbinger. You even banished the nether." He held my gaze. "You've made Draven's Reach safer for this city than it's ever been before."

I laughed in wry realization. "So, you're saying, by doing all those things, I've removed any motivation for people to want to leave?"

All four councilors nodded solemnly.

I sighed. "I take it from your expressions then that none of you disagree with the families."

Their silence was answer enough.

But despite my disappointment, I understood. I truly did. I'd seen for myself how the Powers and players ran amok in the Kingdom, and if I were in the council's shoes, I wouldn't want to leave either. As far as homes went, Draven's Reach was not perfect.

But it was safe.

"For myself, I would love to see the sun one day," Lorn said quietly. "But speaking as the chief of my people, I cannot uproot them from Draven's Reach and take them into what's an uncertain future at best."

"Then you have already made the decision to stay," I said heavily.

"We have," Elron confirmed. "The city will not be evacuated. New Haven will not reveal itself to the Powers at large. We will stay here, where the people will be safe."

"Nor will any soldier wearing the city's livery ever step foot outside the dungeon," Gamil added.

"I understand," I said and began to rise. "Then, I guess we have nothing further—"

"Sit down," Stormhammer growled.

I met the thane's eyes, but his furious gaze did not relent. Nor did I get the impression that it was me he was angry at.

Sighing, I sat back down. "Go on, then. I'll hear you out."

"Notwithstanding our decision," Lorn said, "we are grateful for what you've done."

"Nor do we fail to appreciate who truly safeguards the city," Elron said. "You alone hold the key to this sector."

It took me a moment to parse the First's meaning. "You're referring to the hidden portal." Now that Draven was awake and the shield about the dungeon restored, the hidden portal was the only means of entering the sector.

"Yes," Elron said simply.

My gaze flitted over the councilors. Gamil, Lorn, and even Elron appeared tense. *They want something,* I realized. "What about it?"

The councilors shifted uncomfortably.

Gamil pressed his hands together as he addressed me. "For the safety of the city and its people, we ask that you don't share the portal's location with other players."

I shrugged. "Of course. You have my word that I will not reveal its coordinates to anyone—not unless the council grants me permission to do so."

Gamil closed his eyes. "I won't lie. Hearing that relieves me, but I'm surprised..."

"... surprised that I would give up a resource as valuable as Draven's Reach?" I finished for him. "Or that I won't use it as a bargaining chip?"

"Both," he admitted simply.

I stared at him stonily. "I didn't use the city's safety as a bargaining chip when the nether was at your very door. What makes you think I will do so now?" Did they trust me so little?

Gamil looked away, ashamed.

"We didn't think you would," Elron said gently. "But we had to be certain, you understand."

My expression didn't soften. I wouldn't deliberately endanger New Haven or force the council to help me, but my graciousness did not extend to accepting their rebuff with a smile.

"There is one thing you have not accounted for," I said, moving the conversation on.

The councilors looked at me questioningly.

"The possessed," I said. "I have the new archlich's assurance that the culling of the city's players will stop, but once I leave Draven's Reach, you understand that you will be on your own dealing with them?"

Whether the possessed would even remain in the dungeon was something else I'd not gotten around to discussing with Farren and Adriel, but Castor's example was a worrying one, and I couldn't imagine the council was comfortable knowing that there were potentially others like him back at the archlich's court.

"We have not forgotten the possessed," Lorn said. "We have a plan for dealing with them."

I frowned, wondering what he meant.

"Bah, enough of this," Stormhammer said abruptly. "Tell the lad about the other thing."

My gaze shifted to the thane. "What other thing?"

"Nothing of great import," Elron said with a small smile. "The families may have decided that New Haven's soldiers will not venture beyond Draven's Reach, but they have no say over the decisions of private individuals." His smile broadened. "Nor do they have control over our personal guards."

My eyes widened fractionally.

"What the marshal is trying to say," Stormhammer interrupted, "is that you'll have your thousand soldiers—and a damn sight more—only they won't be marching under New Haven's banner but your own.

"Will that do?" Elron asked.

I matched his smile with one of my own. "Yes, I think that will do. I think it will do nicely."

I leaned across the table. "Tell me about these soldiers," I said intently.

"We've asked for volunteers from our personal guards," Lorn replied. "Men and women willing to serve under you."

"We will outfit them, of course," Stormhammer said.

"Many more volunteered than we could easily accommodate," Gamil added, "and in the end, Elron decided an even two thousand would be a good number."

Two thousand. That was double what I'd asked for, and despite everything else, I couldn't help but be grateful for their generosity.

"The force will be drawn equally from the four council guards and split into individual companies," Elron said. "Five hundred dark elf archers. Five hundred human cavalry. Five hundred heavy dwarven infantry. And five hundred orc skirmishers. All veterans, and all under the command of Algar."

My eyebrows rose. "Algar?"

"He has asked to accompany you," Elron explained, his lips turning down. "And while I'd hate to see him go, I think he will make for an excellent commander of your four companies."

I nodded slowly. "And you're sure the soldiers are all volunteers? None has been coerced or harbors ill-intent?"

"We have made it clear that each and every man and woman will have to swear their oaths directly to you," Lorn said.

"They've also been warned that any mistruths will be sniffed out," Stormhammer added.

I glanced at him questioningly.

"By your companion, Ghost," he explained. "Where is she, anyway?"

"Out shopping with Nyra," I replied absently. I was still trying to wrap my head around the notion that I commanded an army—if a small one—that I spoke more unthinkingly than I should have.

"Ah yes," Elron murmured. "Your new apprentice."

"Who is a player, too," Gamil remarked.

I refocused on the councilors. "Is there a problem?"

The four exchanged glances before finally fielding the question to Lorn. "Minakawa has made... accusations," he said.

My mouth twisted sourly. The dark elf captain was an irritant that kept coming back to bedevil me. "I should have killed him that first day on the wall," I mused aloud.

My words surprised a sympathetic chuckle from Stormhammer, but the other three studiously ignored them.

"What's the idiot saying now?" I asked wearily.

"That your apprentice killed Sienna," Lorn said.

I sighed.

Gamil's eyes narrowed. "Did she?"

"She did," I replied forthrightly. "*She* was the assassin Carnien hired."

That set them aback, and for a moment, they looked at a loss on how to proceed. "Did Minakawa also happen to mention he hired Nyra to kill me?" I asked, letting my question drop into the sudden silence.

Elron's lips tightened. "No. He did not."

"That's how I met her, you know," I said. "In one of the city's alleys after she tracked me down."

"Interesting," Lorn said, rubbing his chin. "Do you mind if we speak to the girl and see if she has proof of Minakawa's wrongdoing?"

"Go ahead," I said. "But be sure it's talk only that you have in mind," I warned. "Nyra is under my protection. No one will harm her."

The orc chief inclined his head. "Understood." He glanced at Elron, who nodded. "Then leave Minakawa to us. We will see to it that he pays for his misdeeds."

"Alright," I conceded. "But if he interferes with my plans again, I will deal with him myself—harshly."

"As will be your right," Stormhammer pronounced before any of the others could comment.

Gamil's brows creased. "Minakawa is only one half of the problem, though. The girl... Nyra, you know she can't remain in the city?"

I flicked my hand dismissively. "That will not be a problem. Nyra will be leaving with me."

"Ah, good," he said, sitting back in relief.

"She truly is a player then?" Elron asked softly.

I nodded. My lips compressed, I studied the councilors. The four surely had to be wondering about the same thing I was. Did it bear mentioning?

It does, I decided.

"You four understand that hiding out in Draven's Reach is only a stopgap measure, right? Sooner or later, more players will be born into New Haven's populace, and some of them will want power of their own."

What will you do then?

"We realize that," Lorn said, sighing heavily. "And we know we can't hide from the Game forever. The city and the people need time, though. Eventually, we will come up with a better solution."

"A better solution," I murmured. I only hoped it wasn't one that ended up with New Haven persecuting its newborn players. Still, I had said my piece, and they had been warned. It was now for the council to decide how New Haven would deal with its future players.

I rose to my feet. "You have my heartfelt thanks for everything, but it's time I took my leave. I still plan on leaving the city today, and before that can happen, there are multiple arrangements I have to make."

I'd planned to outfit only Nyra, Ghost, and myself. Now, it seemed I had another two thousand dependents to consider. And while the four companies of soldiers were a welcome addition, I was sure keeping them fed, equipped, and provisioned was going to give me more than a few headaches.

Lorn held up his hand. "Bear with us a little longer, please, Michael. You see, while you were away, we had a visitor."

I frowned. "A visitor?"

"We've kept him waiting long enough," Stormhammer muttered. Raising his head, the thane barked, "Send him in!"

✻ ✻ ✻

A possessed stepped through the door.

It was no one I knew, but there could be no doubt as to the visitor's nature. A thin red line running front-to-back bisected the human's bald head. At some point, his skull had been cracked open—in what must have been a fatal blow—yet the 'visitor' was still walking around none the worse, and while the injury had been neatly stitched up, there was no disguising the ugly red of an unhealed wound.

My hand dropping to my blades, I drew psi in readiness.

"Woah there, Michael," the possessed said, raising his arms in surrender, "at least hear me out before you kill me."

My frown deepened. There was a familiarity to the man's tone, but I was sure I'd never met him before.

That, though, didn't mean much, considering he was a possessed.

"Analyze me," he said with a knowing grin.

Gathering my will, I did just that.

The target is Regus, a level 179 human.

"Regus," I muttered. The last time I'd seen the former archlich's head of security, he'd been in a dwarven body and serving as Farren's right-hand man.

"You've dropped the disguise, I see," he observed. "Taim's time is done, eh?"

I nodded. "Where's that bloody maul of yours?" I asked, blurting out the first question that occurred to me.

The possessed grinned. "Back in my room. It wouldn't do to come to a parley armed, after all," he said, with a pointed look at my own swords.

My eyes narrowed. "Is that what this is?" I asked, turning sideways to address the councilors too. "A parley?"

Lorn nodded. "Regus is here as archlich Farren's representative. He came through the underground tunnel with a small group of other possessed—" the orc shot the possessed a warning look—"whom, I take it, are still safely confined in their rooms?"

Regus inclined his head. "Of course, Chief. We've not strayed from your instructions."

"We've already had preliminary discussions with Regus," Gamil said, "and we believe we can find common ground with the new archlich."

Stormhammer scowled. "Let's not be too hasty to jump back in bed with those devils. Until Michael confirms everything coming out of this damned creature's mouth, there will be no treaty."

Regus struggled valiantly to keep his expression impassive in the face of the thane's insults, but he couldn't stop his jaw from tightening or his brows from drawing down.

I snorted. If Regus was this easily riled, he was certainly no diplomat, and he was going to have a hard time dealing with the brusque thane. Which begged the question: why had Farren chosen Regus as his representative?

"Why *you*, Regus?" I asked. "Why did Farren send you of all the possessed in his court?"

"Mostly, to deal with Castor." He smiled. "Although I see you've already taken care of the wretch."

I shook my head, not about to be sidetracked. "There are dozens of others back in the court who could deal with Castor—ones *not* tasked with seeing to the court's security. So, why send you?" I persisted.

Regus' smile faded. "Perhaps we should reconvene this meeting for later," he said, directing his words to the councilors. "Michael and I require a moment in private."

"No," I said before Stormhammer could. "Whatever you have to say, it's best if the council hears it too."

The possessed hesitated.

"Sit, Regus," Lorn said, gesturing to one of the empty seats. "Michael is right. There can be no alliance between our people again, until we reestablish grounds for trust."

With a sigh, the possessed strode forward. "I hope you don't come to regret this, Wolf," he muttered under his breath as he brushed past me.

I hope so, too.

CHAPTER 420: A MATTER OF CONSCIENCE

Once we were seated, Lorn gestured to Regus. "Begin, please."

His mien serious, the possessed took his time responding. "Things in the court have not panned out the way we hoped."

I sat up straighter. "What does that mean?"

"You already know about Castor," Regus said. "After his—"

I slashed my hand down. "I only know that Castor was still in the city when I arrived. What I don't know is *why* that was the case." I pinned Regus with a severe look. "Why did Farren allow him to stay?"

The possessed sighed. "The archlich didn't," he replied simply. "Even before Adriel arrived with her report on your meeting with Draven, Farren sent a messenger to New Haven, instructing Castor and his people to return."

"I'm guessing Castor refused," I said.

Regus barked a laugh. "He didn't just refuse. He sent the messenger's head back in a box—which I suppose was a message all on its own."

I pursed my lips. So, Castor *had* rebelled. "That doesn't explain why Farren sent you."

"I was getting to that," Regus said irritably. "Castor's foolish gambit drew attention—as did Farren's response, admittedly."

Lorn's eyes narrowed. "Meaning what?"

"Meaning," Regus expounded, "that the initial group the archlich dispatched didn't just have orders to kill Castor, they were also instructed to burn the bodies—" he shot me a pointed look—"and to crush their finger bones."

"Finger bones?" Gamil asked blankly. "Forgive me, but what's so important about their finger bones?"

His expression opaque, Regus didn't answer.

I frowned, recalling Adriel's words from what was only a week ago but seemed much longer. "The possessed's spirits have never fully separated from their original bodies," I said slowly. "Each of them carries a remnant of their former selves in their new bodies—a finger bone to be precise."

"Destroy the bone, and you destroy the possessed?" Elron—always a quick one—guessed.

I nodded.

"What?" Stormhammer asked, astonished. "You mean to say that all this time all we needed to do to destroy the possessed was to burn their blasted bones? And that would have gotten rid of them *forever*?"

Once more, I nodded mutely. With everything else going on, I'd forgotten about this seemingly arbitrary piece of lore Adriel had imparted until reminded by Regus' words. But I was only too glad to share the information with the council. It would give them some measure of power over the possessed.

A bargaining chip if they ever needed one.

I glanced at Regus. His face was contorted unhappily. He hadn't liked that I'd spilled the possessed's secrets, but he hadn't tried to stop me either, I noted.

Seeing my look, Regus said, "Don't worry. I took care of it."

"Took care of what?" Gamil asked, looking confused again.

"On our way through the tunnel complex, my men and I gathered the possessed bodies and destroyed every last finger bone," Regus answered. "Castor is gone for good."

Involuntary sighs of relief escaped from both Lorn and Stormhammer.

"You mentioned an 'initial group' earlier," I said, guiding the conversation back on track. "That implies yours wasn't the only group sent to deal with Castor. What happened to the first one?"

"They never left. They refused the archlich's orders," Regus stated bluntly.

I stared at him.

"Inconceivable, I know," he said, "but if there is one thing every possessed fears, it's final death. That Farren was willing to inflict such on any possessed—even ones of Castor's caliber—did not sit well with the others."

"He miscalculated," Elron said.

"Badly," Regus agreed.

"So where does that leave us?" Gamil asked.

"The court is... unsettled," Regus admitted. "No one dares to openly defy the archlich, but some are not above resisting passively. They're not actively moving against Farren, but they *are* refusing to comply with his orders."

"Some?" I repeated sharply. "That's pretty vague, Regus. Define some."

The possessed winced. "A significant *some* then. Less than half the court have sided with the archlich." He hesitated.

"What else?" I demanded.

"There is a more rebellious group, too," he added reluctantly.

The picture Regus was painting grew worse with every utterance. "And what are they doing?" I asked tiredly.

"This *small* group has been sabotaging the court's defenses and killing off the archlich's supporters whenever they can," he said.

I gestured to his new body. "Did they get you too?"

"Yes," he replied curtly.

"What has the archlich's response been?" Elron asked.

"Farren has killed the five rebels we caught in retaliation but has stopped short of dealing final death to them," Regus said. "He has refused rehoming any of their spirits, though. Unfortunately, that has not deterred the rest, and matters remain tense."

"Which brings us to you," I said quietly.

Regus nodded. "Farren dispatched me to take care of Castor because there was no one else he could trust to deal with the problem."

"Where's Adriel in all this?" I asked.

"She is at the court in a new golem body and is doing her best to help Farren maintain order," he replied. "But Adriel was never well-liked to begin with, and she can no more fix the problem than Farren can."

"I see." I drummed my fingers on the table. "And is that sum of it?"

"There is one other thing," Regus said, appearing even more reluctant to speak now.

I closed my eyes, striving for patience. "Go on."

"The archlich's new decrees have not gone down well," Regus said.

"What decrees?" Lorn asked.

"The one pertaining to New Haven's players," he replied quietly. "Many disagree."

My eyes snapped open. "Explain."

"There is a, uhm, feeling that the archlich's provision banning the harvesting of New Havener players is overly... generous," Regus said delicately. "Most possessed agree that the way Loskin ended up treating New Haven was wrong, but they also believe the city would not exist without the efforts expended by the court on its behalf."

I spread my hands flat across the table, fearing that if I didn't, I would do something rash.

Eyeing me carefully, Regus continued, "These possessed believe New Haven should continue to pay in, uhh... bodies."

A growl began to rise at the back of my throat.

"In short," Regus said, finishing in a rush, "they want to reinstate the original agreement between New Haven and the court. They propose the underground tunnel be reopened, allowing those who want to leave to do so. Those that remain, though, must continue to adhere to the New Haven-court treaty."

A hush descended on the room.

"So, again, where does that leave us?" Gamil asked finally.

"With things in a mess," I snarled. Bowing my head, I rested my forehead on the table. The others waited for me to go on, but I was too incensed to do so.

After a while, Regus and the councilors resumed talking amongst themselves. My thoughts far away, I let their words flow unheeded over me.

"The damned possessed," I muttered under my breath. "Again." They were a matter I'd ignored for too long, and now it seemed I was paying for my ambivalence. In my defense, though, I'd been expecting the lichs to take care of the problem.

The former scions were Adriel and Farren's responsibility, I had told myself. The possessed were of their making. It was *their* duty to fix things. Not mine.

I was wrong.

I was a scion. Perhaps the *only* scion.

And it was my duty to protect the Pack.

I don't know when I had begun thinking of New Haven as Pack, but all unknowing, the notion had crept up on me. Maybe it had begun when I'd first entered the city, or when Elron had helped me, or when I'd learned of the city's suffering at the hands of the possessed, or maybe it was when I'd taken on my apprentice. I wasn't sure. But I was certain the New Haveners *were* Pack and that I needed to do whatever was necessary to protect them.

There was more to it, though.

The possessed had committed vile deeds, both collectively and as individuals. This was uncontested fact. I had stopped myself from contemplating too hard what that meant, though, and had left it to my allies, Farren and Adriel, to set things right. I knew Adriel's own past was black, and I'd wrestled with the idea of allying with her when I'd first accepted her help.

She, though, had resolved to make restitution for her crimes.

She, though, sought redemption.

But what of the others?

I'd not questioned what price the possessed should pay for the things they'd done—not as a group or as individuals—nor had I considered if any of them actually regretted the dark choices that they'd made.

Truly, how many of the thousand-odd possessed in Farren's court were eager to redeem themselves? If Castor and Regus' tale were any example, the answer seemed glaringly obvious.

Not enough.

My mouth twisted sourly. *There has to be a reckoning.*

The possessed had to be brought in line, or history would repeat itself in New Haven. And if not here, then elsewhere once the possessed left the dungeon.

And I could not let that happen, I realized.

I couldn't allow the possessed to go their own way or remain unbound. They were a danger to everyone, and it was up to me to deal with the problem.

I raised my head. I knew what needed to be done.

"I will take care of the possessed," I said loudly, cutting across the other's chatter.

All eyes turned to me.

"Take care of how?" Elron asked warily.

"I have a plan," I said, waving aside his question. I turned to Regus. "I need you to dispatch a messenger to Farren."

The possessed's eyes narrowed, but he didn't question my right to give him orders. "Go on."

"Tell Farren what's happened here. Tell him he is to lockdown the court. No possessed are to be allowed to leave, either through the exit portal or into the dungeon at large. Understood?"

Regus studied me expressionlessly for a second, then nodded slowly. "I will do as you wish."

"Also, ask Adriel to meet me at the guardian." I would need her help and expertise if what I planned had any hope of succeeding.

"Alright," Regus agreed.

"Good." I turned to Elron. "How soon can Algar and the four companies be made ready to march?"

He pursed his lips but did not ask where I planned on sending them. "They began mustering this morning, and their kits and baggage trains have already been allocated. My best guess? The men will be ready tomorrow morning."

My lips turned down. Tonight would've been better, but there was no helping it. "Then they are to march through the underground tunnel as soon as they're ready. I will give Algar his orders myself."

Lorn glanced at Elron, but seeing that the First was not going to question me, he addressed me himself, "That tunnel leads to only one place: the archlich's court. What do you intend your soldiers to do when they get there?"

I didn't answer.

"Surely you don't plan on throwing them against the possessed?" Gamil asked, aghast.

I shook my head. "I don't. but I *do* expect them to blockade the tunnel and stop any of the possessed venturing into New Haven in the event that Farren's people disobey his orders." I glanced at Regus. "They will have help, though."

"Meaning me?" the possessed asked.

"Meaning you," I agreed. "You and your men will support Algar. Under no circumstances will you allow any possessed to get past you and enter the city."

"What do you intend on doing?" Regus asked worriedly.

"I intend on taking care of the problem of the possessed once and for all. One way or the other, by the time I'm done, there will be no more possessed."

The council meeting drew to a close soon after that.

Despite Gamil, Regus, and Lorn's insistent questions, I refused to share any details of my plans. It was not that I distrusted them, but I was wary of making promises I was unable to keep. But I had meant what I'd said.

When I was done, the possessed would be no more.

Stepping out of the council hall, I found two groups awaiting me. Ghost and Nyra were on one side. On the other was Algar and three officers, all of whom looked vaguely familiar.

"Done already?" I asked Nyra, ignoring the soldiers for the time being.

"Yeah," she replied with a self-satisfied grin. "We got everything you wanted and more." Her gaze drifted to the bald man beside me, and her face paled. "Is that...? Is he a possessed?"

"I am," Regus replied amiably. "And who are you?" Not waiting for Nyra's response, he knelt before the pyre wolf. "You must be Ghost. Adriel told me all about you, but her words did not do you justice. It's a pleasure to meet you, young wolf."

"Now that's a proper greeting," Ghost told me as she and Regus shook paw-to-hand.

"I'll keep that in mind," I replied blandly. *"Did everything go well?"*

Ghost gave a mental shrug. *"As well as can be expected."*

I turned to Regus. "Nyra is my apprentice," I said.

The possessed looked up at me curiously. "Your apprentice? Why would you—" He broke off and, shooting back to his feet, studied Nyra intently.

"Yes," I replied in response to the dawning suspicion on his face, "Nyra is a player."

"She's from New Haven?" Regus asked sharply.

I nodded, keenly observing his reaction.

"Ancients," he muttered. "A player from New Haven. That's the last thing we need right now." He glanced at me. "You know what that means?"

"I do. The possessed are going to want to claim her body."

"What?" Nyra squeaked.

"That's right," he agreed, ignoring the young woman. "Some are going to be baying for her blood. You better keep her hidden until all this settles down."

I shook my head. "I can't do that, I'm afraid. Nyra will be accompanying you back to the court."

"What!" Regus and Nyra exclaimed simultaneously.

Ignoring their outbursts, I went on. "There's been a change of plans," I told my apprentice. "The council has brought to light matters I can't ignore. Regus will fill you in on the details later. But the short of it is that I have to accelerate my own plans."

I grimaced. "The truth is I will travel faster without you, which is why I'm leaving you behind with Regus. Don't worry, though. I will rejoin you soon."

"B-but... but will I be safe with them?" Nyra asked hoarsely, her gaze darting fearfully to Regus again.

"You will," I replied firmly. "I'm placing you in Regus' care. He will personally see to your protection."

The possessed blanched.

"Ghost will also be with you," I added, not looking at the pyre wolf. She wouldn't like being left behind any more than Nyra did.

"*No, Prime!*" Ghost cried, protesting just as I expected her to. "*I should accompany you!*"

"*Not this time,*" I replied adamantly. "*Nyra is Pack, and we both have a duty to see her safe. She is right to fear the possessed. They are dangerous. Which is why you must escort her.*"

"*But what about Regus?*"

"*I trust Regus, but he is still a possessed—and not Pack.*" I paused. "*I don't expect to be gone long. I should rejoin you about a day after you reach the court. Perhaps two if things with Draven take longer.*"

By my estimate, I could make the journey from New Haven to the guardian in about twenty hours, perhaps less, especially if I ran the entire way—something I could do with my high stamina pool.

Nyra couldn't. Even with the help of her focus skill, I expected she would have to frequently stop to rest. The same would also apply to the second leg of the journey, from the guardian to the court.

And after Regus' news, I felt a new urgency grip me.

The possessed hadn't come out and said it, but I got the feeling that matters teetered on a knife's edge in the court. And I couldn't afford for things to tip over the wrong way.

Seeming to sense the direction of my thoughts, Ghost bowed her head. "*I'll do as you ask, Prime.*"

"*Thank you,*" I murmured.

Looking outward again, I found Nyra staring numbly at me. "You will be okay," I said gently. "Besides Ghost and Regus, you will also have Captain Algar to turn to. Will you do as I ask?"

She nodded mutely.

I glanced at Regus. "And you?"

He sighed heavily. "I will, but you don't make things easy, do you, Michael?"

✳　✳　✳

I spent a few more moments relaying my instructions to the trio and then watched them depart, Regus to ready his men and Nyra and Ghost to gather our supplies.

I hoped I was doing the right thing by sending the pair with Regus, but truly, the risk was minimal. At worst, they would lose a life each, and if that happened, Nyra had strict orders not to leave the safe zone until I got there. Ghost, of course, would return to cloak.

On the other hand, if I arrived at the court too late, the consequences could be catastrophic. It would be no small thing to tackle a thousand-odd possessed in full rebellion, even with Farren and Adriel's help.

"I hear we're leaving."

Turning around, I found that Algar and the three officers had walked up to join me. "And I hear you're my new commander," I said by way of rejoinder.

A smile crossed Algar's face, but it was fleeting only. The captain looked too beset by worries for it to last. "Only if you wish me to remain so," he murmured. "Before we go any further, some introductions are in order." He gestured the first officer forward, a familiar-looking dwarf covered in gleaming plate armor from the neck down. "This is Captain Megtir. He commands the dwarven contingent."

I shook the dwarf's mailed hand. "Megtir, I remember you from the prison."

"Aye, aye, milord. You have my everlasting loyalty for getting us out of that hellhole."

"Call me Michael," I murmured.

The dwarf nodded jerkily and stepped back, his armor clanking.

"Captain Zorgulg," Algar said, introducing the slim orc in studded leather armor. He had a javelin sheathed on his back, a sword at his hip, and a dozen more daggers all about his person. "He leads the skirmishers."

The orc was another familiar face. "Zorgulg," I began, only to stop as I mangled his name.

Zorgulg grinned, revealing sharpened teeth. "Call me Zorg."

I inclined my head. "Zorg, then. You were in the prison, too." The captain was the one who'd escaped the torture chamber only to return a little later with the dwarves in tow.

He chuckled. "That was a night to remember."

I nodded. "I have been meaning to ask: how did you manage to free yourself?" I glanced at Megtir. "And the dwarves."

Zorgulg pulled out a slender piece of metal from a tiny pocket sewn on the inside of his sleeve. "With this," he said. "I always have one on hand."

"Impressive," I said, studying the lockpick. "I have a feeling we'll have a lot to discuss in the coming days."

Laughing, the orc stepped back to give way to the dark elf.

"And this," Algar said, "is Sergeant Everard—excuse me, *Captain* Everard, newly promoted despite his protests to command your archers. You've met already, of course."

Saying nothing, the master archer stuck out his hand, and I shook it just as wordlessly.

Algar rolled his eyes at the silent exchange before going on, "And I am in charge of the cavalry."

"Thank you, Algar," I said before addressing the other captains. "I'm sure we will have more time to get to know each other in the coming days, but right now, we're pressed for time."

"It's true then," Algar muttered, his worry resurfacing. "We march tomorrow?"

"Tonight, if you can help it," I said gravely.

He threw me an incredulous look. "But—"

Forestalling him, I relayed Regus' news.

Algar exhaled heavily when I was done. The other three officers listened intently, but none commented.

"I guess this is going to be a bit rushed then," Algar said.

I tilted my head to the side. "What is?"

"The introductions to the rest of your officers." He paused. "And our oath-taking."

I waved my hand, dismissing his words. "None of that is necessary right now. We'll take care of it once all of this is over."

Algar shook his head stubbornly. "The ceremony is important." His gaze flitted to the three silent officers. "Both for the men and you."

"A ceremony?" I asked, staring at Algar. "Really?"

But there was no give in the captain's expression. "It will only take an hour."

I winced. An entire hour. I'd been hoping to leave immediately. I sighed. "Very well, lead on."

One hour later, I was standing in the fortress' courtyard, waiting for the ceremony to *begin*.

I sighed heavily.

"Thinking you should have cut and run?" Elron asked with a grin.

I nodded.

The four councilors were on a raised dais with me, attending as witnesses. Ghost sat at my side. She and Nyra had been roped in, too. Regus and the possessed under him had *not* been invited and were waiting in the underground tunnel to begin the journey back to the court.

"Take heart," Gamil murmured. "Algar looks ready to begin."

Seeing the same, I strode forward to stand beside the new High Captain. It was a new title that I had foisted on Algar in order to cement his position as the warband's commander.

Every army needed a leader—the four company captains could not lead by consensus—and as evinced by today, the warband would quite often need to operate independently. And truly, I didn't want to be saddled with the headache of commanding two thousand men. That was a task Algar was better suited to.

"Companies, attention!" the high captain bellowed.

The two thousand soldiers arrayed in formations before the dais braced themselves. I ran my gaze over the troops. Hands on their weapons, they held themselves stiff under my scrutiny.

The four companies were distinct and easily identifiable. The dwarves occupied the far left of the courtyard. Each was wrapped in a mountain of steel and bore either an axe or hammer. Standing shoulder to shoulder, their lines were neatly dressed and compact.

Beside them were the more slender orcs. Green-skinned giants in comparison to their more diminutive companions, their formation was noticeably less precise. But for all that, they looked no less menacing with their sharpened teeth and deadly javelins.

The human cavalry occupied the right. Both horses and men were nearly as heavily armed as the dwarves, but instead of plate armor, they favored chainmail. Their weapons of choice were steel-tipped lances, shields, and longswords.

Finally, there was the dark elf company. White-haired, dark-skinned, and slouched in line as they were, the archers still somehow managed to convey the same feeling of lethal readiness as the orcs to their left and the humans to the right.

New Haven's army units were not usually so stratified by race, but since the soldiers had been drawn from the councilors' personal guards—which were so divided—Algar and the other captains had decided against further disrupting the norms the men were used to. But despite the companies' differences, every soldier bore a black patch over their left breast.

A patch, still conspicuously blank.

When I'd inquired about it, I had been told by an irritable Algar that there hadn't been time to stitch the warband's insignia onto it yet and had been left wondering what that insignia could be.

"Today, we witness a historic day in New Haven's history," the high captain shouted. "Today, we create something unique, a warband of New Haven's making and yet not. Today, we pledge allegiance to Lord Michael!"

The soldiers roared even as I winced at the title. I was no lord, I'd told Algar, but he had refused to listen, and besides, 'lord' was much better than what he'd first proposed.

"Today," Algar continued, "we will become the first New Haveners in over a hundred years to escape this gorge, entering the underground tunnel built by our forefathers for just that purpose. Not only that but in a few short days, we will leave Draven's Reach entirely, something no New Havener has done since our ancestors first set foot in this dungeon more than a thousand years ago!"

The soldiers roared their approval again—this time in a much louder voice. From their shining gazes, I could tell departing Draven's Reach was a prospect that excited many, if not all, of them. It, I suspected, was the true reason most had volunteered to serve me, but I couldn't fault them for that. I, too, was eager to be done with the dungeon.

"You will be the forerunners of our people," Algar proclaimed. "While the lords and ladies of our great city remain behind in fear, living half-lives, *we* will go and see the new world for ourselves. *We* will venture out and discover what bounty the Kingdom has to offer. *We* will be the ones to show the families that New Haven can prosper in the Kingdom, that our people need not huddle in this dungeon!"

"Aye, we will!" the soldiers shouted back.

My eyebrows flew up, and unable to help myself, I glanced behind me to see what the councilors were making of Algar's speech.

None looked happy.

The high captain's words had caught them as much by surprise as they had me. It was not that I disagreed with the high captain's sentiments. In fact, I believed there was merit to them. Still, I had had no idea Algar felt this way or so strongly on the subject, and from the four councilors' glum looks, neither had they.

I hid a smile, belatedly realizing some of Algar's intent with his ceremony. Algar might have been Elron's right-hand man once, but it was clear the former aide had a mind of his own.

He was telling not just me, but the councilors too, that as much as the warband was comprised of New Haveners, they were *not* New Haven's to command any longer. He was proclaiming his loyalty—and those of the soldiers—in the clearest way possible by breaking with the position of the city's councilors and founding families.

"Lord Michael has done more for this city than any of us had any right to expect," the high captain went on, oblivious of the disgruntled men behind him. "He rid us of the possessed. He freed our leaders. He killed the archlich. He defeated the harbinger. He even banished the nether. Tell me, soldiers, will you follow him? Will you trust him to keep you safe?"

"YES, WE WILL," they roared back, setting the walls of the courtyard itself reverberating with the force of their response.

Algar held up his arms, and after a moment, silence descended. Glancing to his left, where the three company captains stood in silent attendance, he instructed, "Raise the banner."

My eyes narrowed. Banner? What banner?

Everard withdrew a long wooden pole from behind him and, with the help of the other two captains, unfurled the black cloth wrapped around its top half. Lifting it up, he raised the banner high for all to see.

The banner was plain, black, and unadorned except for the single image stitched in threads of red-gold across its center.

I sighed when I saw it.

It was a wolf's face. A laughing wolf that bore a striking resemblance to the smug-looking familiar padding up to me. *"They did a good job,"* Ghost said brightly. *"Don't you think?"*

"That's a bad idea," I muttered.

"Why?" she asked quizzically.

"I'd rather not have my association with Wolf proclaimed so boldly."

"Then you shouldn't have asked Adriel to craft me a wolf's body," she retorted primly.

That was true enough and left me little room to argue. I knew now what insignia was meant to go on the soldiers' black patches—no doubt it was to be the same one decorating the inside of the left breast of my own Cloak of the Reach. *That's where Algar must have gotten the idea from,* I thought morosely.

But it was not too late to get him to change it.

The high captain, though, had resumed speaking. "Soldiers, from this day forward, we are no longer citizens of New Haven." He paused for effect. "We are Bane Wolves! And our allegiance belongs to Lord Michael only!"

The soldiers' cheers were just as deafening this time as the last—which I took to mean they approved of Algar's name. I groaned softly. *Right, so he's given the warband a name.*

Bane Wolves.

The name had a nice ring to it, but for obvious reasons, it would not have been my first choice.

Still, there would be no changing banner, insignia, or name now.

✳   ✳   ✳

It took a minute before the warband settled down again.

When they did, Algar spun to me. It was time for the oath-taking, the only bit of the ceremony that I had been in the know about, it seemed.

The high captain stepped forward, and Ghost lay down, just like we agreed prior to this. If she'd stayed standing, some of the shorter soldiers would have trouble reaching the top of her head. The familiar's role in the ceremony was more crucial than my own. Ghost, and not me, would be the final arbitrator of each soldier's oaths. If they gave their word falsely, she would know it.

Placing his hand on the pyre wolf, Algar looked at me, and I nodded curtly, motioning for him to get on with it. The oath itself was a simple one—I'd insisted on that—and would not take long to enact.

The captain inhaled deeply, then recited loudly for the watching soldiers' benefit, "I, High Captain Algar, commander of the Bane Wolves, pledge myself in service to Lord Michael. From this day on, he alone holds my loyalty."

Bowing his head, Algar fell silent and waited.

"He speaks truthfully," Ghost confirmed.

"I, Michael," I began, refusing to refer to myself as *Lord Michael,* "accept your..."

My words ran aground as a message from the Adjudicator unfurled in my mind.

Algar raised his head, his face a mix of curiosity and worry.

"One second," I murmured, "the Game is intruding."

High Captain Algar has offered you his allegiance, but individual players cannot directly accept a non-player's pledge. You may, however, acknowledge his oath on behalf of your faction. You currently do not belong to any faction, but as an ascendant player, you have the ability to create one.

Do you wish to create a faction now?

"Urgh," I muttered.

"What's wrong?" Algar whispered, looking more alarmed.

"The Game won't allow me to personally accept your allegiance. I have to do so on behalf of my faction."

"Your faction..." he repeated. "Is that going to be a problem?"

I shook my head slowly. "It won't be," I replied firmly and willed my intentions to the Game.

Surprisingly, my response was rejected.

You cannot create a faction without allocating a name to it.

I sighed. "Right, a name..." I muttered. I hadn't included one in my instructions to the Adjudicator, nor did I have one in mind yet.

I certainly wasn't going to go with Bane Wolves. An army of non-players calling themselves that was one thing. A Game faction named the same was something else entirely. *What about...*

The Guardians' Blades? *No, too revealing.*

Soldiers of Yore? *Hmm, too wordy.*

Void Warriors? *More apt but also too easily associated with me.*

Reachers? *Short, sweet.* I liked it, but again, I considered it to be a little revealing, especially considering the name of my Cloak.

Finding myself unexpectedly stumped, I ground my teeth in frustration. I was glaringly aware of the confused expressions on the faces of the onlookers. The soldiers had to be wondering what the hold-up was, and whatever reasons they were coming up with, I was sure it wasn't anything good.

How hard can it be to come up with a name? I wondered.

My gaze fell on Algar. Maybe I should ask him. The captain had done well enough with the warband's name, and his speech had been—

I paused, recalling something Algar had said earlier. He'd called the Bane Wolves forerunners...

Forerunners, I mused.

The name rolled off the tongue and was meaningful, too, if in a way not immediately obvious to most. The Bane Wolves and the others who I expected to join my faction would be forerunners—forerunners of change. Not just for New Haven but for the Game at large.

I like it, I decided. Closing my eyes, I willed my intention to the Game.

Creating faction...

...

...

Faction creation complete.
The <u>Forerunners</u> have entered the Game!

Congratulations, Michael, you have formed a faction!
Factions are the primary means of controlling territory and forming alliances in the Game. Joining a faction is not like binding oneself to a Power. A faction member can join, leave, or change factions without suffering any repercussions from the Game.
A player's spirit signature is also not marked with their faction affiliation, and it is only the faction's leaders who can usually identify its members.
As the sole ascendant player in the <u>Forerunners</u> faction, you have been designated as its leader.

I inhaled sharply, digesting the Adjudicator's words as quickly as possible. Then, opening my eyes, I focused on Algar again. "I, Michael," I said, making sure my words reached the farthest ends of the courtyard, "accept your oath on behalf of the Forerunners faction."

Algar's eyes widened only fractionally at this deviation from the wording we'd agreed upon, and a soft murmur ran through the courtyard. Come morning, I expected the name *Forerunners* would be on every New Haveners' lips.

Another Game message dropped in my mind.

You have accepted High Captain Algar, a non-player, into the Forerunners faction. Algar is free to break his pledge of loyalty at any time and without consequences. As are you. However, until such time as the Forerunners disavow the captain—or vice versa—he will be considered the faction's sworn man, and his actions will reflect on it.

I smiled. "It is done," I said, shaking Algar's hand.

Returning my smile, he bowed deeply before stepping back and allowing Megtir to take his place.

One down.

And only one thousand, nine hundred and ninety-nine to go.

I didn't end up witnessing the oaths of all two thousand soldiers.

After the first hour—during which I only managed to accept the pledges of fifty of the warband's most senior officers—I'd made my excuses and left Algar and Ghost to see to the rest of the ceremony.

Neither could welcome the remaining soldiers into the faction on my behalf, but Ghost could still judge their truthfulness, and for now, that mattered most.

Promising Algar to see things through to completion when I rejoined him at the archlich's court, I said my goodbyes to Nyra and Ghost, then pulled the city councilors aside.

Shooting me curious glances, the four followed me into the vacant room I led them into. I closed the door behind me, and the sound of the courtyard and the still-ongoing ceremony faded.

"What is it?" Elron asked. "Is something wrong?"

I shook my head. "No, nothing like that. I have a favor to ask."

The councilors exchanged glances. "A favor?" Lorn ventured.

I nodded. "But before I get to it, what did you think of Algar's speech?"

Gamil frowned. "It was irresponsible," he said, tight-lipped. "The boy does not understand the risks we must balance."

"Algar can be a little... impulsive sometimes," Elron added. "It is something you will have to watch for."

I grinned. "I don't know how much good that will do. I, too, have been accused of behaving recklessly a time or two." My smile faded. "Still, he is right, you know. You're subjecting your people to a half-life by staying in the dungeon. This gorge is not large enough for the city to flourish, and if you remain, New Haven will turn insular. At some point, you must leave."

"Is that why you've called us here?" Stormhammer asked. "To convince us to leave? Because we already know—"

"No," I said, cutting him off. "I mentioned Algar's speech only to remind you that New Haven cannot continue where it left off and resume life as normal." I held each councilor's gaze in turn. "You will have to begin preparing for the day of your eventual exodus from the dungeon."

All four nodded. "There is sense to what you say," Elron said, "and it's no more than we've agreed amongst ourselves." He paused. "But what does this have to do with your favor?"

"Only this." I inhaled. "I can help you prepare. But to do that, I will have to bring people into the dungeon—people who may find themselves in need of a safe haven from the Game, at least temporarily." I smiled lopsidedly. "Hence the favor."

"What! You want to bring outsiders *here*?" Gamil exclaimed. "After you just gave your word to keep New Haven secret?"

"I didn't promise that," I corrected gently. "I promised not to reveal the location of the hidden portal without the council's approval."

The two were not synonymous. I couldn't see how New Haven and the dungeon's existence could remain secret anyway—what with two thousand of their former residents out and about in the world. Sooner or later, someone would let something slip. Still, while word of the dungeon might get out, no one, not even a Power, would be able to enter.

Not without knowing where the hidden portal was.

"What if..." I continued. "What if I could bring those seeking refuge into Draven's Reach *without* them learning the location of the portal? Would you help them then?"

Doing so would be difficult but not impossible, I thought, especially when it came to non-players.

"Who are these refugees?" Lorn asked.

"Mostly non-players. Humans, gnomes—" I paused—"and wolves."

"Wolves?" Stormhammer asked, his bushy brows shooting up.

"You said *mostly*," Gamil interjected before I could answer the thane. "Who else do you intend on bringing?"

"To transport the refugees here, I will have to reveal the portal's location to at least one other player," I reluctantly explained.

"Why?" Elron asked.

"I am no mage," I replied simply. "I'll need a practiced spellcaster to open a portal and protect the non-players from the nether while we affect the transfer." I held up my hand, forestalling their protest. "The individual in question is someone I trust implicitly. Believe me, I have shared secrets of greater importance with her already—secrets that would see every Power in the Game hunt me more vigorously than they would your city."

For a moment, the councilors said nothing, but from their expressions, I could see they were giving my request serious consideration.

"Where would you settle these... refugees?" Lorn asked finally.

I shrugged. "In New Haven or the archlich's court. Wherever it is, I ask that you be willing to trade with them and aid them."

The four exchanged another round of glances before withdrawing into a huddle. Doing my best not to listen, I waited patiently.

Eventually, they broke apart, and Lorn stepped forward to address me. "We will allow it," he pronounced.

I inclined my head gratefully. "Thank you."

✳   ✳   ✳

I left New Haven shortly after that.

I had a long journey ahead of me, and given the delays I'd already encountered, I doubted I would reach the guardian by morning. Still, I pushed hard. Scaling the sheer gorge walls enclosing the city, I jogged southeast across the plateau. While I ran, I considered the events of the last few days.

Much had changed since I'd entered the city.

I'd gone into New Haven with my path certain. I'd intended on kickstarting the city's exodus, securing the loan of a thousand soldiers, then returning to Draven to see if he'd succeeded, and finally, departing the dungeon for the wolves' valley with my warband in tow.

Now, I was no longer certain things would pan out that way.

I'd gotten both more and less than I'd bargained for in New Haven. I'd not expected the New Haveners to want to remain in Draven's Reach. I'd *hoped* instead to settle them in the wolves' valley after I claimed the sector, thereby forging a long-term alliance with the former denizens of the dungeon.

But there was no denying the council's decision offered different opportunities. With the New Haveners choosing to stay, Draven's Reach became not just a potential training ground but also a refuge for my allies. And considering the sector was now nearly unassailable, it made sense to alter my plans...

Then there were the possessed. I'd had big plans for them too, but after Regus' report, I knew I could not trust them as they were, leaving me no choice but to forge them anew or...

... destroy them entirely.

The future was in flux, and what course I chartered next would depend heavily on whether Draven had succeeded and what Adriel had to say about my plans to deal with the possessed. With only these heavy thoughts for company, I jogged doggedly across the barren terrain.

Hours later, exhausted, I collapsed and slept fitfully, but no more than for a couple of hours. Then, I was back up and running again. Twice more, I repeated the feat until finally, around late afternoon of my thirty-second day in the dungeon, I reached my destination.

✳   ✳   ✳

As I slipped into the dungeon's large central valley, former den of the void tree and the harbinger, and now home only to Draven and the safe zone, I spied the centaur's unmissable frame in the distance.

Draven was turned away, so I couldn't see his face, but sitting cross-legged at his feet was a small figure.

Good, Adriel's got here before me.

Letting my gaze drift from the pair, I searched for a third figure as I jogged closer. But the landscape was otherwise empty. I frowned. Did that mean the guardian's search for Ceruvax had ended in failure?

Damn, I was really hoping—

Seeming to sense something in the air, the seated figure jerked upright and spun around. His eyes narrowed while my own flared in shock.

It wasn't Adriel.

It was an older man with graying hair, a face seamed with age, wiry limbs, and ancient shadowed eyes. His back was unbent, and in his left hand, he carried a staff that topped his own six feet of height. If I hadn't known better, I would have believed it was the Wolf Prime himself I was seeing.

But I did know better. "Ceruvax," I murmured.

Even across the distance that separated us, he heard. "Young pup," he growled. "I should have known…"

In the wake of the envoy's words, a Game alert dropped into my mind.

You have completed the task: <u>Find the last Wolf Envoy</u>! You have rescued Ceruvax from the dungeon in which he has languished for centuries and in a manner most extraordinary. Thanks to your efforts, not only has House Wolf been gifted with a valuable asset, but none of the Powers who have wasted lifetimes hunting the envoy realize he's escaped. Your House remains hidden and continues to grow under your leadership! Well done, scion!

Wolf is pleased, and your Mark has deepened.

My lips curved upward in a smile. I'd found Wolf's envoy! After all this time, I'd finally completed the task, the oldest on my list.

And for a change, something's gone right!

My eyes flickered to the guardian, but he hadn't turned around. I frowned. *Why hasn't he—?* I broke off, finally realizing what the guardian's stillness meant.

He'd gone back to sleep.

I exhaled a troubled breath. Somehow, I didn't think Draven would be slumbering unless the need was great. *Searching for Ceruvax must have exhausted him.* Despite this, the guardian had still honored the boon he had owed me.

I would strive just as hard on his behalf, I vowed. I would find his lost brethren and restore them. Someday soon. I turned back to Ceruvax. The envoy was still watching me through lidded eyes. I quickened my pace.

We had much to talk about.

DAY THIRTY-TWO IN DRAVEN'S REACH

Panting from my long run, I drew to a halt in front of Ceruvax. Unmoving, the envoy studied me while I caught my breath.

You have passed a mental resistance check! Ceruvax has failed to analyze you.

The old wolf rubbed his chin. "Deception?" he guessed.
I nodded.
"Hmm. I have you to thank for my escape from Scharlach, I take it?"
I stared at him blankly. "From where?"
"The dungeon in Nexus where the Shadow Coalition had me trapped."
"Oh." Breathing easier at last, I dropped my hands and stood straighter. "Yes, I brought you here."
The envoy's eyes roved over me from head to foot, darting from ebonheart to the legendary wayfarer items before finally coming to rest on the wolf insignia emblazoned on the inside of my cloak that kept flapping open.
"You've grown since we last met," he said.
I smiled. "I have."
Ceruvax's head jerked upward to study the purple sky. "Where are we?"
My eyebrows rose. "You don't know?"
He shrugged. "I know we're in a dungeon, but not which one."
Frowning, my gaze darted to Draven.
Seeing where I looked, the envoy smiled. "The guardian brought me here and bade me wait. For what he would not say. Then, he fell asleep."
My frown deepened. "He didn't explain?" Technically, Draven hadn't needed to do so. Bringing Ceruvax here was all the centaur was required to do to honor the terms of the boon. But still, I'd expected better of him...
"He didn't," Ceruvax replied mildly.
"And you still waited?"
Surprisingly, the old wolf laughed. "Boy, I can't believe you've grown so much that you think it wise to disobey one such as Draven. When a guardian says wait, you wait."
"I see."
"Besides," Ceruvax added, glancing to the left, "I kept busy."
Following his gaze, I realized with a start the harbinger's corpse was gone. In its place was a mess of gory remains.
"Did you kill it?" he asked softly.
I nodded.
Wordlessly, the envoy held out his hand. Resting on his palm was a single glittering stone as black as the void. Reaching out with my will, I analyzed the item.

This is a netherstone. It is an artifact of unknown rank. You are unable to discern its properties.

"What's a netherstone?" I asked.

"You don't know?" he asked, echoing my earlier question.

I shook my head.

"Curious." Ceruvax's gaze flickered to the aetherstone bracelet on my wrist. "I assumed it was because of the netherstone that you came to this dungeon." He stared at me from beneath bushy brows. "That's the only reason for hunting a harbinger that does not smack of stupidity."

"It's a long story," I said, waving aside his comment. "Are you going to tell me what the stone does?"

Ceruvax held up the glistening orb between his thumb and forefinger. "This little gem can do what no aetherstone can—it can record nether coordinates."

I blinked. "Does that mean you can use it to teleport into a dungeon?"

The envoy chuckled. "I wish, but no. But the stone *can* record the coordinates of a sector lost in the Nethersphere. With it, you can jump directly into the void without using a rift." Frowning, he stared upward at the shimmering barrier surrounding the dungeon. "It's why the stygians never leave harbinger bodies lying around. They don't want scions—or players—jumping freely into their territory. How did you manage to hide that corpse from them?"

"All part of that long story I mentioned," I said blandly.

Shaking his head, Ceruvax tossed the stone at me, and I caught it.

You have acquired a netherstone.

"Thanks," I said, storing the small object in one of my pockets.

"I have a thousand and one questions, boy," Ceruvax said. "But they can wait for later. You've been running hard. I don't want to know from what, but I assume it's unsafe to remain. We should—"

"On the contrary, there are few safer places in the dungeon." I pointed northwest. "The safe zone is not far in that direction." I sank to the ground in a cross-legged stance. "But I'll admit, I'd rather not walk all that way right now. We can talk here."

Ceruvax eyed me askance but didn't demur. "This entire canyon stinks of stygians." He sat beside me, resting his staff horizontally across his knees. "If I didn't know better, I'd say the nether invaded."

"It did," I said seriously.

The old wolf didn't come out and say it, but from his pointed looks in Draven's direction, I knew he thought I exaggerated. How could the nether invade a sector protected by a guardian, after all?

"The guardian was in stasis," I replied. Removing a pair of rations from my backpack, I offered one to the envoy.

Wrinkling his nose, Ceruvax refused. "The new Powers put him to sleep?" he growled. "How?"

I shook my head. "It wasn't the new Powers. Going into stasis was something Draven and his brethren decided to do on their own." I bit into my ration. "When I arrived, there was a hole in the barrier, and stygian seeds were taking root everywhere. There was even a void tree." I swallowed. "It was only a sapling, though."

The envoy kept his face impassive, but he couldn't stop his hands from tightening around his staff. "A void tree. A harbinger. Stygian seeds. And a nest."

He didn't ask, but I could see the question in his eyes. "I didn't defeat them all on my own," I said with a smile. "I had help. And Draven did the rest once we woke him."

Ceruvax bowed his head, pondering my words.

"That's how you did it then," he said after a moment.

"Did what?"

The old wolf looked at me. "Convinced the guardian to pull me out of Scharlach. You earned his favor by clearing the dungeon, didn't you? Then you used your boon to rescue me."

"Something like that," I mumbled, swallowing another mouthful.

Ceruvax shook his head. Whether it was at my audacity or my folly at wasting the boon, I couldn't tell. Looking around, he scanned the valley. "I take it then that the stygian menace has been fully dealt with?"

I shrugged. "In this sector."

"What does that mean?" he asked sharply.

I set down my ration. "Two sectors lead into Draven's Reach. The first has already fallen into the nether. The second is currently in peril. It has a void tree, too." I shuddered. "An older one."

Ceruvax's eyes didn't leave mine. "How do we leave here then?"

"There is a third portal."

"And what lies on the other side of it?"

"I don't know," I said tiredly. "Like the entrances, the exit is one-way. According to my allies, it leads to the Kingdom. However, any information we have on the sector is centuries out of date. I can confirm that the void isn't present there, though."

Adriel had managed to extract that much from Draven. Unfortunately, because Kingdom sectors were outside the guardian network, he couldn't tell us much else about what awaited us on the portal's other side.

Ceruvax rubbed his chin. "Setting aside this curious case of your allies, how did you manage to enter this dungeon—what did you call it? Draven's Reach—if the void is present in both entrance sectors?"

"My Class helped me navigate the way safely through." I shot him a look. "I find it curious, by the way, that you haven't inquired about my Classes, considering your... preoccupation with them the last time we met."

Ceruvax grinned toothily, his first genuine smile since we'd met, I suspected. "I may not be able to analyze you, my young scion, but I can read your Mark as well as any wolf." Remaining seated, he bowed low over his hands. "Hail, Protector. May the Packs flourish under your rule."

Ceruvax has acknowledged your Wolf Mark, accepting your supremacy within House Wolf without contest.

I stared at the old wolf, not sure what surprised me more: the Game message or his words.

Unbending, Ceruvax met my quizzical look. "Your Wolf Mark tells me all I need to know," he said softly. "And not only have you proven yourself to a Pack and earned their loyalty, but you've also begun to tread the ways of Power." His eyes shone. "You've gained an ascendant Class."

I was taken aback. "How do you know that?"

He tilted his head to the side. "I fear whichever Wolf has seen to your education has done a bad job."

I dismissed his words. "There are no Wolves except for me." I paused. "And now you, I suppose."

He leaned forward intently. "Truly? Then who are these allies you mentioned?"

"They're decidedly *not* Wolves," I replied, deliberately keeping my response vague. Now was not the time to bring up the lichs' peculiar affiliations.

"I see," he said, sitting back. "That explains the... gaps in your understanding."

I rolled my eyes. "No need to be coy about it. I know I'm still ignorant of much of the Game. Now tell me. What did you mean?"

"I like you, young wolf," Ceruvax said with a laugh. "I do. Now, listen carefully. There are two paths to ascendancy for adherents of Wolf. The first is straightforward and requires you to advance as a player to rank thirty."

I nodded slowly. "I've often heard minor Powers described as players above level three hundred."

Ceruvax's lips turned down. "We amongst the Houses prefer the term, Young Blood."

"Hmm. Is that the only difference between the two? A name?"

The envoy waved aside my words. "There is more to it than that, which I will tell you all about—" his eyes twinkled—"and at great length. But to get back to your question. There is also a second path to ascendancy, and it is that which I believe you've set yourself on."

"Let me guess... it depends on my Marks?"

He smiled. "Exactly. For a Wolf to acquire an ascendant Class requires two things: the Mark of a Wolf Protector and a Powerful Initiate Mark. And even though I failed to analyze you, I can *see* your spirit signature. Both your Protector and Initiate Marks shine brightly in my eyes." He pointed to the spot recently occupied by the harbinger's corpse. "Then, too, you also told me you killed that. So..."

"So, it's pretty obvious I obtained my ascendant Class," I finished for him.

Ceruvax nodded. "What Class did you choose?"

"Wolf Lord," I replied absently, still pondering what he'd said.

"An interesting choice," he mused. "And your level?"

"Two hundred and five."

The old wolf's eyes widened in astonishment.

"I'm not lying," I said, interpreting his look.

"But... the danger," he began, struggling for the right words. "You shouldn't have... The risks..."

"I know," I replied gravely. "Ascending this early was not deliberate on my part." My gaze slid to the harbinger's remains. "It was an accident—mostly."

Ceruvax laughed hollowly. "An accident?"

"I understand the risks, believe me," I said quietly. "Both those to me personally and my aspirations for House Wolf." I inhaled deeply. "Those risks are why I brought you here."

Any joy the envoy's gaze had held had long since fled, and now he studied me as seriously as I did him. "I think you better start at the beginning, boy."

I sighed. "Make yourself comfortable, then. This is going to take a while."

"Where do you want me to start?" I asked.

"At the very beginning," Ceruvax replied. "From the first day you entered the Game."

I winced. Relaying my tale was going to take even longer than I expected, but I didn't begrudge the envoy his desire to know everything. I was going to ask a lot of Ceruvax in the coming days, and before I did that, I knew I had to win his trust.

Which might not be so easy once the envoy learned the things I'd done. Or not done.

Still, there could be no half-truths today. House Wolf's survival would depend as much on the old wolf as me, and I would not weaken the House's foundations with lies.

"Before we begin, can I analyze you?" I asked.

"Go ahead," he said, unbothered by the request.

The target is Ceruvax, a level 299 were-mage and human. He bears the Wolf Mark: <u>pack-hunter</u>.

I wanted to frown, finding his lack of Marks damning, but I kept my face impassive. "I thought you were an envoy," I said neutrally.

"I was," Ceruvax replied softly.

"Was?"

He met my gaze. "My Prime is dead," he said sadly.

I blinked. "And so..."

"I lost Atiras' Mark that day, becoming unSworn," he confirmed.

This time, I couldn't hold back my frown. "But you have no Power Mark. Shouldn't you—"

Ceruvax laughed, his voice full of old bitterness. "I'm not one of the fortunate few who can evolve, Wolf Lord. I'm not sure what it is like these days in the Game, but in my day, those who could not evolve were looked down upon. Atiras was different, and he made me his envoy regardless."

"I see. And your level?" I asked delicately.

"I will never reach level three hundred," Ceruvax said, confirming my suspicion. "The Game won't allow me to advance further." He exhaled, seeming to expel old frustrations as he did. "But enough of my own history. Begin your tale, please."

I hesitated, glancing from Draven to Ceruvax. It hadn't occurred to me to wonder before, but... how could I be certain of the old wolf's identity? After all, the guardian wasn't around to confirm his tale.

"What's wrong?" he asked, sensing something amiss.

I met his eyes. "How do I know you are who you say you are?" I asked bluntly, deciding to be forthright.

He chuckled, thinking I was joking—only for his amusement to fade when I didn't smile back. "You are serious?"

I nodded.

Ceruvax snorted. "House Marks are nearly impossible to forge, *and* I saw your own Mark too, something no one not of Wolf could do."

"Nearly impossible is not the same as impossible," I murmured, "and being able to see my Mark only means you're a Wolf, not that you are who you claim to be." I had not forgotten the werewolves working for the Triumvirate in Nexus.

"Hmpf. That *is* paranoid, even for someone steeped in deception." He shook his head. "I am no Loken, believe me."

I winced.

The old wolf noticed. "What, don't tell me you've run across the Betrayer?" he demanded harshly.

"If by the Betrayer you mean Loken, then yes." And wasn't that an interesting name for the Shadow Power? "Several times, actually. He seems to have taken an interest in me."

Ceruvax's gaze sharpened. "That's not good."

"I know."

He fell silent for a moment. "Alright, I take back what I said earlier. If Loken has you in his sights, you're not nearly paranoid enough," he said grimly.

I laughed involuntarily.

If the old wolf was an actor, he was a good one. And truth be told, I liked him, but sharing the entirety of who I was was not something I did lightly—with anyone. In fact, I could count on one hand the people who knew everything about me, and if I was going to add Ceruvax to that list...

"A Pact," he said suddenly.

"What?" I asked, looking at him in surprise.

"You're a Power now." Ceruvax smiled. "If a baby one. I propose we enter into a time-limited Pact of truthfulness, with both of us committing to speak no lies. That way, the Adjudicator will stand witness to our words, and we can both be certain of the other's truthfulness. Will that suit you?"

I grinned. "It will indeed."

✳   ✳   ✳

You have sealed a Pact with Ceruvax. For the next 4 hours, he and you will speak no falsehoods.

The terms of the Pact were simple enough, and while it did not guarantee Ceruvax would provide full and complete answers, it did ensure that there would be no lies exchanged.

"I will begin," the old wolf said. "I am Ceruvax," he declared, "former envoy of Atiras and loyal scion of House Wolf."

My suspicions had already dissipated after Ceruvax's proposal of a Pact. Still, I sat easier as his words went uncontested by the Game.

"And I am Michael, wolf lord, wolf protector, voidstealer, and leader of the Forerunners faction."

Ceruvax's eyebrows shot up. "Voidstealer. Is that your Class?"

"Correct."

"I've never heard of it," he admitted.

Taking my time, I described the Class to him.

"You've done well," he said when I finished. "Better than I expected you to have, to be honest." He shook his head ruefully. "From mindstalker to voidstealer, that is a big leap and an achievement most scions would be proud of—even in my day."

I inclined my head. "Thank you."

"Now, do you want to go first? Or should I?"

"You, please." I grinned. "I suspect your own story will be shorter."

"Very well. I assume you already know about the fall of the ancients?" Seeing my nod, Ceruvax continued, "Atiras was one of the first to foresee the danger, so unlike many other Houses, House Wolf was prepared."

He sighed. "Or so we thought. Not even Atiras realized how deeply the rot had spread or how quickly scions would abandon their Houses in favor of becoming Forcesworn." He waved his hand irritably. "I won't bore you with all the details of our defeat, but suffice it to say, one day, while on a mission for the Prime, I was ambushed in Nexus by a group of so-called Shadowsworn. I managed to escape, but only by fleeing into a nearby dungeon."

"Scharlach," I said.

"Yes, this was still early in the war, and at the time, the new Powers were concentrating their efforts on fighting the Primes within the Kingdom, so the Shadowsworn didn't pursue me into the dungeon. Unfortunately for me, Scharlach has only one portal, which serves as both entrance and exit."

"They blockaded the portal?"

"They did." Ceruvax laughed. "I'm sure they didn't anticipate any trouble hunting down a weak-blood like me once they dealt with the bigger threats they considered other scions to be. But Scharlach is huge, almost as large as the minotaur maze, and they erred in giving me time to prepare." He bared his teeth. "Scions have been underestimating me my entire life, and I was neither as weak nor as easy a prey as the Shadow scum expected."

His expression sobered. "Not even I imagined I would evade capture this long, though." He squeezed his eyes shut. "Or that I would survive my Prime's fall. But as trying as these past centuries have been, I'm grateful I survived. I will see House Wolf reborn."

"I hope to witness the same," I said, echoing his sentiment.

Ceruvax shook himself. "That's my tale, in brief. One day, perhaps, I will give you the longer version." He leaned forward intently. "Now, tell me your own story. How did it begin?"

"In the Dark," I said with a lopsided grin. "And with a Power named Erebus..."

✳   ✳   ✳

For the next four hours, I spoke nearly non-stop, taking Ceruvax through every aspect of my journey through the Game. Four hours were not enough, especially when the former envoy kept interrupting.

"It saddens me to hear the dire wolves have grown so diminished," he murmured at one point. "But you say they still have Atiras' astral rings?"

I nodded emphatically.

The rings were the means I had used to enter the Mind Trial, and I'd made certain to mention them to Ceruvax. The former Prime's artifacts were vital to my own plans, and I planned on returning to the subject of them when Adriel finally joined us.

Where is she? I wondered in passing.

"That is good," Ceruvax mumbled half under his breath, unaware of my own musings. "I wonder if the other artifacts survived too..."

...

From there, the conversation moved on to the Awakened Dead. Surprisingly, Erebus' dungeon did not intrigue Ceruvax as much as it had Loken. Nor did the Tartan legion or the wolves' valley, for that matter.

...

"Foolish of you," he muttered when I told him of my attempt to cross the walls around Nexus' safe zone, but he forbore further comment.

...

The arctic wolves elicited another comment. "They're in the guardian tower? How did they end up there?"

I shrugged, having no answer myself.

...

The old gnome, Cyren, drew Ceruvax's interest too.

"You don't know if he is alone in his views on the ancients?" he asked. "Or if there are others who share similar... hopes?"

I shook my head. "It's an avenue I've been meaning to pursue further," I said. "But I've not had the chance to return to Nexus yet."

...

"A forsworn!" the former envoy exclaimed when I mentioned Safyre. "How curious. Did you analyze her?"

"I didn't," I said. "But what does that matter? I know her level and Class."

"Her level is of no consequence, and her Class, while important, doesn't count as much as her Marks do. She forswore her Power, but what about her ties to the Forces? Do they remain in place?"

"I don't know," I admitted.

"Was her class a Forcesworn one?"

Again, I had to deny knowing.

"What about this Kesh, you say, she shelters more forsworn?"

"She does."

Ceruvax's eyes narrowed. "There is an opportunity there..."

...

Unsurprisingly, it was Loken on whom Ceruvax fixated the most.

I told him everything I knew about the Shadow Power. The old wolf listened attentively, his expression uniformly grim throughout—except when I described how I had tricked the trickster.

"Now, what I wouldn't have given to be there for that," he said, a big grin splitting his face. "Being fooled by a young wolf must have been a bitter pill for the Betrayer to swallow."

"Why do you keep calling him that?" I asked with a fond smile of my own at the memory.

Ceruvax's mirth died. "Have you heard of Serpent House?"

I shook my head.

"They were a powerful House. One that delighted in shrouding itself in mystery as much as Wolf did. But despite how close-mouthed the House was about their affairs, they were not able to keep word spreading of one of their rising stars... Loken."

I sat up, my curiosity piqued. Loken had implied he'd been born into a House, but as always with the trickster, there was no telling how far his words could be trusted.

"The feats he was rumored to have accomplished," Ceruvax continued, "the dungeons he was said to have completed, and the foes he'd purportedly vanquished, all of it left little doubt in the minds of the Houses that one day Loken would ascend to Primehood. In fact, many believed he would become the strongest incarnation of Serpent yet and carry his House into greatness."

Ceruvax bowed his head, lost in his memories.

"Then what happened?" I prompted.

"Loken slaughtered his entire House," he said bluntly. "No one knows how he managed the feat, but there is no doubt he did it, killing everyone from the lowliest scion to the Prime herself."

My brows drew down. There was a coldness in Loken. I'd seen it myself, but to murder an entire House? "Is that why he is called the Betrayer?" I asked when Ceruvax said nothing further.

"What? No. A scion slaughtering members of his own House, while frowned upon, was not exactly unheard of. No, what Loken did was worse. Much worse..."

Once more, Ceruvax fell silent. This time, I waited patiently for him to go on.

"He rejected their blood memories," the old wolf whispered finally. "The dead's, I mean. In so doing, he doomed the fallen scions to wander the Game forever and left the bloodline badly crippled."

I contemplated Ceruvax's words. A dead scion was not free. I had bound myself to House Wolf for all eternity and, after final death, would serve the House still—assuming another living scion accepted my spirit essence. What would it mean for me if it wasn't? I shivered. *Nothing good, I can imagine.*

"Why did Loken do it?" I asked softly. "Why did he reject certain Primehood?"

"No one knows," Ceruvax said bleakly. "But on the day that he did, the rebellion began. You see, it was Loken who led the uprising against the Primes."

✳   ✳   ✳

Understandably, there was a lull in the conversation after that, but sooner than I was ready, Ceruvax waved me on, just as if he'd revealed nothing momentous, which, from his perspective, I suppose he hadn't.

It was ancient history to him, after all.

...

Afterward, we spoke of the twins, Teresa and Terence. Ceruvax was keenly interested in both. "Cats," he muttered. "You're sure that's what she said?"

I nodded. He was referring to the bloodline Sulan claimed the twins sprang from.

"I must meet this Sulan too..."

...

"The chalice is important," Ceruvax pronounced when I described the artifact Loken had asked me to steal. "You will have to get it."

He refused to say more on the matter, though.

...

The werewolves were another topic Ceruvax had surprisingly little to say on. "You must bind them to you, of course," he said. "But it is the Wolf Torc that is more important."

"What about the combat trial?" I asked, raising one eyebrow. "Shouldn't I attempt it?"

He eyed me carefully. "I'm not sure that will be a good idea." He paused. "But gaining access to the lycan guard's stronghold will be valuable. If the sea fortress still stands as you say it does, some of the guard's equipment must've survived the looting."

...

Ceruvax had nothing to say about the Bounty Hunters' Guild, nothing at all, and he ventured not a single comment when I'd relayed my now-defunct plans to capture the wolves' valley.

An altogether different group from Nexus drew his interest.

"The stygian brotherhood," he mused. "They did not exist in my day... And you say they are experts on the nether? You must meet this Huntmistress Kartara."

...

"A Prime trapped in Sickening Ooze. It can't be Pestilence Prime, though."

"But—" I began in protest.

"I know for a fact he was slain early on," Ceruvax interjected. "Someone else must have taken refuge there. But who?"

...

Finally, I reached the last leg of my tale and began describing the groups I'd encountered in Draven's Reach. As I expected, he found the dungeon's potential as intriguing as I did.

"You're right," Ceruvax agreed. "Draven's Reach is the perfect base for House Wolf, especially with the city, New Haven, to provide any resources we need. But what about this group called the possessed? You haven't said much of them at all."

I opened my mouth, ready to dig into the subject.

The time allotted to your Pact with Ceruvax has expired. Your Pact is closed!

"Ah," I said, stifling a yawn. Glancing at Ceruvax, I saw his own eyes were turned inward. He, too, had received the notice from the Adjudicator.

"Let's renew the Pact for another hour," I suggested. "There is not much more left to my story."

He shook his head. "You're tired, you should rest. We can pick this up in the morning. I'll keep watch." He paused. "Assuming you trust me to stand guard?"

I rose to my feet. "Of course."

He inclined his head. "Thank you," he said, rising himself. "There is just one more thing to do then."

I looked at him questioningly.

Going down on a bent knee, the old wolf placed his hand in mine. "Wolf Lord," he said formally, "I offer you my unconditional loyalty. From this day onward, I will serve only you."

Ceruvax, a level 299 were-mage, has offered you unquestioning obedience. He will follow any instructions you issue, both inside and out of combat, and in exchange, he asks for nothing. This Pact will terminate on your final death.

Do you accept Ceruvax's offer?

Ignoring the hanging Game message, I stared at the old wolf. "Are you sure you want to do this now? There are parts of my tale you must still hear."

"I'm sure," Ceruvax said, waving aside my protest. "I've heard more than enough to convince me that you are the right one to lead House Wolf." He shook his head ruefully. "You've accomplished more in a few short months than I managed in centuries."

"You were stuck in a dungeon," I pointed out.

"So, were you," he retorted mildly. "But you got out. I didn't."

It wasn't the same thing. I didn't belabor the point, though. "Your oath is too open-ended," I said instead. "It grants me too much power over you."

"Necessary power," he argued.

I began to shake my head, but he stopped me. "I understand your restraint, Michael, and with respect to other players, I even applaud it." He held my gaze. "But I have served House Wolf for over a thousand years. There can be no half-measures to my service. Besides, I hope to be your envoy one day, as I was Atiras'. For that to happen, you must trust me unconditionally. I must be an extension of your will, no more."

He paused. "I cannot claim to know you well yet, but I believe I am right about this much: you will not trust me as you must unless you bind me strongly."

I exhaled softly. "Are you sure about this?"

"I am," he said unflinchingly.

"Alright, then," I said gravely. "In that case, I gladly accept your service, Ceruvax."

You have sealed a Pact with Ceruvax, and he has been sworn into your service as a <u>follower</u>. Total followers: 2 / 100.

Commander ability triggered. You have passed on the secret blood (lesser) trait and 3 attributes to your new follower. Your Magic has decreased to rank 40.

You have accepted Ceruvax, a player, into the Forerunners faction. Ceruvax is free to break his pledge of loyalty to the faction at any time and without consequences. As are you. However, until such time as the Forerunners disavow the were-mage—or vice versa—he will be considered the faction's sworn man, and his actions will reflect on it.

As a result of his new status, Ceruvax's spirit signature has been etched with a new Mark. He now bears the <u>Mark of Michael</u>!

CHAPTER 426: THE ARRIVAL OF DEATH

After accepting Ceruvax's oath, I fell promptly asleep. I'd run halfway across the dungeon—on very little rest—and was exhausted. But no sooner had I set my head down than it felt as if the old wolf was shaking me.

"Michael, wake up."

You have slept for 4 hours.

I didn't open my eyes, the Game message alone was enough to tell me it was too damn early to be rising. "Gimme another few hours," I replied sleepily, trying to tug free from his insistent hand.

"Someone's coming."

That got my attention.

I sat up and blinked blearily. My eyes felt as if they had been stuffed with sand. Rubbing them, I staggered upright. "Where?" I rasped.

Wordlessly, Ceruvax pointed southwards. Squinting my eyes, I peered in the direction but saw nothing. "There's no one—"

I broke off. *Huh*, I thought, studying the figure emerging from the haze on the horizon. *The old wolf has better eyes than I do.*

That or I was still sleep-befuddled.

Widening my eyes, I waited until the figure resolved into focus. A familiar face swam into view. "Ah," I exhaled. "It's Adriel."

"Who?" a perplexed Ceruvax asked.

"We haven't gotten around to discussing her yet." Retrieving a water flask from my backpack, I took a generous sip. "She's a lich."

The old wolf stiffened. "A lich?" he asked, his tone making his distaste clear.

I nodded.

His fingers wrapped tightly around his staff. "From your tone, I take it you're... acquainted?"

I took another sip. "More than that. We're allies."

Ceruvax groaned softly, but not so softly I didn't hear. Ignoring his unhappiness, I kept my gaze on Adriel. She was in one of her younger flesh golem bodies and was walking steadily but with neither haste nor panic, which I took to mean things hadn't devolved in the court yet.

I relaxed. There was still time to enact my plan.

"Lichs are dangerous," Ceruvax growled. "Do you know what they are, what they can do?"

"I do," I replied mildly. I paused, knowing he wasn't going to like what I had to say next either. "She's not just any lich, though. She's a former scion of House Death."

The old wolf's eyes flashed yellow.

I'd not asked Ceruvax explicitly, but from his Class and the change I had witnessed him undergo during our first meeting, I was certain he was a werewolf. "Stop," I said softly. "I trust her as much as I do you."

"Why?" he snarled.

Wordlessly, I reached into my cloak and pulled out a slim glass object. "Do you know what this is?"

"A phylactery," he pronounced, his tension diffusing. "Hers?"

"Yes," I replied, my eyes still on the distant figure. "She gave it to me voluntarily. Not only that, but I wouldn't have managed to kill the harbinger without her. Nor would Draven have awoken if not for Adriel—the guardian has met her, by the way. Then there is Ghost. You recall what I told you about my familiar?"

"The—what did you call her?"

"Pyre wolf," I murmured.

"That's right, I'm eager to meet her. I've never heard of such a creature before. She must be unique."

I snorted. "Who do you think created Ghost's body?"

Silence. "The lich?"

"Correct. Adriel is as committed to seeing the Houses rise again as much as—" my gaze slid sideways to him—"you are."

Ceruvax frowned, saying nothing. But I could see my words had had an effect, and he was no longer bristling.

"You said her name was Adriel?" he asked abruptly.

"Yes, that's right," I said, giving him my full attention this time. "She mentioned having met you. Do you remember her?"

"Perhaps," the old wolf said, rubbing his chin. "If she is the same Adriel I recall, then you're right, she *is* someone we want on our side," he finished grudgingly.

"Good, I'm glad that's resolved." With a smile on my face, I turned back to await the approaching lich.

✳   ✳   ✳

Five minutes later, Wolf and Death were staring off.

Adriel had ignored me completely as she strode up, keeping her gaze fixed on Ceruvax. He did the same, pinning her with a glare of his own.

Hmm, was this what it was like when the Houses met?

But as amusing as it was to watch their silent contest of wills, we had bigger matters to attend to. "It's nice to see you again, Adriel," I said brightly, "and in the flesh once more, too."

The lich's gaze turned slowly my way. "So, Draven did it."

"He did," I replied.

Her gaze flickered to the marble statue behind us. "He is sleeping again?"

I nodded and gestured to Ceruvax beside me. "I take it that introductions aren't required?" I asked lightly.

"They aren't," Ceruvax growled.

"Not necessary," Adriel agreed, her tone just as curt.

I sank to the ground. "Then sit, please. We have much to discuss."

Neither budged.

"Sit," I repeated, my tone less affable.

This time, both complied. "Where's Ghost?" Adriel asked suddenly. "I don't sense her spirit in the cloak."

"She's with my apprentice," I replied, unsurprised that the lich could sense the pyre wolf's absence. She was the Cloak's creator, after all.

"Ghost is doing well too," I went on, answering the question she had left unvoiced. More than likely, it was Ceruvax's presence that constrained her. "She is thriving, in fact. The familiar bonding went well."

Adriel's face spread into a warm smile. "I'm glad to hear that." She tilted her head. "This apprentice... it wouldn't happen to be the player, Nyra?"

My brows rose. "You've heard of her already?"

"Regus' messenger brought word of her to the court—as well as your warning that she is to remain untouched." She arched an eyebrow. "Was that really necessary?"

My lips tightened. "In light of Regus' report, I thought the warning was warranted," I said, an edge to my tone. "Or do you think his tales of the unrest in the court are exaggerated?"

Her face turned grave. "No, I don't."

"Nyra is the girl you took on as your follower?" Ceruvax asked quietly. "The one with a Wolf Mark?"

I nodded, then added as an aside to Adriel. "Ceruvax is my follower too."

Her eyebrows rose again. "I see," she murmured and turned to face Ceruvax squarely for the first time since sitting. "What say we set aside old differences, Wolf?"

"A clean slate is best," he agreed, nodding slowly. "The Houses are dead. Their ancient grievances should remain so too." He stuck out his hand, and taking it, Adriel shook it gravely.

I smiled, relieved to see them treating each other more amicably.

Adriel turned back to me. "So, Michael, are you going to tell me why I am here? I was under the impression we were to meet back at the court."

"The court?" Ceruvax interrupted.

"The archlich's court," I said. "The possessed's main base." Seeing the questions crowding his gaze, I held up my hand. "I know I haven't gotten around to explaining about the possessed yet, but we'll get to them in a bit."

He nodded reluctantly.

"You're here," I said, addressing Adriel again, "because of Regus' report." My face hardened. "The possessed have to be dealt with."

"I don't disagree," Adriel replied, her brows creasing. "But how do you intend on doing that here when all the possessed are back at the court, confined in accordance with your *orders*?"

I grimaced, not missing how she stressed the last word. Had Farren and Adriel chafed under my instructions? Would they resent what else I would ask him to do? I hoped not. Because without the lichs, my plan was dead already.

"Michael?" Adriel prompted.

"Sorry," I muttered. "I was lost in thought." I breathed in deeply. "I brought you here because I have a plan for dealing with the possessed. However, there are a few details that you and I need to iron out." I glanced at the frozen guardian behind us. "I thought Draven would have been able to help too, but..."

"... now, he is asleep," she finished for me. She leaned forward attentively. "Tell me your plan."

"I will, in a minute." I gestured to Ceruvax. "But before I do, you better tell him what the possessed are."

Adriel winced. No doubt she knew how the old wolf would react as well as I. Still, she didn't demur. Gathering her thoughts, she began speaking.

*　*　*

I listened with only half an ear as Adriel described the possessed's nature to Ceruvax. Instead of focusing on the lich's words, I studied riot of emotions crossing the old wolf's face. They devolved steadily—confusion turning to distaste, then disgust, horror, and anger, before finally settling on fury.

"So, let me see if I have this correct," he said, inhaling sharply. "The 'possessed'—" his mouth twisted distastefully on the word— "as you call them, are the spirits of dead scions animating the corpses of slain players? Do I have that right?"

Adriel nodded solemnly.

"And they are *your* creation? Something you and your fellow lichs made?"

"Yes," she said, her tone clipped.

Ceruvax's head whipped around in my direction. "And you condone this?"

"I don't," I said mildly. "And to be fair to Adriel and Farren, they have banned the practice since Loskin's death. No more player corpses will be stolen to fuel the possessed's unnatural lives."

"But how can you suffer the possessed to continue existing?" Ceruvax growled. "What they've done is a perversion. Not just to the Game, but to life!"

I sighed. "I can't."

Silence followed my words.

"What are you saying, Michael?" Adriel asked quietly.

I lifted my gaze to hers. "I thought I could let the possessed be. I thought I could let them make their own restitution for their past crimes. But after Castor and what's happening in the court, I've realized I cannot. They must be judged."

Adriel's face remained expressionless. "Judged or punished? Because from your face, I can tell you've come to a decision already. You've made up your mind, haven't you?"

"I have," I said, not shying away from her gaze.

"What have you decided then?"

"The possessed have to be destroyed."

Chapter 427: A Suitable Reckoning

"You will kill them all?" Adriel asked softly. "All thousand-odd souls? And what about Farren and myself? Will you see us dead too as payment for our crimes?"

"No," I said softly.

She tilted her head to the side, her face still devoid of animation. "No? You will spare us and kill the rest?"

"No," I said again.

She frowned. "I don't understand."

I leaned forward. "The possessed must be destroyed, but they don't need to die unless they desire to. They can be remade—" I paused—"*if*, and this is a big if, my plan can be made to work."

"Tell me," she said.

"Remember what you told me about the possessed's finger bones?"

Her frown deepened. "I'm not following you."

"You said the possessed have to retain some part of their original selves," I elaborated, "because neither you, Farren, nor Loskin were able to fully sever the ties between the dead scions' spirits and their bodies. And because of this, they could only be spirit jumped into similar shells, which, in their case, meant player bodies."

Adriel inclined her head. "That's not exactly how I put it, but yes, the gist of what you've said is true."

"Well, what if you could? Fully separate the possessed's spirits from their old bodies, I mean. What then?"

The lich shrugged dismissively. "That's not possible. If it were, Farren and I would have done so a long time ago."

"But assuming you could," I persisted. "Would you then be able to create flesh golems for the possessed as you did for Ghost?"

"Maybe," Adriel allowed, "but Michael, I told you, I can't do what you're asking. It's—"

"—impossible, I know. But what if I told you I know of an artifact that could do what you can't?"

"An artifact?" Adriel threw me a puzzled look. "It would have to be extremely powerful to do what you suggest."

I smiled. "A Prime forged this one."

Ceruvax sat up abruptly, finally realizing where I was going with this.

"An artifact created by a Prime would certainly qualify," Adriel said wryly. "But I find it hard to believe you've been hiding something like that in your pockets all along."

I chuckled. "I'm not. But I know where to find it. The artifact is called the Ring of Astral Walking, and I had occasion to use it when—"

"—you entered the mind trial," Adriel finished for me. "I recall you telling me." Her eyes narrowed. "This is the same artifact that transformed Ghost into a spirit after she stepped into it accidentally?"

I nodded.

"Describe the Ring and leave nothing out," Adriel instructed.

I glanced at Ceruvax. "You likely know more about the thing than I do. Go ahead."

The old wolf looked oddly reluctant. "What you suggest smacks of desecration. Atiras did not build the rings for this purpose, and I'm not sure he would approve of you using the rings in this manner..."

I opened my mouth, ready to convince him otherwise, but Ceruvax stopped me before I could speak.

"But times have changed, and whatever else he was, the Prime was always pragmatic." He sighed. "Then, too, I cannot deny your idea has potential."

He turned to face Adriel. "Prime Atiras created the Ring of Astral Walking as a gateway to the mind trial. The artifact is formed of two interlocking rings that split when activated." He glanced at me. "From what the wolf lord has said, I'm guessing it's the functioning of the first ring that interests him."

I nodded. "That's right."

"The artifact does two things," Ceruvax continued. "The first ring frees a spirit from its body. The second ring teleports said spirit to the mind trial. The two stages, while interlinked, are still separate."

Adriel frowned thoughtfully at me. "Then what you're proposing is to completely disembody the possessed by sending them through the first ring and for us to rehome the freed spirits in flesh golems before they can be drawn into the second ring?"

I nodded. "Not quite... but close."

She looked at me questioningly.

"The rings are not here," I explained. "They're with a dire wolf pack who are themselves needed to operate the artifact, and I'm not comfortable with allowing the possessed so close to the pack. What I *am* proposing is that we use their finger bones only."

"Then you're suggesting we kill the possessed, extract their finger bones, and take them to the rings for rehoming?" she asked neutrally.

"Yes," I said grimly. "Could it work?"

She bowed her head. "It's audacious, and as the old wolf said, certainly not the use the artifact was intended for. Nor will it be a matter of simply throwing the finger bones into the rings. Each spirit will have to be carefully readied beforehand. But yes, with adequate time and preparation, I think your plan can be made to work."

I sagged in relief. "That's... good."

If Adriel had dismissed my plan, I would've had no choice but to slaughter the possessed, and as inured as I'd become to killing, I was not yet the hardened killer that could deal death without qualms.

Adriel was biting her lip, still working through the details. "You realize, though, that the possessed's rehoming will be permanent? Just as in the case of Ghost, the bindings forged between their spirits and new bodies will be unbreakable."

My lips curved upward. "I consider that an advantage. The days of the possessed living forever by skipping from body to body are over. They will get one life. Just like almost everyone else."

"What about their crimes?" Ceruvax asked suddenly. "Will you make them pay for their misdeeds?"

"Oh, yes, they'll pay," I said softly. "I may intend on granting the possessed new lives, but their slates will not be wiped clean. To make amends, the possessed will spend the rest of their *natural* lives serving New Haven."

✸   ✸   ✸

Adriel and I spent another hour working through the details, not only the mechanics of what needed to be done but how we would convince the possessed to comply. Obviously, some would resist. Both Adriel and I expected it.

They would have to be dealt with—harshly.

Ceruvax did not participate in our discussions. Instead, he sat with his head bowed and lost in thought, only half-listening. There was something about my plan that troubled him, I guessed.

"I will see to it that the rings are not damaged," I said finally, thinking that this was what worried him.

He shook his head. "It's not that."

I studied him carefully. "You can't believe I would let any harm come to the dire wolves? We'll not do this unless Duggar and the elders agree. Their safety will be assured, I promise."

Once more, Ceruvax shook his head. "It's not that, either."

My brows drew down. "Then what is it?"

He sighed. "There may be another way."

I blinked. "Another way to...?"

"... to end the possessed's current state of existence," he said, finishing the thought for me.

Beside me, I felt Adriel's interest quicken.

"End how?" I asked, still staring at the old wolf.

Instead of answering directly, Ceruvax replied with a question. "Do you know what my primary duties as Atiras envoy were?"

I frowned, not making the connection between his question and my own but, willing to humor the old wolf, answered anyway, "I would guess you served as his ambassador to the other Houses."

He nodded. "I did. But that was only one of my functions. I spent as much time mediating internal House disputes as I did external ones."

My frown deepened. Ceruvax was losing me.

Reaching into his robe, the former envoy extracted three objects and placed them before me. The first was a simple tarnished gold ring the size of my palm, the second was a chipped and yellowing wolf skull, while the third was a flat stone disk about the same size as the ring.

Adriel gasped, clearly recognizing the objects.

"Go ahead," Ceruvax prompted. "Analyze the items."

Doing as he bade, I reached out with my will and inspected each object.

The target is the <u>Ritual Combat Circle</u>, an artifact of unknown rank forged by the Wolf Prime Atiras. This item is soulbound to the player Ceruvax and may only be activated by him.

The target is the <u>Skull of Souls</u>, an artifact of unknown rank forged by the Wolf Prime Atiras. This item is soulbound to the player Ceruvax and may only be activated by him.

The target is a <u>Blood Talisman</u>. This is a Game-created item that can be used to awaken a player's blood, bringing to the fore long-dormant memories. When sufficiently infused by the spirits of the fallen, your blood can be made to 'remember' its ancient lineage and perform feats you had not thought possible before.

I gasped, echoing Adriel's earlier astonishment.

I had no idea what the soulbound artifacts did, but the fact that they were soulbound and created by a Prime said enough of their value.

The blood talisman was not something I was likely to forget or undervalue either. I'd come across only one, in the mind trial where I'd used it to choose my first, and thus far, only blood memory.

This talisman was different, yet similar to that other one. On closer inspection, I saw that images of wolves and other wolf-like creatures had been carved into the stone's surface.

"Two soulbound artifacts *and* a blood talisman?" I asked in a half-strangled voice. "What are you doing carrying around all this?"

"They were required to perform my duties," Ceruvax answered.

I rubbed my chin. "I don't understand," I admitted.

"The talisman, you know already of," the old wolf said. "The Skull is a spirit vessel capable of holding the souls of fallen scions—indefinitely if need be." Seeing the sudden hope in my face, he added. "Unfortunately, it's empty at the moment."

"Oh," I muttered. "What about the Circle then?"

"Ritualized combat was how disputes in House Wolf were settled," Ceruvax replied softly.

"You're saying the House's scions fought each other to prove who was right?" I asked. "Isn't that pretty... uhm, primitive?"

"Oh yes, definitely," Ceruvax said with a feral grin. "But then, House Wolf has always prided itself in strength. Weakness was not tolerated, and mistakes often lead to death—even for Everborns like us." Ceruvax smiled. "Atiras—and not just him, but the Primes who came before—believed in the power of final death. They believed a scion never more fully appreciated life as when his life, *all* his lives, were imperiled."

I stared at him incredulously. "Hold on. So, you're saying that not only did they fight, but that they fought to the death—*final death?*"

He nodded.

"That's..." I began.

"Preposterous?" Adriel suggested.

"That's one word for it," I muttered.

Ceruvax chuckled. "Oh, it wasn't all that bad. No one could be forced into ritual combat; the Circle will only work if the combatants are willing. Thus, it has always been a measure of last resort when the parties refused to back down."

"I see," I said, still frowning. "I'm guessing then that the three items work together."

"Correct," he replied. "Ordinarily, the spirit of a scion who fell in the Circle would be absorbed by the victor, infusing his blood. But if, for whatever reason, this did not occur, the Skull could be used to shelter the spirit until a scion was ready to accept it."

"And the talisman would be employed if the victor needed to awaken a new blood memory," I finished.

Ceruvax nodded.

I scratched my head. "Right, I get all that, but getting back to the possessed, what does any of this have to do with dealing with them?"

The old wolf didn't answer immediately. Looking strangely hesitant, he pushed the Circle toward me. He still didn't speak, though.

"Tell me," I said.

Adriel answered in his stead. "I do believe the old wolf wants you to challenge the possessed. He wants you to fight them in the Circle and absorb their spirit essences."

My eyes wide, I stared at Ceruvax. "Is that true?"

He nodded reluctantly.

My head whipped in Adriel's direction. "Could that work?"

She bit her lip. "I'm not sure..."

It was not the straight-up 'no' I'd been expecting. "Explain."

Adriel inhaled. "There is no escaping the Houses," she said. "You know that, or have you forgotten what it means to be an anointed scion?"

I hadn't. The trait's description was unequivocal and left me in no doubt that I was irrevocably bound to House Wolf, even after death. There was still something I did not understand, though. "But the possessed aren't players anymore," I protested. "Surely that means—"

"Means what?" Adriel asked with a sardonic lift of her lips. "That the Game has relieved them of their obligations?" She shook her head. "It has not. They are all still bound to their Houses." Her voice dropped to a whisper. "As am I."

"So, you think the Circle will work?" I prompted when she didn't go on.

She shrugged. "I can't say. There has never been a case like this in my memory." She glanced at Ceruvax. "Unless you know differently?"

The former envoy shook his head. "I don't. But I think it should work because, as you say, they *are* still House-bound."

I stared at him. "Then, you're not certain this will work either?"

He shook his head. "I'm not."

I threw up my hands. "Was your uncertainty the reason for your earlier reluctance?"

"No..."

I said nothing, waiting for him to go on.

"It's the danger that concerns me," he admitted finally. "You are the last Wolf scion. If you die..."

I winced. "I know, but I can't stop doing the things I need to because of the consequences of failure. That way leads to—"

"—defeat," Ceruvax said. "I understand. Still, I can't help but be unhappy about the risk to the House."

Nodding, I rose to my feet and began pacing while I pondered his suggestion. "What happens if I lose?" I asked suddenly.

Wolf and lich exchanged glances. "Well, you'd be dead, of course," Adriel said dryly.

I rolled my eyes. "I know *that*. But I was talking about the victor. What would happen to him or her? Would they absorb my essence? But how could they, when they're not scions anymore?"

The pair shrugged in unison.

"I see. You don't know." I resumed pacing, but only a few moments later, I spun to face the two again. "Assuming this works, would it work against any possessed, even those not formerly of House Wolf?"

Once again, the pair exchanged glances. "It will not," Ceruvax said softly.

"Hmm. And how many of the possessed originate from House Wolf."

Adriel pursed her lips. "I can't be sure, but a few dozen at least."

"Right, a few dozen," I muttered. *Not a lot.* That meant Ceruvax's option wasn't really a solution, not for dealing with the possessed as a whole. "What about the other nine hundred odd?" I wondered aloud.

"You could still face them in the Circle," Adriel answered. "Their spirits might not be able to join with yours." She glanced at the Skull. "But they can still be held for... future scions."

I nodded slowly. While I myself was focused on restoring Wolf, House Wolf was not the only House. Bringing about the Primes' return would also require resurrecting the other bloodlines.

I will have to start thinking broader, I realized.

"So, to summarize," I said, "we have two options. One, rehome the possessed in flesh golems, or two, collect their spirits in the Skull of Souls."

"Option two only applies if we can get the possessed to enter the ritual circle *willingly*," Ceruvax added.

"Nor does going through with the first option negate the second," Adriel pointed out. "You could rehome the possessed now and use the Circle later."

I rubbed my chin. "True," I conceded.

"There is also a third option," Ceruvax said quietly.

Adriel laughed. "Really? You've dreamt up yet another option? You're full of surprises, aren't you, old wolf?"

Pointedly ignoring the lich, Ceruvax stared at me steadfastly.

"Go on," I said. "Tell me."

He leaned forward. "If neither the first nor the second option appeals to you, you could always turn them into werewolves."

✳ ✳ ✳

I gaped at Ceruvax. "Werewolves...?" *Is he being serious?* "How would that work?" I demanded.

"By using were's bite," he replied.

I wasn't convinced. I'd read the trait's description a dozen times already, but just in case, I called it up again.

<u>Were's bite</u>: this trait activates the lycanthropy mutation in your blood. It gives your bite a 10% chance of granting another player the werewolf trait. Depending on the strength of the bitten player's blood and the Marks they bear, this probability will increase to a maximum of 20% or decrease down to 0%.

Were's bite is not a combat ability and cannot transform an unwilling subject. In the event that the bitten player accepts your bite but fails to acquire the werewolf trait, their body will be fatally overrun with lycanthropy.

I hadn't been mistaken, I saw. "The trait's description specifically mentions players," I told the old wolf. "Why would you think it could work on the possessed?"

"Ordinarily, the Game's explanation would be correct," he said, "but in this case, it's not."

I stared at him for a second longer, then sank back to the ground. "Go on, explain."

"I am more than passingly familiar with werewolves," Ceruvax said with a self-deprecating smile, "and I know without doubt it's the wolf blood running in a player's veins that allows them to manifest the lycanthropy trait." He held my gaze. "Usually, a non-player's blood is not nearly strong enough to allow them to become a werewolf. If it were, he or she would be a player."

Adriel's eyes narrowed. "And as we know, the possessed are far from ordinary. They are all housed in the bodies of former players, meaning their blood should be potent enough."

Ceruvax nodded. "Exactly."

I bit the inside of my cheek. "But you said they would need wolf blood specifically. What happens if they have none?"

"I hardly think we'll have any such cases," Ceruvax replied.

Before I could ask what he meant, Adriel added, "No House ever managed to keep its bloodline pure. Today's players likely have the blood of at least a dozen Houses running in their veins. It is only after a scion's blood is awakened that their other bloodlines are subsumed."

I nodded thoughtfully. "And none of the players whose bodies the possessed inhabit have had their blood awakened." I paused, digesting that. "This could work."

"I think so," Adriel said.

"What if they die after being bitten?" I asked.

Adriel shrugged. "That will matter little. In fact, in this case, the possessed's nature will prove advantageous. Unlike with a player, there is no limit to how many times a possessed can be reborn. Assuming the bite fails to take, Farren or I can spirit jump the possessed back into their body once the lycanthropy mutation has run its course, and you can try again."

I exhaled slowly. "It really does sound feasible."

Ceruvax and Adriel both nodded. "It does."

"The only question now is which approach you will choose," Ceruvax said quietly.

It was my turn to shrug. "Why choose at all? Why not go with all three?"

✳   ✳   ✳

It didn't take long to finalize our plans.

We had a long trip ahead of us, though—the archlich's court was half the dungeon away—and Adriel had only just arrived. Her spirit might be housed within a 'flesh golem,' but she was far from tireless. There was another more immediate problem, too.

"What's wrong?" Ceruvax asked, catching me staring at the valley's rim.

"I just realized, I never asked—" I pointed to the sheer cliffs in the distance. "—will you be able to scale that?"

The old wolf glanced from me to the rockface. "Why would I need to do that?"

"There's a plateau up there," Adriel replied, already familiar with my highway. "It's free of dungeon denizens, and our intrepid scion here has been using it to navigate Draven's Reach."

Ceruvax grunted, studying the cliff through narrowed eyes. "I should manage the climb in my half-form." Before I could ask what he meant by that, the former envoy changed before my eyes.

His eyes turned yellow, his teeth grew into fangs, and his ears elongated. Then his entire head turned lupine. A second later, coarse black fur spurted from his skin, and claws extended from his hands.

Fascinated, I watched on.

Anriq had turned into a fully-fledged four-footed wolf during his own transformation, but after waiting another handful of futile seconds for that to happen, I realized Ceruvax's change had come to an end.

"Your half-form?" I guessed.

Ceruvax flexed his clawed hands. "Yes," he replied, the words emerging as half-snarl, half-growl. "Will this form do?"

"I expect so," I murmured and glanced questioningly at Adriel.

She snorted. "I don't need any fancy shape-changing spells. I'll manage well enough with magic."

Not questioning her further, I led the way. "Then, let's go. We'll rest up top when we get there."

✳   ✳   ✳

It took us two days to reach the valley sheltering the archlich's court.

While that was longer than I liked, the time was well-spent with both Ceruvax and Adriel using the opportunity to educate me on as many aspects of House history and Game lore as they could.

In particular, I quizzed the pair on what it meant to be a Power and the paths to ascendancy.

As both Ceruvax and Adriel had mentioned previously, there were two paths to power in the Game: the first was by means of player levels, and the second was through deepening my Wolf and Power Marks.

Neither path was mutually exclusive.

And thus far, I'd been treading both. In fact, according to Ceruvax and Adriel, many ancients in the past had done so too. But to become a Prime, I would need to follow only one path to its eventual end.

The pair had a lot to say on the subject, and after absorbing their words, I painstakingly summarized the information in two drawings.

The First Path to Ascendancy

| Force Sworn • Force Abilities Progression* | | | | | | | House Adherents • Blood Memories Progression** | | | | | |
Ultimate	Ancient	Godlike	Greater	Lesser	FORCE TITLE	LEVEL	HOUSE TITLE	Lesser	Greater	Godlike	Ancient	Ultimate
					PLAYER	1	ANOINTED SCION	1				
						50		2				
						100		3				
						150		4				
			1	2	ELITE	200	HOUSE ELITE	4	1			
			1	3	ENVOY	250	HOUSE ENVOY	4	1			
			2	4	MINOR POWER	300	YOUNG BLOOD	4	2	1		
			2	4		350		4	2	1		
		1	3	4	MAJOR POWER	400	OLD BLOOD	4	3	2	1	
		1	3	4		450		4	3	2	1	
	1	2	4	4	SUPREME POWER	500	ANCIENT BLOOD	4	4	3	2	
	1	2	4	4		550		4	4	3	2	
						600	PRIME	4	4	4	3	1

* Shows the total number of Force abilities that are automatically acquired at each level.

** Indicates the maximum blood memories that can be retained.

The Second Path to Ascendancy

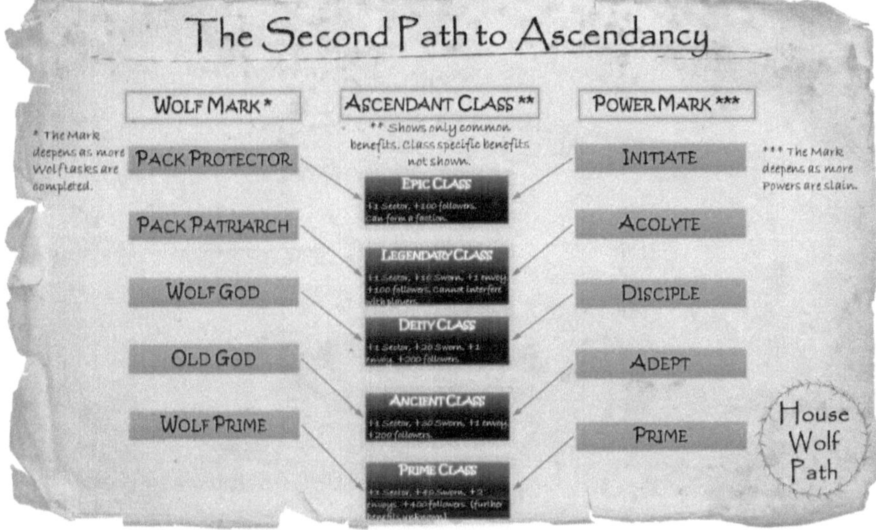

According to Ceruvax, the first path was the one more often favored by the scions of old—and the new Powers, too, unsurprisingly. It was the slower route to power, yes, but it was also infinitely less risky.

The second path required me to repeatedly pit myself against other Powers, which, of course, could quickly turn disastrous—especially for me, a hated scion. Each time I came into contact with a new Power, I risked my secrets being revealed.

But as I already knew, there were Powers, and there were...

... stygian Powers.

For most players, hunting such creatures would be an exercise in foolishness, but for me, the nether and its denizens offered intriguing possibilities.

Still, I made no decisions. Ascending was only a secondary consideration at this stage. Before I could truly bend all my efforts to advancing as a Power, there were a host of other tasks I had to complete.

And first on the list was dealing with the possessed.

CHAPTER 429: INTO THE COURT

Day Thirty-Five in Draven's Reach

It was early morning when we approached our destination.

"That's the archlich's court?" Ceruvax asked, his eyebrows rising as he studied the elegant compound backed up against the dungeon's southern rim.

I grinned. "That was my first reaction, too."

Adriel sniffed. "Being dead doesn't stop one from appreciating finer things."

I glanced at her sideways. "Did you have a hand in the complex's design?"

"Well, of course, I did. I couldn't leave it to Farren and Loskin, could I?"

"Of course not," I murmured as we marched across the canyon.

"There's a ward, I see," Ceruvax observed. "Your work?"

Adriel shook her head. "Farren's."

My eyes drifted to the wrought iron gate at the main entrance. There were no guards on duty this time. Only a single figure. Regus.

"What's he doing here?" I muttered. The possessed should've been in the underground tunnel with Ghost and Nyra.

Adriel followed my gaze. "Farren sent him. And don't worry, the New Haveners are fine."

I looked at her. "You have been speaking to him?" The two lichs had their own means of communicating that allowed them to keep in contact even while halfway across the dungeon from each other.

Adriel nodded. "The possessed are gathered in the central courtyard." She paused. "No one knows you're coming or what you intend yet."

I quickened my pace. Farren knew the plan, of course. What I intended could not be done without his aid, and Adriel had stayed in close contact with him throughout our journey. Yet, even with both lichs' help, there was no guarantee of success, especially with a thousand odd volatile possessed thrown in the mix.

"Before I forget, you better take this." Reaching into my cloak, I withdrew a slim glass object and handed it to her.

You have lost Adriel's phylactery.

She took it wordlessly, one eyebrow arched in question.

"Neither of us knows what's going to happen in the next few hours, and if I'm going to die, I shouldn't do so with that on me."

She smiled. "I won't say everything's going to be alright because I admit, I don't know how things will turn out either."

"Well, at least this should be easier than taking on the harbinger and void tree," I said lightly.

Adriel snorted. "I'm not so sure about that."

"You're certain you don't want us to buff you?" Ceruvax asked. Even the old wolf was looking a little out of sorts. His gaze never settling, he studied the approaching court with the intensity of a hunter—or the hunted.

"No," I said firmly. Some of the possessed would recognize any buffs cast about me, and going into this, I needed them relaxed, not wary, and worried about what I would do next.

Regus uncrossed his arms as we drew to a halt before the gate, and his eyes skipped over us before settling on the former envoy. "You must be Ceruvax," he greeted.

The old wolf inclined his head, though I caught his gaze lingering on the ugly wound on Regus' head.

The possessed swung back the gate and waved us in. "Everything is ready," he reported.

With Adriel leading the way, we passed through.

You have entered a tier 6 protection field. Only entities who have been granted access by the ward's controllers can cross this barrier.

The moment I passed through the barrier, my mindsight rippled out, no longer blocked by the protection field. Letting my awareness expand outward and downward, I began searching the surroundings.

Ceruvax's eyebrows rose. "A powerful ward," he murmured.

Adriel threw him a wry look. "Don't worry, you won't be trapped inside. The ward has been keyed to allow all of us passage—both in and out." She shrugged. "If the worst happens, you will have an escape route."

"And the possessed?" Ceruvax asked quietly.

"They will be trapped," Adriel replied. "Until they figure out how to take down the ward, of course." She glanced at me. "You remember the exit portal's location?"

I nodded. It was also protected by wards that Farren had keyed to us. Using it would be an option of last resort, though, and the lich didn't bother advising me to flee in its direction if things went awry. She knew I wouldn't leave without Ghost, Nyra, and the warband.

I strode up to Regus' side. "How did everything go?"

"There were some problems," he admitted, "But only a few and nothing we couldn't handle. The possessed are gathered and waiting, if a trifle impatiently."

"Farren has done well then." Better than I imagined. "I was half-expecting us needing to run down the stragglers and the disaffected."

Regus chuckled. "Mustering in the square was no great hardship, and truly most were too curious to resist complying with the archlich's orders."

I nodded. "Let's hope keeping them together goes just as smoothly," I murmured. That would be up to me.

He shot me an indecipherable look. "You think this plan of yours will work?"

I studied Regus thoughtfully. It was not an idle question, I knew.

Ceruvax, I, and even Adriel might be able to consider the matter objectively, but for the possessed themselves, it was a question of singular importance.

"I can't say for sure," I replied, making no attempt to hide my own uncertainty. "But there is a good chance it will."

He barked a laugh. "That's enough, then."

I looked at him in surprise.

Regus gestured at his body. "This existence has not been what I thought it would be." He waved his arms, encompassing both the court and the dungeon. "None of it has been. A chance for something better will be good."

I clamped a hand on his shoulder. "I will do my best to see you get it."

✳   ✳   ✳

We navigated the compound without incident.

Adriel had spoken truly, and the streets around us were deserted. As we drew closer to the central plaza outside Loskin's mansion—Farren's now, I supposed—I felt a familiar mind tickle the edge of my awareness.

"*Prime!*" the pyre wolf exclaimed.

"*Ghost,*" I greeted in relief. Despite Adriel's earlier reassurance, having more direct confirmation of her well-being was nice. "*Are you and Nyra alright?*"

"*Yes,*" she replied. "*The possessed have not bothered us. Regus has kept them away.*"

"*That's good. How is Algar and the warband doing?*"

"*The Bane Wolves, you mean?*" she asked, with a teasing note in her voice. "*They're bored and tired of sitting around doing nothing; otherwise, they can't complain.*"

I smiled. "*They are all still in the underground tunnel then?*"

"*Most are,*" Ghost said. "*But Algar and the other captains are in the square with us. What about you? How did things go?*"

My smile widened. "*Better than expected. I found Ceruvax, and he is eager to meet you.*"

"*He is?*"

"*Of course,*" My amusement died. "*But Ghost, listen, things are about to get tricky.*"

She laughed.

"*What?*" I asked in confusion.

"*Prime, things* always *get tricky with you.*"

I chuckled helplessly. "*It does seem that way, doesn't it? Anyway, here's the plan...*"

✳   ✳   ✳

The court's large central courtyard was packed.

Every possessed still part of the court was present, even bitter enemies like Avery. The possessed stood together, yet apart, in one big disorderly crowd—spread out here and clumped together there. According to Adriel, many still aligned themselves according to old House allegiances, which explained the groups.

For this, the possessed's day of reckoning, the lichs and I had agreed everyone had to be included. If we were lucky, our ploy might earn us a bit of goodwill or unsettle the dissenters long enough for my message to get through. But neither of these was the reason why I'd asked Farren to rehome every spirit.

At the end of the day, all the possessed deserved a choice—even those like Avery. The options on offer might not be to their liking, but it was a choice nonetheless and the only one I was prepared to give them.

As we crossed the square's outer edge, passing beyond the buildings bordering it, faces turned our way. A murmur rippled through the crowd as the possessed beheld me. Some recognized me, many didn't. But I was sure by the time we reached the waiting dais, every possessed would know that the player who had killed the archlich was back.

To our left was the archlich's mansion. To our right was the destroyed vault. The damage still hadn't been repaired. In between was the statue fountain. It, too, was a ruined mess. A dais that had been erected for just this meeting waited on the eastern end of the square. With Regus cutting a path through the possessed, we made straight for it.

Ceruvax eyed the scarred and damaged surroundings as we crossed the square. "What did all this?" he asked, ignoring the hundreds of onlookers.

"The harbinger," Adriel replied just as nonchalantly.

"It came here?" he asked, sounding surprised.

"It wasn't my idea," she said, with a pointed look in my direction.

Keeping my eyes fixed on the dais, I ignored the pair. Their chatter might mislead the possessed into believing the two were oblivious to the danger surrounding them, but I knew both were ready to respond to the least hint of trouble.

Farren came into sight. Standing at the fore of the dais with his arms folded behind his back, he, too, appeared at ease, but that was also a lie. The archlich was tense and alert.

Behind Farren were six others. Ghost, Nyra, Algar, and his three captains. I'd thought long and hard about including the New Haveners in today's proceedings, but after listening to Adriel and Ceruvax, I'd reluctantly conceded they needed to be here, if only as witnesses on New Haven's behalf. Their presence, though, would not be without cost, and I only hoped Algar would understand when I broke the news to him.

"Hail, scion of House Wolf," Farren proclaimed loudly.

A palpable hush descended over the courtyard.

I kept advancing, unfazed by the greeting or the possessed's sudden silence. Both were expected. After lengthy and protracted arguments, Ceruvax, Adriel, and I had agreed there was no way we could enact our plan without revealing my House allegiance.

The ritual circle alone would make many of the possessed suspicious, and certainly, none of them could be expected to willingly enter into combat with me unless they understood the stakes. That being the case, we'd agreed that instead of shunning my identity, it was best to use it for what it truly was.

A weapon.

Around me, I felt the crowd's mood change. Where before they'd exuded the watchfulness of cornered prey, now I sensed surprise.

And curiosity.

I could work with both.

I strode onto the dais and joined Farren while Ceruvax, Adriel, and Regus—silent shadows now—peeled off to merge into the line the other six formed behind the archlich. Raising my chin, I looked down at the sea of faces assembled in front of me. I would have to work hard to win them.

And if I could not do that, I would have to secure their cooperation at the very least.

Settling my thoughts, I began. "At this very minute, each of you is likely wondering what game your archlich is playing. 'He can't be serious, can he?' you must be thinking. 'I can't truly be what he claims, can I?'"

I paused. "But there is no game. I am what Farren says I am—a scion of House Wolf."

A murmur rippled through the possessed, and while most took pains to hide their disdain, I didn't fail to mark the many that openly scoffed.

"No doubt you think I lie. I promise you, though, that before this day is done, you will have ample proof I am an anointed scion of House Wolf. For now, all I ask is that you listen."

The whispers grew, but I waited patiently until silence fell again.

"Thank you," I said gravely before continuing. "It is my goal to see Wolf rise again. Even now, the adherents of the House are gathering. And soon, other Houses will follow in Wolf's wake. The new Powers may have defeated the Primes in your day, but the war is not yet done. I—we—will challenge them yet."

The murmurs swelled further this time, sparking some open discussion and even a few shouted comments. The prevalent tone remained that of contempt and derision.

But here and there, I caught a more hopeful voice.

I raised my arms for silence. "I know, I know. You don't believe me. But I'm not asking you to—not yet." The seed had been planted, and it was time to move on. "We will have ample opportunity to talk of the future, but for now, it is the past we must focus on."

It took nearly a minute for the possessed to settle down again.

"I'm not ignorant of your history either," I said when they did. "Adriel and Farren have shared your tales. I *know* you came to Draven's Reach fleeing the new Powers and their rebellion. I *know* Loskin promised you a chance to fight back one day. I *know* you yourselves are scions. And I *know* you came here with the best of intentions."

I paused and swept my gaze across the courtyard, drawing out the silence. "Yet, it all went astray, didn't it?

"You did not carry out any of the brave acts you envisioned. Instead, you preyed on a weak and desperate people. You committed atrocities the likes of which the new Powers performed against your own Houses. You slaughtered players for their bodies. You held an entire city hostage!"

The hush deepened, so much so that the quiet click of Ghost's claws on the dais carried clearly to my ears.

"If we are to challenge the new Powers, it will not be on the backs of the non-players. They will be our allies, not our victims. We will not persecute them, we will not abuse them, and any crimes committed against them will be punished."

I shook my head. "Your misdeeds cannot be forgotten. Nor will they be swept under the rug." I inhaled deeply.

"Before we move forward, there will be—*there must be*—a reckoning."

CHAPTER 430: A CHOICE OF PUNISHMENTS

Predictably, my words did not please the possessed. But I pressed on, ignoring the crowd's dangerous mood. "You are angry," I said. "You are resentful. It does not matter. The possessed are finished."

The crowd swelled in outrage, and this time, not even the threat of the lichs behind me was enough to quell them. Hands were set to weapons, and challenges were issued.

Folding my arms, I watched and waited.

"Silence!" Farren snapped, his voice magically enhanced to reverberate through the court. "You will hear out the scion!"

The shouts subsided, and the mutters died, but I was not fooled—matters stood on a knife's edge. I had riled the crowd deliberately. If our plan was going to work, the possessed had to understand I would not back down and that the lichs wouldn't either. There was nowhere for them to run, no one to appeal to, and nowhere to go.

"This much is absolute," I continued. "Farren and Adriel will not rehome any spirit in another's body after today. It does not matter if you overcome me. And lest you think of pursuing Castor's example, know too that that path is doomed to fail. New Haven is no longer helpless against you. Their soldiers have been taught how to destroy your bodies."

Pausing there, I ran my gaze slowly over the crowd and was met by muttered curses, scowls, and glares. I smiled back coldly.

"The possessed are finished," I repeated, driving home the point. "Whether by a slow death, fighting every step of the way, or otherwise—it is inevitable. You will pay for your crimes."

I let my voice drop, so they had to lean in to hear my next words. "But you will have a choice about how you do so."

I gestured Ceruvax forward, and he placed the three artifacts on the dais. "Your first option is to face me in combat in the ritual circle. Win, and you will go free. You will be allowed to roam the sector until the end of your days. You will not, however, ever leave Draven's Reach. Lose, and the Skull of Souls will gather your fallen spirit to serve another scion of your House."

"Your second option," I went on, not allowing them any questions, "is to become a werewolf. If you go down this path and complete the transformation, you will submit to Ceruvax. He will be your Pack's alpha. Under his leadership, you will serve as New Haven's protectors for however long the city council decides you must."

This had been another matter of considerable debate. Ceruvax had wanted to accompany me when I left Draven's Reach, but for multiple reasons, that was not practical. For one, he lacked deception and wouldn't be able to hide his identity from other players, and while my Initiate Mark made disguising myself more difficult, I could still manage it as long as I stayed away from any Powers.

Then, too, governing House Wolf was the entire reason I'd brought Ceruvax to Draven's Reach in the first place, and he couldn't do that if he were following me around the Game.

No, the best place for him was in the dungeon, training our allies, protecting New Haven, and feeding Draven the energy he needed to stay alert and awake. The last was nearly as important as the first two, and eventually, the old wolf had reluctantly conceded.

"Your third option," I continued, "is to undergo full astral separation using another artifact in my allies' keeping. You will be rehomed into a flesh golem thereafter and conscripted into New Haven's army to serve as long as the marshal decrees."

I paused, but not overly long. There was one more message I needed to impart before I left them to consider their choices.

"There is a fourth option, of course—to fight. But I promise you that if you try that, your bones will be crushed, and your spirits left to wander the Game for all eternity."

I scanned the faces in the crowd again, letting my words sink in. The possessed were looking more subdued now. *Good.* "Now, are there any questions?"

A possessed stepped forward immediately. "Yes," he sneered.

I didn't recognize the face, but the voice was unmistakable. "Ah, Avery. Why am I not surprised? What do you wish to know?"

"What makes you think any of us would be willing to face a brute like you in the ritual circle alone? No one is that daft! And that being the case, all your fancy talk about choice is nothing more than hot air!"

Spreading his arms, Avery swiveled around to address his fellows. "Choice!" he spat. "What choice is this wolfling giving us, really? Choosing how to subject ourselves to a lifetime of slavery under proles—proles, damn it!—is no choice! And I shouldn't need to remind any of you that the bastards will be out for revenge."

"Who said anything about facing me alone?" I asked mildly before Avery could resume his rant.

The possessed spun to face me. "What?"

"The ritual circle is as capable of hosting fights between multiple groups as single-combat bouts," I replied.

It was on this point that my allies had fought me the most. None of them had approved of the idea, but I had been adamant, mostly because I knew there was little chance of convincing the possessed to fight me one-on-one.

I knew if the only choices I left Avery and his ilk were facing me alone or spending a lifetime in servitude, they would opt for option four—rebellion.

In many ways, ritual combat would be no different from that, but in the Circle, the fallen would at least serve a purpose—strengthening the future scions of their Houses. And to get the possessed to commit to such, all I had to do was be willing to face them on my own. Yes, the risk was greater, but as I was learning, nothing worthwhile in the Game was ever achieved without some element of risk.

And facing forty, fifty, or even a hundred possessed alone was a level of risk I was comfortable with.

For a moment, Avery looked stumped. "You will face *all* of us? Alone?"

"All those who choose to enter the ritual circle," I corrected and bared my teeth. "But yes, I will face all the contenders alone."

Avery's eyes narrowed. "No conditions?"

"None," I replied blandly.

"What about your devil dog?" someone shouted from the crowd.

"That's a good point," Avery said, nodding sagely. "I've heard what she did to Castor's people." His eyes glittered. "Did you truly mean alone?" he jeered. "Or will she fight on your behalf?"

I laughed with genuine mirth. Ghost was my familiar, and Ceruvax had assured me that for the purposes of even single combat, the Game would allow her to fight by my side. But this was not the type of fight I wanted the pyre wolf involved in. "Ghost will not participate."

For a wonder, the pyre wolf did not protest, but we'd discussed the matter beforehand, and she understood my reasons.

"Then I will choose option one," Avery said abruptly. "Who's with me?" he shouted without looking back.

Immediately, another three hundred possessed stepped forward.

Behind me, I heard Regus groan, and even the lichs looked worried, but I kept a smile plastered on my face.

I had a plan, after all.

✳ ✳ ✳

"Are you sure about this?" Algar asked for the tenth time.

I threw him an amused look. "Of course I am."

"But four hundred possessed?" he asked, aghast. "And in that Circle? There will be nowhere for you to run or hide!"

The final tally of foes I would be facing had increased as more possessed had joined the initial three hundred, their courage strengthened by the weight of numbers on their side.

I chuckled. "There is little objective difference between facing one hundred and four hundred."

"True, both are ridiculous odds," Regus said, joining us. "Will the Circle even be able to hold that many?"

I glanced into the now-vacant courtyard where the former envoy was setting up the ritual circle. "Ceruvax has assured me it can."

"Hmm," Regus mused, glancing in that direction himself. Three separate groups stood on the outskirts of the square, watching the old wolf work. The first group was the four hundred contenders, although perhaps calling them one group was a stretch.

They'd split into two uneven sides. The first, around three hundred and fifty, congregated around Avery and two elites as they instructed the others on the battle plan.

I snorted. Not for anything would I ever trust a plan that Avery put together.

The other fifty contenders were staring my way, their gazes burning with an intensity I did not understand.

"Who are they?" I asked Regus.

He grunted. "Wolves."

I stared at him.

"Former Wolves," he corrected. "And if I had to guess, they've all decided to enter the Circle to protect you."

"Really," I murmured, my eyes narrowed in thought. I hadn't been counting on any help.

"That's much better," Algar exclaimed in satisfaction. "Join up with them, and you will have a chance."

I shrugged. Even if I could trust the former wolves, I didn't think what Algar suggested was a good idea. I didn't want to argue strategy, though, so I let the matter lie. "So, my claim has been accepted?" I asked Regus. "The possessed believe I'm a scion?"

He mirrored my earlier shrug. "The wolves do anyway. Many of them recognized Ceruvax." He grimaced. "I overheard some of what the old man had to say to them. It was... harsh."

I rubbed my lips. "They realize I will have to kill them?" Assuming they survived long enough for that to matter.

According to Ceruvax, once the Circle was raised, neither side could leave until the other was defeated, and the wolves would definitely not be entering the ritual circle on my team, not after my commitment to Avery to face the contenders alone.

"They do," he said heavily.

I bowed my head, regretting the necessity. House Wolf couldn't afford to lose any wolves, even those who had forsaken it, but the fifty former wolves' lives wouldn't be spent entirely in vain, as they likely knew already. Their spirits would strengthen my blood, awakening further blood memories.

My gaze fell on the second group. These were the possessed who'd chosen to make the transition to werewolves. Numbering over five hundred, they outstripped even the contenders. Farren was with them now, explaining the process they would undergo soon. The last group, comprising less than three scores, was gathered around Adriel. They were the ones who would become flesh golems.

I glanced at Regus. "You're here to fetch me?"

He nodded.

For obvious reasons, everyone had decided it was best I attend to the werewolf candidates before entering the Circle. After all, there was a chance I would not make it out.

I glanced behind me at Nyra and the three captains. Of everyone in the square, the four looked the most lost. My apprentice, in particular, was clinging desperately to Ghost. I sighed. She, too, was not going to be happy with the decisions I'd made. First, though, I had to deal with the warband.

"Be there in a minute," I told Regus, then waved the three captains over to join me and Algar. "How much of all that did you understand?" I asked when the four were assembled before me.

The junior captains fielded the question to their superior. He shrugged. "Not much, but we understood enough to know that you are keeping your promise to see the possessed punished."

I nodded. "There is something else I have to tell you." I paused, searching for the right words.

"The warband won't be accompanying you when you leave," Algar said.

My brows rose in surprise. "How did you—"

"—guess?" Algar finished, his lips twisting in a bitter smile. "It was obvious."

The other captains nodded. "This scion business, whatever it is, sounds like a big deal," Megtir said.

"And since you've not told the council," Zorg added, "it stands to reason that you must want to keep it a secret."

"But it won't stay one if some dumb soldier spills the truth out there," Everard finished caustically.

"I see," I said. So, you *have* figured it out."

Algar nodded. "What I'd like to know is if you planned this all along. Did you know the warband wouldn't be accompanying you before we left New Haven?"

I shook my head. "No. Believe it or not, my strategy for dealing with the possessed was much simpler. I did not know until a day ago I would be revealing my House allegiance."

"On the bright side," Zorg quipped, "at least we know the warband's name is apt."

Algar ignored him. "Being a scion is something dangerous then?" he asked, looking at me searchingly.

"Very," I replied softly. "Once my identity is revealed, every Power in the Game will hunt me."

Algar's eyes widened. "*Every* Power?"

"Every Power," I confirmed. "Draven's Reach is safe, though. No one, not even the Powers, can penetrate the guardian's defenses."

"Your words imply you don't expect your identity to remain hidden," Megtir interjected. "That true?"

"It is. Sooner or later, the Powers will discover who I am." I held their gazes. "Then the war will truly begin."

Everard grunted. "And *that's* when you will need us."

I smiled humorlessly. "You and a million more like you."

Algar nodded solemnly. "We shall await the day then. The Bane Wolves will be ready. You can count on it."

I clasped the high captain's hand. "Thank you, Algar."

"There's just one other thing," he said.

"Go on."

"When you spoke to the council, you seemed pretty adamant about needing one thousand soldiers," he said. "Has that changed?"

"I'm not sure," I admitted. "I have a time-limited task to control a sector. I'd been planning on using the warband to do that. Now, with everything that's happened, I fear that will not be wise."

Algar pursed his lips. "How much time do you have left on this task?"

"About three months," I replied.

"Ample time then," Zorg commented.

I smiled. "Maybe, but I'm no longer certain capturing the valley is even necessary." I shook my head. "Those are worries for another day, though. And truly, if I have no other choice, I'll return for the warband."

"We'll be waiting," Algar said.

"What should we do in the interim?" Megtir asked.

"Stay here," I said, glancing at the gathered possessed. "If everything goes as expected, there will be less than five hundred souls in the court by day's end. That will leave ample room for the warband."

Algar looked around. "It will not be an unpleasant place to be," he admitted. "And we've brought enough stores to last months. Our orders?"

"Train. Expand. Grow," I said simply. "You will have Ceruvax to advise you." I hesitated. "You can also expect more of my allies to join you soon."

Algar's eyes narrowed, but he didn't ask where they'd come from. "How many?"

"A few hundred at least. Maybe more."

"We'll need more housing then," Everard predicted.

Algar nodded. "We'll have to expand the court."

"Building will keep the men occupied at least," Zorg remarked.

"And some walls around this place wouldn't hurt either," Megtir added.

I smiled. "I will leave you to your planning then." I glanced in Nyra's direction. "Now, if you'll excuse me, there is someone else I must speak with."

✳   ✳   ✳

The apprentice watched my approach, her face expressionless. "I heard what you told Algar," she said, raising her chin. "Does the same apply to me?"

"Yes," I said forthrightly.

"You said you'd take me with you when you left the dungeon," she accused.

"I did, but that was before I knew there would be someone here to train you."

Her gaze slid in Ceruvax's direction. "Him?"

"Him," I confirmed. "Ceruvax is a former envoy of House Wolf, and he will be able to give your training more time and care than I can, to be honest." I smiled lopsidedly. "Then, too, here in Draven's Reach, you won't spend most of your time on the run."

"I want to come with you," she insisted.

My smile faded. "It won't be forever. And there'll be others joining you soon."

"Others?"

"Another two young players, at least," I said, thinking of the twins. "And most likely a werewolf and two wolf Packs as well." Bringing them all into Draven's Reach would be a priority. "You'll have plenty of company."

She fell silent for a moment. "Then, you mean to do it."

I looked at her curiously. "Do what?"

"Raise House Wolf. Go to war. Fight the new Powers and all that."

"Yes, but we're a long way from any of that." I held her gaze. "I won't force you, you know. Stay or come, the choice is yours."

Nyra's gaze drifted to Ceruvax again. "Is he really as old as he looks?"

"Even older," I said, deadpan.

"Older," Nyra muttered. Turning back to me, she sighed. "Alright, I'll stay."

"Thank you," I said, relieved. I turned to where Regus was tapping his foot impatiently. "Do you want to come watch? It may be educational."

She wrinkled her nose. "No, I'll stay here with Ghost, I think."

✷　✷　✷

Nyra, it turned out, was the only one not curious enough to want to witness the promised transformation of the possessed into werewolves.

Standing in the center of a crowd, and with Farren, Adriel, and Ceruvax at my back, I faced the first candidate.

Regus.

The former court's head of security had volunteered to go first. I had been less enthused by the prospect than he, but neither lich thought the danger onerous. If need be, they would rehome Regus.

I ran my gaze over the watching possessed, packed tightly together and crowding in on the circle of empty space around me and the others in the middle. Even Avery and his group had come to witness what happened.

We should've done this on the dais, I thought, but it was too late to relocate now. From the avid looks of the onlookers, no one was going to suffer further delays.

I glanced at the lichs behind me.

Both nodded curtly. "Ready," Farren pronounced.

I turned back to Regus. Wordlessly, he went down on one knee and raised his right arm.

I took his hand in mine, baring the flesh at the wrist. I would have to physically bite the possessed, and despite Ceruvax's assurances, I wasn't entirely convinced that what we planned would work, especially not on the first attempt. The Game had stated the probability of success would be no higher than twenty percent, after all.

Farren had explained this to the others, but I knew no one would react well to failure. Nor did I miss the anticipatory gleam in Avery's eyes. He, at least, was expecting me to fail, and in a huge way, too. I suspected this was the only thing that had stopped him and the others from protesting the delay to the ritual combat.

He's probably prepared his speech already, I thought morosely.

I shook off my doubts. There was no use delaying further. *Here goes.* Lowering my head, I pinched Regus' skin between my teeth and tugged— hard enough to tear flesh.

You have bitten Regus! Were's bite activated.
Analyzing the subject's suitability...
...

...

In breathless anticipation, I waited, not daring to wipe away the blood staining my lips or to stop the red rivulets running down the possessed's arm.

Analysis complete.
The non-player, Regus, carries 25 dormant bloodline strains, one of which is of Wolf.
The subject has been deemed acceptable.

I nearly sagged in relief before I remembered the watching crowd. "The Adjudicator has judged Regus a suitable candidate," I reported.

Gasps and cries of excitement rose from all around me. Avery scowled. "That does not mean it will work!" he shouted.

"True," I replied grimly. "But we're about to find out."

The subject has acceded to the were's bite.
Transferring lycanthropy mutation...
...

...

Regus stiffened suddenly.

The next moment, his back arched, and his limbs failed. Releasing his arm, I gripped him around the chest. He continued to thrash, his body simultaneously trying to drag me down and throw me off. I held on grimly.

"His eyes are turning yellow!" someone yelled.

"Look at his hands, they're growing claws!"

"Is that fur?"

Mutation unsuccessful.
The subject has failed to bring the lycanthropy infecting his system under control and has succumbed.
Regus has died.

The possessed slumped, and I staggered forward, trying to hold him upright.

"It didn't work!" Avery shouted gleefully. "I told you fools, it—"

"Shut up, Avery," Farren said mildly. "One more word out of you, and I swear I will crush the life out of your bones."

Not unsurprisingly, the possessed closed his mouth.

Ignoring the byplay, I glanced at Adriel. Regus' spirit had not exited his body as it would've ordinarily, and that was the lich's doing. By some arcane means of death magic, she was forcing his spirit to stay housed within its dead cage.

"I've got him," she confirmed. "Give it a moment. He will come to, once the mutation has run its course."

Nodding, I turned back to the possessed. Regus' eyes were shut, and the pain lines riddling his face hadn't faded. Worse yet, his body remained stuck in a random mix of wolf and human body parts. I shuddered. The possessed's death had been far from pleasant.

At least, it was quick.

A minute passed, then another, and I sensed the crowd grow restless, but I didn't look up. Trusting Adriel, I waited.

Finally, Regus' eyes snapped open.

A moment later, they focused on me. "Again," he rasped.

I hesitated. "You're sure?"

He nodded jerkily. "Do it."

Not questioning his resolve further, I bit down on his wrist once more.

✳   ✳   ✳

It took five tries, but finally, the Game message I was waiting for arrived.

Mutation complete.
The subject's body has accepted the lycanthropy mutation.
Were's bite successful.

"It's done!" I shouted, stumbling back. The possessed was changing before my eyes, his transformation—which thus far had only been occurring in fits and starts—advancing smoothly from one step to the next.

But that wasn't the only change he was going through.

"Look!" one sharp-eyed onlooker yelled. "The wound on his head, it's closing!"

My eyes darted to the new werewolf's bald head. Regus was still in the middle of his change and a wolf's furry coat didn't cover his scalp yet. The commentator was correct, I saw.

The 'pre-death' wound on Regus' head—inflicted when the player whose corpse he inhabited had been killed—was healing, the raw, angry sides closing as if they'd never been.

I inhaled sharply. No possessed could heal 'pre-death' wounds, no matter what magic spells they attempted or how many health potions they quaffed. That Regus could do so now was only due to a werewolf's famed regenerative powers.

Ceruvax had been right. And that meant...

My head whipped around in Adriel's direction, seeking confirmation.

The lich was smiling.

"It worked," she said softly. "The lycanthropy running through Regus' veins has destroyed the finger bone from his old body—just as Ceruvax suspected it would. And that has forced Regus' spirit to mesh fully with its physical shell." She drew in a tremulous breath. "He is whole again."

A grin broke out across my face as I turned back around. A naked werewolf in half-form loomed over me.

Over ten feet in height, Regus was now much taller that he'd been before. His clothes, little more than rags, lay where they had fallen, but with a coat of shiny brown fur covering him from head to toe, he hardly needed them.

"Wow," Ghost exclaimed from where she and Nyra watched on the dais. *"Is this what Anriq looks like?"*

"Something like," I murmured. I met the new werewolf's eyes. Tears swam in them. *He knows.*

"You hear that, Regus," I shouted anyway, more for the crowd's benefit than his. "It worked!"

"I feel it," Regus said, the words emerging as a guttural half-snarl from his snout-like face. Throwing back his head to face the sky, he roared, "I'm no longer a possessed! I'm whole again!"

The crowd broke out in cheers.

"He lies!" Avery yelled. "It's a trick!"

But no one was listening. Ignoring Avery, they congregated around the new werewolf, inspecting him intently. For most, neither Regus' words nor Adriel's pronouncement was necessary. The sight of the werewolf's wounds closing was confirmation enough.

The former possessed was whole again.

That, of course, was the outcome we'd all been hoping for. It had not been guaranteed, not by any means, but it was the entire reason Ceruvax had suggested this approach.

Few things in the Game could stop a werewolf from regenerating. The former envoy had been convinced that if the possessed could be turned into weres, the lycan mutation would take care of the rest of their problems.

And he'd been right.

Turning to the left, I met Ceruvax's gaze. "Well done, old wolf," I whispered.

He heard me despite the crowd's noise. "Did you analyze him?" he asked in a low voice as he stepped closer.

"No, why would—"

"Do it."

Hearing the strange note in his voice, I swung wordlessly back to Regus and did just that.

The target is Regus, a level 179 wolfman.

It is not often that non-players survive an infection of lycanthropy and those that do don't turn into werewolves but wolfmen.

Wolfmen are a species born from a nearly unique set of circumstances, and unlike most other blends of men and beasts, they are more sentient than feral. But despite their origins, wolfmen possess many of their lupine forebearers' traits, including the prodigious regeneration abilities of a werewolf.

"Wolfmen? What are damn wolfmen?" I growled. At first glance, they sounded akin to the ratmen I'd encountered in the Guardian Tower.

"Something I've heard of only once or twice before but never encountered myself," Ceruvax replied. "They're rarer than werewolves."

"Then Regus is *not* a werewolf?" I asked, wanting to be certain. "This is not just him in his half-form?"

"No, this is his *only* form, I suspect," Ceruvax said.

I lowered my head in my hands.

"Does it matter?" Adriel asked from where she'd been quietly listening.

Raising my head, I looked at her. "What do you mean?"

"Werewolf or wolfman, what does it matter?" Adriel asked. "Regus is no longer possessed, and he has a stronger, healthier body than he could ever have hoped for."

"But I promised them they'd become werewolves," I protested. "Not wolfmen."

She chuckled. "I doubt that will matter to Regus—or any of the others, for that matter."

I sighed. "Probably not," I conceded.

"Shall I?" Ceruvax asked, gesturing to the wolfman.

The next part was his—welcoming Regus into the new Pack.

I nodded. "Go ahead."

✳ ✳ ✳

Adriel was correct.

The differences between wolfmen and werewolves fazed none of the possessed, and after witnessing the result of Regus' change, most were eager to undergo their own transformations.

It took nearly the entire day to go through all five hundred candidates. Some went faster. Many took longer. Avery tried to use the time to sway more possessed to his cause, but few bothered listening to him anymore. In fact, it was all he could do to hold onto his existing recruits.

I didn't attempt convincing any of Avery's group to change their minds either. They had made their decision, and it was safer for all concerned for them to go through with the ritual combat than for them to join the wolfmen pack and cause trouble at a later stage.

By the time I finished with the last candidate, Ceruvax's new pack numbered just over five hundred. Only forty possessed had failed to transform. They had been despondent by their failure, but rather than join Avery, most had opted to merge with the third group—those waiting to be rehomed into flesh golems.

"They know what's in store for them?" I asked Adriel, studying the group in question, now numbering nearly one hundred.

She nodded. "They know," she said softly.

I'd given the possessed no guarantees about how long it would take to rehome them, only that they would be. First, I would need to retrieve the Ring of Astral Walking and rejoin the dire wolf pack. Which meant the hundred would be spending a few weeks—at the very least—as disembodied spirits, housed in only their bones.

"Are you ready to face Avery and the others?" the lich asked tiredly.

The wolfmen ceremony had exhausted Adriel and Farren. Both had toiled hard to keep the possessed spirits locked in their bodies while the lycan mutation did its work. I, by contrast, had suffered no ill effects—if you discounted having to endure the coppery tang of blood over and over, that is.

"Almost," I replied. "There's just a few things I—"

I stopped short abruptly.

"What is it?" Adriel asked sharply.

"A Game message," I murmured, turning my focus inward.

By unanimous accord, the wolfmen of sector 73,102 have proclaimed a new leader! Your follower, Ceruvax, is now the alpha of the new Pack of the Reach.

Ceruvax's Wolf Mark has deepened, advancing to <u>Pack Alpha</u>.

"Well, that's interesting," I said, glancing in the direction of the former envoy. The last of the newborn wolfmen had just submitted to him, and by all appearances, the Game's message had also caught the old wolf by surprise.

I chuckled. "Ceruvax has just become the alpha of the new pack, which the Game has labeled the Pack of the Reach. It has a nice ring to it, don't you—"

I broke off again.

Another Game alert was flashing for attention.

You have completed the hidden task: <u>Establish a new line of Wolves</u>! Weres have been around as long as the Game has existed, but nearly every were has been a player, and few are the weres that have formed a species of their own. Your actions today have seen the birth of a wolfmen pack, the first of its kind in the Game's history.

Your spirit signature has been etched with a new Mark! You have acquired the Mark of a <u>Wolf Progenitor</u>. Progenitor Marks are separate and distinct from your main bloodline Marks and are only ever awarded in extraordinary cases.

Your secret blood trait has been triggered! To conceal your bloodline, your new Mark will be hidden.

As a result of your Progenitor Mark, you may undergo another higher evolution. Do you wish to proceed?

"Oh my," I said in a half-strangled voice.

"What is it this time?" Adriel asked, sounding exasperated. "Don't tell me the Adjudicator has more to say."

I nodded numbly. "He certainly does. I've completed a hidden task that allows me to undergo a *second* higher evolution."

Her eyes narrowed. "Did your Power Mark evolve again? Because that would not be good."

I shook my head. "None of my existing Marks have changed." I paused. "But I have gained a *new* one." Lowering my voice, I said, "It's the Mark of the Wolf Progenitor."

The lich's eyes closed to slits. "I've never heard of such a Mark before," she muttered. "Nor of anyone being offered the chance of a higher evolution *without* their Power Mark growing."

"I find it more than a little unbelievable myself," I said and read the full Game alert to her.

"'The first of its kind...'" Adriel quoted in an astonished whisper. "Sometimes, Michael, I wonder what you won't achieve..."

I threw her a half-embarrassed grin. "This is more Ceruvax's achievement than my own. Turning the possessed into weres was his idea."

She waved her hand dismissively. "It was your idea to bring him here in the first place. It seems your gamble is already paying off."

I nodded slowly, though I hardly felt I deserved the credit. I'd summoned Ceruvax to help rebuild House Wolf, not for *this*. This was entirely unexpected!

Ceruvax half-walked, half-ran to join us, the excitement in his expression looking strangely out of place on his usually stern face. "Did you see? I gained an alpha mark!"

Adriel laughed. "Old man, that's not nearly the half of it."

Ceruvax's brows furrowed. "What does that mean?"

Grinning, Adriel chose not to enlighten him.

I rolled my eyes. "It's no more than you deserve. This was your doing, but what Adriel is alluding to is the hidden task I completed."

"What task?" he asked.

I told him.

Ceruvax sat down, looking as shocked as I felt. "That's a magnificent boon," he murmured.

I nodded. "The question now is, what do I do with it?" I glanced to the left, where the possessed of Avery's group were pacing angrily. "And we best decide quickly, because I don't think Avery will wait much longer.

*　　*　　*

Death in the ritual circle would be final, and while I was confident about my chances, I was not so foolish as to enter the fight without maximizing my advantage.

In the present situation that meant completing my second higher evolution and utilizing my last Class point.

While Ceruvax, Adriel, and Farren—he'd hurried over, too—had a whispered discussion about the new Mark and its possibilities, I sat cross-legged and considered my Class point.

I had two options for spending it: slaysight or void thief. Slaysight was at tier four, and void thief at tier three. Considering the number of mages I'd be facing in the Circle, there was a good argument to be made for upgrading void thief and thereby improving my overall magic defenses.

But.

Slaysight was at tier four—only one tier away from being an elite ability—and while the ability didn't need further enhancement to be effective against the possessed, I had a feeling I would need its more powerful variant once I exited the dungeon.

Besides, upgrading slaysight would give me my first elite ability, and the thought of waiting another fifteen levels before the next chance to upgrade it came around did not appeal.

My decision made, I turned my focus inward and willed my intent to the Adjudicator.

Commencing Class upgrade...

...

Upgrade complete. Class points remaining: 0.

Congratulations, Michael! Your voidstealer Class has advanced to rank 12.

You have upgraded your slaysight ability to <u>adept slaysight</u>. The fifth tier of the slaysight ability adds another mental manipulation to your arsenal: <u>paralyze</u>. Additionally, the range, number of targets, and spell duration have increased while the casting time has decreased.

With adept slaysight, you may detect any mind within 200 yards and <u>paralyze</u>, <u>shatter</u>, <u>sleep</u>, <u>terrify</u>, or <u>mentally blind</u> any 10 targets for 1 minute. Paralyze will freeze your foes so they can neither move, cast, nor use any other abilities. The debuff will remain in place even after you've taken hostile action against your targets. Note, a paralyzed foe is completely aware of what happens around him, even though he is unable to interact with the environment in any way. Its activation time is very fast.

This is a Class ability and does not occupy any ability slots.

"Wow," I exclaimed. Paralyze was powerful.

Not only would the ability turn my foes helpless, but it also kept them that way *after* I attacked. None of slaysight's lesser effects could do that, making me doubly glad I'd chosen to upgrade the ability.

Refocusing on my surroundings, I found Farren, Adriel, and Ceruvax staring expectantly at me. I opened my mouth to tell them the good news about slaysight, but before I could, Ceruvax spoke first.

"Are you ready to begin?" the old wolf asked.

Looking at their intent faces, I suspected none of them would be interested in hearing about my new elite ability. *Ah, well.*

"Let's hear it then," I said. "What risks do you see in me undergoing another Class evolution?"

The answer to this was central to my decision on whether to evolve now or not. For obvious reasons, I did not want to wait. What the three had been discussing so frantically was what impact performing a higher evolution would have on my Power Mark.

Growing my Power Mark would not help my cause right now.

As a Power Acolyte, I would be prevented from attacking non-Powers—the same constraint was also applied at level three hundred—and I was far from ready for such to happen.

In fact, for the foreseeable future, I intended on doing my best to *not* kill any more Powers and to remain a Powerful Initiate. There were other ways I needed to grow first.

"There should be no risk," Farren pronounced.

I eyed the archlich. "The word 'should' does not inspire much confidence."

He grimaced. "I know, but that's the best answer we can come up with."

"The truth is you're wading into uncharted territory, Michael," Adriel said quietly. "Even with all the years of Game experience the three of us have between us, we don't know of a single instance of a player undergoing a second higher evolution while still a Powerful Initiate."

"That doesn't mean no one's done it," Ceruvax added, "only that we don't know about it."

"But everything we know of the Game tells us that undergoing a second higher evolution should not trigger a growth in your Power Mark," Farren said. "The relationship is the other way around. It's a Power Mark's growth triggers an evolution."

"So, you *should* be fine," Adriel said, her lips twitching.

I suppressed a laugh. "I guess I *should* be forging ahead, then."

Farren and Ceruvax nodded solemnly, ignoring my amused tone.

I sighed. "So be it." Closing my eyes, I pulled up the earlier Game message. "Here goes."

Do you wish to begin your higher evolution now?

"I do," I replied in response.

Assessing player's suitability...

...

...

Assessment of player's Marks completed.

Warning: you lack the necessary Wolf and Power Marks to evolve your existing commander Class from epic to legendary.

Do you still wish to proceed?

"Hmm," I mused.

"What?" all three blurted in unison. Opening my eyes, I relayed the Game's response.

The trio immediately relaxed. "That's good," Farren murmured.

Adriel nodded. "It all but confirms your Power Mark won't grow."

"It does mean you will have to choose another epic Class, though," Ceruvax pointed out. "Are you prepared to do that?"

"I am." Squeezing my eyes shut again, I willed my intent to the Adjudicator.

Commencing higher evolution...

...

...

Viable ascendant paths determined.

Two new paths lie before you, scion.

Each focuses on a different aspect of Power and, over time, will evolve further to provide improved benefits.

The first path is that of the <u>sire wolf</u> and will grant you the ascendant trait, <u>champion</u>. As a champion, the power of all your blood memories is doubled. You will also gain 30 attribute points and may choose 1 additional benefit unique to your chosen Class.

The second path is that of the <u>den forefather</u> and will grant you the ascendant trait, <u>governor</u>. As a governor, you gain access to a unique branch of blood memories and abilities that focus on sector-wide buffs and spells. You will also gain 20 attribute points and may choose 1 additional benefit unique to your chosen Class.

Which ascendant path will you choose for your second epic Class?

I pursed my lips. The epic Classes on offer this time around were different from those the Game had proposed just a few short days ago. Was that because of my new Mark?

Has to be.

Keeping my eyes closed, I relayed the options to the others.

"Sire wolf and den forefather?" Ceruvax muttered. "I know of no Wolf Prime who has ever been offered those Classes."

I nodded thoughtfully. Ceruvax's remark, while interesting, had little bearing on my choice. I *knew* which Class I had to take this time around.

"Sire wolf," I breathed.

Higher evolution completed!

You have gained the epic Class, <u>Sire Wolf</u>.

Through words and deeds, you have shown yourself worthy of joining the venerated ranks of sire wolves. Throughout the annals of history, less than a handful of Wolves have been graced with such a title. Through this Class, you will gain access to some of the rarest and most potent gifts wolfkin has to offer.

Do not squander them, scion.

Like other champions, the sire wolf is often both the shield and sword of his bloodline. But where most champions frequently depend on their

blood alone, the sire wolf also focuses on strengthening his ancient wolven heritage.

Your secret blood trait has been triggered! To conceal your bloodline, your new ascendant Class will be hidden.

You have gained the base trait: <u>champion</u>. As a champion, the strength of all your current and future blood memories has doubled.
Your champion trait has been triggered! 1 of 1 existing blood memories strengthened. Secret blood has been upgraded.

<u>Secret blood</u> (champion variant): Where ordinarily, secret blood conceals only your Wolf Marks, Classes, skills, and traits, the champion variant extends this protection to your familiar and followers. Their Wolf-related characteristics will be hidden from other Powers and players. If you so wish, you may also conceal your Wolf Marks from other wolves.

You are now a rank 1 champion. The number of sectors your faction may own has increased by +1, the followers you can bind by +100, and the number of active Pacts you may have by +10.

As a result of your new Class, you may choose 1 of the following 4 new ascendant Class benefits:
New benefit: <u>lycan renewal</u>. This trait enhances your shapeshifting blood memories by fully restoring your energy pools whenever you shift form.
New benefit: <u>sire's strain</u>. This trait boosts all your existing and future wolf traits by +1 tier.
New benefit: <u>blood caster</u>. This trait reduces the cooldown of your active blood memories, allowing them to be used more often.
New benefit: <u>elder form</u>. This trait allows you to transform once a day into an elder wolf, the most powerful of all wolven subspecies.

Choose your ascendant Class benefit now.

"Ah," I exhaled.

"Tell us," Ceruvax said, his words almost a demand.

Opening my eyes, I told them about my new Class and the benefits I had to choose from.

"That's no ordinary Class," Adriel said.

"I agree," Farren said. "I know the Wolves have produced some strong Primes before." He glanced at Ceruvax. "But this is unusual even for them."

Ceruvax nodded slowly. "I thought I knew every powerful epic Class variant the House had to offer, but I've never heard of the sire wolf Class." He bowed his head. "Why did Atiras never mention it?"

"Perhaps he didn't know?" Adriel suggested.

The possibility seemed to disturb Ceruvax even more, and his frown deepened.

"We will have to leave analysis of the Class for later," I said, drawing their attention. "I still have the Class benefit to choose."

"You should rule out the two blood options, lycan renewal and blood caster," Farren said. "There's nothing wrong with either, but you don't have the blood memories to make them count."

I nodded. "Agreed. That leaves elder form and sire's strain."

"Elder form," Ceruvax proposed immediately.

I smiled. "I had a feeling you would advocate for that. But tell me, why do you think it's the right choice?"

"There is no more powerful wolf than an elder wolf," he said simply. "In elder form, you can expect all your attributes to increase—significantly." He paused. "They're also about as hardy as werewolves, as mentally adept as dire wolves, and as magically strong as hellhounds."

Farren nodded. "Everything Ceruvax says is true. Not even a lich will take one on lightly."

"I will only be able to change into elder form once per day though," I noted. "But far more damning is how obvious they are."

Ceruvax frowned. "What do you mean by that?"

"I can't imagine elder wolves are common," I replied. I had yet to run across one in the Game.

"That's true," Adriel said. "Even in my day, they were rare. And I can only assume they're grown even more so after the new Powers' victory."

"Which is my point exactly," I said. "How many sightings do you think it will take before the new Powers grow curious about the player who turns into an elder wolf?"

No one answered.

"And how long after that do you think it will take them to make the connection between the form and my bloodline?"

"Your point is taken," Ceruvax said grudgingly. "Perhaps it is best to leave the selection of the ability until your next evolution." He sighed. "And besides, with suitable investment in the 'right' traits, I suspect, sire's strain can become powerful too."

I nodded. "In that case, I best not waste any time. Avery is heading this way." Closing my eyes, I willed my intent to the Game.

You have gained the trait: <u>sire's strain</u>. This trait boosts all your existing and future wolf traits by +1 tier. Currently affected traits include void heritage, voidwalker, arctic wolf, and were's bite.

You have upgraded void heritage to tier 2, increasing its benefits to +4 Dexterity, +4 Strength, +8 Mind, +8 Perception, and +12 Magic.
You have upgraded voidwalker to tier 2. In addition to enhancing your senses and granting you nethersight, the trait also makes you immune to blindness.
You have upgraded arctic wolf to tier 2, increasing its benefits to +10 Constitution, +4 Mind, and +6 Strength.
You have upgraded were's bite to tier 2, increasing the maximum probability of its success to 30%.

I rocked back on my heels, doing some quick math in my mind. In total, I'd gained a whole twenty-eight attributes from my new trait. And that was not even considering the changes sire's strain had wrought on voidwalker and were's bite. Ceruvax was wrong, I realized.

The trait was *already* powerful.

"Old wolf, I think you're in for a shock," I murmured. "Sire's strain is—"

"What's going on here," a querulous voice demanded.

I turned around slowly to face Avery. "We were just discussing strategy," I replied blandly. "Is that a problem?"

He scowled suspiciously. "You better not be attempting to weasel out of the combat. I warn you if—"

"Ceruvax, if you don't mind," Farren cut in, "please take Avery along and see to the Circle's final preparations." He cast a sidelong look at Adriel.

"I'll come along too," the lich said, taking her brother's hint. Turning on her heel, she strode toward the center of the courtyard. "Come along, Avery," Adriel said without looking back.

Looking frustrated, the possessed' gaze flitted between the departing pair and Farren, but he dared not disobey the archlich's direct command, and so after no more than a final glare at me, he stomped away.

I turned to Farren, one eyebrow raised. "I gather you want to talk?"

He smiled. "I do, but the expression on Avery's face alone made that worthwhile."

"I won't deny that I enjoyed it, too," I replied with a grin of my own. "I know we haven't had a chance to talk yet, but—"

"I understand," Farren interjected. "And I won't keep you. I only held you back to discuss one thing." He hesitated, looking more uncomfortable than I'd ever seen him. "I'm not sure when, or even if, we'll have a chance to talk again."

I studied the archlich curiously. "What is it?"

"Do you know why I became a lich?" he asked abruptly.

I blinked. This was the last direction I expected the conversation to go. "Uhm, to escape the new Powers and their—"

"No," Farren said, slashing his hand down. "Loskin did it because he wanted to become Prime, Adriel because she loved Death too much, but me?" He smiled lopsidedly. "I did it to save my sister."

"Ah."

"Loskin always believed he was meant to be Prime," he mused. "He wanted it so badly he was willing to do anything to achieve it." He sighed. "Which is how we ended up here, torturing non-players and harvesting the bodies of baby players."

I bit my lip. Where was Farren going with this? Had the archlich tired of life? Was that what this was about? "Are you trying to say you want to enter the Circle?" I asked slowly. "Because I don't think we can afford to do without you right now."

"What? You think I want to kill myself? No, of course not!" He frowned. "Although I might have to eventually, I suppose."

I fell silent, waiting for him to explain.

"Loskin was wrong, you know," the archlich said abruptly.

Another non-sequitur. "About?"

"It was not him the House watched closely. *He* was not the one destined to become Death Prime."

"You?" I asked, even though the answer felt wrong.

Farren laughed with genuine humor. "No, of course not. It was Adriel."

"I see," I murmured. Now I had more of an inkling what the conversation was about. "You don't want her to replace Kolath as Nexus' guardian."

"I don't. She is too important for House Death to lose."

"But she's a lich," I said delicately. "She told me herself that House Death abhors lichs. That by becoming one, she severed her ties with the House. How can—"

"Don't be a fool, Michael," Farren said mildly.

I stared at him. There was no hint of humor on the archlich's face now. And anyway, Farren wouldn't joke about this.

"Then you believe that whatever she did to become a lich can be reversed?" I asked softly, connecting the dots.

"Yes."

My eyes narrowed. "How?"

"I preserved her body," he said simply.

I waited for him to go on, but when he didn't, I said, "You're going to have to give me a bit more than that."

Farren began pacing. "The details aren't important right now. Suffice to say, I put Adriel's body in stasis." He gestured to the destroyed vault. "Much in the same manner we kept those player bodies on ice, only I did so more... efficiently. If Adriel is strong enough—and I know she is—she can reverse the lich-making ritual and recombine with her body."

I rubbed my chin. "But what makes you think her body is still safe after all this time? It's been centuries." Many centuries.

"Oh, I have every reason to believe it's still safe. I hid the body well. No one will find it."

"Then how do *I* find it?"

Withdrawing a slim object from his robe, Farren handed it to me. "You will find everything you need in there."

You have acquired a sealed missive.

The envelope was formed from thick, expensive paper. The front was blank except for a series of numbers stenciled boldly across the center. Turning it over, I saw a large wax insignia fixed on the back.

"Don't try to open it," Farren warned. "The envelope will destroy itself if you do. The letter is keyed only to Adriel. Give it to her when you reach Death's home sector, the location of which is inscribed on the front."

I nodded numbly, then glanced into the courtyard where Adriel was chatting with Ceruvax. "I'm guessing she doesn't know about any of this?"

Farren snorted softly. "Of course not. And I prefer you not tell her until you reach the sector. Adriel can be... stubborn."

"Right, and conveniently, when I do break the news to her, you won't be around to suffer her wrath," I grumbled.

"There's that, too," he said, smiling fleetingly. "One more thing."

I held back a sigh. "I'm listening."

"Stayne."

I stared at him blankly. "What?"

"The ascendant undead you told Adriel about, remember him?"

"I know who he is," I said irritably. "What does he have to do with any of this?"

"He is important."

"Why?" I demanded.

Farren exhaled. "He is an ascendant and bears a Mark of Death." The archlich held my gaze in case I didn't realize the significance of that. "That is a bloodline Mark. *House Death's* Mark. And by your tale, this Stayne is serving a new Power." He shook his head. "It doesn't make sense. Why would any new Power allow one of their servants, especially an ascendant one, to bear a House Mark?"

"That is curious," I allowed.

"Which is why I need you to investigate the matter further." Farren stared at me intently. "Will you do so? And more importantly, will you help Adriel regain her status?"

"Of course." That I would help was never in any doubt. Somehow, I would find a way to fit it in between everything else I needed to do.

The Adjudicator has allocated you a new task: <u>Resurrecting Death</u>! The archlich has requested your aid in rebuilding House Death. Central to this is restoring the House's scions. Farren has given you the coordinates of Death's home sector as well as the location of Adriel's original body. Help her reverse the lich-making ritual. Primary objective: Make Adriel a scion once again. Optional objective: Solve the mystery of Stayne's Death Mark.

Farren sighed. "Thank you."

I nodded. "You haven't mentioned your own body, you know."

The archlich didn't answer immediately. "I could only save one of us," he said finally. "I chose Adriel."

I inclined my head, acknowledging his sacrifce. "I will do my best to see your work to completion."

✳ ✳ ✳

After our talk, Farren hurried ahead to help Ceruvax and Adriel establish order between the wolfmen and the possessed. The ritual combat would take place in the courtyard itself, with the onlookers watching from the outskirts. By all appearances, everything was ready.

My head bowed, I followed more slowly on Farren's heels. From the right, I sensed Ghost and Nyra approaching, but lost in thought, I didn't look up.

"Prime, there is someone here who wants to speak to you."

Glancing up, I saw that the pair were not alone. A possessed kept pace beside the pyre wolf. My eyes narrowed as I recognized him. He was one of the former wolves Regus had pointed out earlier.

Drawing to a halt, I waited for the trio to catch up.

"Hail, scion," the possessed said, bowing low.

Saying nothing, I waited.

He shifted uncomfortably. "My name is Darius. You may not know this, but we're formerly of—"

"House Wolf. Yes, I heard. Regus and Ceruvax both mentioned you."

"Ah, yes. The envoy." Darius shook his head ruefully. "He is just as I remembered."

"Why did you want to speak to me?" I asked patiently.

"We want to help, with the battle, I mean."

"I will not share my plans," I said softly.

"And I wouldn't ask you to." He inhaled deeply. "I've come to hear your orders."

I kept my face impassive. "Why would I give you orders, *possessed*?"

"You can trust him," Ghost interjected.

I acknowledged her words but didn't tear my gaze away from Darius.

"We want to help you succeed," the former wolf said. "We know it will not make up for everything we've done, but..." He shrugged helplessly.

Sighing, I relented. "How many can you count on?"

"Fifty-two," he replied instantly.

I nodded. "Then keep them together and take out the enemy fighters."

He frowned. "Why the fighters? The mages are the bigger threat. And aren't you forgetting the two elites? They can—"

I cut him off. "I won't explain. Kill the possessed warriors, as many as you can."

He bobbed his head. "As you wish."

"Thank you." I hesitated, then added, "For what it's worth, I appreciate your sacrifice. House Wolf will be stronger for it."

He straightened. "Thank you, scion."

I began to turn away, then paused. "Oh, and Darius."

"Yes, scion?"

"Make sure to tell the others: when they fall under my blade, I will do my best to make it painless."

CHAPTER 434: RITUAL COMBAT

By the time I reached the dais, everything was set up.

The Ritual Combat Circle had been made to expand by whatever magic it employed, and now, the immense ring of tarnished gold encircled the courtyard. The Skull of Souls had been placed inside, atop the fountain's broken statue.

The six hundred non-combatants—eager spectators waiting for the show to begin—stood outside the gold border, their feet brushing against its edges. Avery and his four hundred were already inside the Circle, deployed in orderly squads of ten around the western half.

According to Ceruvax, the Circle's magic would prevent either group of contenders from straying into the other's half before the combat began.

So, I'll have the entire eastern hemisphere to myself, I thought wryly.

"Are you sure about this Prime?" Ghost asked, concern threading her voice. She, Nyra, Ceruvax, Regus, the New Havener captains, and the lichs were waiting for me on the dais.

"I am," I said, as I shook the hands of everyone, genially accepting their well wishes. Reaching Ghost at the end of the line, I went down on one knee and ruffled her fur. *"This must be done."*

She exhaled heavily. *"Show them no mercy then."*

"I won't," I promised. Rising to my feet, I turned to face Ceruvax. "I'm ready."

He clasped my hand. "You remember what I told you?"

I nodded.

"Then go forth and wreak havoc, Prime," he said softly. "And may darkness always shelter you."

I smiled crookedly. This was one battle where I feared the shadows would do me little good. Other than for the fountain itself—which was miserably small—there was nowhere to hide inside the Circle. But I understood Ceruvax's sentiment, and I inclined my head in acknowledgment.

A moment later, a Game message unfurled in my mind.

Ceruvax, the custodian of the Ritual Combat Circle, has assigned you to team Wolf. Do you accept?

Willing my response to the Adjudicator, I shot the former envoy an inquisitive glance. "What did you name the second team?"

"Scum," he replied blandly.

Chuckling, I jumped off the dais and approached the circle. I had nearly no preparations to make. The Circle would allow no precast buffs and would prevent any spells or abilities from being used until the battle officially commenced. All my equipment would work normally inside the circle, but I could not fortify myself with enchantments or potions beforehand.

Which suited me more than it did my foes.

All two hundred mages inside the circle were without protective shields, and I could see how nervous they were about that. If I had to guess, the mages—and not just them, everyone else too—would be spending the first few seconds of the battle frantically seeing to their buffs and defenses.

I didn't intend on bothering with any of that, at least not straight away.

Standing on the outer edge of the circle, I ran my gaze over the aptly named Scum and analyzed them one by one, identifying my targets.

"What's wrong, Wolf?" someone yelled. "Afraid to enter?"

Not about to be rushed, I paid the heckler no heed. I wasn't entering the battle blind, of course.

Courtesy of Adriel, Regus, and Farren, I had detailed information on every possessed they deemed a threat, their capabilities, and their weaknesses. Adriel and I had gone over everything extensively during our two-day journey to get here. Of course, we'd not known which particular possessed I'd be facing, nor had we bothered going over the possessed's physical descriptions, only their names.

Which was why I was standing here now, putting faces to names with analyze.

The Scum, on the other hand, knew far less about my capabilities, and if I knew Avery, he'd probably overstated the extent of his knowledge about me to the two elites.

They would be unprepared. I wouldn't be.

Completing my analysis, I turned my attention inward. There was one last thing I needed to do—spend my remaining attribute points.

Deception was the key to winning the battle.

There was no way I could go toe-to-toe with four hundred possessed. And my usual strategy of lurking in the shadows would not work either. There were damn few hiding spots in the courtyard.

That, though, did not mean there was nowhere to hide.

Four hundred people made for a sizable group, after all. One big enough to hide in—especially if I was not wearing my own face. All I would need to do was resist detection.

Which is why I threw my thirty new attribute points into Perception.

Your Perception has increased to rank 90. Other modifiers: +4 from items.

I didn't especially need the added Perception to deceive the Scum. My rank nineteen deception was good enough to defeat the senses of all but a few key individuals—and I'd already marked *those* for early elimination.

But deception would also be the key to my survival once I left the sector, which was why I needed to train the skill and invest in its governing attribute while I still could.

I set my hands onto the hilts of my sheathed blades. I was finally ready. *Let's do this*, I thought and stepped over the Circle's gold border.

✳   ✳   ✳

You have entered a Ritual Combat Circle. A dampening field is active in this Circle. Your mana, psi, and stamina abilities have been inhibited.

Analyzing contender...

...

...

No active buffs found. No time-limited spells present.

Warning: death in the Circle is final. You will not revive if you fall within its field of effect. Exit the Circle immediately if you do not wish to risk final death.

Ignoring the Game message, I strode deeper into the Circle.

The battle will commence in 1 minute, at which time the dampening field will be deactivated.

Once combat starts, there can be no retreat until a victor is determined. A barrier will be erected around the Circle, preventing outside influences from affecting the battle's outcome. You have until the start of the combat to retreat if you so wish.

Coming to a halt in the center of my half of the Circle, I bounced lightly on my feet. Most of the warriors facing me had drawn their weapons already. They stood poised on the edge of their side of the circle. Their intent was obvious. Once the clock ran down, they would rush across.

Judging the distance carefully, I drew back. I couldn't afford to be caught out by an errant charge.

"Look! He's afraid."

"Stupid wolf, what was he thinking?"

"He's mine!"

"Not if I get him first!"

The battle will commence in 30 seconds.

Ignoring the hecklers, I let my gaze rove beyond them. Darius' people were massing behind the first line of warriors and looked ready to cut them down—a fact not lost on the possessed warriors—causing many to turn about and face the former wolves.

The Scum's archers and spellcasters had retreated to the far rim of the Circle, and some already had their bows and staffs pointed skyward. I eyed the weapons. They could prove troublesome.

Avery and the two elites were at the center of the casters' formation. Predictably, Castor's former protege was sticking close to the pair. The first was a ranger named Whyte, and the second was a sorcerer called Mersk.

Only one was a serious threat, though.

The battle will commence in 15 seconds.

It was time to get ready. Lifting my hands from my sword hilts, I set them on the belt strapped across my chest and drew two items.

Then, I crouched down low, waiting.

The battle will commence in 5 seconds.

4...

3...

2...

1...
Fight!

I exploded into motion.

Everyone else did, too.

A wall of sound rolled across the Circle, the twang of a score of bows competing with the chants of the mages and the yells of the fighters. Half of the possessed warriors hurtled across the ground at me. The rest held the former wolves at bay. Mages lobbed missiles or whispered furiously, and archers fired arrow after arrow.

Flinging away the stone bottle in my right hand, I rolled across the ground as the missiles hissed across the sky—a sky distorted by the shimmering haze of a protective dome. The Circle's barrier was in place.

You have ignited a smoke bomb, creating a smoke cloud.
You are hidden.

Dark gray clouds ballooned out from my feet, concealing me from sight, but also obscuring my own vision too. Still, I didn't need to see.

I had my target's location fixed with mindsight.

I continued rolling, keeping my motions as erratic as possible while I spun psi. The charging warriors drew closer. But they worried me little. Even the descending projectiles would soon be of no consequence.

The gray cloud I'd created would do more than confound my foes' attacks, it would distract them, too—and leave them futilely searching for me where I was not.

A heartbeat later, my spell was ready, and I released it.

You have teleported into Whyte's shadow.
A hostile entity has detected you! You are no longer hidden.

I emerged from the aether behind my target and with my hands already in motion. The ranger spun around, instantly sensing my presence. His longsword came up, ready to fend off a blow.

But it was not a blade I leveled at him. It was a ring.

My right arm darted upward—palm up and facing Whyte—while my left hand opened, dropping the second stone bottle.

Mage's surprise activated. Spellhold casting released. You have trigger-cast seeking storm.
You have ignited a smoke bomb, creating a smoke cloud.

Ten forked tongues of lightning arced out from my hand at the same time as gray smoke mushroomed up from my feet.

Whyte has failed a magical resistance check!
You have critically injured Whyte!
You have critically injured Whyte!
You have critically injured Whyte!
...
Whyte is <u>stunned</u>. Duration: 6 seconds.

Castor's tier five spell, kept safe all these days in the ring on my hand, ripped through the ranger's defenses as if they weren't there, inflicting pure air damage and pushing him back into the billowing cloud.

"He's here! He's here!" Avery shrieked. "Get him!"

Ignoring the possessed, I drew ebonheart and advanced. My foe's chest and hands were a smoking wreck, but he was still very much alive, and he needed to be dealt with.

Mersk's homing fireball has hit you. Damage resisted by void armor!
Avery's scorching ray has missed you.
Garnet's color spray has missed you.

The second elite's attack staggered me, but my void armor rebuffed it, and it failed to do any damage. The other attacks, poorly aimed, were likewise ineffective. Nor did I need fear follow-up volleys. Until the dense plumes of smoke were cleared, I was as invisible to the possessed as they were to me.

Still, I knew I had only a few seconds at best.

But that was all the time I needed. Locating the stunned ranger by mindsight, I lunged blindly forward.

You have injured your target.

My first strike found only meaty flesh, but that was alright. It gave me a sense of how my target lay, guiding my second attack.

You have killed Whyte.

"Where is he?" Avery yelled. "Mersk, you see him?"

"Shut up and let me work," the elite growled. "I need to banish this smoke!"

I rolled off the body, leaving ebonheart buried in the corpse. The black blade was too distinctive to keep carrying around. Rising to my feet, I pulled out two more stone bottles and, without hesitation, flung them toward Avery and Mersk.

You have ignited an acid bomb and a fire bomb.

"He's after us! Run!"

I didn't stop lobbing bombs. Deception was the key. But a bit of chaos wouldn't go amiss either. Pulling out more stone bottles, I threw them in random directions.

You have ignited 4 ice bombs and 3 acid bombs!

"He's to our right!"

"No, he's attacking from the left!"

"You fools! You're both wrong. Retreat and regroup!"

I grinned, listening to the sound of pounding feet—as many were heading blindly in my direction as away from me. My foes were panicking. They'd spent too long as possessed and had grown used to being immortal. Now, faced with the threat of death—*real* death—they were running scared.

Sadly, it wouldn't last.

But while it did, I had time to prepare. Removing the Cloak of the Reach, I let it drop to the floor. It, too, was easily recognizable and would have to be left behind. Drawing on my stamina, I wove a spell quickly.

You have cast facial disguise, assuming the visage of Limond, a level 110 human scout. Duration: 3 hours.

My chosen face was that of a nondescript human possessed. He was still alive somewhere in the Circle, but I had his location fixed in my mind, and he wouldn't remain that way for long.

But first, it was time for me to regroup, too. Pressing the central stud on the belt around my waist, I released its magic.

You have activated the simple mode enchantment of the belt of the chameleon.

Clothes rippled upwards from the artifact to cover my leather armor in sturdy black pants, a white cotton shirt, and a brown duster jacket. Then, affecting the same panicked expression that my fleeing foes would be wearing, I dashed out of the smoke.

You have cast heightened reflexes, load controller, and trigger-cast quick mend.

"Where is he?" a possessed asked.

"Stop asking me, Meg!" another replied. "For the last time, I don't know!"

"Well, *someone* must know where the scion is, Bev," Meg replied reproachfully.

Nearly a minute later, the possessed were still searching for me. The gray haze had been cleared, and more than one revealing spell had been cast.

Despite this, I went unfound.

My deception and Perception were both too high. Whyte had been the possessed with the best chance of seeing past my disguise, and now he was dead.

"Are you sure about that?" Bev asked. "I heard they found his cloak and sword."

Meg shrugged. "The scion must have lost them. Or someone must have stolen the stuff."

"Nah, I think the fool is dead," Bev replied.

"He can't be," Meg retorted, "or the Circle would have deactivated by now."

Bev had no response to that.

Meg lowered her voice. "You don't think the scion is pretending to be one of us, do you?"

"Don't be daft," Bev scoffed. "We all know what he looks like! He must be hiding somewhere."

"But I heard he can change faces," Meg protested.

My lips twitched, but I managed not to laugh. I was in the middle of a group of possessed ordered to run around the Circle and find the 'Wolf.' The chatty pair were in front of me, and safe in my anonymity, I'd spent the past minute casting my buffs.

Now, it was time for me to act again.

"Maybe he's with Darius' group?" Meg suggested, resuming the conversation.

"Bloody wolves. Always sniffing their way into trouble," Bev replied before clutching his sides in amusement.

Ignoring the lame joke, I considered Meg's words. It was an interesting idea. Not to actually hide amongst the former wolves but to use them—both as decoys and to trim the enemy's ranks.

Glancing to my left, I studied the battle raging on the other side of the Circle. Darius' group had been whittled down to half its original size and was fighting defensively against the larger force arrayed against them. But from the number of bodies lying nearby, they'd claimed more than their fair share of victims.

Time to help.

Reaching out with my will, I targeted the possessed warriors on the former wolves' right flank.

You have cast slaysight.
You have paralyzed 10 of 10 targets for 60 seconds.

Across the distance, I saw a squad of possessed freeze in place. Despite the suddenness of the change, Darius' people didn't hesitate and hacked into the helpless warriors with a vengeance.

Excellent.

Turning my attention to the other side, I drew more psi and cast again.

You have cast mass charm.
You have charmed 10 of 10 targets for 20 seconds.

My will flooded the minds of another possessed squad, overwhelming their mental defenses and forcing them into submission. *"Attack,"* I ordered, directing my new minions to assault their former comrades.

Possessed cut down possessed, and chaos broke out on the former wolves' left flank.

I hid a smile. *That was easy enough.*

The sudden change in the warriors' fortunes did not go unnoticed by the rest of the Scum, though.

"He's with the wolves," someone shouted.

"I told you," Meg hissed.

"You shouldn't sound so happy," Bev grumbled. "Our glorious commander is ordering *us* there."

"Oh. Damn."

Our squad swerved abruptly left, and I realized the pair were right. We had been picked to reinforce the warriors. I grimaced. The wolves wouldn't serve much purpose as decoys if I were *actually* present nearby.

Time to relocate.

Extracting another handful of smoke bombs from my bomber's belt, I threw one down. Then, drawing faithful, I thrust the blade into the back of the hapless Meg.

You have killed Agameg with a fatal blow.

✳   ✳   ✳

Jump. Kill. Jump. Kill.

That's how I spent the next few minutes, reseeding the Circle with chaos until the Scum lost track of my true position again. Then, assuming another face, I faded back into anonymity.

And charmed and paralyzed more warriors.

Unsurprisingly, my tactics frustrated the enemy. I could smell the terror and anger rolling off them, but they couldn't find me no matter what they tried.

Left without a target against which to direct their anger, the mages stayed inside their protective bubbles and wasted their time casting spells of revealing.

Eventually, though, the last of Darius' people died, and I knew it was time to change tactics.

There were about three hundred possessed left in the circle, two hundred of whom were mages. I could go on killing the remaining ninety warriors, but that would leave me with nowhere to hide because, as effective as my deception abilities were, I couldn't use them to imitate a mage's shield.

"Now what?" I heard a possessed demand angrily. "We've killed every last damn one of those wolves, and we've still not found the blasted scion!"

No one had an answer for him.

The two hundred mages had drifted back to the center of the Circle and were gathered around the fountain in a loose crowd—the earlier discipline that had kept them in orderly squads of ten had long since vanished. The ninety warriors—me included—intermingled with the mages, our weapons held laxly in our hands.

Everyone was worried and afraid but at loose ends, too.

Surprisingly, the possessed hadn't twigged onto the fact that I was hiding amongst them. I knew, though, that with the wolves defeated and the Scum no longer preoccupied, someone would figure out what was going on. It was only a matter of time.

Still, I didn't attempt to rush proceedings.

The lull in the battle suited me just fine. The longer the fight dragged on, the less alert my foes would be. Then, too, the mages couldn't be happy about keeping their defenses up. Spells cost mana, and every bit they wasted now was a little less that they would have to throw at me when the conflict inevitably resumed.

And in the meantime, I could begin altering the battlefield to my liking.

Meandering lazily through the crowd, in a manner that appeared random—but was, in fact, meticulously planned—I placed my booted heel over the crystal I'd dropped and linked it to the trigger in my pocket.

You have connected a trap element to a remote-control trigger.
A tier 3 blot of darkness trap has been successfully configured!
Remaining trap-making crystals: 4 of 200.

I'd already planted eighteen darkness traps, each linked to its own remote trigger, and had only three more to go.

"He's here," Avery said abruptly.

"Well, of course, he is," Mersk replied grumpily. "Otherwise, the Circle would be down."

"No, I mean *here*—as in hiding as one of us."

Concealing a sigh, I paused in my step and, like everyone else, turned to look at my 'fellow' possessed suspiciously. For all Avery's arrogance and simpleminded tactics, he was also annoyingly perceptive at times. Casually concealing the trapper's wristband beneath my sleeve again, I began drawing psi.

"What makes you say that?" a warrior yelled.

"Have you forgotten Taim?" Avery retorted. "Not even Castor saw through his false visage. The scion is a doppelganger. He must be."

"A doppelganger?" Mersk asked skeptically. "That's a stretch."

"How else do you explain us not finding him?" Avery challenged.

I didn't wait for Mersk's reply. It was time to bring the discussion to a close. Releasing the spell, I held ready, I targeted the largest group of warriors.

You have cast mass charm.
You have charmed 10 of 10 targets for 20 seconds.

"Kill," I instructed, pitting them against the closet mages.

"It's more likely he is—" Mersk began.

"Aiyee!" a bespelled warrior yelled, hacking at the black bubble of a nearby witch.

"Damnit, Joff, what are you doing?" she cried.

"He's bewitched," another replied.

Mersk spun around, surveying the burgeoning skirmish behind him.

"The bastard has done it again," Avery snarled as more mages came under attack.

"What do we do?" someone yelled.

"Kill them!" Avery ordered grimly.

"What? Are you sure? But they're *our* people. Surely, we should—"

"Do it," Mersk interjected. "Whatever they were, they're a liability now. Kill them." The elite ran an opaque gaze over the rest of the warriors, and I could almost see the thought running through his mind.

They're liabilities, too. All the warriors were.

The smarter fighters picked up on the elite's thoughts, the same as I did, and backed away. The others stupidly followed his commands and hacked into their former comrades.

It's time to quit the field, I decided.

Using the renewed turmoil as cover, I threaded through the mages, cutting a swift path toward the fountain.

Too intent on slaying the charmed possessed, no one paid any heed to me or the other fleeing possessed. As I drew closer to the statue, I flicked my left hand forward, sending the stone bottle I held arcing over the crowd.

You have ignited an ice bomb, freezing 2 of 10 hostiles.

"The scion is attacking!" someone yelled.

"Where?"

"To the north!"

The bomb did minimal damage, but then, inflicting damage was not my intent. For a single moment, all eyes were turned either north, searching for me, or south, on the charmed warriors—leaving me and the fountain free of observation.

Ducking down, I wrapped myself in the smattering of shadows beneath the broken statue.

285 hostile entities have failed to detect you! You are hidden.

I was safe.
For now.

✳   ✳   ✳

**2 blot of darkness traps have been successfully configured!
Remaining trap-making crystals: 0 of 200.**

It did not take the possessed long to kill the ten bespelled warriors, but by the time they did, I had set my last two traps—at the base of the fountain itself—and was ready to charm the next ten.

Yet, I held back, curious to see if Avery and Mersk would do what I expected them to.

"Now what?" a hulking brute named Igural asked.

"Now, we make sure the scion can't use our people against us anymore," Mersk replied.

Igural scratched his head. "How do we do that?"

"How long have we known each other?" Mersk asked, ignoring the warrior's question.

"Ten centuries? Twenty?" he replied with a shrug. "I dunno, it's been too long."

The elite sighed. "Too long sounds about right." He lowered his staff. "Goodbye, old friend."

"What are you—"

A mass of tentacled vines writhed out of Mersk's staff—he was a life and fire magic specialist—and wrapped tightly around Igural, covering his nose, mouth, and eyes and trapping his arms against his chest.

Then, inch by inch, the thorny growths squeezed the life out of the trapped warrior.

Igural has died.

"Damnit, Mersk, what did you do that for?" a possessed demanded.

The elite turned dead eyes upon him. "It was necessary."

Before the possessed could question Mersk further, Avery raised his head and shouted. "Every non-mage dies now!"

"What—"

"You can't be—"

"It's them or us!" Avery shrieked, overriding the dissenters. "If you don't like it, you can join them. But one way or the other, we'll leave no one for the scion to hide behind, nor anyone for him to trick into betraying their own!"

The protests died.

And the slaughter began.

✳   ✳   ✳

I gave it thirty seconds.

An entire half-minute while I watched the mages butcher the warriors. The battle was not entirely one-sided, though, and here and there, I saw spellcasters being taken down.

Yet, I knew the warriors could not win even if I intervened, which I intended to do, only not in the usual manner.

I could not show myself—if I did that, I was sure the possessed would forget their own conflicts to focus on me—which meant I couldn't follow my favored approach of battering against the spellcasters' defenses until they failed.

Thankfully, I had other options.

A mage's shield came in multiple variants. The most popular one, though, was the type that blocked all damage—everything from physical damage to magic spells, from light to dark damage, and from psi damage to poisons.

It undoubtedly gave spellcasters a powerful advantage and explained why many players were drawn to Magic and Faith Classes.

Magic did have its downsides, though. A mage's spells often required verbal and somatic components. This made their casting both 'noisier' and slower than my own psi abilities.

Spellcasters were also—with a few notable exceptions—unable to kill their foes with 'fatal blows' like warriors, archers, and rogues often did. The damage a spell or psi ability did was usually not as concentrated as that inflicted by a physical weapon.

I'd known all of this, if not consciously, then subconsciously through my own experiences in the Game. Yet, it was only after my many talks with Ceruvax and Adriel on the subject—we'd discussed more than history during our two-day journey—that understanding of these particular Game dynamics had crystalized in my mind.

My understanding of magic had grown in leaps and bounds.

And that had made me realize I had another potent weapon in my arsenal to use against spellcasters.

Shatter.

Shatter was a slaysight ability that weakened a target's mental defenses, and while a mage's magic shield was not a psi shield per se—it did not hide their mindglows or stop me from teleporting onto them—it *did* prevent them from sustaining psi damage. What it boiled down to was that the more popular defensive magic spells had a psi component.

A psi component that I could destroy with shatter.

Shatter wouldn't take a mage's entire shield down, but it would leave their minds vulnerable to subversion. This, however, did not mean using shatter was without risk.

The target would sense my attack—there was no way to hide the mental intrusion—and while that didn't mean they would automatically locate me, they *would* know the general direction from which the attack came, much like someone shot by an arrow would know from where the bowman had fired.

Still, the mages were distracted at present. Something I intended to use against them.

Best I get started then. Drawing psi, I searched out the weakest spellcaster.

CHAPTER 436: SHATTERING THE ENEMY

The target is...
The target is...
The target is Nevin, a level 121 dark elf.

Him.
The dark elf in question was one of the weakest possessed I'd analyzed, and if shatter worked as I expected, he wouldn't put up much resistance.
Fashioning a spear of my will, I flung it against the possessed.

You have cast slaysight (shatter).
Nevin has failed a mental resistance check!
You have weakened your target's mental defenses by 70% for 60 seconds.

Thirty yards away, the dark elf staggered back. His eyes wide, the mage spun around to stare in the direction of the fountain.

A hostile entity has failed to detect you! You are hidden.

My face set, I shaped a second psi spear and tossed it at the possessed.

You have shattered Nevin's mental defenses! Remaining duration: 58 seconds.

The dark elf's mouth worked soundlessly. *He's about to scream*, I thought. I didn't intend on giving him the chance, though. Massing more psi, I swamped the mage's mind with my will.

You have paralyzed your target for 60 seconds.

Nevin froze, his mouth open, and his eyes unblinking. I drew more psi. Ideally, I would've wanted to bespell the mage immediately after shattering his defenses, but alas, charm was a significantly slower spell than slaysight.
A few seconds later, the spell was ready, and I drove my will into the doomed mage's mind, replacing one bewitchment with another.

Nevin is no longer paralyzed.
You have charmed your target for 20 seconds.

The dark elf's mouth closed with a snap, and obedient to my will, he swiveled around and sent magical fire coursing toward a nearby mage.
"Dem, watch out! Nevin's joined the warriors!"
"The bastard, I'll kill him."
Chuckling to myself, I turned away in search of another target.

✷　✷　✷

By the time the last fighter fell, seventy mages were dead, most of whom had died due to my intervention rather than the doings of the hapless warriors.

I'd picked my targets meticulously, choosing relatively low level mages whose defenses I could overwhelm quickly. Even so, I could tell Mersk, and Avery realized something was amiss, yet they were unable to pinpoint what. After all, all my victims' magic shields were visibly intact.

But, while the outcome was better than expected, it still left me with one hundred and twenty foes to deal with.

And I was nearly out of tricks.

That was not to say I wasn't confident about my chances against the remaining mages. Yes, one hundred and twenty spellcasters were a lot, and yes, magic was unpredictable, but truly, I had feared the fighters more. There was little I could do to stop a warrior's charge or a ranger's arrow—except get out of the way, and that was not so easy when there were scores of attacks to worry about.

Against spellcasters, on the other hand, I had my void armor to depend on. It gave me advantages most wouldn't expect. All of which went a long way to explain my confidence. That was not to say I expected things to be easy, though.

A hundred and twenty mages were *a lot*, after all.

"Well, glorious leader, what now?" I heard a witch ask, her mouth twisting unhappily.

"Yeah," another muttered, "this was *supposed* to be easy."

"And look at us now. Almost three hundred down, and no closer to winning."

Mersk scowled. "It will be easy; the scion has nowhere left to hide."

"Then where is he?" an angry mage shouted.

"Bah!" Avery spat. "We'll find the bastard. Recover your mana, then we'll hunt the scion and put an end to him once and for all."

"That's what you said before," the witch observed sourly.

It did not require any great intuition to know the possessed were near breaking. Avery, Mersk, and a few more might still be confident about their chances, but the others were wavering. All it would take was another well-placed blow.

It was time to shatter the enemy—and in more ways than one. Drawing in psi, I picked my target.

"We should rest in cycles," Avery suggested. "Do you want to take the first watch, Mersk, or should I?"

You have cast slaysight (shatter).
Mersk has failed a mental resistance check!
You have weakened your target's mental defenses by 10% for 60 seconds.

The elite's eyes widened.
Smiling grimly, I hit him again.

You have reduced Mersk's mental defenses to 80%! Remaining duration: 58 seconds.

"Mersk?" Avery prompted.

The elite's eyes narrowed. "The bastard is attacking my mind."

Avery's brows drew down. "Where is he?" he demanded fiercely.

The elite turned about to face the fountain. "He's—"

You have reduced Mersk's mental defenses to 70%! Remaining duration: 56 seconds.

"I'm over here," I said mildly, using ventro to make it appear as if I was at the southern end of the Circle.

One hundred and nineteen mages spun in that direction.

"Or am I here?" I asked, letting my voice emerge from the east this time.

You have reduced Mersk's mental defenses to 60%!

"No, you fools, he's playing tricks!" Mersk hissed, stalking closer to the fountain. "Don't listen to him." Raising a finger, he pointed unerringly in my direction. "He's there!"

You have reduced Mersk's mental defenses to 50%!

The mages spun back to face the fountain, but instead of attacking as the elite no doubt expected, many backed away while the more fearful scattered.

Multiple hostile entities have failed to detect you! You are hidden.

I laughed. "There's no escape," I said from the west.

You have reduced Mersk's mental defenses to 40%!

"Imbeciles," Avery growled, even as mana gathered in Mersk's hands. "Reveal him!"

Obediently, a handful of mages began chanting. Ignoring them, I stayed focused on the elite.

You have reduced Mersk's mental defenses to 30%!
Stone has cast revealing light.
Ensyn has cast pulse of scouring dark.
You have failed a magical resistance check! Multiple hostile entities have detected you! You are no longer hidden.

"There he is!" Avery snarled as the shadows fled from me. "Get him!"

Dozens of possessed lowered their staffs and wands in my direction. They didn't worry me, though. Mersk did. He'd not stopped furiously whispering the words of whatever spell he'd begun earlier.

Breaking off my attacks against the elite for a moment, I began another casting.

You have cast windborne.

A wave of destruction descended upon me—fireballs, ice missiles, lightning bolts, darkness rays, and so on. Trusting in my void armor to handle those I failed to dodge, I hopped onto the windslide and spiraled upward.

You have evaded 36 hostile spells.
Your void armor has repelled 6 magical attacks!
Your void armor has reduced the damage sustained from 9 magical projectiles.
Void armor charge remaining: 58%. Your health has decreased to 53%.

Agony tore at me as I was simultaneously burned, chilled, shocked, and bludgeoned. But as horrendous as the pain was, it was far from debilitating.

And importantly, I'd survived.

I squeezed my eyes shut for a heartbeat in silent relief. The possessed had had their chance and squandered it.

Depressing the trigger held tightly in my left hand, I vanished from sight again.

A blot of darkness trap has been activated.
Multiple hostile entities have failed to detect you! You are hidden.

"God damn!" Avery shrieked. "How could you idiots miss!"

Borne aloft by the air ramp, I floated through the billowing clouds of darkness. Errant spells passed me by, flung more in hope than anything else. Paying them no heed, I kept my gaze fixed on Mersk.

He hadn't broken off from his casting.

Time to hit him again.

You have reduced Mersk's mental defenses to 20%! Remaining duration: 35 seconds.

"Reveal the scion again!" Avery snapped.

The elite raised his hands in the air. His spell was done, I suspected. Anticipating what was coming, I wove psi in readiness.

"I'll take care of this," Mersk roared. "Die wolf!" The elite brought his hands down.

At the same instant, I blinked.

Mersk has cast meteor shower.
You have teleported into Gagin's shadow.

Fire and brimstone hammered down from the sky, obliterating not just the fountain but every possessed in close proximity. I was not there, though.

Celon has died.
Zurash has died.
...
....

The mage in whose shadow I'd jumped whirled around, his eyes round with fear. I ignored him, having no interest in killing him just yet, and triggered the remote in my other hand.

A blot of darkness trap has been activated.
Multiple hostile entities have failed to detect you! You are hidden.

At the appearance of the second black cloud, Mersk spun around, his eyes swimming with hate. He realized he'd missed. I smiled grimly. Mersk, too, had had his shot. Now, it was my turn.

You have reduced Mersk's mental defenses to 10%! Remaining duration: 27 seconds.

The elite raised his staff. His hands were shaking. *He knows it's over.*

You have shattered Mersk's mental defenses! Remaining duration: 25 seconds.

Vines shot out of the end of the elite's staff and raced across the intervening space between us, but before they could reach me, they sagged lifelessly to the ground as my next spell took effect.

You have charmed Mersk for 20 seconds.

"Attack," I rasped, pointing the bewitched elite at Avery.
Not waiting to observe the outcome, I rushed forward. In less than twenty seconds, Mersk's mental defenses would renew themselves, and before that happened, I had one last spell to enact against him.
I burst out of the dark cloud, my feet flying over the ground.
Avery's hand snapped up. "There he is! Get—"
He broke off as a bar of liquid heat rammed into him.

Your minion's scorching fire has hit Avery.
Avery's shield has blocked your minion's attack.

"Mersk, what are you doing?" Avery screeched.
A second jet of flames hit him.
I drew psi. Around me, possessed yelled—some in fear, some in anger—and a few even leveled their weapons at me. I kept running, staying focused on my target.
More angry flames laid into Avery, and finally realizing he wouldn't talk sense into the elite, he began retaliating against Mersk.
It was already too late for that, though.

Avery's shield has been destroyed!

Perfect, I thought. I was less than six yards from the defenseless mage. *"Kill,"* I ordered, setting Mersk against another possessed while I dealt with the other Scum leader.
Only four yards separated me from Avery now. His staff held loosely, the possessed stared at me with a stunned expression.
If only you had learned wisdom earlier.
Leaping the final three yards, I covered the remaining distance to Avery in a single bound. Faithful flashed out. The possessed made no attempt to dodge, and the bright blade plunged straight through his heart.

You have killed Avery with a fatal blow!

I landed atop the corpse as a spattering of spells hit me from the rear. Ignoring them, I rolled clear. It was time for the second half of my gambit. Releasing the psi I held ready, I flung it at Mersk.

Mersk is no longer charmed.
You have paralyzed your target for 60 seconds.

"The bastard has killed Avery!"
"Mersk is bewitched!"
"By the Powers, what is this Wolf?"
Terror was running rampant through the remaining mages, but there would be enough time to deal with them later. For now, it was the elite I had to take care of.

You have teleported into Mersk's shadow.

Removing yet another stone bottle from my bomber's belt, I smashed it against the ground.

You have ignited a smoke bomb, creating a smoke cloud.
You are hidden.

It was time to end things.
Raising faithful up high, I began hacking into the elite's shield. Sooner or later, I would win through.
And that would truly mark the beginning of the end for the Scum.

CHAPTER 437: RECONFIGURING

The elite died without protest.

Using a combination of backstab and whirlwind, I made short work of his defenses, and before his paralysis or the smoke cloud could dissipate, I slit his throat with faithful.

You have killed Mersk with a fatal blow.

Backing away from the corpse, I listened intently. There were still one hundred and eighteen mages alive. Individually, they weren't a threat, but together, they could be problematic.

None were nearby, though.

I frowned. I couldn't see the remaining possessed, but I could tell from mindsight and the sounds and smell carrying to me they'd retreated to the rim of the Circle. Dropping into a crouch, I crept to the edge of the gray cloud and peeked out.

My senses had not lied.

The mages had broken out into ten uneven groups, the smallest numbering eight and the largest twenty, and as far as I could tell, they'd divided themselves along factional lines. Arrayed around the Circle's perimeter, they were making no attempt to attack or even approach the area around the fountain.

Well, that's inconvenient, I groused. *So much for my safety net.*

If the mages weren't going to come to me, I might be forced to go after them and leave behind the traps I'd seeded around the center. Rising to my feet, I stepped clear of the gray clouds.

Multiple hostile entities have detected you! You are no longer hidden.

Even though I stood in full view, none of the mages attacked. *Huh. They've truly gone on the defensive.*

It was not exactly what I'd been hoping for. I'd been expecting more panic, less reasoning. And while the tactics the possessed had opted for were not the best—an all-out attack would've suited them better—they could still prove troublesome.

What will they do if I use shatter again? I wondered.

Would the possessed attack the mages I charmed? Given how they huddled against the rim, I guessed not. But that was alright. There were other ways to use charm.

And other ways to deal with the mages too.

Looks like I'll be doing this the hard way, then.

Stepping back into the smoke cloud, I set about replenishing my health and void armor.

Once I was ready, I would take the fight to the possessed.

✳   ✳   ✳

You have fully restored your health, mana, and psi.

You have cast facial disguise, heightened reflexes, load controller, fade, and trigger-cast quick mend.

It was the work of only a few minutes to restore myself and renew my buffs. The smoke cloud had long since dissipated, but the mages still didn't attack.

It seemed I would have to make the next move. Taking my time, I took stock of what I had to work with.

You have reached level 210 and have 11 attribute points available.

Your thieving has reached rank 14, telepathy rank 21, insight rank 22, and deception rank 20.

You have 0 x trap elements, 10 x smoke bombs, 7 x fire bombs, 4 x acid bombs, and 10 x ice bombs.

I rubbed my chin considerately. Despite my lack of traps, I had plenty of bombs—enough to execute an escape if necessary.

I'd also gained five levels from the battle, which translated into a tidy sum of attribute points. I didn't have to think too hard about how to spend them either. Perception had been boosted enough, and my Mind was already quite high, which left only Dexterity.

Your Dexterity has increased to rank 84. Other modifiers: +24 from items.

Right, that leaves only one more thing to take care of.

Striding across the field with affected nonchalance, I headed to where I'd dropped ebonheart and the Cloak of the Reach. The soulbound items were exactly where I'd left them.

Casually, I re-equipped both.

Finally ready, I surveyed the battlefield. All ten groups of mages stared warily back at me, their defenses up and their weapons clutched tightly in their hands.

For just a split-second, I contemplated charming the possessed to come to me—that or returning to the center of the Circle and waiting them out. Exhaustion would get the better of the mages sooner than it did me, and they would be forced to sleep.

But neither idea appealed. *Let's get this over with.*

Bared blades in hand, I strolled toward the smallest possessed faction, a group of eight. It was better to start small. They inched back further. *Would the adjacent groups attack?* I wondered idly. If they did, things would certainly get interesting. I kept walking.

Fifteen yards. Fourteen. Twelve.

The group began chanting in unison.

I didn't hurry, but I did draw psi.

A bar of flames shot out of a witch's staff. I dodged to the side, but that only put me in the path of a jet of sparkling ice.

You have sustained water damage.

Your void armor has reduced the damage incurred by 45%.

The ice dissipated, the damage it had dealt not even enough to cause me to wince, and I resumed walking.

Storm clouds gathered overhead, and a bolt of light rushed down. Lunging forward, I rolled clear, but as I regained my feet, six churning balls of blackness crashed into me.

Ork's hunting orb of Dark has hit you!
Ork's hunting orb of Dark has hit you!
Ork's hunting orb of Dark has hit you!
Void thief triggered! Void siphon and negate activated!
Jaim's 3 hunting orbs of Dark have failed to harm you. You are immune to this spell.

I laughed—in genuine humor and not just for show—despite being staggered back by the focused blows. Two of the casters had employed the same spell on me, and while the first trio of orbs had certainly hurt, the second had done nothing.

Thanks to my void armor, I'd become immune.

Resuming my advance, I ducked beneath three whirling 'somethings'—successfully—but that only allowed the incoming attacks from the casters on my flanks to close in unimpeded.

Your void armor has repelled a Shadow cord!
Your void armor has partially resisted the effects of a Light cord!
You are <u>light-bound</u>. Duration: 3 seconds.

"I got him," the caster in question crowed as the tendril of dazzling light wrapped around my torso.

I grinned. "Not for long, you don't," I replied and released the psi I held ready.

You have cast windborne.

I formed the windslide beneath my feet and was immediately thrust into motion despite the ties of binding Light.

The Light caster's eyes rounded with shock as he was unceremoniously jerked off his feet by the taut cord. Cursing and yelling, the other mages flung yet more spells at me, but I'd woven the ramp of air in a devilish path around them, and they missed more often than not.

You have evaded Hogen's freezing cone.
You have evaded Zalmain's horrid tentacles.
Yasmin's blood swarm has injured you (damage reduced by 5% due to void armor).
You have evaded...

...

Trusting the windslide to keep me safe—relatively safe, anyway—I risked a glance at the adjacent group of possessed. While both sets of mages watched the skirmish avidly, neither group appeared intent on interfering.

So be it.

Refocusing on my current foes, I waited for the Light caster's debuff to run its course or for my own spell to end.

You are no longer light-bound.

The debuff dissipated first. Not hesitating, I flung myself off the windslide and atop the closest enemy. I hit him feet first, causing his protective bubble to turn over, and before the mage could recover, I struck at him with ebonheart and faithful, both blades a barely-seen blur as they rushed forward and back.

Your target's shield has blocked your attacks.
Your target's shield has blocked your attacks.
Your target's shield has been destroyed!

Amazingly, it took only three hits to penetrate the mage's defenses. And a fourth to dispatch him.

You have killed Firmath with a fatal blow.

I didn't stop to celebrate. Throwing myself to the left and out of the way of the next wave of incoming magical projectiles, I laid into the next mage.

You have cast whirlwind and piercing strike.
Your target's shield has blocked your attacks.
Your target's shield has blocked your attacks.
You have killed Xain!

Three strikes alone sufficed to secure my foe's death the second time around.

I smiled grimly. Things had not panned out as I had hoped after Mersk's death, but ripping apart the remaining mages looked like it was going to be child's play. At this rate, I'll be done in an hour.

Stepping through the aether, I searched out my next victim.

✳ ✳ ✳

Thirty minutes later, I was done.

None of the splintered factions of possessed proved a challenge, not even the largest group of twenty whose ranks I first thinned from afar using shatter before tackling more directly.

I supposed the ease of the contest explained why killing all one hundred and eighteen mages netted me only one player level. The level disparity between me and the possessed had grown too large, it seemed, and even their strongest spells were negated before they could offer any serious threat.

But despite my lackluster player progression, my skills had advanced appreciably.

You have reached level 211.

Your dodging has reached rank 19, shortswords rank 20, and two weapon fighting rank 17.

Your mediation has reached rank 21, and telekinesis rank 18.

Your channeling has reached rank 20, elemental absorption rank 11, null force rank 7, null life rank 3, and null death rank 5.

Withdrawing my bloodied blades from the last corpse, I lifted my gaze upwards as the shimmering dome around the Circle vanished.

Congratulations, Michael, you have survived your first ritual combat, carrying Team Wolf to victory!

My lips twitched at the somewhat anticlimactic message, but I'd survived, and that was what mattered. More so, I saw that the previously vacant orbs of the Skull of Souls were glowing. The artifact had fed well, no doubt. Sheathing my swords, I straightened to meet the onrushing spectators.

"Well done, Prime!" Ghost sang, her words ringing loudly in my mind.

"Thank you, Ghost," I replied, watching her race across the courtyard towards me. Nyra trailed her closely while the others followed more sedately.

"M–michael, that... was..." Nyra began as she panted to a stop before me.

"Horrible? Gruesome?" I suggested, running my hands through Ghost's coat.

Nyra raised her eyes to mine, her face shining. "No, not at all. It was beautiful."

I suppressed a laugh. *"This one will do well as an assassin."*

"She certainly is bloodthirsty enough for it," Ghost agreed.

"I'm sure Ceruvax will have something to say about that," I replied. *"The old wolf doesn't strike me as the type to enjoy gratuitous killing. He'll—"*

I broke off. Another Game message was clamoring for attention. Smiling expectantly—perhaps the Adjudicator had a reward in store for me—I turned my attention inward.

You have killed or co-opted the last of the former sector boss' minions. The dungeon will now reset to its original configuration. The new sector boss and his minions will respawn in 1 hour.

Warning to all players still in the dungeon: collect any unclaimed loot and exit the dungeon before the final chamber is resealed.

My grin faded. *One hour? Really?*

Nyra gasped. "Michael, did you see—?"

I nodded grimly. "I did." I didn't understand the message's reference to a 'final chamber,' but I was sure Adriel and Farren would enlighten me.

Lifting my gaze, I saw the others had arrived. Their faces solemn, Ceruvax, Adriel, and Farren drew up beside Ghost and Nyra. I wanted to immediately blurt out my questions about the surprising alert from the Adjudicator, but there was an expectant air about the trio.

Ceruvax was also carrying the Skull of Souls, I saw. Catching my gaze, he mouthed the word, "Wait." He, too, of course, had received the Game message.

Trusting the former envoy's judgment, I stayed silent while the wolfmen, the hundred possessed waiting for rehoming, and the New Haveners formed a tightly packed circle around us.

Raising his chin, Ceruvax began speaking. "Hail, scion!" he pronounced formally.

"HAIL SCION!" the wolfmen, the possessed, and the lichs echoed.

Whatever was going on had a hint of ceremony about it, and once more, I was reminded that my new allies belonged to a different era. As former scions, they had no doubt witnessed other ritual combats in their past lives and knew better than me what to expect.

"You have faced your foes in the sacred Circle and triumphed," the old wolf continued. "Your victory has earned you the right to their blood memories." Going down on one knee, he held up the Skull of Souls to me.

Sensing it was expected, I placed my hand atop the artifact.

Commencing the Ritual of Infusion...

Before I could think how to respond, the light in the eye sockets flared, the jaws creaked open, and an unseen force gripped my palm, keeping it fastened to the top of the wolf's skull.

A heartbeat later, an ethereal mist streamed out of the artifact and assumed a person's hazy outline for a split second. My eyes narrowed.

Is that Darius?

The spirit gave me no chance to confirm my suspicions, though, and in the next instant vanished, sucked into my own body.

You have absorbed the essence of a fallen scion.
Your blood awakening has begun...

A second spirit emerged from the Skull. Then, a third. One by one, I absorbed their essences. With every infusion, I felt my awareness expand. Alien thoughts skittered across my mind, and my body thrummed with a strange energy I knew was not mine.

The fallen scions I absorbed were nothing like those I'd encountered in the trial of the Mind. Those had been young, untried. These spirits were not that. Older, experienced, they were measurably stronger.

And each stirred my blood more vigorously.

Energy raged within me, an inferno that only gradually subsided after each infusion. My nerves tingled, my skin was rubbed raw, and my organs protested. On and on it went until I felt full to bursting. Squeezing my eyes shut, I endured as best I could.

And just as I felt I could take no more, the ritual drew to a close.

Ritual of Infusion complete.

Congratulations, Scion, 51 fallen of your House have gifted you their essences, infusing your blood sufficiently to recall either 3 lesser blood memories or 1 greater blood memory. To determine the form your awakening will take, consult a Blood Talisman.

The Skull released me, and I staggered back.

Nyra yelped.

I turned to her. "What's wrong?"

"Your eyes, they're glowing!"

"It'll fade," Adriel reassured her before I could grow concerned. The lich glanced at me. "Right now, I'm sure you're buzzing with energy. But that'll pass once your blood absorbs the spirits' essence."

I nodded slowly.

Stowing away the skull, Ceruvax stepped forward. "In the meantime, there is something else you need to attend to urgently."

I opened my mouth.

"It can't wait," he said, "and you're on the clock."

Adriel and Farren looked at Ceruvax curiously but didn't ask him to explain.

"Alright. What is it?" I asked, expecting him to pull out the Blood Talisman.

Instead, Ceruvax waved Regus forward. "We'll have to cut things short," he told the wolfman. "Pare it down to the bare bones."

The former possessed nodded curtly and went down on one knee. "I, Beta of the Pack of the Reach," he growled in the manner I was coming to recognize as the normal speaking voice of the wolfmen, "pledge myself and the Pack in service to the Forerunner faction. From this day on, it alone holds my loyalty."

"I, Michael," I replied firmly, "accept your oath on behalf of the Forerunners faction."

You have accepted the Pack of the Reach into the Forerunners faction. As non-players, the wolfmen are free to break their pledges at any time and without consequences. As are you. However, until such time as the Forerunners disavow the Pack—or vice versa—they will be considered the faction's sworn people, and their actions will reflect on it.

Regus rose to his feet, and I shook his hand. "Thank you, my friend."

"It is you who deserve our thanks," Regus replied. He smiled, baring his sharpened fangs. "After your performance in the Circle, none in the Pack doubt that you will succeed in restoring the ancients. You and the alpha honor us by allowing us to join the cause."

I waved aside his words. "It was nothing. I only did—"

"It was not nothing," Farren interjected sharply. "Even in our day, few would have managed such a feat."

Ceruvax nodded. "The lich speaks truly."

I inclined my head, heartened by their words. "What's next? Do I use the Blood Talisman?"

The old wolf frowned. "It depends on what the Game message meant. There may be no time."

Adriel's brows rose. "No time?" she echoed.

"The Adjudicator has just informed us the dungeon will reset in one hour, at which time the final chamber will be resealed," I explained. "Do you know what that means?"

"Reset to what?" Farren asked carefully.

"To its original configuration," Ceruvax said. "After which a new sector boss will spawn."

"Ah," both lichs exclaimed simultaneously.

"That's not good, I take it?" I asked.

Farren rubbed his chin. "It depends on how you look at it. I've been wondering when—and where—the new sector boss will spawn. It is nice to have confirmation of both."

"But?" I prompted. "There is a 'but,' right?"

"There is," Adriel confirmed. "The dungeon's original configuration includes the sub-level beneath the court. It forms an entire underground complex all on its own."

"Incidentally, it's the sub-level," Farren added, "that prompted the idea of the New Haven tunnel."

I frowned. "This sub-level is the same one housing the exit portal?"

"It is," Regus growled.

I sighed. "And let me guess, the sub-level is also where the sector boss spawns?"

Adriel nodded. "Correct. But the more pertinent point is that the exit portal is in the final chamber." She paused. "You will need a completed Emblem of the Reach to open it."

I groaned, finally seeing the cause of their concern. "So... either I leave in an hour—before the chamber reseals—or I spend days hunting down the emblem's mosaic pieces?"

Regus grunted. "More like weeks."

"You could collect the old pieces from Gamil," Algar said, speaking up for the first time.

I nodded slowly. "But that, too, will take days." Even using the underground tunnel, New Haven was not close.

Stepping forward, Ceruvax placed something in my hand.

You have acquired a Blood Talisman.

"Don't use it now," he warned before I could say anything. "Take it with you."

I shook my head in denial. "It's safer with you. Rather I use it here, than—"

"You can't," Ceruvax interjected. "Not unless you want to spend more time in the dungeon."

I frowned.

Seeing my confusion, Adriel asked, "Do you remember your first blood awakening?"

I did. It had been painful, and it had felt as if my blood had been on fire. "I do, but I'm not sure what that has to do with anything."

"You'll understand soon enough," the lich replied. "How long did you sleep after the first awakening?"

"Hmm, I can't remember. A few hours, maybe? But that was more due to the trial of the mind than anything else."

Adriel shook her head adamantly. "It wasn't just the trial that exhausted you. Blood awakenings are strenuous. They will drain all your energy pools and more besides. Depending on the strength of the blood memories you're recovering, you can expect to be out from anywhere between a half day to a week."

I stared at her. "A week?"

She smiled. "Don't worry. Those only apply to the ancient memories, which you don't have to concern yourself with just yet."

"But even a lesser memory can knock you out for hours," Farren added.

I sighed. I didn't want to spend another day in the dungeon, much less a week. "Alright, I'll take the Talisman with me." I glanced from face to face. "Then I guess this is goodbye. For now, anyway."

Regus bowed his head. "Safe travels, scion."

Ceruvax shook my hand. "Return safely to us. In the meantime, you can rest assured House Wolf will grow in your absence."

"Don't forget what we spoke of," was all Farren had to say.

Algar stiffened to attention. "The warband will await your return."

"No goodbyes from me," Adriel said. "I'll be coming with you, of course." She stepped back, pulling Farren with her. "Now, if you'll excuse us, my brother and I must attend to something before we leave."

Inclining my head in acknowledgment, I turned to Nyra. She was the only one who hadn't said anything.

"I'm coming too," she blurted.

My brows shot up. "But I thought—"

"I know I said I would stay," she said rapidly. "But seeing what you did in the Circle changed my mind. Can I learn all that here?"

I opened my mouth to answer, but she resumed speaking before I could. "I don't think I can. The skills I need aren't available here."

"You can always—" I began.

"And besides, Ceruvax agrees with me," she added stubbornly.

I threw the old wolf a reproachful look.

He shrugged. "She's right. I cannot teach her to do what you do. And certainly not in this dungeon."

I sighed. "Alright, you can come."

✳   ✳   ✳

Congratulations, Michael, you have discovered an exit from the Endless Dungeon. This portal leads directly from sector 73,102 to the surface of the Forever Kingdom. This location is a key point and has been added to your Logs.
The dungeon will reset in 10 minutes.

Fifty minutes later, Nyra and I were in Draven Reach's final chamber, staring at the shimmering curtain of white hanging before us.

The exit portal.

"What's keeping Adriel?" I muttered for the tenth time.

"Patience, Prime," Ghost replied, sounding amused. *"She'll be here."*

The pyre wolf was back in spirit form. Not knowing what we'd face on the other side of the portal, we'd both agreed it was better for her to make the transition while tucked away in the Cloak of the Reach.

"She should have been here twenty minutes ago!" I said, frustrated. "What could—"

At the approach of soft footsteps, I spun around.

"I'm here," Adriel said.

I stared at the oversized pouch she was carrying. "What's that?"

"For you," she said, placing it in my hand.

You have acquired a small bag of hiding. This bag is enchanted with a tier 6 concealment ward and contains 100 possessed finger bones.

I blinked. "This is what kept you?"

She nodded. "Farren and I worked as quickly as we could, but killing a hundred possessed, extracting their finger bones, and setting their spirits to sleep does not go quickly," she said wryly.

"I see," I said, feeling suddenly churlish for my impatience. "Why don't I see their spirits hovering in the air?"

"Well, for one, they're dormant," the lich replied. "And for another, the bag is shielding them from detection."

"Ah, wise that," I said, stowing away the pouch and turning about to face the portal. "We're all ready, I take it?"

"I know I am," the lich said with a small smile. "It's been too long since I set foot in the Kingdom."

Nyra nodded mutely, looking too nervous to say anything.

I inhaled deeply. It had been thirty-five days since I'd entered Draven's Reach. I'd ventured into the dungeon with only escape in mind. Yet, I'd found so much more.

An entire city of non-players.

A new Pack.

A familiar.

Other scions. Powerful allies. A former envoy. A restored guardian. What's more, I'd grown immensely, both in terms of my understanding of the Game and the nature of power.

I'd entered the dungeon with the nebulous goal of restoring House Wolf.

I was leaving it, not only with a plan, but the means of executing it, too.

I exhaled. "Right, let's be off then." Stepping forward, I crossed through the shimmering curtain.

Transfer through portal commencing...

...

...

Leaving sector 73,102. Entering the Forever Kingdom.

✳   ✳   ✳

THE END.

Here ends Book 6 of the Grand Game.
Michael's adventures will continue in **Ancient Debts**.
Get it here!

I hope you enjoyed the story! If you did, please leave a <u>review</u> and let other readers know what you think.
<u>Click here to leave a review</u>.
Happy reading!
Tom Elliot.

MICHAEL AT THE END OF BOOK 6

Player Profile: Michael
Level: 211. Rank: 21. Current Health: 100%.
Stamina: 100%. Mana: 100%. Psi: 100%.
Species: Human. Lives Remaining: 4.
Ghost's Lives Remaining: 3.
True Marks: Powerful Initiate.
True Marks (hidden): Worthy Adversary, Wolf Protector, Wolf Progenitor.
False Marks (fabricated): Lesser Shadow, Lesser Light, Lesser Dark.
Followers: 2 / 200. Active Pacts: 0 / 20.

Faction Data: Forerunners
Office held: Faction Leader. Sectors claimed: 0 / 2.
Players pledged: Ceruvax.
Non-players pledged: Pack of the Reach (500), Bane Wolves warband (2,000).

Active Buffs
denotes boosts affected by items.
Damage reduction (reduces damage incurred only):
Life: 15%. Death: 25%. Air: 55%. Earth: 55%. Fire: 55%. Water: 55%.
Shadow: 35%. Light: 35%. Dark: 35%. Nether: 100%. Physical: 46%*.

Resistances (negates damage and/or rebuffs spell effects):
Life: 7.5%. Death: 12.5%. Air: 27.5%. Earth: 27.5%. Fire: 47.5%*. Water: 27.5%. Shadow: 17.5%. Light: 17.5%. Dark: 17.5%. Nether: 70%*. Physical: 0%.

Benefits derived from Items
Damage: +30% damage (ebonheart), +40% damage (faithful).
Abilities: perceive tier 6 spelled wards (sorcerer's coif), move soundlessly (wayfarer's boots), hands immune to hazardous substances (wayfarer's gloves), spellhold: empty (mage's surprise), psi-feed (psi bracelet).
Immunities: tier 2 entanglement (unbound ring), tier 2 mind spells (stillness ring).
Skills: +4 ranks stealth (ranger's armor).

Attributes
Available: 2 points.
Strength: 28 (20)*. Constitution: 32 (24)*. Dexterity: 108 (84)*.
Perception: 94 (90)*. Mind: 135 (123)*. Magic: 66 (46)*. Faith: 0.

Classes
Available (Michael): 0 points.
Available (Ghost): 10 points.

Primary-Secondary-Tertiary tri-blend: voidstalker (fabricated). voidstealer XII (hidden).
Ascendant Class: wolf lord (rank I, hidden), sire wolf (rank I, hidden).
Familiar: stygian pyre wolf III (unique, hidden).

Traits

void heritage II (wolf, hidden): +4 Dexterity, +4 Strength, +8 Mind, +8 Perception, +12 Magic.
voidwalker II (wolf, hidden): improved senses in all conditions, nethersight, immunity to blindness.
arctic wolf II (wolf, hidden): +10 Constitution, +4 Mind, +6 Strength.
were's bite II (wolf, hidden): 0 to 30% chance of granting another player the were-trait.
sire's strain (wolf, hidden): boosts your other wolf traits by +1 tier.

anointed scion (bloodline, hidden): bound to House Wolf.
secret blood (bloodline, hidden): conceals the wolf blood of yourself, your followers, and your familiar.

beast tongue: can speak to beastkin.
Marked: can see spirit signatures.
inscrutable mind: +8 Mind.
mental focus IV: increases effectiveness of Mind skills by 40%.
budding explorer: all key points in newly discovered sectors logged.
spell illiterate: cannot cast mana-based spells.
potion resistance II: potency of potions reduced by 2 ranks.
spirit talker: can speak to spirits.
bold blood: +1 attribute per level.
higher evolution: can evolve Class beyond master ranked.
commander: can share bloodline traits or blood memories with your followers.
champion: increases the strength of blood memories.
spirit familiar: can bind a willing spirit as your familiar.
mage-host: +10 Mind, +10 Magic.

spirit familiar (Ghost): mirrors player attributes and level, and shares ability slots with them.
psionic being (Ghost): retains telepathic skills and abilities from her former incarnation as a dire wolf.
free spirit (Ghost): can roam an unlimited distance from her host, but only within the same sector.
born again II (Ghost): grants your familiar 2 additional lives, will resurrect in spirit vessel.

Skills

Available skill slots: 0.
light armor (current: 159. Constitution, basic).

dodging (current: 192. Dexterity, basic).
sneaking (current: 208. Dexterity, basic).
shortswords (current: 201. Dexterity, basic).
two weapon fighting (current: 173. Dexterity, advanced).
thieving (current: 141. Dexterity, basic).

chi (current: 179. max: 1230. Mind, advanced).
meditation (current: 211. Mind, basic).
telekinesis (current: 184. Mind, advanced).
telepathy (current: 214. Mind, advanced).

insight (current: 221. Perception, basic).
deception (current: 204. Perception, master).

channeling (current: 204. Magic, basic).
elemental absorption (current: 110. Magic, master).
null force (current: 77. Magic, master).
null life (current: 31. Magic, master).
null death (current: 51. Magic, master).
nether absorption (current: 200. Magic, master).

magma maw (Ghost) (current: 61. Magic, master).
stygian claws (Ghost) (current: 78. Strength, master).
ash armor (Ghost) (current: 65. Constitution, master).
telepathy (Ghost) (current: 77. Mind, advanced).

<u>Abilities</u>
<u>Constitution ability slots used:</u> **10 / 24.**
load controller (10 Constitution, expert, light armor).

<u>Dexterity ability slots used:</u> **56 / 84.**
crippling blow (Dexterity, basic, shortswords).
minor piercing strike (5 Dexterity, advanced, shortswords).
improved backstab (10 Dexterity, expert, sneaking).
improved trap disarm (5 Dexterity, advanced, thieving).
superior lockpicking (5 Dexterity, advanced, thieving).
superior set trap (10 Dexterity, expert, thieving).
whirlwind (5 Dexterity, advanced, two weapon fighting).
greater fade (15 Dexterity, master, sneaking).

<u>Mind ability slots used:</u> **71 / 123.**
superior mass charm (10 Mind, expert, telepathy).
stunning slap (Mind, basic, chi).
windborne (10 Mind, expert, telekinesis).
heightened reflexes (10 Mind, expert, chi).
twin astral blades (5 Mind, advanced, telepathy).
long shadow blink (10 Mind, expert, telekinesis).

quick mend (10 Mind, expert, chi).
fortified mind (10 Mind, expert, meditation).
astral bite (Ghost) (5 Mind, advanced, telepathy).

<u>Perception ability slots used:</u> **36 / 90.**
superior analyze (10 Perception, expert, insight).
improved trap detect (5 Perception, advanced, thieving).
conceal small weapon (Perception, basic, deception).
superior facial disguise (10 Perception, expert, deception).
superior ventro (5 Perception, advanced, deception).
lesser imitate (5 Perception, advanced, deception).

<u>Other abilities:</u>
adept slaysight (hidden) (Class, elite, telepathy): paralyze, shatter, sleep, terrify, blind.
superior void thief (hidden) (Class, expert, any void skill and telepathy): steal, siphon, negate.
manifest (Ghost) (Class, basic).
diresight (Ghost) (Class, advanced, telepathy).
direshield (Ghost) (Class, advanced, telepathy).

Known Key Points

Kingdom Sector 1 (Nexus) safe zone.
Kingdom Sector 12,560 (wolves' valley) nether portal and safe zone.
Kingdom Sector 18,240 nether portal 1 (guardian tower), and nether portal 2 (Draven's reach).

Dungeon Sector 101 (scorching dunes) exit portal and safe zone.
Dungeon Sectors 102, 103, and 104 (haunted catacombs) exit portals and safe zones.
Dungeon Sector 105, 106, 107, 108, and 109 (guardian tower) exit portals.
Dungeon Sector 14,913 (candidate's dungeon) exit portal and safe zone.
Dungeon Sector 73,102 (Draven's Reach) one-way entrance portal, safe zone, and exit portal.

Aetherstone Bracelet Stored Points

sector 24,401 safe zone.
sector 12,560 (wolves' valley) safe zone.
sector 18,240 nether portal 1 (guardian tower).

Equipped

<u>Weapons</u>
ebonheart (+30% damage).
faithful (+40% damage).

<u>Armor & Clothes</u>
sorcerer's coif (perceive tier 6 wards).
ranger's kit (+40% damage reduction, +4 ranks stealth).

bomber's belt (2 x acid bombs, 3 x smoke bombs, 2 x ice bombs, and 3 x fire bombs).
belt of the chameleon (5 x rank 4 nether protection crystals, 11 x rank 4 disease protection crystals, 9 scent concealment crystals, 5 x mental concealment crystals, 4 x rank 6 disease protection crystals, 2 x rank 5 poison protection crystals, 1 x rank 4 strength enhancement crystals, 0 x rank 4 dexterity enhancement crystals, and 2 x rank 4 magic enhancement crystals).
wayfarer's boots (legendary item, +8 Dexterity, move soundlessly).
wayfarer's gloves (legendary item, +8 Dexterity, hands immune to hazardous substances).
cloak of the Reach (legendary soulbound item, +10 Magic, +20% fire magic resistance, +20% nether magic resistance).

<u>Rings & Accessories</u>
goliath's ring (+8 Strength).
acrobat's ring (+8 Dexterity).
sharpshooter's band (+4 Perception).
hale stone (+8 Constitution).
savant's ring (+4 Mind).
troll's talisman bracelet (+6% damage reduction).
gift of the unbound ring (immunity to tier 1 and 2 entanglement spells).
band of stillness ring (immunity to tier 1 and 2 Mind spells).
aetherstone bracelet (3 / 5 stored locations, 2 stones charged).
simple potion bracelet (2 / 3 full heal potions).
mage's surprise (+10 Magic, spellhold: trigger-cast tier 5 spells).
psi bracelet (legendary item, +8 Mind, psi-feed).
veteran's trapper's wristband (0 / 200 trap-making crystals) (<u>triggers</u>: pressure plates, sound glasses, tripwires, motion pins, and remote control. <u>elements</u>: lightning, poison clouds, fire, spring-coiled daggers, bear-trap clamps, small explosives, blots of darkness, and ice. <u>guides</u>: reflect, split, and funnel.)

<u>Other</u>
backpack, large bag of holding (200 slots), **hunter's alchemy stone.**
pioneer's compass (soulbound, attuned to safe zone).

<u>Ghost</u>
shadow's friend (+4 ranks stealth).

<u>Backpack Contents</u>
<u>Money</u>: **23 golds, 5 silvers, and 3 coppers.**
10 x field rations.
2 x flasks of water.
2 x iron daggers.
1 x bedroll.
goblin writ of safe passage.
bounty letter authorization.

1 x coil of rope.
tavern bill of ownership.
Tartan token.
Vivane token.
Kesh Emporium access card.
cat claws.
spectacles of ward seeing (detect tier 4 wards).
BHG ID (junior member, 1 / 10 active jobs).
simple map of Nexus.
1 x rank 6 cure disease potions.
dungeon notes.
commune rod.
greater trap detect ability tome.
enchanted leather armor set (+20% damage reduction, -35% Dexterity and Magic).
2 x acid bombs, 7 x smoke bombs, 8 x ice bombs, and 4 x fire bombs.
2 x rank 4 cure poison.
mirror shield (reflect tier 4 spells).
phoenix's feather shaft (soulbound).
small bag of hiding (tier 6 concealment ward).
a simple shovel.
1 x blue mages robes, 1 x black mages robes.
stygian shortsword, +3.
stygian shortsword.
netherstone.
a sealed missive (from Farren).
Blood Talisman.
small bag of hiding containing 100 x possessed finger bones.

Miscellaneous Loot

4 x legendary items.

Alchemy Stone Contents

(14 / 500 ingredients stored).
4 x orbs of petrification, 10 x Shadow ectoplasm.

Bank Contents

<u>Money</u>: 1,655 gold, 0 silvers, and 0 coppers.
2 x full healing potions.
2 x full mana potions.

<u>Tavern Money</u>: 9,850 gold, 0 silvers, and 0 coppers.

Open Tasks

Heist in the Dark (steal chalice from the Power, Paya).
A Perverted Trial (stop the Triumvirate abuse of the Combat Trial).
Brokering Peace (establish peace in sector 12,560 within 4 months).
Brotherhood Obligations (report to the brotherhood after 4 months).

Restore the Nexus Guardian (replace Kolath with Adriel).
Revive the Guardians (awaken Draven's brethren).
Locate the Lost Prime (find the hidden Prime).
Resurrecting Death (make Adriel a scion again).

BOOKS BY TOM ELLIOT

BY TOM ELLIOT

The Grand Game (series page)
Book 1: The Grand Game: ebook | audiobook
Book 2: Way of the Wolf: ebook | audiobook
Book 3: World Nexus: ebook | audiobook
Book 4: House Wolf: ebook | audiobook
Book 5: Wolf in the Void: ebook | audiobook
Book 6: A Scion's Duty: ebook | audiobook
Book 7: Ancient Debts: ebook | audiobook
Book 8: The Lost Reclaimed: ebook (coming soon)

The Grand Game Box Set (series page)
Book 1-3: Birth of a Player: ebook
Book 4-6: Rise of an Elite: ebook
Book 7-9: The Making of a Power: ebook (coming soon)

The Grand Game, Elana (series page)
Book 1: Empyrean's Rise: ebook
Book 2: Empyrean's Flight: ebook

Annals of the Runeguard (series page)
Book 1: Proving Grounds: ebook

BY ROHAN M. VIDER

The Dragon Mage Saga (series page)
Book 1: Overworld: ebook | audiobook
Book 2: Dungeons: ebook | audiobook
Book 3: Sponsors: ebook (coming soon)

The Gods' Game (series page)
Crota, the Gods' Game Volume I
The Labyrinth, the Gods' Game Volume II
Sovereign Rising, the Gods' Game Volume III
Sovereign, the Gods' Game, Volume IV
Sovereign's Choice, the Gods' Game Volume V

Tales from the Gods' Game
Dungeon Dive (Tales from the Gods' Game, Book 1)

AFTERWORD

Thank you for reading the Grand Game!

If you enjoyed the book, please consider leaving a review on <u>Amazon</u> <u>[click here]</u>. I'm already working on Michael's next adventure.

If you have any questions, comments, or want to support my writing, please feel free to contact me through my site, <u>TomLitRPG.com</u> or <u>Discord</u>.

Alternatively, if you wish to learn more about the world of the Forever Kingdom, understand the system of the Grand Game better, or are just looking for the latest news on the Grand Game, please visit my site at <u>TomLitRPG.com</u> or signup up here for my: <u>Newsletter</u>.

Regards,
Tom
Support my writing on **PATREON**
<u>Amazon Author page</u> | <u>Goodreads</u> | <u>Facebook</u> | <u>Reddit</u> | <u>Discord</u> |

Definitions

Accord: old agreement between new Powers ceding control of Nexus to the Triumvirate.

Adjudicator: controller and arbitrator of the Grand Game.

alchemy stone: a device used to store alchemical components.

ancient: old Power.

anointed scion: a scion who has bound himself to a bloodline.

ascendancy: process of being a Power.

ascendant: descriptor often applied to Game aspects involving higher evolution.

ascendant undead: term the Adjudicator used to describe Stayne, meaning unknown.

blended Class: a combined Class.

blood awakening: the process of recalling blood memories.

blood infusion: the absorption of the essences from former scions.

blood memories: gifts from your forebears containing the power of the ancients themselves.

bi-blend: a combination of two melded Classes.

bloodline: reference to the ancient from which the player is a descendant.

Circle: aka Ritual Combat Circle.

civilian player: a player without a class or combat abilities. Civilians do not have a player level.

class-unique skill: a skill that is unique to a Class and can only be acquired through a Class stone.

closed sector: a landmass that does not physically border another, making the area inaccessible except by portal.

composite spell: a multi-stage spell made up of two or more individual spells.

controlled sector: a sector owned by a faction. Ownership of a sector gives the faction's players increased privileges in the region.

Class: a defined path or vocation that gives a player access to specific skills.

Class evolution: the advancement of a Class, generally to a better-ranked one, due to particular traits, skills, or Marks acquired by the player.

Dark: one of the three Forces.

Darksworn: a player pledged to the Dark who values the self over the collective.

deathwish: An ability that is triggered in the instant between a creature being dealt fatal damage and the spirit fleeing the body.

Elite: a tier five player, i.e. someone above level two hundred.

ebonblade: soulbound weapons found in the Twilight Dungeon.

envoy: a trusted representative of a Power authorized to speak on their behalf.

Endless Dungeon: A section of the Nethersphere where dungeon mechanics are active.

Everborns: term used to describe players.

evolution: the advancement of a player's core characteristics.

familiar bond: a permanent spirit binding between a spellcasting player and a creature, allowing them the transfer of Game-gifted knowledge from host to familiar.

follower: a player that has pledged themself in a binding vow to a Force or Power.

Force: Light, Dark, Shadow. The building blocks of the cosmos and energy in its rawest form.

Forcesworn: Collective term referring to Darksworn, Lightsworn, and Shadowsworn players.

Forever Kingdom: the world of the Nethersphere and Kingdom.

forsworn: a sworn who has betrayed their Power.

Game: refers to the Grand Game.

gatekeepers: holders of ancient lore, guardians of the ancients' trials.

half-form: the in-between state where the player is in a mix of his two forms (man-form and beast-form).

House: House of the Ancient.

House of the Ancient: a grouping of followers pledged to one Prime.

Kingdoms: the collective name given to sectors located in the aether.

lycan: werewolf.

ley line: magic threads connecting nether sectors.

Light: one of the three Forces.

Lightsworn: a player sworn to the Light that champions the cause of the many, even to his own detriment.

marshmen: mysterious dwellers in the saltmarsh district.

meld: the process of combining multiple Classes into one.

mindglow: the visible signature of a mind as seen with mindsight.

neutral sector: a sector unowned and unclaimed by any faction or Force.

Nethersphere: collective name given to the sectors in the nether.

Netherspawn: stygian creatures.

nethersight: ability that allows stygian to see through free-floating nether.

new Power: one of the Powers that usurped the ancients.

oath breaker: one who has broken a Pact.

Pact: a binding enacted between a Power and player, overseen by the Adjudicator.

Power: an evolved player.

power word: a blood memory ability.

Prime: head of ancient bloodline. An ancient.

Prime Conclave: a gathering of Primes referred to by Kolath.

Primehood: the act of becoming a Prime.

rift: unstable portal from the nether. Ley line created by stygian seed.

scav: short for scavenger. A player who loots kills not his own.

scion: one bearing the blood of an ancient.

scion abilities: the abilities Michael had earned during the Wolf trials: astral blade, chi heal, mind shield, shadow blink.

seeking spell: spell that distinguishes friend from foe.

Shadowsworn: a player pledged to Shadow.

stolen spell: a spell acquired from another and cast using their skills and attributes.

soulbound: an item that remains with the player after death.

sworn: as in sworn servant. A sworn is a follower of a Power who has sufficiently deepened their binding Mark to benefit from the binding.

the real: reference to the physical realm.

trap-making crystal: crystal in trapper's wristband. Can be manifested as different trap components.

trials of the ancients: tests created by the Primes for their successors.

tri-blend: a combination of three melded Classes.

trigger-cast: a spell held in readiness and invoked under specific conditions.

unsworn: not a sworn servant, and not bound to a Power.

upgrade gem: a game item used to advance an ability a single tier.

voids: informal term used to reference players who possess a void Class.

void Classes: a rare subset of Classes that specialize in damage reduction.

void's chosen: term by which the stygians address the stygian seeds.

void fathers: void trees.

windslide: ramp of air formed by windborne spell.

were-trait: a trait carried by all were-players, fueling their ability to shapeshift.

weres: short for werewolves and other were-players.

wolfmen: hybrid species, non-player werewolves.

wolf trials: ancient trials created by Wolf Prime.

wolfkind: used interchangeably with wolfkin.

KEY CHARACTERS & FACTIONS

FACTIONS

Albion Bank: major non-aligned bank in the Forever Kingdom.
Awakened Dead: A Dark faction.
Axis of Evil: An alliance of Dark factions.
blackguards: Policing force in the Dark quarter.
dawn brigade: Policing force in the Light quarter.
gray watch: Policing force in the Shadow quarter.
Mantises: A Dark faction of assassins.
Marauders: small Shadow faction.
Shadow Coalition: A power bloc of Shadow, made up of like-minded Shadow Powers.
Tartan: the faction of Tartar, the god-emperor.
Tartan legion: the military forces of Tartar.
Triumvirate: A unique faction composed of Light, Dark, and Shadow that control Nexus.
Unity Council: the governing body of Light, made up of all Light-affiliated Powers.

GUARDIANS

Draven: centaur construct in Draven's Reach.
Kolath: mysterious construct in the Guardian Tower.

GUILDS AND NON-FACTIONS

Bane Wolves: mercenary band out of New Haven.
Bounty Hunters Guild (BHG): headquartered in the plague quarter, mercenaries.
Information Brokers: a gnomish organization in the plague quarter.
Pack of the Reach: wolfmen pack.
Kesh Emporium: merchant company owned by Kesh.
Stygian Brotherhood: headquartered in the plague quarter, experts in all-things-nether.

HOUSE WOLF

Atiras: Dead Prime Wolf.
Ceruvax: Former envoy of Atiras.

NON-PLAYERS

Adriel: lich, Farren's sister.
Arden: Gnome information broker.

Algar: human captain, New Haven.
Avery: New Haven magister.
Castor: Possessed mage.
Cilia: First amongst the dark elves of New Haven.
Cyren: Gnome senior information broker.
Elron: dark elf marshal, New Haven.
Everard: dark elf master archer, bane wolf.
Farren: lich, Adriel's brother, new archlich.
Gamil: New Haven shopkeeper.
Lorn: Orc Chief in New Haven.
Loskin: Archlich.
Megtir: dwarven captain, bane wolf.
Minakawa: dark elf captain, New Haven.
Regus: court's security chief.
Sunfury: A phoenix.
Sienna: Human lord in New Haven.
Stormhammer: Dwarven Thane in New Haven.
Zorgulg: orc captain, bane wolf.

Players

Anriq: werewolf criminal.
Barac: crusader, male centaur.
Beorin: senior BHG member, dwarf.
Bornholm: Michael's companion from Erebus' dungeon, dwarf.
Cara: alias given to Kesh's agent in plague quarter by Michael.
Dathe: unknown werewolf player.
Devlin: Viviane's guard, unknown aquatic species.
Ent: guard outside emporium, armsmaster, giant.
Eyes: The BHG HQ doorkeeper, species unknown.
Jasiah: duelist, human male.
Genmark: ward architect, gnome male.
Gintalush: mantis assassin, insectoid.
Hannah: BHG client liaison officer, human female.
Kartara: huntmistress at Stygian Brotherhood Chapterhouse.
Kesh: master merchant, owner of the emporium, human woman.
Lake: guard outside emporium, berserker, giant.
Michael: protagonist.
Misha: Marauder tracker, aka the Hound.
Moonshadow: aeromancer, male elf.
Morin: Michael's companion from Erebus' dungeon, the painted woman.
Nyra: sniper, Michael's apprentice.
Orlon: Triumvirate knight-captain in the plague quarter, human.
Pitor: rank 15 warrior, Kalin sworn, human, Marauder sub-boss.
Richter: constable in Triumvirate citadel, human civilian.
Saya: apprentice alchemist, tavernkeeper in wolves' valley, gnome.
Shael: red minstrel, half-elf.
Simone: sharpshooter, half-elf female.

Stayne: Erebus' henchman.
Stonebeard: Triumvirate captain, dwarf.
Talon: the captain, Tartar's envoy.
Tantor: Michael's companion from Erebus' dungeon, high elf male.
Teg: Michael's escort in citadel, human.
Terence: rank 2 human fighter, swordsman.
Teresa: rank 2 human fighter, blade devotee.
Tevin: Marauder knight.
Toff: player outside haunted catacombs, ogre
Trion: Triumvirate holy knight, Herat sworn, human.
Trexton: herbalist in Triumvirate citadel, Simone's contact, dark elf.
Wengulax: mantis assassin, blade dancer, human.
Wilsh: Blackguard captain, human.
Yzark: Marauder boss.

POWERS

Arinna: Light Power.
Artem: Shadow Power. Goddess of nature.
Erebus: Dark Power, leader of the Awakened Dead faction.
Herat: Light Power, member of the Triumvirate.
Ishita: Spider goddess, Dark Power, member of the Awakened Dead.
Loken: Shadow Power.
Kalin: Minor Shadow Power, faction leader of the Marauders.
Menaq: Dark Power, leader of the Mantis faction.
Muriel: Light Power contesting Wolf Valley.
Mydas: Shadow Power, member of the Triumvirate.
Paya: Dark Power, junior member of the Awakened Dead ruling council.
Rampel: Dark Power, member of the Triumvirate.
Tartar: Dark Power, also known as the God-Emperor.
Viviane: Power owning the Albion Bank.

WOLFKIN

Aira: dire wolf dame.
Barak: dire wolf elder.
Cantur: half-mad wolf.
Duggar: dire wolf alpha.
Oursk: dire wolf sire.
Leta: dire wolf elder.
Monac: dire wolf elder and former alpha.
Moonstalker: Oursk's pup.
Shadetooth: Oursk's pup.
Snow: arctic wolf pack alpha.
Star: Snow's mate.
Stormdark: Oursk's pup.
Sulan: dire wolf healer.
Suva: dire wolf elder.

LOCATIONS

bounty hunters guild headquarters: in the plague quarter.
court of the dead: archlich's stronghold. Also court.
Dark quarter: eastern side of Nexus.
global auction: auction in the safe zone.
guardian tower: public dungeon.
haunted catacombs: public dungeon.
information brokers office: in the plague quarter.
Kesh Emporium: merchant house in the safe zone.
Light quarter: western side of Nexus.
market square: square housing global auction.
New Haven: city in Draven's Reach.
plague quarter: southern side of Nexus.
saltmarsh district: area in the southeast of plague quarter.
scorching dune: public dungeon.
Shadow Keep: central castle in the Shadow quarter.
Shadow quarter: northern side of Nexus.
Sickening Ooze: dungeon in saltmarsh.
Sleepy Inn: Michael's tavern, aka Wyvern's Roost.
Southern Outpost: tavern in plague quarter.
Wanderer's Delight: hotel in the safe zone.

www.ingramcontent.com/pod-product-compliance
Lightning Source LLC
Chambersburg PA
CBHW051603100726

47898CB00001B/204